We Other

Why did I laugh to-night? No voice will tell
No God, no Demon of severe response,
Deigns to reply from Heaven or from Hell

John Keats *Why Did I Laugh Tonight?*

The Author

Sue Bentley lives in Northamptonshire. She is the author of over seventy books, published in her own name and using a pen name. She is a bestseller both as herself and as another persona. Her books for younger readers have sold over two million copies and have been translated into over twenty languages.

We Other

Sue Bentley

Sue Bentley

Published in the UK by Everything with Words Limited, 3rd Floor, Premier House, 12-13 Hatton Garden, London EC1N 8AN

www.everythingwithwords.com

A CIP catalogue record for this book is available for the British Library

ISBN 978-1-911427-02-5

Printed and bound in Great Britain by Clays Ltd, St Ives plc.

Acknowledgements and Dedication

I would like to thank my agent Caroline Montgomery for her continuing support. Along with her professionalism, her kindness, solid advice, good company and much shared laughter over the years, she has made the challenging business of bringing this book to life immeasurably easier than it would otherwise have been. The wait has been well worth it!

All writing is difficult, but having people one can trust to give an honest opinion, cheer one up when the writing is not going well, and provide tea and sympathy when needed (very often, in my case) is invaluable.

I would like to thank Graham, my best friend and life-partner, for patience, support and understanding. And for helping to provide what I need to flourish in my chosen craft. And, not least, for knowing exactly when I just need a hug.

Thanks to my two lovely sons, Daniel and Alon and their families for just being there and enriching my life. Two of my grandchildren are of an age to enjoy this book. I hope they do!

Special thanks also go to Alon Bentley for helping me to turn a figure from one of my paintings into the wonderful artwork on the cover of We Other. And also for his continued support and enthusiasm for the book.

I have fond memories of the writing group and how we three would meet to offer constructive criticism of work in progress, while being sensitive to each other's delicate writers' ego. You know who you are, ladies. I know you are as delighted as I am that We Other is finally being let loose upon the world. My thanks and blessings to you both. Still miss those meetings.

And I would like to thank Mikka, my publisher at

Everything With Words. For believing in We Other - for her enthusiasm for the characters, her encouragement and patience when life's interventions held up delivery of promised text, and not least, her kind comments. One can never have enough of those.

A final word of thanks to the authors who inspired me and fostered within me a love of fairies both good and bad, folklore and richly imagined worlds. Who first prompted me to believe that I could write a book about something Other than the Everyday. It was while reading the works of Enid Blyton, C.S. Lewis, 'B.B', Katharine Briggs, the late Tanith Lee, amongst many, many others, that the flame of a future writer sparked into life and flickered within me.

I have written many books, but this one is particularly close to my heart.

Their Royal Host

Glimpse them from the tail of your eye
Where the land meets the sea. Beauty of
White horses slender, cresting the waves. Tossing silver
spindrift manes
Their jewelled hooves make silent spark-trail.

See their gathering when twilight beckons
And night and day enmeshed, blessed glimmers.
Peeping from shadows, they swirl and caper. Cat's
eyes agleam.
Pointed faces and innocent fingers, over-long.

Watch them feasting at the turn of the seasons.
When apple shine and fruitcake spices beguile.
Spider-silk clad, with feather capes and golden caskets,
they beckon.
Smiling offer gifts, but beware their bloodied teeth!

Sue Bentley

A beginning...

I met a lady in the meads,
Full beautiful—a faery's child,
Her hair was long, her foot was light,
And her eyes were wild.
– John Keats, *"La Belle Dame Sans Merci"*

MIST WREATHED THE ground in the forest clearing, a grey pall that was resisting the invasion of dawn. Fingers of light stole through the branches of an ancient oak, filtering onto the tangled net of undergrowth, before playing gently over the face of the man who was sprawled there.

His eyes opened. He groaned. Head throbbing with pain, he pushed himself into a sitting position and looked around. Dew had soaked into his jeans and T-shirt. He shivered. He must have been lying there for hours. Trees almost blocked out the sky and filled his vision on all sides. To his right lay the trunk of a fallen giant, half buried beneath a thick growth of ferns and lichens. Leprous fungi bloomed from its crumbly dark crevices.

He watched a large beetle with impressive horns, its carapace gleaming blue and green like a magpie's wing, as it laboured across the leaves that carpeted the ground. Frowning, he tried to get his bearings. None of it was familiar. How had he managed to lose his way and stray this far into the forest? The last thing he remembered was walking home alone from his mate's birthday celebration at the Red Lion.

Alice was still uncomfortable in crowds, so had chosen to stay at home. 'But, you go,' she had encouraged. 'No sense in both of us being miserable.' She was insistent, kissing him deeply to show that she meant it and was not just trying to be brave. He had held her close, his head resting on her soft dark hair that smelt of the musky perfume she wore. 'Really? You don't mind being here by yourself? Ivy's not much company.' Alice's grandmother was a successful artist. She was passionate about painting, but had little time for anything else, even her teenage granddaughter who was still so fragile and struggling to come to terms with her grief. 'I hate to think of you brooding and getting all upset without me here.'

Alice smiled up at him. 'I won't. What's the point? It's not going to bring Mum and Dad back, is it? I have to get used to that. I'll light a fire in my bedroom to cheer the place up and then curl up with a book.' Her lips curved in the way that sent a jab of heat to his belly. 'I'll still be awake when you get back.'

They kissed again. He felt excited at the thought of slipping up to her room and making love in her bed, maybe spending the night there. Ivy Stark knew nothing of their affair. She probably wouldn't approve of the hired help fraternising with her granddaughter. And then there was the six year age gap, but that didn't matter to him or Alice. They planned to get a place together and were already saving up for the rent on a flat in the nearby town.

'Go on, now. Have a good time,' Alice urged, giving him a playful push. 'Love you.'

He grinned as he stepped out of her embrace. 'Love you more.' It was a thing they said. He promised to have just a couple of drinks and then come straight back to her.

And that's what he had done. Or so he thought. The Red Lion was bursting at the seams with birthday guests arriving from all over the district. A huge bowl of punch had pride of place on the table. His mates were a raucous lot, but good-hearted and he enjoyed their familiar company, even though they teased him about Alice.

'When are we going to meet her then?'

'She must be special if you're keeping her a secret.'

'She is,' he told them with quiet pride. His Alice. The love of his life.

He had stayed at the party for a little over two hours before walking home under a cloudless starlit sky to Ivy's rambling old Victorian mansion. So how come he was here?

As he scrambled to his feet in the forest, he felt a bramble snag his cheekbone. He pressed a hand to the scratch and was straightening up, when he caught a movement. There was something in the mist. A figure. And it was moving towards him. As it drew closer, he could see that it was a woman, tall and slender with very long straight hair and wearing a vaguely old-fashioned looking long gown. A fall of some shimmering stuff fluttered outwards like a cape from behind each shoulder.

Was she coming home from a fancy dress party? Maybe she was lost, like him. He was about to call out to her, when his breath hitched. She had disappeared for a moment and then re-appeared. He blinked hard. The tall elegant form seemed to be breaking up, flickering in and out of focus, like a faulty hologram.

That's when he knew he was imagining things.

'Yeah, right! It's Princess Leia. Help me, Obi-Wan Kenobi!' He grinned at his stupidity. Just wait until he caught the joker who had spiked his drink. He had a fair idea which of his mates was responsible. Raking a hand through his untidy brown hair, he took a step forward. Time to get going. Alice was expecting him back hours ago. He pictured her waiting in that dark, draughty bedroom, frantic with worry.

Another shift of focus. Suddenly, without seeming to move, the figure of the woman was in front of him. She appeared to be as solid he was. But something was definitely out of kilter. His eyes were playing tricks, because expressions seemed to shiver and flow over her face, as if she was lying on the stony bed of a fast flowing stream and he was looking down at her through the water. With a rustle, like a collective indrawn sigh, the leaves on the nearby trees all turned in her direction. There was not a breath of wind, but boughs bent and branches extended towards her, as if pulled by invisible ropes.

She laughed then, a bell-like sound and bowed her head as if acknowledging their obeisance.

The hairs on the back of his neck prickled. Did alcohol and drug induced hallucinations come with a sound track? Maybe he was still asleep and having a dream, within a dream, like in cheap horror movie? He pinched himself. No, definitely awake. What then?

She was lifting dainty feet, swirling and dipping in a dance. Where her long hair brushed the ground, drifts of flowers sprang up. Their petals were like dark red velvet, their centres clustered with jagged, black stamens ringed about a protuberant pistil.

You've got to be kidding! He needed to get away. Have a shower, sober up, straighten his head out.

A complex perfume drifted towards him. Moss and spice; mixed with ripe fruit, sweetish and rotting and violets and dust. He gagged as he felt the thick sweet scent pouring down his throat like honey.

The woman was spinning round and round. Dew drops flew outwards and then upwards, to form a rainbow corona that tinkled sweetly before dissolving. Her skin glowed softly. Throwing back her head, she laughed again. This time, the sound was like glass breaking. It sent a spear of dread through him. There was a movement behind her. What he had taken for a floating cape at her shoulders sprang up, opened in rapid telescopic jerks as if worked by some silent mechanism.

She has…wings? As he stared in disbelief, they beat against the air, buzzing faintly and glinting like stained glass in the early morning sun.

'Oh, I get it! It's a trick.' He whipped round, looking for his mates who were obviously hidden in the trees. 'You bastards! You got me! Where did you find her? She's very convincing. Come on out! Joke's over!'

'Silence! Did I give you leave to speak!'

Her voice was a sibilant whisper. He turned, looked at her again. And saw black ink flood the entire area between her eye-lids. Two obsidian almonds, fixed upon him, a metallic glint showing in their depths. Between her parted lips he glimpsed small pointed white teeth.

He felt the skin on his skull tighten with terror. The taste of that honeyed perfume lingered in his mouth. It grew stronger. Fumes of it were clouding his thoughts. 'What…what's happening? Have you poisoned me…?'

She smiled. It was not pleasant. 'And break such a pretty toy?'

'I…I don't understand.'

'Oh, you will.' She turned her head slowly, deliberately looked away.

He gasped as a sense of loss wrenched at his guts. It was as if all joy had fled and he stood on the edge of a precipice. In the depths below him, loathsome things swirled. The sun had no warmth and the earth had turned cold.

And then she turned her head, looked at him again. He was mistaken. Her eyes were a startling turquoise. Gold dust encircled the pupils. Her milk-white skin was almost transparent, her mouth a pink flower. Her smile dazzled him. A blessing. The long, long hair lifted, twining and twisting about her neck and shoulders of its own accord, while her wings thrummed.

Her beauty made his heart ache. He trembled, wanting her to look at him forever.

A sly look crossed her face. She spoke sweetly. 'What am I to call you, pretty hot-blood? Will you give me your name?'

'Robin…Morgan. Rob.' He couldn't tear his eyes from her. 'And you? What's your name?'

She only laughed. 'When I call you to me, Robin Morgan, you will come.' Her image flickered, wavered. Began to fade.

'Yes. Yes, I will. Any time.' He nodded, eagerly. 'But wait. Please. Don't go…'

But she was no longer there. The mist had cleared. Sunlight flooded the glade and birdsong filled the air.

Blinking, he shook his head. The bramble scratch on his cheek was smarting. He rubbed at it absently. In a daze he started walking, not noticing where his feet trod. He had thought himself deep in the forest, but in a few moments he was walking down the lane towards Ivy's large house and grounds.

Alice was waiting. His chest swelled with love for her as he thought of taking her in his arms. She would be angry at his lateness. It would be fun, making up. They had such plans.

He had reached the gravel drive, when he was suddenly violently sick. Bending over, he threw up a quantity of clear slimy water. Something lodged in his throat and he coughed, choked and spat out a gush of fibrous stuff. He frowned, looking down at the three dark red petals that lay on the ground. God, he must have been really drunk. It looked as if he had gulped down most of the garnish floating in the punch bowl.

A smile of embarrassment played around his lips. He never could hold his drink. His mates were going to rip the piss out of him for being such a lightweight. Actually passing out and sleeping it off under a bush! Priceless!

CHAPTER 1

Seventeen years later. Present day...

JESS CLOSED THE front door behind her as quietly as she could, in case her mum's boyfriend heard her leaving. She hurried along the walkway and took the stairs down to the entrance of the high-rise flats. Outside, she glanced briefly towards the bus stop where some teenage kids from her class at the community college were waiting. Thrusting her hands deep into her jeans pockets, she trudged away in the opposite direction. The college, the latest in a run of similar schools over the years, had a strict policy on student attendance. She would scribble a sick note later, forging her mum's signature as she had been doing since she was seven years old.

The space around the flat had once been a garden, with flowers in neat beds, clipped hedges and benches. Now it was a wilderness of weeds and cracked paving stones that stuck up at odd angles. Still, Jess loved the fresh green smell of it here, the sense that small things were moving under the earth, immersed in their own world. Something about it felt more real, more authentic than the ugly blocks of concrete and glass housing that made up Limefields estate where she and Alice had been living for the past year and a half.

It hadn't seemed too bad at first. They had lived in far worse places. But then Mum had met Leon. Things had been going steadily downhill since. Jess walked on past the rusting whirly lines no one ever used, heading for a path sloping downwards between high banks that rose up on either side of her. Empty food containers, cans and broken glass littered the grass. A patch of bare scorched earth surrounded what remained of a mattress, its exposed rusty springs looking like a burned carcass.

It began to rain. The clean smell of it lifted Jess's spirits as she flicked her hood up to cover her hair. She came to the familiar graffiti covering the entrance to the underpass. Someone had spray painted a new design over the older faded stuff. The androgynous manga character - black, white and rich shades of purple - looked almost three dimensional.

Jess felt drawn to its enormous eyes and stylised triangular face, surrounded by a shock of impossibly spiky hair. She wondered if the artist lived nearby. Someone who was into graffiti and manga might be worth talking to. *Which was more than she could say for most of the kids around here,* she thought, kicking idly at a puddle which was skinned with an oily metallic sheen.

'Oh, great!' She grimaced with annoyance as she felt the wetness soaking into her left foot. As she lifted it, the front section of the sole peeled away and flopped free. She sighed. The battered Doc Martens were her last pair of wearable footwear. She had a few coins in her pocket, although nowhere near enough to get the boots repaired. She weighed-up the risk of returning to the flat and borrowing a pair of Leon's trainers. He had so many pairs of them lying about that he probably wouldn't notice, and it would give her time to trawl the charity shops. It wasn't easy to get women's size 9 footwear and the DMs had been a lucky find. She didn't expect to be able to replace them easily.

When she left the flat, Leon had been sprawled on the sofa,

wearing only his jeans while watching daytime TV. He had scratched his bare chest and looked at her in that way that she didn't like. He had been doing that a lot lately. She made sure she kept out of his way when her mum wasn't around. She had heard the two of them shouting late into the night during another of their alcohol fuelled fights, so knew from experience that Mum would not emerge from the bedroom until late afternoon; her worn pink velour tracksuit hiding new purple marks, layered over the green and yellow ones already streaking her arms and legs.

Jess doubted that she would be able to get back into the flat unnoticed, so gave up on the idea. Her stomach growled reminding her she was starving. A brief inspection of their fridge had revealed a stack of lagers and a half-empty carton of milk growing green mould. She had eaten nothing but half a wilted lettuce and two tomatoes since yesterday. Her stomach felt as if it was touching her backbone.

A couple of metres into the tunnel under the road, she came to the rough shelter formed from cardboard boxes, where the homeless guy with the filthy raincoat slept. Mike's waist-length dreads were matted into solid lumps that hardly moved when he walked. Jess usually stopped to chat with him, but this morning he'd already gone, probably to the shopping centre to beg for just enough money to buy a few hours of oblivion.

She wrinkled her nose against the reek of pee as she took hold of a relatively clean corner of cardboard and tore a piece off. Leaning against the curved wall, she unlaced her boot, folded the card into shape and then slipped it inside. It felt awkward and lumpy against her toes, but it would do for now.

A few moments later, Jess emerged onto the busy dual carriageway and the 24 hour garage where gangs of kids from the estate hung out at night. The fizzing and jangling of metal here was almost overpowering. It was an effort to move through the cacophony. She coughed at the scald of traffic fumes in her throat and felt the bitter sting penetrating deep into her lungs. Taking a small atomizer from her pocket, she squirted the mist into her mouth. The hit of aromatic oils was soothing, easing her tortured throat and chest.

Better. At least, as good as it ever got. Pollution levels had to be skyrocketing, because her asthma was worsening. Not that she had ever been officially diagnosed. They had moved house so often that Mum had never bothered to sign on with a doctor's practice, so Jess had missed out on all the normal tests and check-ups and had never had any inoculations.

'Doctors don't know everything, darling,' her mum had slurred once, tossing a letter from one particularly efficient school nurse into the waste bin. 'You've never even caught a cold. You're a tough little kid. Clever too. That plant stuff you make yourself takes care of your asthma, so what's the problem?'

'But all the other kids are getting their jabs,' Jess had protested, still bothered about being singled out as 'different'. Her mum arched one eyebrow at her in a 'so what?' gesture, blinking in slow motion. Jess recognised the signs that she was well on her way to a binge. Sometimes Mum didn't drink for a few days, but then she would start and it could go on for a week or two, as she drank to keep the level topped up. The more tanked-up she was the more carefully controlled were her movements. Her mum had walked towards Jess as if she was strung tightly with invisible strings like some sad inverted puppet, and then all at once the strings were cut and she flopped onto the sofa and closed her eyes.

'Stop pestering me. You're like a bloody broken record.'

She pinched the area at the top of her nose between trembling fingers. 'My head's banging. I need to lie here for a while. Just…do what you want. Sling it, OK?'

So Jess decided that she didn't fancy having needles stuck in her anyway and wrote a letter of refusal in her mum's handwriting, signing it Mrs Alice Morgan. The letters became a habit, a means of getting out of lessons, being excused from stupid pointless sports and avoiding groups of kids who taunted her because her uniform was too small and crumpled. Until her too frequent absences brought her to the attention of the Educational Welfare Officer. Visits from a stern-faced woman followed, warning of court proceedings and a large fine if Mrs Morgan allowed Jess to keep skipping school.

Soon after that, she and Mum did another moonlight flit to escape the bailiffs, so the matter of her school attendance was solved. She didn't go at all and Mum didn't make her. It wasn't until they settled in the block of high-rise flats on the Midlands housing estate that the authorities caught up with them. Now Jess attended the community college and kept her absences to a minimum.

The supermarket she was now making for was sandwiched between a turf accountant and a newsagent. Entering via the automatic doors, she glanced at the bored-looking security guard. There were two of them who worked shifts. This one was her least favourite. He was short and thick set with a florid jowly face. His gut bulged out over the waistband of his trousers and flecks of dandruff peppered the shoulders of his navy uniform jacket. She could smell the stale ash on his clothes from here.

Jess unzipped her fleece as he came forward to bar her way. She looked down at him from her lanky height, as his eyes raked her ripped jeans and top with threadbare patches from being laundered so often, and the tangled dark hair that protruded from the hood and hung in rat tails onto her chest.

The guard's lip curled. 'How come you're not out the back, thieving from the bins?'

'Wrong time of day for it. And I don't steal.' *Not that often anyway.* She had been about seven years old. There had been no food in the house, no money to buy any and Mum was face down in a stupor on the sofa. Desperation had driven Jess to go out and lift what they needed from the nearest supermarket. Her best ever haul had been a litre-sized carton of milk, a bag of apples, a jar of instant coffee, a loaf, and a slab of cheese – most of the stuff for her mum who often forgot, or didn't bother, to eat. But then she had discovered the huge bins, where food with short sell-by dates was regularly dumped. It was even respectable to take stuff from there, these days.

Jess shifted her weight onto one leg. Stuck out her hip. 'Supermarkets throw away tonnes of good food every day. Freegans, like me, help them reduce their carbon footprints by re-distributing the stuff they waste. It's a public service. You should thank me.'

He rolled his eyes. 'Yeah, yeah. Don't give me that hippy dippy shit. As far as I'm concerned it's still shoplifting. If I catch you with your snout in a skip, I'll kick your skinny arse. Why aren't you at school anyway?'

'Teacher training day,' she lied.

'Funny that. Haven't seen many other kids around.'

'Had your eyes tested lately?' she asked sweetly.

He gave a short humourless laugh. 'Go and try to buy some booze or fags, why don't you? Give me an excuse.'

'Never use them. That stuff's poison.' Her eyes glinted with mischief. 'Look what it's done to you.'

He flushed deeply. 'Watch your mouth. And put that hood down, or you're not coming in.'

'Keep your wig on.' Jess flicked back the hood. Grabbing a basket, she sauntered towards the nearest aisle.

She knew he would follow her. It was hilarious how he thought she couldn't see him, peering from behind special offer displays. She wandered up and down aisles, plucking tins and packets at random, doling them into the basket, before retracing her steps and replacing every one of the unwanted groceries. She enjoyed winding him up until she got bored of it.

Jess noticed a teenage girl wearing a dark coat, looking at a rack of crisps. There was something familiar about her, but she gave it no more thought as she stopped beside a display of fruit and veg. Red peppers and tomatoes were piled next to lettuces, cabbages and salad leaves in a dozen shades of green. Citrus fruit and mangoes were placed next to apples, pineapples, berries. It was a feast of riches.

Her mouth watered at the sight and she felt a faint prickling all over her skin, but this was pleasant unlike the scour of chemical and iron-burn. Since she was a tiny child, she had been hyper-sensitive around living things – trees and plants prompted the strongest response. She had a similar reaction, but to a lesser extent, with fresh fruit and vegetables, which diminished as the pear, cucumber or whatever dried up and lost its vitality.

There! From the corner of her eye Jess caught a slight movement, as if something that was *almost* visible was hovering above the display of neatly piled carrots, before zinging away. And again – a trembling visual shift above some glossy purple aubergines, as if some tiny amorphous *thing* had moved and left a faint wavering trail on the air, which faded as soon as she blinked. She had watched a documentary on TV about people who could see words as colours, days of the week as shapes or personalities. Synaesthesia, it was called. The brain, apparently, was 'wired' differently in some people.

She had seized on the explanation. That was her then. Sorted. She rather enjoyed the idea of being special.

Still, she had kept these experiences to herself. Not even her mum knew. But lately there seemed to be a sharpening of this Sense, as she thought of it - a sort of inner shift. The happenings were becoming more frequent and if she concentrated hard, the vague impressions would sharpen. Worried that she might be forced to acknowledge the reality of what she was experiencing and have to take some action, Jess took pains to consciously ignore them, which seemed to keep them at a manageable level.

She was doing that now, as she began filling two plastic bags with the cheapest apples - when something exploded out of them and zoomed right at her. She heard a faint clashing and then a tiny buzz that could almost have been a voice close to her left ear as whatever it was circled her head three times. Jess jumped back in alarm, batting at the air with one hand and trying to avoid being stung by the wasp or bug she couldn't see. She felt something tug at her hair and shook her head hard. There was what sounded like a tiny shriek and another flickering tremor in mid-air – this time like a torn silvery thread - and the thing was gone.

Shaken, Jess stood there in silence. The air around her was crackling faintly and the ends of her nerves seemed to be tingling. What felt like minutes, was actually only seconds before the normal noises of the supermarket crowded back in. She forced herself to calm down. Stupid to get so worked up about an insect.

An insect doesn't tug your hair or shout in your ear.

Her default strategy was well ingrained and came to her rescue now. 'I won't think about it. I won't,' she murmured, realising that she had been holding her breath. Woodenly, she added a jar of honey to her basket, before making her way to the checkout.

The girl on the till was chewing in a bored manner. There was a flat popping sound, as she burst a pink bubble between her lips. Jess caught a sweetish whiff of gum as she handed her some coins and accepted the change.

'Ta. Have a nice day,' the girl intoned, automatically.

Pocketing the money, Jess forced a smile. Her stomach was rumbling so loudly she was sure the person in the queue behind her could hear it. She imagined sinking her teeth into the crisp juicy flesh of an apple, scooping flower-scented honey into her mouth. It was all she could do to stop herself from running out of the shop.

The guard stood near the exit, glowering at her, folded arms resting on his paunch. Beads of sweat dotted his face. Jess could smell his unhealthy sweat, bitter like burnt onions.

The second she was outside, she ripped the plastic bag open, grabbed an apple and bit into the skin. The juice was a taste explosion in her mouth. Munching luxuriously, she crossed the road.

The damp cardboard in her boot chaffed her bare toes, but the discomfort barely registered when measured against the heaven in her mouth. She decided to go and sit in the park to eat her feast beneath one of the enormous horse chestnut trees. For some reason her asthma was always better there, not worse as might be expected. Birdsong would be a bonus.

After that she had no real plans. She didn't own a laptop or tablet, so maybe she would hang out in the library, where they had free internet access. She could surf for a while before browsing their display of manga.

She had not gone far, when an urgent female voice called out.

'Hey, wait! Stop!'

Jess turned, surprised to see the girl from the shop, the one who had been looking at the crisps. The girl was red-faced running towards her, with her dark coat flapping open.

Drawing level, the girl smiled. 'I'm glad I caught you. You forgot this!' She waggled a packet of instant macaroni cheese in the air.

The girl was small and rather dumpy, her round face half-hidden behind unflattering glasses. 'Isn't mine. I don't eat that stuff.'

'Oh, sorry. I thought…' A crop of pimples on the girl's chin stood out palely against her flushed skin. 'Um…I'd better take it back then.'

Jess shrugged. 'Wouldn't bother.'

'But that's stea - '

'Evening the score?' Jess interrupted. 'One in the eye, for the big chain rip-off merchants?'

'Erm…' The girl seemed unsure whether Jess was joking. Her face brightened. 'I know you, don't I?'

'Do you?'

'Yeah. You're Jessica Morgan. I'm in your class. Lisa. Lisa Simpson.' Behind the thick glasses, her pale blue eyes looked large and distorted. Her reddish-blonde hair was curly and clustered around her ears.

Jess grinned in recognition. 'Like in Homer and Marge's daughter, right?' That's why she had thought the girl was familiar earlier. She recalled that Lisa sat at the back of the class. A quiet girl, who took pains not to draw attention to herself.

'Didn't anyone ever tell you that you shouldn't wear your uniform when you're bunking off?' She indicated the pleated grey skirt, white blouse and school tie, visible under Lisa's open coat.

'What?' Lisa glanced down at herself. She grinned suddenly. 'Oh, I'm not bunking off. I go for extra tuition on Mondays. Dyslexia and speech therapy. They were both cancelled today, but no one told me. Typical.' A particularly nasty spot under her bottom lip wobbled as she talked. It was difficult not to stare at it.

Jess swallowed the last piece of apple. One wasn't nearly enough to take the edge off her hunger. She was desperate to cram her mouth with honey along with the fruit. Water was squelching unpleasantly against her toes, despite the cardboard wadded in her boot. Slouching against a lamp post, she curled one leg round the other, balancing on her dry foot. It was raining harder now. She needed to get undercover, finish eating before she fainted or threw up.

'Well...I'll see you around.'

Lisa made no attempt to move. 'Want to get a coke...or something? My treat,' she said shyly.

Jess's plans definitely did not include being saddled with the class misfit. But Lisa was grinning hopefully, her rather plain face totally transformed. 'OK then,' she agreed, surprising herself.

Lisa clapped her hands like a child being handed a party goody bag. 'Faberoozy! Where shall we go?'

Faberoozy? Jess blinked. *Is she for real?* 'I was going to the park. We could sit inside the café.'

'Oh, I love the park,' Lisa said happily. 'Especially the bird cage walk. The old peacock just died of a heart attack and his mate died too, of a broken heart. Isn't that just totally sad? I cried when I read about it. Anyway, they've just got *three* new peacocks. I've been dying to see them. One of them is an albino. How cool is that?'

'Well it's different.' Jess wasn't sure that she could handle so much ebullience. But she was quite interested in seeing the peacocks. They were about to set off, when she had a thought. 'Do you want that pack of instant mac cheese?'

'The what?' Lisa seemed surprised to find herself still holding the packet. 'Oh, this? No.' She handed it over.

Jess's eyes gleamed. 'Back in a tic!'

She sprinted back across the road to where the supermarket guard was visible through the glass window. Frowning, he moved forward as the automatic doors opened with a faint whoosh to admit Jess. She stood in the entrance, but didn't go in.

'You again!' He knuckled his hands on his hips, ready for battle.

'Catch!' Jess lobbed the packet at him. It was a lucky shot and hit him square in his bulging gut. It couldn't have hurt much, but his expression of fury was deeply satisfying.

'I didn't nick it, in case you're wondering. Someone dropped it outside. I'm doing my duty and returning it.' Jess beamed at him, with all the mock sincerity she could muster. 'Oh and you needn't bother with the thank you letter. It was a pleasure!'

As the guard's face darkened, Jess winked at him.

'I can get you banned,' he blustered. 'One word to the manager. That's all it would take…'

'Whatever!' Jess sauntered past Lisa who was watching with her mouth open and a look of scandalised admiration on her face. *That girl really needs to get out more!* Realising that Lisa wasn't following her, she looked over her shoulder. 'Are you coming or what?'

Lisa scampered forward like an eager puppy. They set off together, the carrier bag with the apples and honey inside banging against Jess's leg. Suddenly they both saw the funny side. By the time they had rounded the corner, they were breathless with laughter.

CHAPTER 2

IN THE FLAT, Alice was surfacing slowly from a deep sleep, her thoughts clouded and muzzy as if her head were stuffed full of cotton wool. The room was dim, filled with dusty grey light. It could be early morning or late evening, she couldn't tell which.

She thought she could hear a baby crying. Was it real or just her imagination? She wasn't sure. But it sounded hungry.

The sound multiplied as the baby grew more distressed, each cry stretching into a low angry mewling before the infant gathered breath into its tiny lungs for another scream. Struggling to get her bearings, Alice was gripped by emotions that were as fresh as when she first experienced them.

Which of her baby daughters was crying?

She couldn't tell their sounds apart yet. But she knew that the one who was still sleeping would wake up in a moment and then they would cry in tandem, her twin girls Jessica and Stella.

Since they were been born a few weeks ago, in the bedroom overlooking the woods, Alice had only managed to snatch odd hours of sleep. She felt exhausted with the endless round of feeding, nappy changing, rocking to sleep. There were so many baby clothes to wash and get dry, too.

This wasn't what she had expected when she had come to the West Country to live with her grandmother, Ivy after her parents had died. Ivy Stark was a stranger to her, pre-occupied with her career which was really starting to take off. At nearly seventeen, she had been a quiet serious girl, marred by loss and loneliness. Ivy did nothing but paint.

It was Rob who rescued her. He had kind hazel eyes that sparked with humour. Rob was a man, where up until now she had met only boys. His mixture of passion and gentleness mixed with calm practicality was irresistible.

She was already a few months pregnant when her grandmother found out about them. Ivy was furious. She didn't consider Rob, who worked for her as a gardener and handy man, good enough for her only granddaughter. As if she really cared. But she was grateful that Ivy allowed Rob to keep his job and allowed them to continue living at Windroth until they could afford to move. When their twin girls were born, Alice was happy. Her new family gave her life purpose. The shadow of grief that still hung over her began to lift.

The baby gave another wail. Her breasts tingled. 'Mummy's coming, darlings,' she whispered, running her tongue around parched lips.

Why was her mouth so dry?

Alice struggled to sit upright, stupefied by exhaustion. She flopped back against the pillow, blinking gritty eyes, conscious of the ache in her neck from where she must have been sleeping in an awkward position.

What was Rob doing? He wasn't in the bed beside her.

Of course, he must have got up already. He would be in the kitchen, spooning dried baby milk into sterile bottles, adding boiled cooled water and squirting a few drops on the inside of his wrist to test the temperature. When he returned, she would put one baby to the breast, while he gave the other a bottle and then they would swop. Turn and turn about. It was a good system and kept both babies happy.

Only one baby was still crying. It was a miracle that the other hadn't woken. Which one was it? Stella or Jessica?

It bothered Alice that she couldn't tell. She wished Rob would hurry up. Her light-headedness wouldn't seem to clear. Everything was confused and she thought she might fall if she got up quickly.

She would ask him to pick up the baby and bring it to her, so she could feed it in bed.

She frowned as something moved in the shadows across the room. For a moment she thought she had glimpsed a figure bending over one of the cots. It was tall and slender with elongated limbs that glowed with a faint radiance. Now it was moving away in a series of fluttering jerks, like a dancer caught in the beam of a strobe light.

Alice blinked hard. The figure was gone. It must be the lack of sleep playing tricks with her vision. A sudden cold draught prickled her skin. She shivered, her teeth chattering although the room was cosy enough. Rob had built a fire in the big old fashioned fireplace, which they kept banked-up all night, and found a pair of thick figured velvet curtains in the attic.

Alice rubbed at her eyes. The bedroom door opened. A man stood there, silhouetted by the light from the hallway.

Rob. Relief washed over her. Rob was here, at last.

The sound of the TV floated into the room. Alice frowned, puzzled. They didn't have a TV at Windroth.

Around her, the bedroom morphed into a featureless box with mould-blackened and peeling wallpaper. A venetian blind with bent slats hung lopsidedly at the small window. There was no high-ceiling with ornate plaster carving, no figured velvet curtains, no red turkey carpet on the floor.

And no matching pink cots, containing Jessica and Stella.

She became aware that she was lying on a mattress on the floor. A grubby duvet, mottled with circular brown-edged marks covered her thin body.

Rob had bent down to lift Stella from the cot. The sound he made reminded her of a wounded animal. And how she had known instantly - why only one baby was crying.

Stella was cold. Her tiny chest unmoving. The stillness surrounding her, absolute.

Ah, no. My poor sweet darling. The floor rushed up to meet her, her cheek struck the side of the cot with bruising force. But Alice didn't feel it.

The pillow beneath her cheek smelt of vomit. A jumble of clothes, cans, and pizza boxes littered the floor. On the wine box that served as a bedside table, lay a plate cemented with the remains of beans on toast. A cigarette had been stubbed out in the middle of it.

'Hey, shit for brains! Are you ever going to bloody get up and cook my breakfast?'

Not Rob's voice. Leon's.

'Stella. My baby girl…' she whimpered.

'Oh, for Christ's sake. Not this shit again, you daft bitch. You should keep off the effing vodka if you can't handle it.' Leon ran a hand over his unshaven jaw as he knelt beside her. He grabbed her face, digging his fingers into her jaw as he pulled her up into a sitting position. 'Knock, knock. Anyone in?' he said softly.

Alice looked at him with blurred vision.

Grunting with exasperation, he pushed her, twisting his hand so that he pressed her face downwards into the pillow. She dragged in a breath to tell him to stop, and felt the fabric sucked tight to block her mouth and nose, cutting off the air. She sagged, couldn't find the will to struggle. She wouldn't beg. Not this time. Even though she knew he would let her up if she did.

The blood drummed in her ears and her vision turned red. She felt herself starting to shut down.

Go on then. Do it.

Lifting his hand, Leon brought it down in a hard punch. The air whistled past her ear. At the last moment she heard the whump! as his fist connected with the pillow. When she still didn't react, Leon laughed. He stood up and strode towards the doorway.

'I'm going out,' he said, slamming the door without a backwards glance.

CHAPTER 3

In Faery – Fifteen years ago human time –
or the blink of an eye...

NINKA WAS TRYING not to listen to the struggling hob's squeals. It wasn't the tiny faery's death that bothered her; the matter of life and death in the Shadow Court was like everything else there, twisted and uncertain. It was the lengthy pleasure that Tweeter took in his task that she found so upsetting.

Added to this, in the midst of it all, Catelysma was jouncing her newest plaything on her knee. No one knew where the pretty baby had come from and no one was foolish enough to ask her. It looked too well cared-for to be a forest foundling. But it was of no concern to any of the fey gathered here that a mortal might be grieving her baby's loss; mortals were fecund, if short-lived, and the mother could easily have another. The infant's rounded features, flushed pink cheeks and soft, peach-skinned limbs were drawing murmurs of admiration from all those in attendance.

As Ninka looked more closely at the fitted garment that covered the baby from its neck down, her heart gave a lurch. Although muddy and grass-stained it was just possible to see the original pink colour and the faint design of dancing animals. Immediately, she guessed where it had come from.

'She shall be known as, Aerith,' Catelysma decided, a smile of satisfaction playing over her perfect features.

There were nods of approval from the scrags and boggarts clustered in the shadows. A grey fantasy drifted past, smoke-like limbs trailing and its mournful features wearing what passed for a smile.

Aerith smiled and gurgled, unconcerned by the narrow eyes blinking at her from spiteful cat faces.

Ninka felt a shiver of fear for the little mortal. How soon before the Dark Lady tired of her and she became prey to the ravenous scrags and red caps? She watched as Catelysma placed a golden ball in the baby's lap and made a languorous gesture with one slender white hand, setting a glamour on the ball, which instantly became a fluffy golden rabbit.

The infant's lips pursed. She blew a loud raspberry as she clapped her chubby hands with pleasure.

'How delightful, she is!' Catelysma purred. 'Eyes like cornflowers and tender pink lips.'

Nods and smiles rippled round the court. Ninka found herself smiling too. Aerith was indeed charming, but then new-born mortals brought into Faery usually were - at first.

'Some pity...I beg.' The wounded hob gave a loud moan, as Tweeter continued working with his curved bone blade.

Some of the faery host tittered with amusement. A few yawned. Many paid no attention to the little hob's suffering, which was commonplace enough. They preferred the rare novelty of watching Catelysma petting the pretty infant.

Was the Dark Lady thinking of that other half-ling babe - the Forbidden? And what had become of it? Was it dead, and if so, did she mourn it? Was this what the show of maternity was all about? Ninka's thoughts began to wander.

The details of that event in the forest, which she alone had witnessed by accident, were imprinted deeply upon her. It would have far-reaching implications for the Shadow Court, the solitary fey and beyond if what she knew ever came to light. But that knowledge was caged within her, where it must stay buried, until the time was right for disclosure. If Catelysma had even the slightest inkling that any fey knew her secret – well, Ninka knew that her life would be worth less than a dandelion seed blowing on the breeze.

A bloated-bellied scrag nudged her, jerking her out of her reverie. 'Pretty toothsome thing, ain't it?'

'Yes, very,' she said neutrally.

The scrag's eyes gleamed and Ninka turned away from the blast of its meaty breath. 'Tender bones,' it mused.

Like most of the fey, Ninka normally cared little for mortal playthings that were so easily broken. But there was something about Aerith. She was an engaging little creature, unafraid and sunny-natured. For the first time, it bothered her that innocence could be corrupted so carelessly.

Catelysma glanced her way and Ninka quickly lowered her eyes, veiling her expression. It was not wise to show too much interest or to become too attached to anything. At the Shadow Court finer emotions too swiftly became currency.

The hob was wailing piteously now. 'Mercy. Ah, mercy,' it sobbed.

Catelysma had laid her cheek against the fuzz of blonde hair that clothed the infant's small skull. She lifted her chin, her face clouding.

'Be done with that now.'

'Ladyship.' Tweeter clenched uneven mud-coloured teeth in an ingratiating grin. Raising the blade, he thrust hard.

The hob shuddered, was silent.

Ninka would have liked to think that the Dark Lady had spoken up out of pity. But she knew she was simply impatient to find out whether her latest experiment had worked. She felt mixed emotions when she looked at Catelysma. She feared, sometimes hated, the tall, slender faery who ruled uncontested over the Shadow Court, but her humble sensibilities could not help but be moved by Gentry beauty. The Dark Lady, a ravishing beauty, her milk-white skin, the waterfall of shifting pale green and silver hair brushing the ground behind her as she walked. Her slanted eyes a dazzling turquoise ringed with gold, but Ninka knew how they could change in an instant.

Tweeter had now filled a goblet, carved from rock crystal, and was mincing towards Catelysma, every inch the attendant courtier. The effect was rather spoiled by his awkward rolling walk as he balanced his powerful upper-body on a pair of stringy, knock-kneed legs that ended in goat's feet.

He handed Catelysma the glass of warm red liquid. 'I hope the flavour delights you, Ladyship. The hob, which chose to sacrifice itself for your pleasure, ate only newly sprouted wood sorrel leaves for the allotted portion of time.'

Catelysma twirled the crystal glass, so the rays of sunlight penetrating the thick leaf canopy above the court's garden played over it. She took a dainty sniff and swirled the thick liquid, before finally sipping.

'Mmm,' she murmured, considering. She swallowed and then ran her tongue around her shell-pink lips.

Everyone waited. Nearby, another tiny hob hovered in the air, trembling, its wings shedding powdery faery dust. Kors and puckles sprawled in the grass. A boggle-eyed brownie and three slender pixies sat rigidly on a fallen log.

The tension in the Shadow Court was that of a coiled spring.

Catelysma's face betrayed nothing.

Tweeter shifted impatiently. 'Good, is it, Ladyship?' he simpered.

'You do not have permission to speak.' She stared coldly at him until his grin slid towards dismay and then dawning fear. Tipping the goblet, she poured the red stream onto the ground. 'It tastes insipid. You have failed me again. What will you do to make reparation?' she asked sweetly.

Ninka saw sweat break out on Tweeter's face. 'A thousand pardons, Peerless One. I do not deserve your forgiveness,' he burbled. 'I shall cut strips from my skin and eat them, while dancing on hot coals. I will blind myself in one eye with a thorn…'

Catelysma gave a stifled yawn. 'If you can't be more inventive, do not bother.'

There were mutters and cries of disappointment from the watching host at the loss of the chance of some more entertainment.

'Silence!' The Dark Lady glowered. 'You, Tweeter, will find another for my purpose. But not a hob this time.'

She cast her gaze round the assembly. Ninka steeled herself to remain still as all around her faery kind shifted nervously. Some of them looked rigidly at the ground. Others shrank inside their skins like fungi collapsing in a rainstorm. Elsewhere, black eyes, sharp faces and snouts melted further into the shadows.

'A pixie, I think,' Catelysma mused. 'Instruct it to feed only on violets – the flowers, not the leaves,' she said, fanning long fingers in the air. 'And you alone, Tweeter, shall gather the flowers, while they are yet fresh with dew.'

Tweeter sighed with deep relief and bowed low, so that the bones of his spine showed pale through his hairy, lemon-coloured skin. 'As you command. The sole purpose of my miserable existence is to serve you.'

Catelysma sighed absently, already bored. She stranded a tress of shining, silver-green hair through her fingers, fingering the strings of emeralds woven through it.

The pixies on the log seemed frozen in terror. Then one of them lost her nerve. With a strangled cry, she flexed glassy dragonfly wings. But before she could rise into the air, the Tweeter's muscular arm shot out and grasped her round her slim neck.

The pixie squeaked with terror and wet itself.

'The next volunteer!' Tweeter said, triumphantly.

The pixie's long toes scrabbled at the floor and her wings clattered desperately against Tweeter's body. He reached down and roughly tore them from her shoulders, before trampling them into glittering shards beneath his sharp hooves. Moaning faintly, the pixie was borne away towards a dark corridor with walls of woven brambles.

Ninka's heart moved with pity, but there was nothing she could do.

The pool of hob's blood on the moss carpet at Catelysma's feet looked dark and syrupy. She felt slightly sick with disgust, but knew better than to reveal the fact.

'Dismissed. All of you!'

As the rest of the court melted away into the forest, Ninka began sidling behind a birch trunk, eager to be about her work. The rush matting in her forest dwelling was in need of replacement. She planned to investigate a patch of sedge along the lake's edge in the grounds of...

'Not you. Approach me, hudskin,' Catelysma said softly.

Her mouth dry, Ninka backed up and then scurried forward. As one of the solitary fey, she retained a degree of freedom and was allowed to come and go freely, but she was still bound to obedience by the blood oath she had sworn.

'How may I serve you, Majesty?'

Catelysma lifted the infant beneath its arms and held it in

the air. 'Take this from me. It's messed itself and smells *very* bad. Wash it, perfume it and find it some garments.'

'Yes, Majesty.' Ninka took the little warm body in her arms. A pungent stink of dung clung to it and she almost gagged. The baby raised a pudgy hand and touched her face. It gurgled happily. An unexpected tenderness rose within her and she had to force herself not to smile in response. 'Do you wish me to return Aerith to you at once?'

'No.' Catelysma dusted off her hands. 'You will take care of it. Find it a bed and furnish quarters for it. I give you leave to find a helper if the task is beyond you. But mistake me not, the responsibility for Aerith falls to you.'

Ninka felt a surge of panic. *What shall I do? I have no knowledge of these things.* 'Very well, Majesty.' She started to move away.

'Wait! Come closer.'

Ninka stopped and moved forward on her short sturdy legs, but the baby hampered her movements, so that she was forced to kneel awkwardly.

Catelysma flexed her fingers, a crafty smile hovering around her lips. 'How fancy you look today. I mislike it.'

Ninka fought down a cry of dismay. She had taken pains that morning to weave her few strands of coarse hair with ribbons of spider silk and blue forget-me-knots, so that the scalp lock hung down in front of one pointed ear. The summons to court had caught her by surprise. She had forgotten to pull on her usual cap of woven rushes. It was a mistake she was about to pay for, she realised, as she bowed her head in resignation.

The first stab of pain made her eyes water. Helpless tears slid down her broad cheeks and dripped off her chin as Catelysma grasped each coarse hair between finger and thumb and plucked them out at the roots, before scattering them to the ground in a jumble of petals and spider silk.

Ninka gulped back a sob. She did not know why it pleased Catelysma so much to do this on a regular basis. The fact that every single one of the sparse hairs would re-grow during the night didn't make each experience any less humiliating.

Catelysma plucked out a final hair with a flourish and then reached out and wiped her bloodied fingers on Ninka's squirrel-skin tunic. 'There. That's *much* better. You may leave now, little hudskin.'

'You are very kind, Majesty.'

Trembling with distress and closing her ears against the Dark Lady's mocking laughter, Ninka stumbled away to wash and change the infant's moss-lined loin cloth before its stink polluted the entire court.

CHAPTER 4

Present day

JESS STOOD IN the park, looking into the peacocks' cage. The rain had stopped for the moment. Lisa had been right. One of the birds was a classic mix of blues and greens, one a brownish female and the third was an albino with ruby eyes. They were all rather small and tatty-looking. Huddling together, they perched on the small dead tree sticking up out of a shallow square pit, which contained barely a scraping of sand. A yellowing yucca plant with dusty, strap-like leaves stood in a pot on the far side of the cage.

Jess felt her anger rise. 'Look at this place! The poor things need something to rummage about in. Like a bit of fresh earth or even a tray of grass.'

Lisa nodded. 'I saw this TV programme about an animal park. They hid grapes and stuff inside logs, so the monkeys had to find it.'

'Yeah? If we have to keep animals as prisoners, the least we can do is make sure they're happy.'

'We could find a park keeper to ask about it,' Lisa suggested, craning her neck to look back down bird cage walk. 'Mum used to bring me here when I was little. There was always someone cleaning out cages or planting flowers.'

Jess indicated a nearby flowerbed where a few straggly pansies were competing with the weeds. 'Must have been before the credit crunch.'

Two mums with little kids in buggies had stopped to look at the canaries in the cramped cage opposite.

'I wish we could do something.' Lisa turned away as if she couldn't bear to look at the peacocks in their bare pen any longer. She started walking slowly towards the café, which was visible in the distance.

Jess hesitated before following her. She stared into the cage and became aware of a strange thickening in the air around her. A space seemed to open up inside her. *Green.* The word seemed tangible, to reverberate through her like the sound of a bell followed by a strange sensation. A dream-like impression of something approaching through a forest, a weighty presence rushing towards her and exploding into a rain of light.

What? Jess rocked back onto her heels with astonishment.

Now she felt something flowing *outwards* from her, formless as smoke. Inside the cage, a tiny point of light, the glowing tip of a bonfire night sparkler, was fizzing round the dead tree on which the peacocks perched. It darted along the dry branches, zig-zagged down the shrivelled trunk and then seemed to disappear in the region of the roots.

And then Jess – blinked. In a nano-second, the world righted.

She could hear the drone of a plane overhead, the canaries whistling, mums chatting and one toddler's shrill voice complaining that it wanted to get out of its buggy.

What the hell just happened? It hadn't felt like all the other times when she had sensed odd things. This had felt…personal: like she was actively involved. But that was too scary even to consider. Anyway, nothing had actually happened. An odd feeling, a trick of the light, it didn't add up to much. It was probably low blood sugar. She *really* needed to eat that honey.

Jess's gaze travelled towards the dead tree where the peacocks perched. Two clumps of bright green leaves were sprouting from the branch. They hadn't been there earlier, had they?

The albino peacock sidestepped along the branch and nibbled a dainty crescent from one of the leaves. It turned towards Jess, pinning her with ruby eyes. Jumping to the ground, it stalked towards her, the elegant, crowned head bobbing in time with its movements.

Jess bent down everything forgotten in the pleasure of seeing the bird up close. It was healthier-looking and more handsome than she'd first thought. Delicate shades of violet-grey and cream shaded the white feathers.

The albino bird stretched out one scaly leg, inclined its neck and fanned its wings to bow to her, as gracefully as a courtier in a costume drama.

'Look Mummy. That big white bird's doing tricks!'

Startled, Jess stood up. She hadn't noticed the little boy run up to stand beside her. Inside the cage, the peacock had straightened up. It was still watching her with one pink eye, as if expecting a response.

She raised a hand in confusion, waved. 'Um…Hi!' she said, lamely.

The peacock dipped its head as if in acknowledgement, before turning and disappearing inside the sleeping enclosure.

The child's mother was standing beside her son. 'It's a wild bird, darling. They don't do tricks.'

'But it did. I saw it!' The boy's earnest face crumpled and

his lips quivered. 'That lady saw it too! Tell Mummy, lady!' He reached up, grabbed a handful of Jess's fleece and tugged it hard.

'Now don't be rude.' The woman looked embarrassed, as she removed the fabric from her son's clinging hand. 'I'm sorry. He has a very vivid imagination. It's his ADHD. Attention Deficit Hyperactivity Disorder, you know? He gets obsessed about things.'

'I did see it,' the child yelled, stamping his foot. He was scowling now, pressing his lips together.

Something within Jess reacted to the mournful little face. She knew how it felt to be different. 'Your little boy's right. The peacock was behaving oddly. Maybe it was re-homed from a circus or something.' *Unlikely. But it could happen.*

'See, Mummy!' The boy's face lit up. 'I told you!'

'So you did. Well, goodness me. What an old clever clogs you are…' The voices faded as the mother and son moved away.

Jess saw that Lisa had stopped to wait for her. She signalled to tell her she was coming. She threw a final glance at the dead tree. The clumps of green leaves had gone, maybe eaten by the other peacocks, maybe they had never been there - except in her imagination.

But she couldn't shake off the feeling that some kind of line had been crossed. First the cry in her ear and that tiny tug on her hair in the supermarket. Now this. Two off-kilter events in such a short time were unprecedented. She straightened her skinny shoulders, wishing there was someone she could talk to.

You're on your own, girl. Just like you've always been.

As she quickened her step, the loose sole of her boot flapped annoyingly. Despite the cardboard, her foot was soaked. Jess and Lisa went to sit at a plastic table in a window booth.

The warm fug of damp clothes, recycled air and cheap cooking oil enveloped them. Rain was again drumming on the glass roof of the café, pattering on the concrete outside.

A large cherry coke, with ice, stood untouched on the table in front of her. Jess took a slim pale object out of her pocket, opened it and used it to slice up another apple. The jar of honey was open on her lap. She dipped each apple slice into it before eating it.

Lisa eyed her with interest, as she slotted fries into her mouth in between bites of her cheeseburger. 'You're not an animal activist are you?' she asked worriedly. Jess gave a short laugh. 'Nah! I just don't like things being caged, unless they're injured or couldn't survive in the wild. But we don't live in an ideal world, do we?'

Lisa looked as if she had never given the matter much thought. 'Are you a vegan or something? No offence, but you have to admit, what you're eating is, well…a bit odd.'

'Don't knock it, 'till you try it! And vegans don't eat honey. It's an animal product.' Jess wrinkled her nose, munching. She smiled to show that she didn't mind Lisa asking; even though she had heard every kind of comment about her eating habits over the years. 'I can't do chemicals. Most food makes me sick. It's a pain – literally. So I stick to fruit, veggies and nuts.' She licked honey off her fingers and then wiped them on a paper napkin. 'Do you want my coke? I only asked for it, so they'd let us sit here out of the rain. Thanks, anyway.'

The ice clinked as Lisa pulled the paper cup towards her and took a long swallow. She wiped her mouth on the back of her hand. 'Food allergies. I thought maybe you were one of Stacey Weaver's crowd. You know, the class golden girls who all want to be size zero models.'

'Those lame brains!' Jess made a sound of disgust. 'Posting

Facebook messages and Tweets about how many times they've stuck their fingers down their throats in one day. No thanks. Who wants to be a model? It's a pathetic meat market. I've got too much respect for myself!'

Lisa sighed. 'It's all right for you. You're tall and skinny and really striking. You should try being me. People treat you differently when you're big. I wish I was allergic, but nothing ever makes me sick. I could eat a whole chocolate cake in one go. Dad says I'm on a 'sea' food diet. I see food and I eat it.'

It was an old joke. Jess had heard it before, but she laughed anyway. 'Women can be any size they like, Lisa. Boys with brains don't date stick insects, they like curves.'

Lisa grinned. 'I suppose.' She sounded unconvinced. She pushed her glasses more firmly up her nose, leaving a greasy fingerprint on one of the lenses.

Jess finished her last apple, wiping the slim pale blade, before folding it away into its leather sheath.

'Isn't it illegal to carry a knife?' Lisa asked, frowning. 'Don't let anyone see it. You could get into serious trouble for bringing that to school.'

Jess shrugged, unaccountably touched by the girl's concern. She wasn't used to anyone caring what she did. 'It's a letter-opener. See, the end is blunt and rounded. I got it from a car boot sale.'

Lisa looked relieved. 'Can I see?'

Jess unfolded it again and handed the object to her.

'It's beautiful.' Lisa admired the tiny carved leaves that twisted in a spiral down the length of the blade. 'What's it made of?'

'Some kind of bone, I think. The woman at the boot sale thought it was plastic, so I got it cheap. I like it because it's old. Maybe Victorian.' *And because I hate using metal cutlery. It feels hot and makes my skin sore.* But Lisa didn't need to know that. The girl already knew more about her than any other kid in college. Jess didn't want to totally weird her out.

Lisa handed the 'knife' back. Jess pocketed it.

They fell into a companionable silence. Which was a novelty for Jess. She could feel her prickly defences softening. It was a strange sensation. For the first time in ages, she felt relaxed; almost, but not quite, carefree.

Lisa chewed, swallowed the last of her burger.

Jess was staring absently at the steamed-up window. She stretched out her index finger to catch a drop tracking a wobbly line down the pane. When she looked back, Lisa was staring fixedly at her splayed fingers. Jess controlled the urge to jerk her hand back and cover it with her wide cuff. She'd always been self-conscious about her big, loose-boned hands and large knuckles.

'Piano fingers. Family trait,' she said lightly. 'Shame I can't play a note.'

Lisa smiled. 'You could wear loads of rings. Really big ones, if you wanted.'

Jess's lips twitched. 'You're definitely a glass half-full kind of person aren't you?' Folding her arms, she rested her elbows on the table and leaned forward. 'So, do you live round here?'

'In a terrace opposite that awful Limefield Mansions place. It's a posh name for such a horrible area.'

'That's where I live,' Jess said, amused.

'Oh, sorry. I didn't mean... Some of those flats are...er quite nice.'

'Nah! You were right first time. They suck.' She picked up a sachet of unopened tomato sauce, enjoying the sensation as she squidged it between finger and thumb. 'It's a poxy estate. I hate it. Mum and I, we've got plans to leave here.' *Who was she kidding?* She'd have to persuade Mum to get rid of Leon first. He was like a leech, bleeding them dry, contributing nothing. Under his influence, her mum was drinking more heavily and hadn't worked for months. Jess refused to believe that this was it – there had to be more. 'Which one's your house then?'

Lisa told her. 'We could go there, if you haven't got anything else to do,' she said shyly. 'Mum and Dad won't be back from work for ages.'

Jess considered her options. She should go back and check on her mum, but chances were she'd get no sense out of her today. She usually waited until lack of money forced Alice to stop drinking for a few days, before venturing anything more than two word conversations. Leon might have gone out to one of the pubs he frequented. But he could just as well be at the flat with some of his low-life friends, playing cards and smoking dope. She hated the way the sickly smell permeated the place, tainting her hair for days.

Either way, there wasn't a whole lot to go home to.

Lisa watched her face, as if trying to divine her thoughts. 'I'll understand if you don't want to…'

Jess shrugged. 'Might as well.'

Lisa smiled, brightening. 'Cool! My brother Zac's got a new games console. We can borrow it.'

'Sounds good. I have to go into town for something first. OK, with you?'

'Sure.' Lisa licked her finger, wiped it round the inside of the empty fries carton and sucked the last greasy crumbs into her mouth. She peered out of the café window. 'Looks like the rain's stopped again. So, where we going?'

Jess dumped the plastic bag and empty jar in a bin. She took the remaining few coins out of her pocket. 'Charity shop,' she decided. 'The scruffy one near the church. It's the cheapest.'

* * * * *

An hour later, Jess and Lisa walked back through the under-pass, taking a short cut across Limefields to Lisa's house. Jess had a pair of brown men's zip-up ankle boots tucked beneath one arm.

It was even gloomier than usual under the concrete cavern. The vaulted opening at the far end was almost indiscernible against the louring sky, giving them a sense of being in some parallel underworld.

Lisa wrinkled her nose, looking nervously at the mess of cardboard stacked haphazardly against the curved wall. 'I never come through here. Smells like a toilet. And that bloke with the filthy coat and awful hair scares me.'

'Who Mike? I've had a few chats with him. He's a bit of an oddball, but seems harmless.'

'I'll take your word for it. There's no way I'd dare to talk to him.' Lisa gave a tiny shudder. 'Why would anyone choose to live rough? I mean - couldn't he get a job or something?'

Jess felt a stir of irritation. She was beginning to like Lisa, but they were poles apart in terms of life experience. The girl's judgemental comments grated on her. 'Maybe Mike didn't choose,' she said, tersely. 'All kinds of things can happen to throw people off track.'

Lisa looking puzzled 'Like what?'

'Well – divorce. Some people never get over it, do they? Or you might lose your job and get turned out of your house. Then there's poverty, depression, addiction...' Jess paused, not really wanting to get any deeper. It was starting to feel too close to home, but she felt a perverse urge to shock Lisa. 'Anyway, sleeping rough's no picnic. Blokes like Mike are an easy target. There was a craze of happy slapping, a few months back. Gangs of kids beat up drunks while filming it on their mobiles, then posted in online. Last winter, one old homeless guy died after someone kicked the shit out of him and left him lying outside in the freezing cold all night.'

'Really?' Lisa's eyes widened in alarm. The colour had left her cheeks. 'That's terrible! Let's hurry up and get to the main road!'

Jess felt an immediate stir of guilt. *Why am I acting like I'm the guardian of this girl's social conscience?* She ought to know by now when to keep her mouth shut. Her outspokenness had got her into trouble more often than she could remember. No wonder the kids in class avoided her. Lisa was the first girl she had felt like hanging out with in months.

'My mouth runs away with me sometimes. Take no notice. And don't worry. OK?' she said more gently. 'The police have sorted things. Everything's quietened down around here. Community officers keep an eye on trouble makers. Anyway, most of the pu...' she caught herself, about to say pushers and pimps. '...problems,' she corrected herself, 'are on the far side of the estate. It's quiet where you live. You should be fine.'

Lisa still looked pale, but managed a shaky smile.

'I've got to get out of these skanky wet boots,' Jess said, grimacing. 'They're driving me mad.' She found a cleanish patch of concrete floor, sat down and began to unlace the DMs. 'God, this floor's as cold as a witches tit!' she complained.

Lisa spluttered with laughter. 'You say such funny things!'

'Yeah? I crack myself up sometimes,' Jess said dryly. She pulled on the brown charity shop boots and then stood up. Dusting down her jeans, she regarded her new footwear, flexing her long toes as she had in the shop. 'Not great, but not bad, eh?'

'If you don't mind stuff somebody else has already worn.'

Jess bit back a grin. Going to the charity shop had been a new experience for Lisa, one she didn't seem eager to repeat. 'Beggars can't be choosers.' Picking up the discarded DMs, she swung them by their laces as they set off again.

Lisa hurried to catch up with her. A weak sun was pushing between rain clouds as they emerged from the underpass and began trudging towards the u-shaped blocks of high-rise flats. The narrow roads in Limefields were busy with working girls and kerb crawlers at night, but it was quiet and almost deserted at this time of day. Jess led the way down a short alley to a row of garages. A gap in a fence brought them out opposite a building site on a residential street. The hoarding surrounding the site was peppered with graffiti tags.

Jess paused to check that no one was watching. She swung back her arm and tossed her old boots over the hoarding. 'Bye old friends! We've had some good times together, but it's time to part!'

Lisa laughed, but there was a forced sound to it. Jess recognised the girl's expression from one too many uncomfortable encounters. The smile froze on her face. 'What?' she said, more sharply than she'd intended.

'N…Nothing.' Lisa shuffled her feet as she looked down at the pavement.

Jess thought she knew the sub-text. *You were fun for a while. But you're not the sort of person I want be seen with.* She was used to the pain of rejection, but she hadn't seen this one coming. Lisa had seemed different. That would teach her to let her guard down. Her disappointment had an edge of anger.

'OK I get it. No hard feelings. See you around.' She spun on her heel, ready to march away. But a hand on her arm stopped her.

Lisa's fingers gripped tight. 'Don't go! I didn't mean

anything. I'm always getting stuff wrong and putting my foot in it.'

'That makes two of us! I have a tendency to act like a cross between a complete dork and...um a complete dork!'

Lisa giggled. 'What are we like? Come on,' she urged. 'My house is one from the end of the road. It's got a red door.'

Of course it has. Jess felt a silly smile hovering around her lips as she followed Lisa. Her new boots were pinching a little, but she couldn't suppress an absurd feeling of happiness. *I am totally out of practice with this friendship shit.*

Lisa's house, a narrow-fronted, three-storey terrace was a revelation. Pastel wallpaper in each room, furniture worn but comfortable, flowered curtains fastened with shiny cords that ended in big tassels. Everything neat and spotless, with a faint smell of lemon polish.

Jess could see at once that it wasn't just a house. This was a home. She and Mum had lived for so long in chaotic rooms, shabby bed-sits, once in a squat, that she had forgotten what home looked like.

She felt grubby and ill at ease. Unconsciously, she combed her fingers through her dark hair, feeling them snag on the tangles. Lisa invited Jess to leave her fleece in the hall. She hung it on a hook, embarrassed by the shabby top she wore underneath. At least it was clean. She had spilled blackcurrant juice down her only T-shirt and had yet to wash it.

Lisa was bustling about making coffee for herself. She poured Jess a glass of orange juice. They took their drinks into her bedroom. 'I'll just go get Zac's new console.'

Jess sat on the bed and sipped her juice. The duvet and matching curtains had a design of pink spots. An entire wall of shelves held books, box games and jig-saws. Dolls were everywhere, even lining the top of a wardrobe. A threadbare

and obviously well-loved teddy bear sat against the headboard. On top of a chest, a mirror was draped with glittery
scarves and strings of beads. It was the kind of bedroom Jess
would have loved when she was nine years old. Creepy and
cute at the same time, it was the kind of room in horror
movies where dolls suddenly came to life and gnashed
sharpened teeth.

When Lisa returned with the console, they sprawled on
her bed to play computer games. The duvet was marshmal-
low soft and the childish room was very warm.

The sound of a key jangled and a door banged shut downstairs. 'Lisa? You in here?'

'Oh, blimmin' heck. It's Zac!' Lisa jumped up as if she had
been burned, already unplugging wires and gathering up the
console. 'He'll go ballistic if he finds I've borrowed his stuff!'

'You go downstairs,' Jess offered. 'Keep him talking, while
I put it back.'

She crept along the hall to Zach's bedroom. The door
opened without a tell-tale creak. Jess slipped inside and
quickly deposited the console on the bed. There was a
sweetish, faintly chemical smell in the room, similar to nail
polish remover. The fumes clutched at her throat. She
muffled a cough against her sleeve, knowing that she ought
to leave at once, but she couldn't help looking around. She
had never been in a teenage boy's bedroom. It was smaller
than Lisa's, more sparsely furnished. Apart from a bed and
wardrobe, the room was taken up by a desk, topped with a
bulky PC set-up with a stack and separate speakers. Heavy
metal posters hung on the back of the door. CDs, DVDs and
comic books were stacked against the walls.

A quick look revealed them to be gothic manga. Jess had

been into that stuff in a big way, a while back, but had been forced to leave her collection behind after she and Alice beat a particularly hasty exit from a flat while avoiding a debt collector. She was reaching for one of the comics, when she saw the cardboard box full of spray-cans beneath the bed.

Zac was the graffiti artist. It was he who had painted the new manga character she had admired, near the underpass entrance. Jess's interest in him quickened. There was a sound behind her. She whirled round.

Zac Simpson's clear blue eyes were hard and unfriendly. 'What the hell are you doing in my room?'

CHAPTER 5

In Faery – a while ago in Human time –
or the blink of an eye…

NINKA'S PANIC AT the thought of caring for the court play-thing was starting to lose its edge. She had carefully sifted the Dark Lady's words for hidden entrapments and found none. *"You will take care of it. Find it a bed and furnish quarters for it. I give you leave to find a helper, if the task is beyond you. But mistake me not, the responsibility for Aerith falls to you."*

Good, thought Ninka, there had been no mention of having to stay at court with Aerith. And she was not specifically *ordered* to press another into her service, but was given leave to do so, if she felt it necessary.

'Pshaw!' a small explosive sound escaped her. 'Have I needed help with anything these many long years, since the last of my kind fell to the royal hounds? I should say not! And would I welcome any of the fawning court fey to my hearth, so that he or she could carry back tales of me and my doings? I should think not!'

Muttering softly to herself, she entered the hill, striding through halls and down sloping corridors as she made her way to the kitchens. Hopefully, Crowle would know what to feed the young mortal. The cook had looked kindly on her, since she made him a salve for his feet, ogres being much prone to bunions and ingrown toenails.

Her arms were already aching. She wondered how in all of Faery she was going to carry the baby as far as the forest. Aerith lay against her chest, her head tucked under the crook of Ninka's chin. The pale hair, soft as thistledown, tickled as she stirred and began to grizzle.

'Hush, now. All's well,' Ninka crooned, but the baby cried harder.

She quickened her step, but by the time she puffed down the stone steps and into the cavernous room the baby was bawling, her face red and her arms and legs working angrily. It was all Ninka could do to keep hold of her.

'Here, here. What's this?' Crowle lumbered forwards, arms extended and crouching to be on a level with Ninka. 'Give us the mite here.'

Limp with relief, Ninka handed Aerith over. 'Her loin cloth needs changing.'

'I should say it does.' Crowle's broad snout wrinkled. 'Who's a little pongo then?' he crooned. 'Phew!'

'Aerith's a 'she', not an 'it',' Ninka corrected.

Crowle threw her an amused glance from under beetling brows as he balanced the squalling child along the length of one meaty forearm. 'That right? And how is it that you have charge of it…her?'

'Catelysma has made her my responsibility.'

'A weighty task you have indeed,' Crowle mused. 'I'm surprised the Dark Lady concerns herself with such a tiny scrap of mortality – unless there's something special about Aerith. Where was she got from? D'you know?'

Oh, yes the little mortal was special indeed. Ninka shrugged, but said nothing.

A powerful faery with a dangerous secret. And her mortal lover who had unwisely tried to tear himself free, when his young wife became gravid. Ninka alone knew the full extent of what had transpired, but she would not speak of it to any fey. Because once the tail end of *this* thread of secrets was picked free, the entire spool would begin to unroll. And, ancient powers protect her, what a poisonous tangle of thorns it would become.

Crowle was moving across the stone floor towards a wooden chest with many drawers and compartments. Procuring a length of woven fabric, he draped it over his free arm. 'Nip outside then and get me some sphagnum, my treasure,' he said equably. 'There's plenty of it growing around the stream.'

Ninka went gladly, the child's cries still ringing in her ears. Curious that she found the sound so troubling. She went out of the back door, glad of a moment's respite. The kitchen garden was quiet, the only sound coming from the spring, which bubbled up between rocks and gathered in a clear pool.

When she returned with an armful of springy pale-green moss, Crowle had already stripped and washed the infant's nether regions. It lay on the wooden table top, kicking its chubby bare legs as he gently patted it dry with enormous hands. Deftly, he lined a piece of cloth with soft moss, before knotting it around the baby's loins.

'There we go. Who's as sweet as a gilly flower then?' he crooned, gently chucking the baby under her chin with the tip of one huge finger. 'You don't want to be wearing that bit of old rag. Look what Crowle has made for you.'

He had cut a hole in the centre of a piece of clean nettle hemp and was now slipping it over the baby's head and securing it with binder twine. While he admired the make-shift dress, Ninka swooped down and picked up the discarded pink suit that was lying crumpled on the flagstones. Without really knowing why, she tucked it down inside the neck of her tunic.

Sobs still shook the infant's little chest. They subsided as Aerith gathered breath for a moment and then let out a shriek that lanced new panic through Ninka's veins. Tears trickled from the corners of the tightly screwed eyes and ran down the peachy cheeks.

'Good set of lungs,' Crowle approved.

'Is she hurting somewhere, do you think?' Ninka wrung her hands, surprised to feel her own eyes pricking with tears of sympathy.

'Gentry love you, no! The mite's hungry, that's all.' The ogre's laughter boomed round the cave, his yellow tusks showing in his lower jaw.

Ninka blinked uncertainly, still unnerved by Aerith's gummy cries. How did so much noise come from a small being? You would never think there was enough breath for it. 'We must feed her then. Will she suck mashed leaves? Or shall we crush worms and beetles in water for her. Look - she hasn't teeth to chew meat.'

'All's in hand.' The ogre's speckled amber eyes glittered with humour. 'Fabe's speeding to the nearest mortal farm to steal milk. She'll return presently.'

'Milk? Of course. Mortals are hot-bloods, like cervids, canines and coneys that give suck to their young.' Ninka felt foolish for not having worked this out for herself. But then she had never been much concerned about the other court play-things; most of the human infants hadn't lasted all that long anyway. The awful responsibility of having this one solely reliant on her made her feel light-headed. How would she know what to do? What if Aerith got sick? Once they were deep in the forest, Crowle would not be at hand to give advice. 'Will…will I have to steal milk for her until she is old enough to go out and get it for herself?'

The ogre nodded. 'Yes and No. She'll need milk for a short time, but then she'll come into her teeth, so you'll know to start weaning her. Feed her soft pap at first. Soft fruits, pounded with honey, mashed vegetables, grain patties. She'll soon manage more and before you know it she'll be eating whatever you eat.'

Ninka let out a breath of relief. She could do this. She smiled at Crowle. 'How do you know all this?'

He grimaced. 'In the old days, we used to be partial to the odd slice of roasted mortal. My father kept a stable of them for the kitchens. I had the care of the newborns.'

Just then there was a silvery clatter of wings. The scullery fey, a slender pixie, with rosy colouring, appeared at the kitchen entrance. 'Farmer weren't around, so I milked the nanny myself.' She handed a small pottery jar to Crowle.

Crowle nodded. 'Well done, Fabe.'

Blushing, the little scullery fey tucked her cloud of pink candy-floss hair behind her ears. Her long dangling toes brushed the floor as she drifted towards the sink, where she swirled soapwort into warm water and began washing a huge pile of wooden plates and dishes.

Crowle showed Ninka how to dilute the milk with water and pour it into a small pottery vessel, with a long spout. He sat her down, placed the baby in her lap and tipped Aerith back so that her head was resting in the crook of Ninka's arm. 'That's it, my treasure. Put the spout to her lips.'

Tentatively, Ninka did so. Aerith thrashed her head about, her lips bumping against the vessel. At first a lot of milk spilled down the baby's chin, but after a few tries, she latched onto the spout and began sucking greedily.

Ninka glowed with pride as she heard the sounds of swallowing. Aerith began making little grunts of content-ment. 'It is working.'

Soon all the milk was drunk. Aerith's head fell back and the spout slipped from her lips. Worn out with crying and sucking, her eyelids fluttered. Ninka picked her up and laid her across her shoulder. There was a rumbling noise and then a wet-sounding explosion close to her ear. She jumped in alarm.

'Something's wrong with her!'

Crowle chuckled. 'That's just air coming up from the baby's belly. All's as it should be. Rub her back. That's it. You'll soon get the hang of it. Infants don't do a lot, besides supping, sleeping and shitting.'

Ninka beamed, her confidence growing. 'I should take her to my home now. Can I take the rest of the milk and the sphagnum?'

'You can and welcome. It'll do you for a day or so. But it's a long way for a little personage like yourself to carry a heavy baby.' He turned to Fabe who was now hovering nearby, and watching everything with great interest. 'Fabe, go and get the dog cart we use to carry roots in leaf fall. Line it with a bit of hay.' The scullery fey fluttered off to do his bidding. 'It'll be easier to push Aerith in the cart. I'll send Fabe to collect it when we need it again.'

'I am grateful to you,' Ninka said warmly, knowing better than to thank a faery.

'A pleasure,' Crowle said. 'You and the little mortal will do very well together. Just - take care to watch your step, my treasure. She's Catelysma's pet, remember.'

Ninka nodded, trying not to think of all that could mean.

She looked up as Fabe reappeared with the little wooden cart and smiled her thanks. Aerith barely stirred as she settled her in the cosy hay nest. As she took the shafts in hand and set off, pulling the cart behind her, her heart felt lighter than it had in many a long, lonely year.

CHAPTER 6

ZAC LET THE door swing behind him. It didn't quite close. Jess smiled apologetically. 'Oh, sorry. Is this *your* room? I was trying to find the bathroom.'

Zac didn't return her smile. She could feel him weighing her up. He was nothing like his sister. She guessed he was about seventeen. Tall and broad-shouldered, his dark blond hair brushed his collar. There was a sprinkling of freckles across his nose and short stubble covered a square jaw. He wore jeans and a navy and white check shirt over a grey T-shirt.

'Lisa was just telling me about this cool girl in her class, who she invited to the house. But I didn't expect it to be you. What's the catch?'

'Excuse me?'

'Don't bother playing dumb. We both know Lisa's not the kind of person the other college kids are queuing up to hang out with. Not without strings, anyway. She can do without your sort putting ideas into her head.'

'My sort? And what sort's that?' Jess said, softly.

Zac's grin held no warmth. 'I've seen you around. Don't tell me you got that face and pale skin from staying out of the sun. You're on something more than just wacky baccy. What is it, coke? Heroin?'

'All of it! And you can add speed and horse knock-out drops to the list! Oh, yeah, and I strangle kittens in my spare time!' She narrowed her eyes, looking at him with dislike.

'You don't even *know* me. Where the hell do you get off, judging me?'

'Come off it! Everyone knows that bloke your mum's shacked-up with has been done for possession of drugs.'

Jess hadn't known, but it didn't surprise her. She shrugged. 'And that's my fault?'

'Whatever.' Zac shook his head slowly and then glanced round the room. 'Maybe I should check if anything's missing.'

'It's not, but I don't expect you to believe me,' Jess said flatly. 'You've got me all wrong.'

'I don't really care.' Zac paused and ran a hand through his hair. 'This isn't about you. Look - Lisa's a sweet kid.' He lowered his voice. 'It's been difficult for her to fit in at college. Things are starting to work out for her. The last thing she needs is to get mixed up in any trouble. Do me a favour and stay the fuck away from her.'

Jess felt her temper igniting. 'Or what?' she said, quietly.

'Or you'll bring down a severe sack of shit upon your head. That's a promise.' Zac's light-blue eyes glinted, dangerously.

'You arrogant prick!' Jess shouted, all constraint forgotten. 'What makes you think I'm scared of you? You mean *that* to me!' She snapped her fingers in his face.

Zac grasped her wrist and jerked her towards him. She twisted and her bony shoulder banged into his collar bone. She heard him wince. His face was almost on a level with hers.

'Don't test me, right? I've got friends.'

Light-headed with fury, she yanked her hand free.

'I don't give jack shit about you or your lame friends. And I wouldn't hang around with your lame-brain sister if you paid me!' she yelled at him. 'Why would I need a pathetic puppy trailing round after me? Everyone in class takes the piss out of her...' she stopped, the door which Zac has left ajar was moving.

In the doorway stood Lisa. The stricken look on her face told Jess that she must have heard most of the conversation.

She groaned inwardly. 'Oh no! Lisa. I didn't mean...'

Zac grabbed her by the shoulder and swung her back round to face him.

He looked almost smug. 'I think you should go.' He poked her in the chest, with one hard fingertip. 'Now!'

Taken aback, Jess swayed. Heat flooded her veins. Fire and ice shot up her backbone. She seemed to see the room through a flickering heat haze.

There was a sudden bang followed by a loud hissing sound. Blood spurted from under the bed and sprayed on to the carpet. Jess choked back a cry as more of it fountained up from behind the headboard, staining the wall. Lisa was screaming at the top of her voice.

Red – shocking in its brightness, was everywhere. Zac was spattered and so was his PC, the contents of his desk and everything piled against the wall opposite.

The peardrop reek of cellulose filled the room and scoured Jess's throat. Sourness rose from her belly. She convulsed in agony. Dimly, battling not to throw-up or black-out, she realised what was happening.

Not blood. Paint. One of the pressurised spray-cans under the bed had exploded.

Finally, the hissing stopped and silence fell. The room looked like an abattoir.

'What the...' Zac moaned, tearing at his hair as he took in the devastation. 'Christ! Look at my stuff! It's ruined...'

A thin sound like a kitten mewling came from Lisa. She

had taken off her glasses and there were pale circles round her eyes on her otherwise scarlet face.

Jess felt the urge to laugh hysterically. She staggered backwards, gagging on a sob and somehow fell out onto the landing, where she bent over, retching helplessly. She spat, coughed, spat again. Red-streaked snot dribbled down her nose. She cuffed it away with her sleeve. Finally, she was able to draw a pained, shaky breath.

She headed for the stairs, stumbling down them, two at a time. Her fleece was hanging in the hall. Grabbing it from the hook, she flung it on as she dragged open the front door. Fresh air flooded in easing her agony.

'Jess?' Lisa called from the top of the stairs. 'Wait!'

She didn't reply. What was there to say?

*   *   *   *   *

Jess hurled herself into the flat and stood there with her back pressed against the closed front door. A bike with no saddle or front wheel leaned against the crumbling plaster wall. The hurt and betrayal that had marked Lisa's face, she couldn't shake it off. Zac had hurt her but she had only herself to blame for her what she had said. Their tentative friendship was over. She trembled, her thoughts in turmoil. Her feelings had taken her by surprise. Her life had always been unpredictable, but lately it seemed to be spiralling out of control. She wasn't sure what to do about it. There was no one she could confide in. No one she trusted.

And that spray-can...

'Jess? You're home early.' Her mum came out of the sitting room, a can of lager in one hand. Her gaunt face was pale. There were dark puffy circles beneath her eyes. She leaned against the door jam. Her dark hair was scraped back, a few greasy strands tucked behind her ears. 'Look at the state of you! You know there's no money to buy new clothes. Why can't you be more careful?' And then her voice changed as she seemed to focus. 'Is that blood? What's happened? Are you hurt?'

'No. It's red paint. Art class at college. Just leave me alone.' She tried to walk past, but her mum moved awkwardly to stand in her way.

'Something's wrong with my little girl, isn't it?' she asked, reaching out to caress a lock of Jess's hair. 'Do you want to talk about it?' Her smile held a trace of the sweetness Jess remembered from their early years together.

Even though she was used to her mum's quicksilver changes of mood, Jess felt her anger slipping. Stupid to foster hope when she knew better, but she still did. She couldn't help longing to curl up on the sofa with Mum. Talk, laugh, maybe leaf through the pile of crappy celebrity gossip magazines Alice filched from the recycling boxes neighbours put out weekly.

She could detect the peculiar smell that meant Mum was so tanked up she was sweating alcohol out of her pores. She might seem normal, even appear to be making sense, but the shadow creature, unleashed by the alcohol, was completely in control. Jess could see it looking at her now out of the blank bloodshot eyes. Blank, but still somehow – wounded.

Which was what she found almost unbearable.

'What's the point of talking?' she snapped. 'You won't remember anything I've said when you're sober.'

'Don't talk to me like that!' Alice slapped Jess across the side of her face. Grabbing her by the shoulders, she shook her as if she was a rag doll. 'Who do you think you are, eh? Well

I'll tell you.' Each word was punctuated by another shake. 'You're just a bloody know-all kid! I can do what I like – get it? I've only had a couple to help me relax.'

And the rest. Jess's ears rang from the blow. Clenching her teeth, she reached out, jerked the can from her mum's hand.

'Give that back!' Alice clawed at her, eyes wild.

Jess shook her off. She was taller by almost a head and much stronger. Marching into the kitchen, she emptied the lager down the kitchen sink.

Alice stumbled after her, bare feet making a faint sucking noise on the sticky floor. 'You little bitch!' Her shoulders slumped and she started to cry. 'I'm a terrible mother. You don't deserve this, Jess. I am going to stop. You see if I don't. That's my last drink. Promise. Fresh start tomorrow. OK? Cross my heart and hope to die.' She made the sign on her chest with her index finger.

'You can't do it by yourself. You're sick. You have to get help,' Jess said blankly.

'I know I should. I'm weak and pathetic. Leon says I'm ugly and useless. A waste of space. He's right.' She laid her head on Jess's shoulder.

'Leon's full of it.' Jess stroked her mother's hair with one hand, feeling the base of the small skull resting in her cupped palm. The emaciated body smelt stale and her breath was sour.

She felt responsible for her mum, but also acutely aware of her own helplessness. For a long time, she had felt she was the adult and Mum was the child. She was bone-weary of the merry-go-round of their existence. Mum promised not to drink, sometimes managing to stay dry for a week or two. On one occasion, she was dry for a couple of months, but then started drinking again. It didn't seem to matter whether she was happy or sad, worried or carefree. Alcohol was the only constant in her mother's life.

And with Leon always chipping away at her, Mum had gradually lost the will to even *try* to stop drinking. Jess wished he'd just do a Rob – take a hike and never come back.

Alice pulled away, still murmuring and sank heavily onto a kitchen chair. 'If only your dad was here. He shouldn't have left us…'

Jess took a deep steadying breath. She filled the kettle, making sure not to touch the metal with her bare hand.

Head in her hands, her mother kept talking in a low monotone. 'It was Stella dying that did it. If she had lived, Rob would have stayed. He blamed himself. I never understood that. How could it have been his fault? But he insisted it was. Something he had done, God knows what. I begged him to tell me, but he wouldn't. Said it was too terrible and I wouldn't believe him anyway – no one would. And what was the point because it wouldn't change anything. Maybe it would even make things worse.' She made a sound of disgust. 'As if they *could* be worse!' She paused, dragged in a harsh breath. 'Rob was in a bad way. Wouldn't eat. Couldn't sleep. Hurting himself too. Scratches on his arms. Hundreds of them, criss-crossing the skin. We'd been good together. I thought we were forever – whatever happened. But he said we were safer without him. Christ, was I ever wrong about him…'

Safer? Jess had been reaching for the jar of coffee, the only thing in the cupboard apart from a box of Leon's cheap sugary cereal, when the word snared her attention. *Why safer? And Rob was self-harming because of something terrible he had done? Curiouser and curiouser, says Alice.*

How come her mum had never mentioned that before?

Alice's version of her twin baby sister's cot death and her father's desertion didn't usually change, there were never any fresh details. Unlike her recall of more recent events, which was consistent only in being unreliable. From what dark recesses had Mum dredged up this new stuff about Dad?

Jess sensed a ring of truth. She had to agree that something didn't sound right about her dad's reactions. What could he have done, that was so bad that he was driven to punish himself by cutting into his arms in that alarming way?

Shaking her head in puzzlement, Jess poured boiling water onto instant coffee and added sugar. She didn't expect she would ever know what happened. Rob Morgan was the only one who knew the truth. They hadn't heard a word from him in fifteen years. For all she knew, he was dead.

Mum's voice had taken on a familiar bitter note, '…I really loved him. He was a beautiful man. Hazel eyes – like yours, although yours are greener. He was kind and generous. Funny, too. Always laughing. I've never felt like that about anyone before or since. But he turned out like all the rest. Taking off, without a word. And after he promised that he'd always look after me. 'I'd say, "I love you" and he'd say, "I love you more." Bastard! Men are all the same. No bloody backbone…'

Jess knew this part of the routine. Once Mum started in with slagging off her dad, and having a go at men in general, it could go on for ages. Her attention wandered. She nodded absently at appropriate moments. For herself, she couldn't muster any emotion beyond resentment. Rob Morgan's disappearance had trapped them all in time; her Mum, most of all.

Exhibit A; A big empty space where a husband and dad used to be.

Jess placed the mug of coffee on the chipped formica topped table. 'Milk's off. You'll have to have it black.'

Alice lifted the cup and sipped. She pulled a face. 'It's vile.' She wrapped her hands around the cup to warm them. 'Stella was a beautiful baby. Golden curls and skin like cream. Chubby little limbs. Ten minutes older than you. And quiet. She hardly ever cried, except when she was hungry...'

Yeah, I know. My dead baby sister was a saint.

'...unlike you. You'd scream until you were blue in the face. So demanding!' Her mum looked up and gave a fond, blurred smile. 'So different, with your long arms and legs. All that fine black down on your skin - just like a little monkey. It rubbed off after a few days. No one would have taken you and Stella for twins...'

Jess folded her arms and leaned back. She was sitting on the chair that Leon had kicked in a rage. The wonky leg creaked beneath her. She did occasionally wonder why her dad had never bothered to find them. Wasn't he at all curious about her, Jess? The twin in his likeness, the alter-ego of the golden child who had died so tragically? It seemed impossible that she'd once *had* a twin sister. Twins had a special link, a bond, didn't they? Even non-identical ones. Shouldn't she feel like the broken half of something once whole? The fact was, she didn't feel *anything* about Stella. How do you mourn a sister you've never known? She wished that she could grieve, if only for her mum's sake; then she might be connected to some small part of Alice's pain. A pain that had coloured and tainted both of their lives.

While still somehow excluding Jess.

Her mum shuddered, pushed her half-drunk coffee away. Wiping her eyes, she got up and went silently out of the kitchen. Through the open door, Jess watched her weave her way back towards the sitting room, before closing the door behind her. She got to her feet and went into the hall. *Stupid to court disappointment.* But she had always been the kind who couldn't resist picking a scab.

Seconds passed. Then - there it was. The tiny soft popping, as a ring-pull can was opened.

Jess shrugged, fatalistically. Well, she had got what she expected. Where was the logic in being upset? But logic had nothing to do with it, of course. 'I'll be in my room. See you later,' she said, bleakly.

There was no answer.

In her bedroom she stripped off her clothes, dismayed to see that they were heavily splashed with red paint. She hunted through the stuff strewn on the floor, dragging out a crumpled black cotton shirt with frayed cuffs and a pair of creased black combat trousers. She put them on, and then took the soiled clothes into the bathroom where she attacked them with a bar of soap and a nailbrush. Ten minutes of hard scrubbing and rinsing, made no impact on the paint splatters. With a sigh of exasperation she draped the wet garments over the balcony railings to dry.

As she was going back to her bedroom, Leon came in the front door. He wore a new, camouflage army-style parka over grey jeans and expensive trainers. Jess tensed instinctively, weighing up his mood.

His grin revealed the gap in his nicotine-stained front teeth where an incisor had been knocked out during a fight. Stubble shadowed his thin cheeks and a scrawny beard, plaited and bound with a leather thong, hung from his chin. There were piercings at his eyebrow and nose. The nose ring was a recent addition, the skin around it was red and inflamed.

'All right?' he asked.

A good mood. For now. Jess nodded, still wary. 'Yeah.'

'Where's your mum?'

She hated the way he moved his mouth so that the stud in his tongue clicked against his bottom teeth. She pointed towards the sitting room.

Leon took a plastic bag filled with dried leaves out of his pocket. Shrugging off the parka, he draped it over the crippled bike. 'You want some? It's good stuff. A mate of mine grows it.'

Jess shook her head. 'No thanks.'

'Oh, yeah. I forgot. You never touch drugs or drink. You should. It might loosen you up a bit.' Leon's eyes, the colour of withered-grass narrowed with mockery. Click, click went the stud as he folded and unfolded his thin lips. 'Prissy little bitch. Where do you get off looking at me as if I've just crawled out from under a stone?'

Jess suppressed a flicker of fear. Showing weakness only incensed him. Leon was slightly-built, with bony rounded shoulders. She was taller than him by a few centimetres, but he was a lot stronger than he looked. She had seen the damage he could cause when he lashed out.

'Well you said it.'

Leon frowned and then he suddenly laughed. 'You crack me up! Sometime, you and me are going to have a long talk about that smart mouth of yours. That's a promise.'

'Don't hold your breath,' Jess drawled.

Click, click. Winking at her, Leon opened the sitting room door. She heard him say, 'Here I am, babe! I've got us a treat. Who's the daddy then...'

Jess quivered with dislike.

The old Alice, fiercely protective and resourceful would never have looked twice at a loser like him. There had been a change in her over the last few months, since Leon arrived on the scene. She seemed more fragile as if some inner part of herself was shrinking. Jess had been worried about her mum for a while, since she started finding bottles hidden in cupboards and behind furniture. Alcoholics were mostly in denial. They often drank themselves to death – slowly. Jess knew this because she had read about it in a library book. Mum needed to get onto a programme if she was ever going to be strong enough to face her demons. But how was that going to happen when their life was characterised by instability?

They had met Leon in the bus station café, where they were sitting hunched over hot drinks; coffee for Mum, hot water with lemon for her, dreading closing time because they had nowhere to stay. Four plastic carrier bags, holding everything they owned after they'd done a moonlight from their last place, were stuffed beneath the table. Leon sat at the next table. After more hot drinks, which he paid for, he had offered to help find them a place. He had a friend who knew about an empty flat. Jess had misgivings. She had disliked him on sight, but she was all too aware that her mum had a heavy cold. One night sleeping rough in the local park had made her cough worse. Leon had been as good as his word. The following day, they moved into the flat in Limefield Mansions.

It was small, cramped and badly in need of redecorating, but Jess was able to make sure Mum rested and kept warm. Leon dropped by with food, cold remedies, kitchen stuff and bedding; all gratis, having fallen off the back of a lorry. He was charm itself. Jess still didn't trust him, but they'd run out of options. What was she supposed to do?

After three weeks, she started thinking that she and Mum could make a go of it. She began looking for a part-time evening job, had even found a convenient self-help group for people with drink problems. She returned from college one day to find the curtains closed. Leon sat on the sofa with his feet up on the rickety coffee table Jess had rescued from a skip. Techno music filled the flat. He and Alice were working through a stack of six-packs.

Leon had looked up at Jess with a self-satisfied smile. His tongue rolled the stud against his teeth. Click, click. He knew she had seen through his act, but didn't care. The battle lines were drawn between him and her. It was only a matter of time.

Leon didn't go home that night or the night after. He became a permanent fixture.

Now Jess heard her mum's voice rising querulously from inside the sitting room. And then Leon's deeper tones. 'Don't worry about that snotty little bitch, OK? I'll roll a spliff, you'll feel better…'

She didn't wait to hear the rest of it. A wave of depression swamped her. She went into her room and bolted the door.

CHAPTER 7

SUNLIGHT SLANTED THROUGH the front window of *Farmer & Sons, Family Hardware*. It framed what was not so much a display as a jumble of the products on sale. Electrical goods stood on cardboard boxes, the lettering bleached to a uniform beige. Rolls of deckchair canvas brushed shoulders with cards of wooden clothes pegs, paintbrushes and plastic tea-strainers. Outside on the pavement, baskets in all shapes and sizes were piled alongside buckets, brushes and mops. The shop stood halfway along what had once been a busy street, but a by-pass a few years back had directed the bulk of traffic onto the new ring road. Since then, many of the once-thriving businesses had re-located or morphed into residential dwellings.

Inside the shop, Caleb Farmer was sweating beneath the thick canvas apron that his dad insisted he wore over a T-shirt and cut-off jeans. He was tall, over six feet, but the apron reached past his knees. He had to wrap the tape twice around his waist to secure it. Still, he was resigned to wearing it; taking it off would only prompt another row.

He bent forward to rest his lean muscular arms on the wooden counter top. The surface was clammy to the touch. A breeze blowing in the open door smelt of hot pavements, dust and parched air. At the back of the shop, an ancient floor-mounted fan rattled and whirred, making the atmosphere just about bearable. Caleb had recently broached the subject of installing air con and found it dismissed out of hand. Never bothered by changes in temperature, his dad, Neil Farmer, was oblivious to the discomfort of others.

Besides money was tight right now. Caleb knew just how tight. A letter from the bank had slipped beneath the kitchen table and been left there. Caleb had read it before returning it to the small bedroom his dad used as an office. Repayments on the business loan were four months in arrears. The bank manager was keen to schedule a meeting with Mr Farmer to discuss his options.

Caleb sighed, heavily. He knew he had to find the courage to tell his dad about his decision to leave, but there never seemed a good time to bring up the subject. Everyone assumed he'd carry on working in the family business, but he knew he wasn't cut out for it. He had one talent – he could draw well, and it was all he wanted to do. He had secretly applied, and been accepted, on a course in art and design. By now he should have been in his first college term. But things hadn't worked out that way. Pa Farmer had retired suddenly due to ill health. The burden of responsibility for the hardware business had fallen onto his dad's shoulders and by default onto his own.

Loyalty to Pa Farmer and his dad had warred with Caleb's ambitions. Reluctantly, he put his own needs second. But after a few months standing behind the counter, he felt like he was slowly being crushed. The thought of working in the hardware shop, year after year, and taking it on when *his* dad retired filled him with horror.

Irritably, he pushed back a lock of his collar-length dark-brown hair. He had been at the counter since seven thirty that morning. Dad insisted on opening early to take advantage of the people walking past on their way to work, as Pa Farmer had always done. So far today, Caleb had sold a packet of six brass cup hooks and a brush for cleaning teapot spouts. Both to an old lady who had limped in with a red, plaid shopping trolley in tow. She told him she was on her way to buy budgie seed from the Homes and Garden superstore in the newly built industrial estate. 'You ought to get a pet care section. Then I wouldn't be needing to go so far on me poor ole legs,' she complained.

More stock? Caleb cast a jaded glance round the shop. To his right there was a rack hung with screwdrivers, window blinds, rolls of replacement washing line and insect spray. On the counter, a box of novelty car air fresheners leaked a ferny, chemical smell. Some of this stuff had been here for years. If they added anything else, he suspected the whole place might collapse like a badly tied bundle of sticks.

Forcing a smile, he counted out change into the old lady's palm. 'I'll mention it to Dad. Thanks for your custom. You have a nice day now.'

Mid-morning arrived at a snail's pace. A few office workers hurried past on their way to buy sandwiches from the bakery at the end of the street. Two young women, wearing short skirts, strappy high-heeled shoes and too much make-up, called in at lunchtime. They worked at the new hairdresser's near the flower shop, they informed him animatedly, along with a lot of giggling.

Caleb was glad of the distraction, although he was uneasy in the company of attractive young women. Not enough practice. It was something he hoped to remedy as soon as he could break free of the shop. One of the women, with blonde hair was quite pretty. After a bit of good-natured banter, he sold her a plastic sandwich box. Before she left, she invited him to, 'Come in to the salon sometime, yeah? I'll do you an Indian head – for free. That's a massage – in case you're wondering!'

Her friend had laughed as Caleb felt himself redden. 'Thanks. I'll remember that,' he lied. 'Don't work too hard.' He lifted a hand, returning their waves through the shop window.

He smiled to himself. Their flirty chatter and high spirits had been a pleasant diversion.

Half an hour later, bored witless, he considered sweeping the floor or washing the front windows. What was the point? Nothing was going to change the fact that the shop was a dinosaur.

Reaching under the counter, Caleb took out his sketchbook and pencils. He turned to a drawing he had begun earlier in the week. An imaginary landscape of bleak towering rocks, dramatic skies and contorted trees with a skewed perspective, all flat planes and sloping lines. He set to work, adding patches of cross-hatched lines, becoming absorbed in a world of his own.

No more customers came in. After a while, he laid down his pencil, fetched a cold drink and stood in the open doorway. The church bells on the spire, visible above the house opposite struck two. A faded, blue and white painted sign on the end wall of the house was still decipherable. It stated that *Nightly Bile Beans keep you healthy, bright-eyed and slim.* Caleb felt a stir of depression at this visible remnant of a by-gone age. Sometimes, he thought his whole life was spent inside a time-warp. Crumpling the can, he lobbed it into the bin at the kerb.

Back inside the shop, he could hear the drone of the radio in the upstairs flat, where Dad was struggling with the monthly accounts. Mum was visiting friends across town. Before returning she would do the week's shopping and call in at the wholesalers. He hoped she wasn't doing too much. She looked tired and drained lately.

At the counter, he added finishing touches to the drawing, before holding it at arm's length. The quality of the black pencil marks, some thick and forceful, others delicate and scratchy, gave the monotone drawing the appearance of a woodcut. There was a sense of something brooding about it, as if he had captured the exact moment before a storm. It wasn't bad, he decided. This dramatic style was a new direction for him. He flipped back through some of his latest drawings, all of them in a similar vein. Promising. He was on to something.

It was hotter in the shop, now that the sun had moved round to the front of the building. A trickle of sweat ran down his chest. He rubbed at his T-shirt with one hand, too lethargic to bend down and slip the sketchbook under the counter.

Caleb wrinkled his nose against the familiar fug of cardboard, rope, candles, hot metal and beeswax. The shop probably smelt much the same in Pa Farmer's day. He sat down, propped his chin on one hand and drifted off momentarily. The next thing he knew Dad was striding towards him. Caleb straightened and attempted to look alert. His eyes fell on the sketch book, lying in full view.

'Are you winning with those accounts?' he asked with forced brightness.

'Bloody books never balance,'

'You should let me put everything on computer. It'll save time in the end.'

'Yeah, yeah.' Neil Farmer stood with his hands thrust into the pockets of his trousers, his cheeks red, his forehead shiny with sweat. His hunched posture and the way he held his head jutting forward made him seem shorter than his son, although they were of similar height. Strands of grey flecked his dark-brown hair. There were lines of discontent either side of his mouth. 'Anyway, how's business?'

He hadn't noticed the sketch book. Relief flowed through Caleb. 'Been a bit slow.' *That's the understatement of the century. It's been dead. Like every other day.*

Neil nodded. 'Mondays are always quiet. I'm thinking of putting a sign in the window. Ten per cent off all homeware. That'll bring them in.'

Caleb had been listening to similar comments for months. He was tired of his dad's refusal to face facts.

'That new Homes and Garden store's undercutting us massively. We'd have to reduce the stock by fifty per cent, to compete.'

Neil's lips tightened. 'So now you're an expert? You can barely bloody tie your own shoes and you think you know more than me!' He sighed, as if with weary patience at Caleb's denseness. 'It's not all down to cost in this business. People want personal service and advice. That's always been our strength. The kids on the tills in that store are still wet behind their ears.' He made a sound of disgust. 'Wouldn't know the difference between a crosshead and a Philips screwdriver if their lives depended on it!'

That was his cue. He was expected to give way, nod and bow to Dad's greater knowledge. That would have been the sensible thing to do. 'I don't know if people are still bothered about that kind of thing...' he began.

Neil turned to face him full on, hazel eyes hardening. 'That's right. You don't bloody know,' he said, as if Caleb was simple-minded. He stared fixedly. 'I was working in this shop with your grandpa when I was ten years old, so give me some credit for knowing a few things. This shop's got everything the DIY enthusiast wants.'

Caleb's temper flickered. He wasn't a kid anymore. He'd be nineteen next birthday. 'People haven't got time for do-it-yourself. They're too busy commuting or holding down two jobs. The new buzz phrase is GSI – get-someone-in.'

Neil glowered. 'Buzz words, is it? Think you're so bloody clever don't you, with your smart mouth? Trying to tie me up with words. Is that where your fancy education has got you?'

'I'm just trying to tell you how it is. Mum's dog tired, but you hardly notice. She shouldn't be on her feet all day. The shop's like a mill stone round all our necks. She knows it, but you're too stubborn to see it...' he broke off. He'd gone too far.

'Don't you tell *dare* me how to treat my own wife! Been talking about me behind my back, eh? The two of you?' Neil's voice was dangerously quiet. There was a pinched look to his mouth. His nostrils were white. 'You've always been as thick as thieves. I wanted a son, but I got a mummy's boy. It's her fault you're so bloody soft and useless. You think the world owes you a living.'

Stung by the unfairness of it, Caleb lost all restraint. 'No, I don't! I could be at college now, but I chose to work all hours in this shop. Whatever I do, it's never enough for you. Well, I've had it! I'm leaving. I'll get a job in something doing drawing and design. It's what I'm good at. I'm going to build a new career.'

Neil's lip curled in a sneer. 'Oh, yes. Where's that then? In some bloody poncy, parallel universe?'

'There are jobs...in advertising, publishing or PR. I'll...I'll need to find out the details of course...' Caleb faltered, hating the way he always felt diminished by his dad's scorn. 'Design's important in...in everything. There are on-line businesses opportunities. Ask anyone.'

His dad gave him a scathing look. 'How long are you going to stand there talking out of your arse?'

Caleb felt the heat rising in his face. He set his chin stubbornly. 'I mean it. I'm not staying here.'

Neil clenched his fists. 'You bloody young idiot!' he roared. 'When you've had years of experience, like I have. I *might* listen to you. But right now, I'd advise you to concentrate your efforts on the shop. Knuckle down. Learn a few things from your betters, instead of wasting your time dreaming. And sodding drawing!'

Shaking with anger, Caleb shouted back. 'Look around you for God's sake! This shop's had its day! It's dying on its feet. You're the only one who can't see that!'

They stared at each other in silence. Caleb was the first to relent. 'Look. I'm sorry, I didn't mean it to come out like that...'

A sly looked passed over Neil's face. Suddenly, he whirled round. Leaning across the counter, he grabbed the sketch book and hurled it to the floor. It landed on one corner. The spine broke, spilling pages everywhere. He kicked out savagely, stamping down, heavy work boots crushing the pages and mashing the scattered drawings.

Caleb watched, disbelieving, too shocked to react at first. 'Don't, Dad! Stop it!' he shouted, his voice cracking with distress.

Neil ignored him.

Caleb looked at the face that was set like granite, the expression that brooked no argument. Since when had they been able to discuss anything? There was only Dad's way; no one else's opinion mattered. He should have known he was wasting his time. His chest burned, emotion almost choking him.

Neil stopped suddenly, calming himself with a visible effort. He stood with bunched fists, looking down at the wreck of the sketch book. Slowly, he uncurled his fingers, his breath escaping him in a long hiss.

'I'm warning you. Watch your step from now on, boy,' he said heavily. 'You're needed here. You'll do your duty. And damn well learn to like it.'

Caleb didn't trust himself to speak. A gust of cool air from the labouring fan reached him. It seemed to him to cement the coldness that had slipped between then. He felt something retreat inside him and lowered his eyes.

Neil took this as a gesture of defeat. He flicked a hand towards the back room. 'Check that new delivery off against the invoices, before you shelve it. And you can forget about taking a lunch break.'

Caleb pressed his lips together, swallowing the impotent hatred that burned in his chest. He walked round the counter. Silently, he bent down to pick up the remnants of his sketch-book.

'Leave that!' Neil rapped.

The drawings were beyond saving. Straightening up, he headed for the back room and closed the door behind him. Pressing his backbone against the cool, hard wood, he blinked away furious tears. He didn't know how he was going to manage it, but after today, he was more determined than ever to get away.

CHAPTER 8

'NICE TO HAVE you back, Jess,' said Mr Blackwell, looking over the top of his glasses. 'I trust you're feeling better now?'

'Yes, thanks. It was a jippy tummy. Must be something I ate. I was leaking both ends at once for almost three days. And then I started my period. You should have seen...'

The teacher winced. 'I get the idea.'

Worked every time. Mention anything to do with women's intimate body fluids and most male teachers freaked out. She climbed onto the coach and scooted across to sit in a window seat. Her class was going on a trip to the Royal Academy as part of their studies about modern painters. Which was why she had decided to come into college, instead of bunking off until after the weekend. Art class was one of the few things she enjoyed. Besides she had never been to London.

Jess stared out of the window, as the coach filled up with her fellow students. No one came to sit in the empty seat beside her, but that was nothing new. It meant she wouldn't be forced to make polite conversation.

She felt a slight apprehension about seeing Lisa. The first time that she could recall having any feelings whatsoever about her fellow students.

Stacey Weaver got on, with Debs Cranford trailing behind her. Stacey had new extensions in her blonde hair. It spilled over the shoulders of her blue satin puffa jacket. She wore so much lip gloss that her mouth resembled a pink slug.

'I see the Goth wannabe has graced us with her presence,' Stacey said loudly as she sat in the seat behind Jess.

'Ooh, we are honoured!' Debs laughed, joining her friend.

In another mood, Jess might have said something cutting. She craned her neck to see whether Lisa was walking down the road and had just decided that she wasn't going to show, when she saw her small rounded figure climbing the coach steps.

All the seats were taken, apart from the one next to her. Lisa hesitated and then sat beside her and crossed her arms.

All around them voices were raised in conversation. Some were huddled around mobile phones, playing games, others plugged in ear phones to listen to music.

Jess took long steadying breaths, acutely aware of being encased inside the metal vehicle. Despite the insulation of wood and plastic walls, the low-level screech of iron was setting her teeth on edge. Bunching up her jacket, she placed it so that she could lean her bare arm against it without her skin jangling from contact with any exposed metal. With the windows closed and couple of hits from the atomiser in her pocket, the stench of diesel was just about bearable.

Stacey Weaver's shrill voice sounded from behind her seat as she laughed at something Debs said. Two guys in front of Jess were discussing their musical tastes. The sound of traffic rushing by was a background hum. Jess glanced sideways at Lisa, wondering how to break the silence. The other girl's cheeks were blotchy and the area around her nose and chin roughened and flaky. Lisa's spots looked worse than when Jess had seen her a few days back.

'What's wrong with...'

'White spirit,' Lisa murmured, after a pause. 'To get the

red paint off. I had to scrub hard. My skin's still stinging. I'm putting cream on, but it hasn't helped.'

Jess held out her atomiser. 'Here, try this.'

'I'd rather not,' Lisa said primly.

'Oh, go on. Live dangerously,' Jess, insisted, nudging her.

A tiny smile lifted the corners of Lisa's mouth as she took the atomiser. She removed her glasses and closed her eyes. She sprayed her face, hesitantly at first and them more liberally.

'Mmm. It feels lovely and cool. Smells nice too. What's in it?'

'Just water and essential oils. It's my own blend. Keep it. I've got a spare in my school bag.'

'You don't have to give it to me.' Lisa tried to hand the atomiser back.

'I know. Peace offering. OK?' Jess gently pushed Lisa's hand away. 'Listen. I didn't mean what I said to Zac. I was angry, because he was talking to me like I was scum. And he had the cheek to warn me off you – like I was a disease you could catch. I lashed out and said that stuff about you. It was just scoring points. Stupid stuff. You weren't meant to hear it.'

'Zac doesn't like me being friends with you.'

'No shit?' Jess rolled her eyes. 'I got that message! Who does he think I am – the love child of Rasputin and Countess Bathory?'

'Countess who?'

'She was this Hungarian noble woman who killed girls and drank their blood. Like a female Dracula.'

'Nice!' Lisa pulled a face. 'How do you know this stuff?'

Jess shrugged. 'I like reading weird stuff. You know? Anything twisted, with an edge. That's why I was keen to come on this trip and see the Krasts.'

'The what?'

Jess grinned. 'Didn't you read the print-out? Krast is an

78

artist. She was famous a while back, but she's pretty much a recluse now. There's an exhibition of her stuff on at the RA, where we're going.'

Lisa looked blank.

'The exhibition is a retrospective of Krast's work over twenty years. According to the print-out, the paintings are "disquieting images of nightmare worlds." Sounds a whole lot more interesting than the impressionists!'

'What's wrong with the impressionists?'

'Nothing, but there's such a thing as overkill.' She mimed a yawn.

Lisa grinned. She took off her glasses. Squinting slightly, she began cleaning them on a corner of her school blouse. Jess could see faint traces of red paint on the frames. Without her glasses, Lisa's face looked open and vulnerable.

'I tried to tell Zac you're nothing like he thinks you are, but he wouldn't have it,' Lisa was saying. 'He's always looked out for me. That's just the way he is. He pretty much has a total downer on you. On your mum and her boyfriend, anyway.'

'Look - I'm not saying I haven't got problems. But they're *my* problems and I'll deal with them. I would never involve anyone else, so you're safe. I'm used to taking care of myself and I like it that way. To be honest I don't care *what* Zac thinks. I'm never going to hang out with him. But…we had fun the other day, didn't we…?'

Lisa nodded, as she replaced her glasses.

'…and all I can say is. I'm sorry if I upset you. Truly, I am. I promise not to be an idiot again. Or at least, I'll try not to be. I can't guarantee it, since idiocy is my best subject. Second to sarcasm…'

By now Lisa was giggling. 'So – are we still friends?' she said, shyly.

'What do *you* think? Come here you!' Jess surprised herself by giving Lisa a hug. Girl-bonding was a first for her and it felt weird, but good weird.

'Oo-of! You're squashing me!' Lisa spluttered, hugging her back. 'You don't know your own strength!'

'OK get off now. That's enough!' Jess said, only half-joking.

There was an explosive snort from behind them.

'Oh my God! The skanky Goth and Lisa lard-ass are *snogging*!' Stacey Weaver's mocking voice floated through the coach.

A shout of laughter came from Debs. 'Yuck! And double yuck! I think I might chuck my breakfast!'

Lisa jerked away from Jess, face flaming and shoulders hunched. In two seconds, the girl had morphed back into an insecure jelly. Jess's temper rose on Lisa's behalf. She turned and looked through the gap between the backs of their seats, staring coldly at Stacey.

'I don't give a shit what you say about me. But if I hear you call Lisa *anything* like that again, you'll be very, very sorry,' she said quietly.

'Says who? Anyway, she is a fat lard-ar...' Stacey stopped, as Jess continued to hold her gaze. The colour drained from her cheeks. 'Hey! It was just a joke!'

'No it wasn't. You're a nasty, poisonous bully. Apologise,' Jess ordered.

'In your dreams...'

Jess smiled without warmth, her eyes never leaving the other girl's face. There was a tingling sensation in her skin and she was aware of a subtle shift in the air around her. There was a sense of something building. It didn't feel like anger. 'What was that? I didn't hear you,' she said softly.

'I said. In. Your. Drea...' Stacey's voice cracked and died.

She was trembling, her lips white. 'What I meant to say was. I'm sorry! Really, really sorry. OK? What more do you want from me?'

One of the guys discussing music in the seat in front of Jess looked up. 'Hey, Stace! Can you be sorry a bit quieter?' he said dryly. Some other students sniggered.

'I don't want anything from you,' Jess said, looking away. 'Just stay out of my face. And leave Lisa alone, or you'll have me to deal with.'

'F…fine by me!' Stacey had recovered some of her bravado. 'I'd have to be mad to want to hang out with you two *freaks*!'

Jess glanced at the girl again, steadily. The tingling in her skin increased.

A pained look crossed Stacey's face. She suddenly jumped up, her hands pressed to her lap. 'Get out of the way Debs, quick!'

'Hey! There's no need to shove me!' Stacey scrambled past her and whispered to Mr Blackwell.

'We'll be coming up to the Services soon. We'll take a fifteen minute break. Can you wait that long?' he said.

'No! I'm bursting. Can't you tell the coach driver to hurry or something?'

'Certainly not! You should have told me if you had a medical condition.'

'I haven't!'

'I've got a plastic bottle you can use,' someone suggested helpfully. There was a general burst of laughter.

Stacey was now scarlet, clenching her legs together and jiggling about. 'Shut it, you lot!'

Jess laughed softly to herself, feeling that odd prickling sensation fade. Lisa was studying her with a bemused expression.

'What?' she asked her, spreading her hands.

'How do you do that?'

'Do what?' Jess asked, puzzled.

'Be scary, without really doing anything,' Lisa said. 'I wish I could do it. You just *looked* at Stacey and she was so terrified she almost peed herself.'

Jess shrugged. 'Stacey's a drama queen.'

A few minutes later the coach pulled into the services. The moment the door opened, Stacey raced down the steps and dashed towards the toilets to a chorus of cheers. Some people were getting off, going to buy drinks or burgers, but Jess and Lisa decided to remain in their seats.

Reaching for her bag, Jess fished out the arts supplement she had hurriedly torn from a newspaper in the college library that morning. On the front, was a feature about the Krast exhibition, entitled, "Jaded beauty challenges our perception of reality". She opened the double-page spread, her eyes drawn immediately to the photograph accompanying the feature. It was a detail, from one of the artist's most celebrated paintings.

A tall slender figure was just emerging from the shadows beside a fragment of drapery. Shoulder-length, dark red hair lay like a bird's wing against the angular face. Elongated eyes, slanted upwards at the corners, were lowered, lending the figure an air of mystery. The softly glowing face and one pale, long-fingered hand were the only places of light in a deep-violet darkness.

There was something beautiful and compelling about the image, but Jess felt herself involuntarily recoil from it. An aura of power and danger seeped from it. Who had been the model, she wondered. *And why does it seem familiar in some way?*

It wouldn't be long now before she saw the painting in its entirety. Would the rest of it have such a strong effect on her?

Suddenly, she didn't want to read any more about Krast. She would let the paintings speak for themselves.

'You might like to see this.' She passed the page to Lisa. 'It's about the exhibition we're going to see.'

'Oh right.' Unfolding the page, Lisa began reading.

Jess relaxed back in her seat, freshly aware of the fizzing and clashing of the metal all around her. There was a concentrated stink of diesel from the nearby fuel station. Another squirt from her spare atomiser helped to ease the burning pain in her lungs. She closed her eyes. The roar of the traffic on the motorway as it sped past the coach was faintly soporific. She let the sound of it wash over her and allowed her thoughts to blur and turn inwards.

Dark red hair, white skin covering angular delicate bones, eyes to the ground. Something fierce and wild in the expression. And the eyes, when they were raised, would be mismatched...

CHAPTER 9

SALLY FARMER WAS dishing out salad onto three plates, each already containing sliced ham and a hard-boiled egg. Thursday the shop closed at one.

She had put a cloth on the table. White linen embroidered with flowers, a wedding present from Ma Farmer. Instead of the everyday plates and mismatched mugs, she had set out pretty china plates and cups and saucers. A glass dish of hulled strawberries, sprinkled with sugar, and a dish of cream stood next to a small green vase which held pink rosebuds.

She usually made cheap, filling meals from basic ingredients. They hadn't had any luxuries for months.

Caleb's surprised face made her flush with pleasure and she reached out to lightly touch his hair. 'Oh, it's only salad. You don't want anything too heavy in this weather.'

A door slammed downstairs. He heard his dad's heavy footsteps on the stairs. Dad was back from the chamber of commerce meeting with Pa Farmer, who despite his fragile health retained an interest in the shop.

'Oh, good. Perfect timing,' his mum said.

The door opened. Neil paused in the doorway. His mouth thinned as he glanced at the table.

'What's this in aid of?'

'I thought it would be a nice change for us to have lunch together. You have to push the boat out now and then or life's not worth living.'

Neil grunted. 'Pa's feeling much stronger. More like his old self, if anyone's interested.' He went to the sink and washed his hands in silence before coming to the table.

'I'm glad to hear that.' Sally looked up as he sat down, her smile wobbling a bit. 'Ham and egg salad, all right for you?'

Neil nodded shortly. Picking up his knife and fork, he began to eat.

'Tea, Caleb?'

The atmosphere had changed perceptibly. Caleb tried to ignore the tight knot of tension inside him.

Sally looked at her husband. 'How about you, Love?'

Neil was tearing at a piece of ham with his fork. He paused, let out an audible breath and then continued chewing. Without looking up, he jabbed his knife in the general direction of his cup and saucer.

Caleb steeled himself not to say anything. Mum was trying so hard. It wouldn't hurt his dad to show some appreciation.

She poured tea, added milk and sugar, moved the cup and saucer closer to his plate. 'Would it hurt you to unbend, just this once?' she said, mildly.

Neil looked up at her, incomprehension on his face. A muscle ticked in his cheek. 'You've no damned idea, have you? Throwing away hard earned money on bloody flowers and strawberries!' He put down his knife and fork. Reaching for his tea, he gulped noisily. As he replaced the cup he banged it down with unnecessary force. The fine china rang in protest. Tea slopped over the saucer and made a spreading brown mark on the freshly laundered cloth.

'Oh,' Sally made a small sound of dismay and rose to her feet. 'Never mind. I'll get a cloth.'

He did that deliberately, Caleb thought, shocked. He might not always agree with his dad, but he'd always respected him for his strong principles. He'd never thought of him as petty.

'Leave it be, woman,' Neil said sharply.

Unperturbed, Sally ran the cold tap. Returning with a damp folded cloth, she placed it under the tea stain. 'Best to do it now, before the stain sets.'

Neil jerked back his chair, the slatted back creaking in protest. 'For Christ's sake! Do you have to make such a fuss?'

Caleb saw the hurt look on his mum's face 'You shouldn't talk to her like that,' he said.

Neil rounded on him. 'Don't you *ever* tell me what to do!'

Caleb opened his mouth to speak, but caught his mum's eye as she shook her head imperceptibly. Caleb schooled himself to remain silent. Neil stared fixedly at him for a moment longer, triumph and contempt warring for supremacy on his face. Caleb's eyes fastened on a fleck of pink ham caught in the corner of his dad's mouth. He felt a surge of dislike so strong that his hands trembled.

Neil breathed out noisily, picked up his knife and fork and once again began eating in silence. Caleb struggled to keep his temper under control. He saw himself getting up, telling Dad what he thought of him and storming out. But he forced himself to remain seated. Another row would only result in his being made to stay at home for the afternoon, doing some mind-numbingly mundane task.

He chewed automatically, without tasting anything. In the silence, the clattering of their knives and forks against the plates set him on edge. He accepted a dish of strawberries, but he didn't really want them. He poured cream and had just begun eating them, when his dad made a great show of scraping his chair back from the table and standing up.

'I've got work to do. We can't all be idle,' Neil said pointedly, before leaving the room. His steps sounded on the stairs.

'I don't believe him!' Caleb shook his head slowly.

Sally patted her son's arm. 'He'll come round. He doesn't mean it.'

Yes, he does. He's always been the same. I hate him.

Down by the river he threw himself onto the grass, opened a new sketchbook took out a pencil and settled down with his thoughts. The peace and beauty of the place sank into his bones. Sunlight flashed on swirling eddies and ripples of water, glinting off the dragonflies hawking for insects. He felt the tight knot inside him unwinding as he worked, oblivious to everything but making marks on the page. In a short time, he had drafted the bare bones of another of his startling imaginary landscapes. Clouds, rocks and trees seemed carved out of the negative space on the page.

Caleb laid the drawing aside. A good start, even better than the ones Dad had destroyed. Maybe he would get a portfolio of drawings together, show them to someone whose opinion he trusted. His old art teacher might give him some pointers about what to do next. He clasped his hands behind his neck and dozed in the dappled shade of the willow. Sunlight flickered across his face, turning his inner vision red and gold.

A fresh breeze was rustling the silvery undersides of the leaves, when Caleb sat up. As he pushed himself to his feet his stomach growled with hunger. It must be almost time for supper. Time to head off home, he thought, with reluctance.

Caleb swallowed, tasted bitterness. Well, not for much longer. Because he *was* going to leave. Soon. It was becoming a question of survival. *Yeah, right!* So where was he going to go? There wasn't any one who'd let him doss on their sofa for a few weeks. And he would need money, not dad's occasional hand-outs, to rent even a tiny bed sit. If he left, he'd be totally on his own. No chance of any support from Dad or Pa Farmer.

He set off homewards with dragging feet and churning thoughts, his mood souring. It didn't take long to reach the shopping centre. He was always surprised by how close the river bank was to bustling humanity. For one mad moment, he imagined living by the river. Why not? He wouldn't need much – a small tent, a sleeping bag a few changes of clothes. But he knew it was unrealistic. Besides the river was too close to home; he wouldn't put it past Dad to track him down and physically drag him back there.

He reached the fountain. The mums and toddlers had long gone. Smartly dressed office workers had replaced the earlier shoppers at the pavement café. Well-groomed young women with glossy hair chatted and laughed with young men with designer stubble and open-necked shirts.

Caleb threw a bleak glance towards them. He had nothing in common with any of them. The sun was little more than a silver glow behind white clouds as he threaded through side streets. He was just passing the 24-7 on the corner, its entire window obscured by a yellow and orange sticker, when a small figure emerged and stepped right into his path.

Deep in thought, Caleb was slow to react. It was hardly a collision. He felt something light and insubstantial brush against his arm and then seem to fall away. There was a cry of dismay as the figure crumpled onto the pavement, amidst soft thuds and rustles of shopping.

'Oh Gosh! Sorry!' Horrified, Caleb saw cartons of milk, loaves of bread and packets of butter rolling out of plastic bags into the gutter. 'I didn't see you. Are you hurt?' he asked the old woman who was lying there.

'Why don't you look where you're going?' she said crossly.

Holding onto the shop window ledge, she levered herself painfully to her feet.

Caleb rushed to help. A smell of bitter almonds, musty clothes and camphor moth balls engulfed him. 'Shouldn't you stay still? You might have broken something.'

'Nonsense!' She grabbed his arm with a bird-claw hand. Leaning against him, she motioned imperiously towards the low front garden wall of the house next door to the shop. 'Over there. I need to sit down.'

Caleb topped her by a head and shoulders. She was hardly more than a bag of bones inside her dark, shapeless dress and could easily have belonged to a previous century, except that peeping out from beneath her hem he could see the toes of grubby trainers. Her fingers were digging painfully into his bare arm and he suppressed a wince. When she released her grip after collapsing onto the wall, there were white pressure marks on his tanned forearm.

She had long white hair. A lock of it had slipped from the bun, pinned low on the back of her neck. As she tucked it behind one ear, her loose sleeve fell back to reveal a sinewy wrist, knotted with veins, and covered with spotted skin like the foxed paper of old drawings he had seen in junk shops.

'There. Um...feeling a bit better now?' He patted her shoulder awkwardly.

'Don't talk to me as if I'm an idiot!' she snapped. 'I might be old, young man, but I've got all my faculties.'

He spread his hands helplessly. 'Sorry.'

'Hmph! Save your breath, if that's all you can say. Take it from me, sorry never fixed anything.'

'Sor...' Caleb began reflexively, before he managed to stop himself. He stood there at a loss, looking down at the small seated figure. What a crabby old thing she was. He ought to walk away and leave her to it. It would serve her right, if he did. But he was still worried that she might have an injury. Old people had brittle bones, didn't they? She ought to get checked out at A&E.

'Wait here. I'll call for an ambulance!'

He was half-way to the shop doorway, when the woman shouted to him.

'Come back here, at once!'

Caleb turned, surprised by the strength of her voice.

'Did you hear me, young man? I do not like to repeat myself. Come here.'

Still looking over his shoulder, Caleb backed-up slowly. He kept his voice level with an effort. 'All right. Calm down. Are you sure you don't want a doctor to check you over? You might have broken something.'

He saw now that she was very pale. All the lines of her face drooped downwards as if with regret or disappointment. Her lips were folded inwards. It looked as if someone had run a gathering thread around them and pulled it tight. Only her eyes, dark points in their pouches of violet-shadowed flesh, were vibrant and alive-looking.

'I can assure you that I am simply shaken up.' She gave a grunt of annoyance. 'Hardly surprising, since I've been almost mown down by a lumbering great boy!'

'Excuse me,' Caleb said, stung. 'But you weren't exactly looking where you were going either! *You* almost tripped *me* up.'

The dark eyes snapped at him, but he thought her pursed mouth relaxed a fraction in what might be a smile. 'Make yourself useful then. Pick up my groceries.'

Caleb felt an answering flicker of humour. He resisted the urge to click his heels and snap to attention. There was something indomitable about the old lady. He couldn't help but admire her spirit. Bending down he gathered up the cartons of long-life milk, loaves of white bread and packets of butter and packed them neatly into the two carriers. He straightened up to find that she was watching him closely, her sharp eyes, measuring, probing.

'I'll help you home with your shopping, if you like,' he offered on impulse.

She looked surprised, but if he was expecting thanks he was disappointed. She nodded shortly, pushing herself to her feet. 'Very well. Come on then.'

'No problem.' It couldn't be far. She was on foot, so he assumed she probably lived in the sheltered housing, just off the main road. Caleb shifted his holdall to a more comfortable position on one shoulder, wrapped the carrier bag handles round one hand and extended his arm to the old woman.

'One moment.' Reaching into the pocket of her long black dress she took out a collapsible walking stick. Leaning on the stick, she linked arms with him. They set off. For a while they walked in silence and then she asked, 'What's your name, young man?'

'I'm Caleb. Caleb Farmer,' Caleb said.

'Farmer, eh? From *Farmer & Sons Family Hardware*?'

Caleb nodded. 'That's me.' *Worst luck.*

'I thought you looked familiar.'

He turned to her in surprise, sure that he'd never seen her before. 'Do you come into the shop?'

'Used to, when your Pa Farmer ran things. I don't get out so much these days.' She squinted up at him. 'You're Neil's boy. I remember him at about your age, serving in the shop. Same build, dark hair and hazel eyes. You're just like him.'

'No, I'm not. I just *look* like him,' Caleb said, before he could stop himself.

'Like that, is it?' Her black eyes flashed with humour, quickly replaced by irritation. 'Slow down, boy! I can't keep up with you.' She dragged at his arm.

He hid a smile, checked his stride. 'Sorry.'

She gave a small, dry chuckle. 'What a great one you are for apologising! Why so much regret in one so young?' A strand of long white hair had come loose. It drifted across her face like a wispy cloud across the moon. 'Told you already. Sorry's a wasted word. I've no truck with it.'

Caleb's interest in the old lady quickened. She was spiky, quick to find fault, equally quick to give voice to her opinions, but her directness was refreshing, after the torturous drip, drip, drip of Dad's brooding anger and sly mind games. He liked her, he decided. At her age, she had earned the right to be awkward.

'You can call me, Caleb, if you like,' he said.

'Fair enough, Caleb. I'm Ivy. Ivy Stark.' She grinned, displaying an even row of small, yellowed teeth. 'You can call *me*, Mrs Stark.'

CHAPTER 10

JESS WALKED BENEATH the Krast archway into a large space with a vaulted ceiling and marble pillars.

The first painting was a woodland scene, a chocolate box confection of fluffy bunnies sitting round the feet of a little girl with rosy-pink cheeks. Tiny goblin faces, with bright eyes in creased brown cheeks, peered from gaps in the bushes. It was pretty, colourful and accomplished. And Jess hated it. The next few paintings were no better. From the legend next to each, Jess learned that this was Krast's early 'illustrative style'. The artist had enjoyed some small success, her work being sought after by publishers of children's books and greetings cards.

Visitors were grouped three deep around some of the paintings. They had to wait to get close enough for a proper look. In one painting, a boat full of laughing children was being towed across a lake by butterflies holding silk ribbons. In another, a winged figure hovered above the surface of a pool, while fish poked out their heads in greeting.

'Oh, these are so gorgeous.' Lisa enthused, bending forward over the rope barrier to have a closer look at the fine brushwork.

'If you like that sort of stuff,' Jess murmured, grumpily.

Krast's early work was unbelievably twee and cutesy. How could this be the same artist who had produced the painting that contained that enigmatic figure? The whole of the first gallery was filled with work in a similar vein. She decided to skip it and go straight to the later work. Leaving Lisa cooing over some ducklings that sat in the lap of a smiling faery stringing dew-drops into a necklace, she wandered into the adjoining gallery. The colours seemed less bright, the parades of goblins and toadstools painted with less conviction. The artist was losing interest in her work.

And then looking through the opening into the final gallery, Jess caught sight of a large painting hanging by itself. Her breath quickening with excitement, she walked rapidly towards it.

There was a small crowd of people in front of the painting. She could only glimpse details through the shifting bodies, but she knew it was *the one*. She hung back, wanting to prolong the moment when she stood face to face with that figure wrought from shadows. *Leave me alone with it. Go away. All of you.* Oblivious to the air around her tingling and shimmering, in a way that was beginning to feel familiar, she stared at the painting. As she moved forward, time seemed to shift into slow motion. A slew of sound echoed hollow and discordant in her ears as every person standing in front of the painting turned in a single movement. They looked at Jess with glazed eyes, before drifting sideways in a single body, moving as if in the steps of some tightly choreographed dance, and melting from the gallery. Everyone else had somehow left too, she realised. She could see people strolling around the other galleries through the archways.

But here, she was alone.

In the sudden stillness Jess caught her breath. The painting was revealed to her in its entirety. Or as she thought oddly, *it* revealed *itself* to her. She was not disappointed by what she saw.

The painting was of a large room, perhaps Victorian in design. Jess would have said Gothic. Windows with small glass panes and stone surrounds were set into plain walls, with ornate plaster coving. The furniture was dark, heavy and richly carved.

A woman wearing a dove-grey dress, lay on a four poster bed, her dark hair tumbled across the silken pillows. She was pale and there were shadows beneath her closed eyes. Her face was pinched with sadness or grief. Something, a tiny wrapped parcel lay beside her – the details of it were unclear, but inside the gauzy wrapping could be glimpsed the glassy outline of a complex form. A chrysalis? One of the woman's arms lay across her body. The other drooped downwards towards the patterned red carpet, her slim fingers pointing towards a group of nightmare figures, both large and small.

Jess bent closer to see them more clearly. A knobbly-faced creature with sharp teeth in its red slash of a mouth was riding a terrified mouse, its spurs drawing blood. Two slim white-haired girls, their skin covered with intricate designs and holding hands, stood looking over their shoulders, smiling prettily. Their backs were completely hollow. A parade of tiny men and women, some cat-faced, some with beautiful vivid features, and some with legs ending in hooves and claws and dressed in garments made of skins and leaves were dancing around a hedgehog writhing on a thorny spear.

Inexorably her eyes were drawn to the tall figure who watched from the shadows; shadows, which she saw now, were formed by the folds of dark figured-velvet curtains that hung at a casement window. The exhibition posters had not captured the richness of that dark red hair; there were strands of purple, maroon and vermillion amongst the tresses. Nor had they caught the startling luminosity of the white skin, which glowed softly as if lit from within with a pale greenish-fire. Or, the thought suddenly intruded upon her, the phosphorescence of something rotting at the bottom of a dark trench. That pale, pale skin was stretched over high-cheekbones, a blade-like jaw and sharply pointed chin. The thin line of the sensual lips could have been drawn with the tip of a feather.

Involuntarily Jess shivered moving forward, gripped by fascination. She studied the figure's cast down eyes, imagining it lifting its chin and staring out at her. What would she see in its gaze? Satisfaction, tenderness, concern? It was not plain whether he or she was guarding the woman on the bed or spying on her. And was the woman in the grey gown sleeping or dead?

The painting seemed to vibrate with loss, suffering and a sense of secret menace. She felt a tear slide down her cheek. Impossible that this was the same artist who had painted that earlier stuff. What could possibly have happened to Krast to bring about such a radical change of style?

The painting was entitled *Royalty's Revenge*. Curious title. It seemed to hold a mystery as did the painting itself. She read on. After producing dozens of sickly-sweet paintings and illustrations, Krast had faded into obscurity. There was a gap of some years, before she exhibited six new works; the first of them being *Royalty's Revenge*. The radical new style of these paintings attracted the attention of the art world. Paintings in similar vein followed; all of them to critical acclaim. Many of them were now in private collections; a selection had been loaned for the current exhibition.

Jess repositioned herself in front of *Royalty's Revenge*. Something about it held her in thrall. It was an effort to finally tear herself away in order to look at the other Krasts on display.

They were all stunning; filled with ethereal creatures, dancing, feasting, playing together, sometimes tormenting animals, or each other. In the last one, she spotted the same tall, compelling, red-haired figure. Again, he or she was poised as if just about to emerge from the shadows. This time the figure stood beneath an oak tree that swarmed with tiny beings holding glowing fireflies. One hand, long-fingered and oddly bent and seeming to have extra joints, cupped the figure's chin, as if he or she were deep in thought. The beautiful face was shaded down one side, softening the angular features a little. Those thin lips were lifted in a vulpine grin and the single long eye, slanting upwards at the outer corner, blazed out of the canvas. It was a bright gold.

Green. Emerald green. The other eye, unseen in the shadows.

Jess wandered back and forth between the final paintings in a daze of wonder. All of them held a twisted beauty. Krast's later work was a progression into genius touched with the darkness that had begun with *Royalty's Revenge*. Each one was a masterpiece.

No new visitors entered the gallery, although the others were becoming more crowded, as Jess could tell by the buzz of noise and glimpses of movement. She was grateful to be left alone. After looking at each of the later works, she finished up at *Royalty's Revenge*, the painting which held a special fascination for her. She let out a long breath that seemed to tremble on the air like the visible after-shock of having shaken the dust out of a heavy rug.

'That one's really horrible, isn't it?' Lisa said at her shoulder.

Jess jumped visibly and turned to her friend. 'Oh! I didn't hear you come in.' Over Lisa's shoulder, she saw that visitors were beginning to file in again. 'Horrible? That's not a word I'd use.'

'I don't s'pose *you* would.' Lisa grinned wryly. She had

wrapped her arms around her body and was running the palm of one hand up and down the outside of one upper arm. 'These paintings give me the creeps.'

'Do they? I love them,' Jess said, absently, still caught in the spell they had cast over her. 'This one's my favourite. I could look at it forever. I'd buy it, if I ever won the lottery.'

'Can't say I'm all that surprised,' said Lisa in a knowing voice.

Jess narrowed her eyes, searching for the hidden joke or clever comment. 'What do you mean?'

Lisa, becoming the target of a direct gaze, blushed as usual. 'Well…well it could be you there, couldn't it?'

'Me?' Jess said, puzzled. 'What are you talking about?'

'The woman lying on the bed. She looks like you.'

'No way!' Jess gave a short laugh.

She turned back to the painting and saw what Lisa meant. How could she have missed the resemblance? But then she had been more interested in studying that striking red-haired figure and had only spared the woman on the bed a cursory glance. Now something struck her forcibly.

The sleeping woman with tumbled dark hair didn't actually look that much like her. But it was a mirror-image of her mother. Which was obviously impossible. Why would Alice be the subject of any painting, especially *this* one?

CHAPTER 11

THE FIRST TIME Caleb helped Mrs Stark home, he'd assumed she lived fairly close to the shop where they had literally bumped into each other. It hadn't taken long to realise his mistake. It still amazed him that she had walked all the way into town with only her fold-up walking stick to aid her, and then still shaken-up after her fall and with Caleb carrying her shopping, she had walked all the way back again.

But now that he knew her better, he was less surprised by anything she did. She was nothing if not determined. Despite her physical frailty Mrs Stark had a will of iron.

Pushing aside trailing branches that caught at his hair, Caleb emerged onto a weedy gravel drive that was slowly disintegrating into overgrown flower borders. What had once been a sweeping lawn in front of the enormous house was now a waist-high meadow. Layers of wild flowers, cream, pink and purple, moved in the breeze like skeins of folded silk. Windroth Hall rose up to meet him, a ship above foaming waves. Caleb paused for a moment to look at it and admire its faded grandeur.

An impressive porch, topped by a gothic arch of crumbling stone, framed a front door of some dark, heavy wood, studded with tarnished metal. There was a lion's head doorknocker and handle, which he guessed no one had used in years. Most of the windows were intact, but here and there boards were fastened against missing panes. Stone urns, either side of the porch, were clotted with weeds.

Shifting his holdall to balance its weight, Caleb cut round to the back of the house. Trees and over-grown bushes had encroached on what had once been a sizeable vegetable plot. A smile crossed his face as he registered the newly planted square of earth to one side of the kitchen door. He was proud of his small efforts to bring life and usefulness back to the garden. The herbs and salad vegetables were doing well, despite that fact that Mrs Stark invariably forgot to water them. It didn't matter how much he reminded her, she was consumed by the single thing at the centre of her existence. Painting. She had no time or energy for anything else.

'Hi! It's me, Caleb!' he called cheerily as he pushed open the kitchen door and stepped into the huge room.

Sunlight streaming into the windows picked out peeling battleship-grey walls. It was still chaotic in here, but nothing like when he had first seen it. Then the wooden table and huge old dresser had been invisible beneath an accumulation of years of empty cans, bottles, packets and dust. Now the table was scrubbed clean. Chairs were tucked under it, ready for use. The red quarry-tiled floor, once piled with overflowing black bin bags, was clear.

The wild flowers he had placed in an antique-looking jug on his last visit had shed dried petals like tiny screws of paper all over the table top. The sink was stacked with a week's worth of dirty crocks. Used tea bags, coffee grounds and bits of toast had been flung on top of them. A bottle on the draining board held a couple of centimetres of greyish liquid, topped with a skin of greenish fur. A sour smell leaked from the open swing-top bin. From the blow flies buzzing in and out of it, Caleb guessed it would be crawling with maggots.

Mrs Stark seemed not to notice these things. If *he* didn't clear up, it would stay like this and rapidly get worse again. With an edge of impatience, he took off his backpack and unloaded the groceries.

'Mrs Stark!' he called again. 'I'm here!'

'You don't need to shout. I'm not deaf.'

Caleb looked up and saw her small figure in the doorway. It was those trainers she always wore that enabled her to creep up on him like that.

'Hi. How's the painting going?' he said, smiling.

'Slowly. Painfully. As always,' she said, in a matter of fact tone. Over her habitual black dress she wore a loose smock, so streaked and crusted with layer upon layer of paint that it was impossible to discern its original colour.

'What are you working on today?' Caleb asked, hoping that she might trust him enough by now to show him. Mrs Stark was loath to discuss her work.

'I've just started something new,' she said neutrally, which was more information than he'd expected. She came forward and flopped into a chair. Today, her long white hair was gathered into untidy coils, pierced through and anchored by a worn-out paintbrush.

Encouraged, Caleb sought for a question that wouldn't be too probing. 'Are you...working to commission?'

'Not – in a manner of speaking,' she said cryptically.

Her eyes were shadowed with weariness. There was a smudge of light blue paint above one hollow cheek. 'Why do you always have to work so hard? Can't you choose your own pace if you haven't a client snapping at your heels?' Caleb filled the new electric kettle he had brought with him from the shop. Apart from an ancient electric toaster, she had only an old kitchen range, which obviously hadn't been working for years.

Mrs Stark closed her eyes briefly, the lids pale and fretted with reddish-purple veins. 'It's not a question of choice,' she whispered so low, that he barely heard her.

He frowned. Was she talking about the artistic impulse? The drive to create images as a way of making sense of one's world? He could understand that, recognising something of it in himself. But there was an underlying bitterness in the way the old lady spoke. Her deeply lined skin looked sickly today, almost transparent. He thought she had lost weight.

'Looks like you haven't spent much time in here lately,' Caleb said, his gaze sweeping the kitchen.

Mrs Stark blinked at him in incomprehension. 'Why would I?'

'To make a meal or proper sandwich?' *Instead of the buttered toast and tea she seemed to live on.* 'Maybe take time to sit and eat, while listening to the radio or enjoying the garden from the window?'

She made a dismissive gesture. 'Food's just fuel. I can eat and work at the same time...' she tailed off, her head cocked as if she had caught a sudden noise. Drawing herself up, she sat in an attitude of concentration.

'What?' Caleb paused in the act of finding mugs and tea bags. He thought he heard a rustling sound and then an odd, high noise a bit like the chattering of starlings as they swept down to their evening roost in the reed beds near the river. But it was far too early for birds to be roosting. Besides, the sound was *inside* the house. He thought a fleeting expression of alarm crossed her face.

'It is nothing,' she said quickly.

'There *is* something. Listen.' It was coming from overhead, where she had her studio. He looked up towards the ceiling. 'What's that?'

'Mice I expect. Don't fuss, Caleb!' she snapped. 'This is an old house. It was built over the ruin of a far older building. There is a maze of cellars and all manner of gaps in the bricks where creatures can get in.' She rose to her feet, unable to hide a wince as she flexed her narrow shoulders. 'I have to get back to work.'

Mice wouldn't make so much noise. It was more likely to be rats, Caleb decided. They had some sturdy traps in the shop. He made a mental note to bring some with him next time. He'd bait them for her, keep an eye on them and remove any that got caught. Didn't want dead rats stinking the place out.

He watched Mrs Stark moving stiffly towards the door that led into the large entrance hall, wondering if he ought to attempt to detain her. He suspected that she shut herself away in her studio for days at a time. She kept the door locked, even when working, but he'd once caught a glimpse from the open doorway when he'd taken up a tray of tea.

That brief glance had shown him that the studio was a large, light room, as jumbled and chaotic as the kitchen had once been. Paints, brushes, jars, bottles, used palettes and other paraphernalia littered every surface, obscuring outlines of tables, chests of drawers and cupboards. Paint was splashed everywhere. Even the walls had been used as an extended palette. The impression was of a place where work was executed in bursts of passion or great concentration, as if Mrs Stark had to work swiftly to complete a painting before the original impetus, or her strength, petered out. Stacks of completed canvases leaned against the walls and were piled face down on the floor. In one corner, there was a lumpy red velvet couch, where Caleb guessed she slept. And then she had grabbed the tea tray and slammed the door shut.

'Mrs Stark! Wait a moment,' he called, on impulse. 'Let me make you something to eat. You can take it with you.'

She turned back to look at him and her face softened. 'Perhaps I am hungry,' she said, as if it was a surprise to her. 'Very well.' She came back to the table and sat down again. 'I appreciate your bringing me shopping and visiting, Caleb. A young man like you shouldn't be wasting your time in the company of a shrivelled old bird like me. You must have a million other things you'd rather do.'

'Actually, I haven't,' he confessed with a grin, taking butter and cheese from the ancient fridge. 'I've selfish reasons for coming here. I used to sit by the river on my afternoons off, but it's much better here. So many fascinating things to draw. And I like talking to you.'

'Flatterer!' Mrs Stark snorted. 'You never mentioned that you like drawing?' she lifted a brow in enquiry. 'Are you an artist, too?'

'Kind of, I suppose. It's what I want to be anyway. Some hope though.' He couldn't hide the note of bitterness in his voice. 'Dad's always banging on about how I have to carry on the family business. He says scribbling is for dreamers and wasters. No money to be made from it. But I hate the shop. It's choking the life out of me. It's such a relief to come here. No one knows where I am or expects anything from me. I can just be myself for a few hours...' he paused, feeling his colour rise. He had revealed more than he had intended to.

Mrs Stark was nodding thoughtfully. 'Ah. Your artistic tendencies are the cause of friction?'

Caleb rolled his eyes and blew out his breath on a long low whistle. 'Yep! You could say that. That and the fact that the shop isn't making any money! We've got crippling debts, but Dad refuses to sell up.' As he buttered bread with one of her heavy silver handled knives, he told her about the row they'd had a while back. How Dad had stamped on his sketchbook as if he could stamp out Caleb's inconvenient talent. How he could hardly bear the long hateful silences, punctuated by barbed comments. How Dad played him and Mum off against each other. He told her how he felt sick with guilt, because it just wasn't in him to build his life around the hardware shop, like Dad and Pa Farmer had done. His chest felt tight and there was a tremor in his voice as he finished speaking.

Mrs Stark was silent for a long time. At last, she said, gently, 'Will you show me your drawings?'

Caleb blinked at her in surprise. She was serious, he could see that. He had wanted someone to cast an expert eye over them, hadn't he? But now that the moment was here, he wasn't so sure. What if she told him he had no talent? He didn't think he could bear it. He cut the sandwich into quarters and put it on a dark-blue, gilded china plate, before placing it on the table.

'All right,' he decided. 'There's not a lot to see. It's new stuff.' He dug into the holdall and handed her the sketchbook, before he could change his mind,

'Thank you.' Mrs Stark opened the book. Her expression was neutral as she examined the six recent drawings.

Caleb waited, feeling as exposed as if his skin had been peeled back to reveal his inner workings. The back of his neck prickled with heat.

She leaned forward to lay the book open fully and take a closer look. 'You did all of these, here? At Windroth?'

He nodded.

She sat with her finger and thumb cupping her chin. With her head on one side, and the paintbrush's grizzled bristles sticking up out of her loops of white hair, she resembled an alert, crested bird. Caleb's discomfort increased. He was dying to know what she thought, but too scared that she didn't like them to prompt an opinion.

When she finally looked at him again, she was smiling. 'Your drawings have an unsettling, brooding quality. They are very accomplished, for one so young. It's excellent work, Caleb. Have you ever tried to sell anything?'

'Er...no,' Caleb said, hardly able to take in what she was saying. *She liked them! She really did.* 'I wasn't sure they were good enough. I thought about getting a portfolio together. Maybe showing it to my old art teacher. But it'll take a while. Dad trashed so many finished drawings.' Every time he thought of it, his anger rose again, hot and heavy. 'I go off by myself on my day off, so Dad can't complain about what I'm doing. He thinks I've given up drawing. I'm letting him, for now. But I couldn't stop, if I wanted to. It's when I feel most alive. You know?'

Ivy Stark was listening closely, her eyes were curiously bleak. 'Oh, indeed I do. None better. You have the divine discontent of the true artist, Caleb. One has to become obsessed with one's craft, to progress and grow one's talent. Having such talent is a mixed blessing. Take care. It can easily become a curse.'

Before he could ask what she meant, she bent her head to the sketch book again. Caleb felt his self-consciousness increase. He squirmed inwardly as he saw that she was studying one of his drawings more closely.

It was a skewed perspective of Windroth Hall, drawn in silhouette against a stormy night sky. He had set the horizon high up, so the building was close to the top of the page. The larger part of the drawing was of the sweeping meadow, where moonlight silvered grass stems and daisy heads and the spoke-like stems of wild Angelica made slanting shadows in the foreground.

Mrs Stark sat up. She made a little sound of satisfaction. 'This one. You've caught something of the brooding character of the house. I'd like to buy it. I shall give you...' She named a figure that made his jaw drop.

'But that's far too much. I can't accept it!'

'Don't be a fool. Of course you can,' she said stoutly. 'You have real talent, Caleb. Do you think I'd waste my time telling you that, simply to feed your ego? I thought you knew me better.' Her mouth twisted in a dry smile. 'Take my advice. Never sell yourself short.'

'Look. If you're trying to give me some money as a roundabout way of paying me because I help with the shopping and gardening and stuff, there's no need. And that electric kettle's old stock. Dad won't even notice it's gone,' Caleb protested, making a gesture towards the work surface. Which wasn't quite true. He was going to pay for the kettle out of the money Dad sometimes gave him. 'I told you, I like coming here.'

Ivy Stark lifted her chin, revealing loose folds of papery skin. 'Do you find it so hard to believe that I like your work?' She looked fixedly at him until he finally shook his head. 'Good. Because I can't abide false modesty. That's settled then. I'll get the money. Do you want a cheque or cash?'

Caleb was still reeling from the unexpectedness of it. 'Well, if you're sure, Mrs Stark. Um...cash, please.'

She nodded shortly and went out of the kitchen. He heard her shuffling steps on the wooden floor of the entrance hall and then a door sounded faintly somewhere in the maze of rooms inside the house. He knew better than to follow her. She had made it plain that the interior of the house was out of bounds.

Caleb slipped his hands into his jeans pockets as he stood waiting. He'd never had much money of his own. Dad didn't pay him regular wages, on the basis that it was payment enough that Caleb lived at home rent free with all meals provided. Now and then he was given enough money to buy magazines or go and see a film at the multiplex. But it had been weeks since any had come his way. He had spent his remaining few coins on the sketchbooks and in the cafe. He suspected that the business finances were getting worse and with relations between him and Dad strained, hadn't liked to inflame the situation by asking for money.

The amount Mrs Stark was paying him for the drawing of Windroth Hall would be the most he'd ever had. It amounted to the equivalent of nearly six weeks' proper wages; as far as he could judge. It might even stretch to the down payment on a flat.

CHAPTER 12

JESS MUNCHED HER way slowly through six bananas as she lay on her stomach on the grass. She'd found half a box of them in the bin behind the supermarket; a few were squashed but the rest of them were fine to eat. In her shoulder bag, she had more bananas, carefully wrapped so they wouldn't bruise.

Overhead, the leaves of the horse chestnut rustled softly in the warm breeze. Sunday and the park was full of people enjoying the sunshine. The smell of cut grass swirled round her along with the sounds of children playing and dogs barking.

She took the exhibition catalogue out of her bag and began leafing through it. It had been simple enough on the day of the school trip to slip one up her school jumper on the way out.

Music filled the air, as an electric folk combo at the bandstand started up. The mood was warm and lazy. People were sitting around on fold-up chairs drinking beer or wine. Others were sprawled on blankets on the grass. Jess tapped her foot in time to the music as she studied *Royalty's Revenge* for the twentieth time.

She had committed to memory every detail of the painting and knew she was becoming obsessed by it. It wasn't just that the woman on the bed bore an uncanny resemblance to Alice, it was everything; the details of the room, the rich colours, the silken pillows and that mysterious androgynous figure half emerging from shadows. And then there was the strange swaddled object that lay beside the sleeping woman. She was still puzzling over that. What could be inside it? She thought she could make out corded veins or ligaments, perhaps the hint of thin cramped limbs, folded insect-like, but it was hard to tell. The wrappings were made of something hazy, like light shining through mist that obscured and yet half-revealed the contents.

The whole painting resonated with secrets. It reminded her of medieval religious paintings, full of symbols, which people of the time would have been able to read. There were discoveries to be made about *Royalty's Revenge*, she was sure of it. But so far they eluded her.

And why was she so certain that the shadowy red-haired figure had one gold and one emerald eye?

A long shadow fell across her. Jess gave a start and looked up to find Lisa's brother peering down at her. She hadn't seen him since their encounter at the Simpson's house. Zac's blonde hair was flopping forward over one eye. She could smell the weed he was smoking. From its familiar tang, she knew that it was strong stuff. Leon had mates who grew the plants, so always had his own supply.

'I hope you're not expecting to meet up with Lisa,' Zac said.

'Nice to see you again, too,' Jess said sarcastically. She knew Lisa had gone shopping with her mum and then was visiting her grandmother.

'I thought you had a big thing about not doing drugs.'

He grinned wryly as he blew out smoke. 'I meant the hard stuff. *You'd* know more about that, of course.'

Jess felt a stir of annoyance, but didn't rise to the jibe. She looked down at the catalogue lying face down in her lap, hoping that he'd take the hint and get lost.

'Cool T-shirt,' he said.

She was wearing the long-sleeved, paint-spattered T-shirt, having decided that the indelible red stains actually looked pretty cool over the faded black and white design. She hadn't bothered to iron it, but had just pulled it on over her black combats. She wondered whether Zac had managed to clean the paint splatters from his room and rescue his DVDs and manga collection, but decided that she didn't much care.

Zac twisted his head sideways. 'What's that you're reading?'

She folded her arms over the catalogue protectively. 'Nothing you'd be interested in.' She raised her eyes to his. 'Why are you being so friendly all of a sudden?'

Zac shrugged. 'Lisa tells me you stuck up for her when some kids had a go at her about being overweight. Look, I've got nothing against you two hanging out together in class. Don't s'pose you can avoid each other. But remember what I said about being best buddies. She doesn't need a friend like you. Nothing personal. OK?'

Jess didn't reply. Arrogant prick.

He slouched off and went to join a group of guys who stood waiting a few metres away. A couple of them were looking in Jess's direction. She saw one of them, who wore a baseball cap and had a large plastic bottle of cider under each arm, say something to Zac. He glanced back over his shoulder at her and they all laughed mockingly.

Jess bridled and her temper flared. Leaping to her feet, she gave them the finger. 'Sit and spin! Tossers!' she yelled.

The boys whooped, jostling Zac as they trudged away to sit on the grass. Jess watched them, annoyed with herself for rising to them. A woman sitting with her three kids looked at her disapprovingly. 'What?' Jess glowered at her and the woman turned away.

She felt rattled and exposed. The quiet solitary afternoon she had planned in the park was ruined. She decided to go and find somewhere less public to sit and was stuffing the book into her bag, when her hand brushed against the wrapped bananas. There were still loads of them in her bedroom, far more than she could eat. She changed her plans and marched purposefully across the grass towards birdcage walk. The brown ankle boots were worn-in now and felt comfortable. She had decorated them with permanent black felt tip and was pleased with the way the black whorls and squiggles worked with the red paint splashes.

As she passed the peacocks' cage, Jess noticed that the 'dead' tree was now covered in fresh green leaves. She remembered the strange feeling she'd had when she and Lisa had come to the park. How she'd had the impression that she'd somehow *caused* green leaves to grow on the bare branch and the way the albino peacock had appeared to bow to her. Which was patently ridiculous. And yet…there were other things. She shook her head. No, she wouldn't think about that stuff. Didn't she already have enough problems?

She walked on, out of the park gates and soon came to the 24 hour garage at the start of the dual carriageway. There was the usual discomfort from traffic fumes and the zinging metal that jarred her already strained nerves, but she quickened her steps and veered off down the slope that led to the entrance to the underpass. The sound of traffic was magnified beneath the vaulted tunnel, but at least she was able to breathe more easily. Even the ever-present, stench of ammonia didn't bother her. It was fairly light as bright sunlight was penetrating some way into the cavern from each end. Her footsteps rang on the concrete as she approached the cardboard structure in the centre of the tunnel.

'Hey! Mike! You in there?' she called.

There was a dry rustling from the depths of the cardboard as sheets of newspaper were pushed aside. She heard muttering and then a head appeared, fringed with stiffened outgrowths, like some coral-dwelling sea creature. It was followed by a pair of shoulders and then the rest of Mike emerged. He wore a filthy army great-coat over dusty, colourless trousers that bagged over his worn boots. A fringed, checked scarf was muffled around his neck and knitted fingerless gloves covered his hands.

He blinked owlishly and grinned, displaying surprisingly white teeth. 'Can't a bloke get a lie-in on a Sunday?'

'Nope!' Jess grinned back, fishing in her bag. 'I thought you could use these.' She gave him the parcel of bananas.

'Thanks.' Mike clasped them in grimy fingers. The dirt seemed to have sunk into the pores of his long narrow face, so that the skin visible above his untrimmed beard had a faintly polished look to it, like the seat of a worn pair of black trousers.

Jess caught his smell. It was strong but not unpleasant, like a mixture of earth and leaf mould, overlaid with a sweetish almost spicy scent – a forest in autumn. The tunnel might stink of pee, but Mike didn't.

He bustled about, digging beneath the cardboard. Pulling out a couple of flattened but reasonably clean cushions, he placed them on the floor. 'Take a pew.'

'Thanks.' Jess sat down, cross-legged. She leaned against a piece of cardboard, while Mike found a tiny single-ring stove from somewhere. He poured water from a ridged plastic bottle into a cleaned-out soup tin. Turning his back, he bent over the stove. Jess heard a faint crackle as the burner ignited and he set the water to boil.

She watched as he produced two clean jam jars and then

took a brown paper package from his pocket. Crumbling dried leaves, he added them to the hot water. The smell of herbs floated into the air.

'From the allotments at the back of the garage,' Mike explained. 'Couple of blokes there let me help myself to fresh water and whatever's in season. I give them a hand with weeding, clearing up, burning rubbish – stuff like that. Pretty much keeps me going.'

'Bartering.' Jess nodded. 'We are supposed to be living in a global village, but you wouldn't know it around here.'

'Mmm.' Mike raised his eyebrows, in a 'so what' gesture. She supposed the outside world wasn't that important to him. He lived a life alongside society, without taking much of a part in it. He tipped the straw-coloured liquid into the jars and then handed one to Jess. 'Careful it's hot.'

She noticed that the wrists exposed in the gap between his gloves and the frayed coat sleeves were very pale and fine-boned. Beneath all the layers of clothes and the matted hair and beard, Mike was stick thin.

She cupped the tea in her hands and sipped. Peppermint and lemon balm. It was very good, strong and aromatic.

'So how long have you lived under here?'

'I come and go. Maybe a year and a half, all told.'

'Same as Mum and me.'

'Is that right?' Mike sipped his tea. 'Do you like it here?'

Jess wrinkled her nose. 'We've lived in worse places than Limefield Mansions.'

'Sorry to hear that.'

She shrugged. 'Yeah, well. You get what life hands out, don't you?'

Mike nodded, solemnly. 'True enough.' His expression softened as if he were looking inwards.

'We're not staying here though. I've got plans,' Jess said, surprisingly herself. She didn't usually talk about her home-life.

'Oh?' His eyes widened. They were bright, like black beads – robin's eyes – and surrounded by smooth unlined flesh. Jess was struck by the fact that he was much younger than he appeared to the casual eye. But there was also a maturity about him, as if he had lived for a long time or experienced a great deal. For some reason, she felt that she could trust him.

She breathed in the fragrant steam of her tea. 'I'm waiting for Mum to get fed up with Leon sponging off us and chuck him out of the flat. She gets depressed and drinks too much. Leon's no good for her. He drinks even more than she does. It was better when we were on our own. She didn't drink all the time then. But she has a knack for picking guys who let her down. Some of them have been OK, but most didn't want a kid hanging around. Leon's the last of a bad lot. Sorry...' She grinned. 'I'm waffling on a bit.'

'I don't mind.'

They drank the tea in companionable silence. Mike didn't comment or offer advice. He just waited for her to continue. Encouraged, Jess carried on unguardedly

'I don't know where we'll go. Maybe somewhere in the country. I hate towns and busy roads. Carbon emissions and stuff, you know? I'm allergic to the pollution. The air burns my lungs and it's hard to breathe. And the metal. You can't get away from it. It makes a constant noise that makes my head ring. ...' She paused, self-consciously.

Mike was listening closely. 'It's the iron. City living is hard for our kind,' he said, softly and with great intensity. 'We're not shaped for it. Change has come too fast for us and is coming ever faster.'

'I'll be leaving college in a few months, so it doesn't matter if we take off. No one's going to add me to a missing persons list. I'll get a job somewhere. Find a way to help Mum quit drinking. I can take care of both of us…' Jess hadn't been fully listening, but then the strangeness of Mike's last comment filtered through. *Our kind?* She gave him a searching look. 'What do you mean? *We're* not shaped for city living?'

Mike's expression changed. There was a long pause, while she waited for his reply. She thought he was about to tell her something important. Then his bright eyes flickered away briefly, before coming back to rest on her face, and the moment passed.

'Outsiders. Those who don't fit in. That's what we are, right?' He gave her a knowing wink. 'It takes one to know one.'

He was being evasive. But she nodded. She knew all about not fitting in. She sensed that Mike was angry about something. Well, he had a right to be. Here she was, bleating on about her pathetic mundane life, when at least she had a roof over her head. Mike must have more than enough troubles of his own. She wanted to ask what had driven him to take to the road, but was fearful of probing too deeply and offending him.

'How old are you, Mike?' she asked on impulse.

'Younger than the stones and older than the trees!'

Jess laughed. 'It's usually women who are sensitive about their age.'

'Is that a fact?' Mike shrugged, his narrow grin, exposing just the tips of his teeth. Seen that way they looked sharp and somehow feral. He stood up abruptly. 'Finished with your tea?' When she nodded he took the jar and swilled it out with leftover hot water before tipping it onto the ground. He did the same with his own jar and then neatly packed away the tin, jars and little stove in a cardboard box.

'You've forgotten the matches,' Jess prompted, looking around for the box he must have dropped, but she couldn't see one.

'Mmm.' Mike smiled enigmatically as he tucked his belongings into the depths of his cardboard home. 'Right.' He rubbed his gloved palms together. 'Since I'm up and awake, I'm off for a walk over to the allotments. I've promised to give someone a hand with their new shed.'

'I should be going.' Jess rose and shouldered her bag. 'Thanks for the tea.'

'Any time.' He stood watching as she walked towards the vaulted exit in the direction of Limefield Mansions. 'Thanks for the bananas!' he called out.

'You're welcome!' Jess lifted her hand in a wave but didn't look round.

She didn't see Mike stroking his beard thoughtfully as he watched her until she was out of sight. He took off his fingerless gloves to reveal large loose-boned hands that seemed to have extra joints. He flexed them and then held his palms facing each other. A tiny point of light appeared in the gap. It grew and burst into flame. Mike massaged the flame, until it tightened into a ball and then brought it up to his mouth, where it danced on his tongue for an instant before he swallowed.

He wished that he could tell Jess about the things that would help her cope here, but it wasn't his place. He would do what he could to watch over her, as the little hudskin had requested. It was little enough that Ninka asked of him. He was happy to do her this small service. Besides, it suited him to be able to move back and forth mortalwise in the dangerous circumstances. Out of sight, if not out of reach. Beyond that? Well, all in good time. Ninka had told him nothing about the mortal and sworn him to secrecy, but he knew someone with the mark of the fey about them when he saw them. It was plain that the girl had no idea. Poor thing.

Well - blood would out. Sooner or later, Jess would discover the truth by herself.

Dusting off his hands, Mike pulled the gloves back on.

'Not much longer now, Jess,' he said softly.

CHAPTER 13

JESS HELD HER mum's hair back as she hunched over the toilet. She was retching helplessly and Jess saw that the vomit was streaked with blood.

She helped her to stand and then flushed the toilet with her elbow. 'Come on. You'll have to lie on the sofa. I haven't done the bed yet.'

Trembling and hollow-eyed, Alice shuffled along to the sitting room. She was hunched over, her arms wrapped around her middle. 'I just need another drink...' A string of drool hung from her bottom lip, glistening on the red line of the new scar.

Things were getting worse. But what did you do with someone when they wouldn't admit they had a problem?

'You've had more than enough. Anyway, there isn't any drink in the house. You need to drink some water or you'll be in hospital with that stomach,' Jess said through gritted teeth. *I hate this so much.* Forcing herself to stay calm, she filled a glass and held it out to her mum.

'Stop telling me what to do,' Alice murmured irritably. 'I don't want bloody water!' Her windmilling arms caught the glass and swept it to the floor, where it caught the edge of a lager can and smashed. Water pooled on the carpet amid broken glass.

'For God's sake! I'm trying to help you!' Jess yelled. She ran for cloths and a brush and then quickly cleared up the broken glass before Mum stumbled on a piece and injured herself.

She couldn't face another humiliating incident, like that of three weeks ago, when Alice had fallen over and cut her chin on a broken wine glass. The flesh had split open like ripe fruit and Jess couldn't stop the bleeding. It was late at night and Leon had passed out on the sofa. She'd had to beg a lift to the hospital from someone in a neighbouring flat and then sit for hours in A&E with Alice who was so out of it, she was barely conscious. It was all Jess could do to stop her falling off her chair. She'd had to stop herself slapping Mum's hands down, when she kept plucking at the gaping wound.

'Bloody leave it alone!' she'd hissed in frustration, irritated by the pitying glances and knowing looks of other patients. A large proportion of those waiting for treatment were noisy, aggressive drunks, covered in blood and causing havoc. Jess hated the fact that Mum didn't look that much different.

When they finally returned home, with sterri strips placed ladder-like on her mum's cut chin, it was just getting light. Jess was exhausted and near the end of her tether. To her relief, Mum had immediately passed out next to Leon and woken the following morning with no recollection of the events.

Now she looked down on Alice, who had subsided into a sobbing heap on the sofa. Luckily the wound had healed cleanly and wouldn't leave much of a scar. She gave her a handful of tissues, tucked a pillow beneath her head and covered her with a blanket. 'Stay there, OK?' she ordered.

Alice's lips quivered. 'Where else would I go? I'm useless. I don't know why you bother with me...'

Jess had no time today for alcohol-induced self-pity. She was going to be late for college, again. Lisa was back from two weeks' holiday with her parents. She wanted to catch up with her, but she couldn't just leave Alice in this state.

Dispiritedly, she wrapped the broken glass in newspaper and dumped it in the over-flowing kitchen bin before stripping the vomit-stained sheets from the bed and stuffing them into a black bin bag. She scrubbed the mattress with hot water and washing-up liquid, the only cleaning fluid she could find and then opened the bedroom window in the vain hope that the fresh air would dry and freshen it.

In the sitting room, Alice was snoring gently, her puffy face younger-looking and vulnerable in sleep. Jess turned Alice onto her side, so she wouldn't choke on her own vomit if she was sick again. Bundling the bin bag under her arm, she went out of the flat and along the walkway. The lift was out of order again, so she took the stairs down to the basement laundry. With a hollow sound, the door clanged open into a large square room smelling of mildew. The walls were made of grey breeze blocks. It was cold and gloomy under the strip lights, one of which was buzzing and flickering intermittently.

The laundry was little-used, since almost all the tenants had installed their own washing machines. The machines and tumble-dryers here were covered in graffiti and mostly trashed, but a couple still worked. Two plastic garden chairs were placed beneath a cheap, melamine-topped work surface.

She had forgotten to bring the bottle of washing-up liquid with her. The wall dispenser, containing small boxes of washing powder for sale, was empty. No point in forcing the thing open. She stuffed the bedding into the machine, selected the hottest boil wash and hoped for the best.

It would be a while before the washing was done. She didn't relish sitting down here by herself staring at the walls. It would be safe enough to collect it later. It would take a desperate thief to want to steal two sicked-on sheets. She decided to go in to college and see Lisa. It didn't matter how late she arrived, since she was already on report for poor attendance. The thought of having to do a lunchtime detention made her toes curl up with boredom, but it would be worth it. She was surprised by how much she had missed Lisa.

Her decision made, Jess was walking towards the laundry door, when it opened.

'Thought I'd find you in here,' Leon said. 'Fancy some company?'

Jess hid her unease. Leon didn't do 'nice'. Not unless it served his own self-interest. 'I was just leaving. I've got college...'

'I don't why Alice bothers about you going. I learned all I needed to know on the streets. Stay here. We can get to know each other better.' Leon rotated his tongue stud against his bottom teeth. Click. Click. The tiny sound set Jess's own teeth on edge.

'I don't think so.' Jess would have pushed past him, but he stood squarely in the doorway, blocking her exit.

'That's not very friendly now.' Raising one hand, he rubbed the stubble on his chin with the backs of his bent fingers.

Jess made herself smile. She attempted a joke. 'I'm surprised you even know the way down here. Laundry's not exactly your thing.'

Leon was very particular about his clothes, insisting on them being washed, ironed and folded properly. The flat could be filthy and the cupboards empty, but outwardly he was always clean and smart. He wouldn't lift a hand himself though. Alice did all their laundry and when she was incapable, Jess did it for her. Not because she wanted to, but because Leon would take it out on her mum if he found a single food stain on a shirt.

He grinned. 'Yeah, well. You don't have two dogs and bark yourself, do you?' His lips worked. Click. Click.

'I need to go. Lisa's…waiting for me.'

His voice was softer, wheedling. 'So see her later. What's the rush? I told you, you and me were going to have a long talk. I'm just in the mood.'

'I'm leaving, now!' Jess took a step closer, hoping he would move aside. 'I mean it. Get out of my way!'

Leon's dull-brown eyes sparked with anger. 'Now you're pissing me off. Who do you think you're ordering about?'

He moved forward, kicking the door shut behind him. Jess felt a stab of panic. No one was likely to come down here and disturb them. The walls were so thick, that she could scream at the top of her voice and no one would hear. There was a fire exit on the opposite side of the room. Would there be time to run for it and get out before he caught up with her?

She backed up slowly, still deliberating. Terror curdled her stomach.

Leon moved quickly. Before Jess realised what he intended, he grabbed her with one arm and pulled her close. His free hand swept downwards to cup the slight curve of her buttock.

'Get your hands off me!' she yelled into his face.

Leon laughed. She smelt the alcohol on his breath. His hand flashed up and grabbed a hank of her hair. 'Or what? You'll run to mummy? You should be grateful to me, you weird bitch. Who else is going to want you?'

Jess winced at the pressure on her roots as he wound his fingers more tightly in her hair. The pain made her eyes water. She could smell the sourness of his body beneath the cheap aftershave.

'Lucky that I like weird, eh? You've been winding me up for weeks. Giving me looks and then playing hard to get. So how about it?'

'In your dreams!' Jess sneered.

'You can drop the act now. OK? You've got me. Question is…what are you going to do about it?'

Her scalp screamed in protest as he hauled her across the room. 'Ow! That hurts! Shit! Let go of me you bastard!'

Leon kicked her legs from under her. Jess went sprawling and landed with all her weight on her wrists. She crumpled and felt her cheek strike the floor with bruising force. Before she could get up, Leon pounced and dragged her over onto her back. He sat astride her and looked down into her face with a triumphant grin.

'Nothing to say now?'

Jess tasted bile in her throat. Her heart was pounding. Everything hurt and she couldn't think straight. *Help me – someone.*

Leon leaned closer, grabbed her face in one hand, his fingers digging into her cheeks. 'Knock, knock. Anyone in?' he said softly.

Jess screwed up her face and closed her eyes as she felt his breath on her cheek. If he tries to kiss me, I swear I'll bite him. She felt anger pushing at the edges of her fear and, suddenly, the helplessness dissipated. This is not happening. I won't let it. *Something in the air around her crackled faintly. There was an internal gathering, a soundless click of ignition. Subtle energy flying outwards.*

A soft pattering noise, like dry leaves falling to the forest floor, as tiny objects landed on her face. They were hot and stung her skin.

Leon gave a howl of pain. Jess felt an easing of pressure as he shifted his weight onto his knees, rising up to leave a small space between their two bodies. She opened her eyes. He had clapped one hand to his face. A thin line of blood was pouring down his cheek, more flowed from his slit nostril.

'Argh! What the fuck…' he burbled, through bloody teeth. In his open mouth, blood was welling up like an underground spring breaking the surface. He swallowed, gagged, spat bloody gouts onto the floor.

Jess fluttered fingers up to where a tiny, hurting object was caught in her eye socket and pinched the hot metal bead between finger and thumb. Not a bead. A stud, complete with its screw-on fastening. Leon's tongue piercing. A tiny piece of flesh was lodged in it. She twisted her head, saw the two bloodied steel rings that had bounced onto the floor beside her. And understood.

Leon's facial piercings had been torn from their sheaths of flesh; just as if a giant magnet had extracted them wholesale. *Had she done that? Was there some kind of distilled energy in her rage which when unleashed spawned a self-protective force? Oh, God what was happening to her?* Grimacing with disgust, she threw the stud across the room.

Leon was still moaning softly in pain and confusion. Jess saw her chance. She bent her knees and thrust against the floor, at the same time lunging upwards with all the power she could muster in her thighs and hips. And slammed Leon in the balls. A high-pitched scream escaped him as he collapsed sideways. Jess kicked herself free of him and was on her feet in an instant.

She looked down at him as he lay with his hands bunched between his legs. Tears leaked from his eyes, mingling with the blood running down his face. Jess dropped to one knee beside him. He looked up at her, lips stretched back from his teeth.

'You like weird, eh? You've no idea, how weird I am!' she hissed, her voice shaking with intensity. 'I want you out of the flat. Get your stuff and go. Or I'll go to the police. Tell them you attacked me. I mean it. I know you've got a record. You'll go down this time. What do you get for attempted rape? Two years? Three?' Her eyes bored into him. She rapped him on the head with her bony knuckles. 'Knock. Knock. Have you got the message? You'd better be gone by the time I get back.'

Leon cringed, closed his eyes, nodded.

As Jess walked towards the door, Leon retched helplessly. 'You'll pay, you bitch. Oh, God you'll pay and pay. I'll make sure of it,' he sobbed.

'Whatever! Just get the hell out of my life!' Jess opened the door and slammed it shut behind her.

CHAPTER 14

JESS RACED BACK upstairs, legs trembling. She dragged open the door onto the walkway and stood there taking deep steadying breaths. She was shaking all over and her stomach cramped as if she was about to be sick.

Leon's smell, his touch seemed to linger on her skin. Her scalp was bruised from where he had dragged her across the floor by her hair. She was aware of a coppery taint on her lips and when she wiped at her mouth, her hand came away smeared with his blood. *And his piercings had somehow ripped free.*

A shudder of revulsion ran through her as she spat onto the floor. She was desperate to have a shower and scrub away every last trace of him. But that would take time and she didn't want to risk running into a recovered and dangerous Leon. Better to leave him nursing his empty threats; hope he'd call into the flat later to get his stuff before disappearing.

But what of Alice?

There should just be time to check on her, before Leon staggered upstairs. She found her still dead to the world. Should she try and wake her? But where could she take her, while she was in this state? Alice would be safe enough. Leon's viciousness was single-minded. Any thoughts of revenge would be centred on *her*. It was actually better this way. A comatose Alice wouldn't rage at Leon or cry, or plead with him; the usual incitements to violence. If all went to plan, by the time her mother surfaced that evening, Leon would be gone.

She bent and kissed Alice's cheek. 'We don't need him. This is for the best. I promise.'

Her face in the college cloak room mirror: left side, swollen, already turning blue , eye partly closed.

Lisa's voice trailing off as she took in her appearance, 'Jess? I thought I saw you come in…'

'Yeah? Sorry about the dramatic entrance. I planned to get here early. But there was a slight glitch.' She dabbed her face gingerly unable to suppress a grunt of pain.

'Are you OK?' Lisa squinted at her through thick glass lenses. As Jess lowered her hands, her pale eyes widened in horror. 'Oh my God! What happened? You look terrible!'

'Thanks!' Jess said wryly. 'I head butted the floor. Helped by my mum's scumbag boyfriend.' She told Lisa how Leon had cornered her in the laundry room, omitting the part about his mysteriously ruined piercings. She still wasn't ready to go there. It threw up too many questions. She felt panicky at what she might uncover.

'He tried to come on to you? That's so gross. He must be twice your age!'

'I don't think that came into it. At least I've got a good reason for being late. I can say I fell down some stairs. Say I've been to A&E. No one's going to question that when they see my face. No detention for me today. Yay!'

Lisa didn't laugh. 'This is serious, Jess. Leon *attacked* you! That's GHB. People get locked up for that!'

'GBH,' Jess corrected, feeling an absurd urge to giggle. 'Stands for grievous bodily harm. I don't think it was quite that bad.' *It might have been though,* she thought feeling queasy.

'Your face is black and blue. You're going to have a terrible shiner. I think you really *should* get checked out. Why don't

I come to the hospital with you, after school?'

'Thanks. But no. We'd have to wait for hours to be seen. You'd have to tell your parents where you were. And Zac's bound to hear about it. Which would confirm what he already thinks. I'm the devil's spawn, remember?' She grinned then wished she hadn't. Her hand flew to her injured cheek. 'Ouch! Remind me not to smile for the next couple of weeks.'

Turning her back on Lisa, she peered into the mirror to examine her half-shut eye more closely. She caught the movement in the reflection as Lisa stepped closer, felt a gentle touch on her left shoulder.

'You've got a big lump near your shoulder blade.'

'Have I?'

Jess bent one arm, curved it backwards, and felt around with her long fingers until they connected with a raised area that was protruding above the low scooped back of her vest. It was a vertical ridge around six centimetres long. 'I must have knocked it when I was grappling with Leon.' She pressed the bump experimentally. It was a little sore, but nothing to worry about. Suddenly self-conscious about standing there with her scrawny arms and flat chest on show, she reached for her shirt. 'I think I'll live,' she said, buttoning the front.

Lisa made a sound of exasperation. 'Why are you acting like this is no big deal? OK, hospital's out. I get that. You should talk to Mr Blackwell. He's a bit strict, but he's pretty good when there's real trouble. He might be able to help.'

'No way! Next thing, it'll be social services. Been there, done that. It just makes things worse,' Jess said sharply. At the look on Lisa's face, she softened her voice. 'Besides, I really *can* cope. I've been doing it long enough. I'm a survivor, right? In a strange way, I'm glad this happened. If it gets Leon out of the picture, it'll be worth it.'

'If you say so.' Lisa rolled her eyes. 'You've obviously made up your mind.'

'Yeah.' Jess suppressed a groan as her injured cheek throbbed insistently. 'There is one thing you could do.'

'Of course. What is it?'

'Buy me a carton of fruit juice from the vending machine?'

* * * * *

'Don't tell me. You walked into a door.' Mr Blackwell regarded her over the tops of his glasses, an uncharacteristic twist to his lips.

'No, I fell down some stairs,' Jess said. 'I was carrying my school bag, so I couldn't put out my hands to save myself. I've been checked out at A&E. The doctor said I haven't broken anything. Lucky wasn't it? Anyway, I'm fine now. '

Despite Jess's protestations, he insisted she saw the school nurse. 'Health and Safety. The subject is not up for discussion. Understood?' he said firmly.

Jess nodded, knowing when not to push it.

'And if there's anything you want to talk about, in confidence, I'm a good listener.' He patted her arm.

'OK.'

'I mean it. Don't forget.'

She nodded again. And walked away quickly, before he could ask awkward questions or, worse still, she burst into stupid tears. Outside the treatment room, she and Lisa paused.

'You needn't wait. I'll see you back in class,' Jess said.

'I'll come in with…'

Jess held up her hand. 'No, really.'

Lisa sighed. Shaking her head, she wandered away.

Inside the treatment room, Jess submitted to a facial

examination and answered the nurse's questions. She didn't mention the tender lump on her back. It was no big deal and would be fine after a day or so. After a few minutes she left with a couple of pain killers and a dressing taped over her eye.

On the way back to the classroom, she ducked into the cloakroom. She flushed the tablets down the toilet and, on impulse, took her atomiser out of her school bag and sprayed her face, lifting the dressing to include her eye. The relief was immediate. She wished she had thought of it before. She was tempted to remove the dressing, but on second thought smoothed it back into place. It would satisfy Mr Blackwell and stop him from asking any more questions.

Back in class, Jess faced the curious looks and nudges with a blank stare.

'If you ask me it's an improvement!' Stacey Weaver commented, tossing her blonde extensions over her shoulder.

Debs Cranford tittered. 'That's the worst pirate impression I've ever seen!'

Lisa rounded on them both, fists clenched. 'Shut up! Both of you!'

Taken aback, Stacey and Debs fell silent.

Jess blinked in surprise. She caught Lisa's eye as she slid into the seat next to her and raised her eyebrows in amusement.

'Well, they really annoy me! Always picking on people. If they can't say anything positive, I wish they'd keep quiet!' She took out a book and slammed it onto the desk

The moment the bell went for the end of lessons, she and Lisa filed out of the classroom and headed for the bus stop. They sat in companionable silence for the short journey.

Jess was no longer in pain. Her face seemed less swollen to the touch. She peeled the dressing off her eye experimentally.

'It's hardly even bloodshot.' Lisa leaned closer. 'I had a black eye once, for three weeks. The bruises went green and then yellow before they disappeared. I swear yours are fading already!'

'Told you it looked a lot worse than it was. The cold water must have helped and I sprayed my face with my atomiser.'

'That squirty stuff works like magic. Remember my face after I'd scrubbed that paint off? The redness and swelling went down overnight. You should start selling it. That's how that woman with all those shops selling bath bombs and stuff got started. She's made millions.'

'Maybe I will.' Jess pondered how long it would take to shop-lift all the bottles of essential oils she'd need.

As the bus neared their stop she fell silent, beginning to worry about what she would find when she got back to the flat. They walked along together until they reached the corner where they usually went their separate ways.

Lisa shuffled her feet looking at the ground. 'There's a Bridget Jones movie on this week. I...I wondered if you fancied going and seeing it?'

Jess preferred darker and more cerebral films, but was pleased that Lisa has asked her. Especially as it meant she was defying Zac. *You'll be a rebel yet, Lisa!*

Lisa's eyebrows dipped in a frown. 'If you'd rather do something else...'

'Nope. A movie's good. Sounds like fun.'

'I could meet you at the cinema. That way Zac won't see us together and make a big deal of it. He's such a dork.' She shook her head. 'I still don't get what he's got against you.'

'He's just looking out for you, I suppose. But what he doesn't know won't hurt him, Right?' She resisted the urge to tell Lisa that her hypocrite brother had been smoking weed and drinking with his friends in the park a few weeks ago. She wasn't going to spoil the moment by telling tales.

'How about Saturday?'

'Hmm. It's Thursday today. I'll have to consult my diary.' Jess looked down at her open palm and mimed turning electronic pages with the index finger of her other hand. 'I have a busy social schedule. Ah, I seem to have a *teeny* window on Saturday. I can just about fit you in. What time?'

'You idiot!' Lisa giggled. 'Meet you there at seven?'

'I'll be there.'

'Bye then. See you at college tomorrow.' She wore her happiness easily, all on the outside, an unfamiliar warmth and a childish smile.

Jess watched her. Such a novelty to have a friend after being a loner for so long. She could get used to it.

As she neared the flat her mood soured, her pulses quickening with apprehension as she thought about what she might find there. She shouldered her school bag, hardly conscious of the slight discomfort as it brushed against the sore bump between her shoulder blades.

CHAPTER 15

CALEB HAD BEEN busy today. Ivy noticed him rummaging about around the base of the kitchen wall and the drain. He had a bag, which clanked as if something metallic was inside it, and in his other hand he had a jar of peanut butter. When she asked what he was doing, he tapped the side of his nose and grinned at her.

'I'm sorting something for you. You needn't worry about it. OK?'

'Strange boy!' Ivy laughed, amused by his secrecy. The way he performed small tasks for her without being asked to was touching.

She left him to it, and went off to her studio. Shoulders slumped, she ascended slowly, gripping the stair rail and heaving herself up onto each step. Caleb and everything else was now forgotten, as she thought of the work awaiting her.

The day passed in a blur of broad brush strokes on canvas, colour-mixing, blending, drafting new shapes with oil paint diluted with turpentine, as she strove to capture the essence of her ever more demanding models.

'Be still!' she hissed at one of the little beasts, a hedgehog-like creature with a snub snout, long legs and tiny pale-blue wings, which was worrying at her ankles. It subsided with a little grumble of complaint and fluttered up to perch on the curtain rail.

Ivy noticed a new being amongst the faeries today. Its pale bones were visible beneath swathes of luminous glowing flesh which trailed behind it, like the tendrils of a jelly fish. It had a sweet feminine face with a mild expression. Smiling encouragingly, Ivy beckoned it forward. Over the next couple of hours, she painted the creature into the corner of a new composition.

She became aware of a nagging discomfort in her left hand and on raising it, saw that the fingertips, worn nearly to the bone from frantically blending paint on the canvas, had begun to bleed again. Crossing to a side table, she rifled through the clutter of paints and brushes for a roll of dressings and scissors and awkwardly taped her sore fingers.

By the time the day had lengthened into the pearl gold of late afternoon, Ivy was exhausted. The faeries had grown bored and were either asleep, resting, or doing despicable things to each other in the shadows. They seemed to sense that she was unable to go on working. One by one, they faded or disappeared with faint popping sounds. The beautiful jelly fish woman was the last to leave. She blew Ivy a kiss, and waved goodbye, the exposed bones of her delicate hand flexing.

Left to herself at last, Ivy loosed a long shuddering sigh. Her wrists felt so tight that she could barely flex her fingers and the muscles in her forearms were on fire. The familiar pain was worse than usual. Helpless tears sprang to her eyes, as she slowly massaged each aching hand in turn. After a while the pain eased slightly. She opened a window, before cleaning her brushes. The sound of skylarks met her ears, their fluting notes trailing on high, lifted her jaded spirits.

Below her, Caleb came into view. He was pushing his bicycle back along the narrow trough, which had been tramped through the waist high grass by his comings and goings. Seeming to feel her eyes on him, he twisted round to smile and raise a hand, his palm flattened in a 'see you soon' gesture.

Ivy waved back, smiling.

The sunlight glinted on his dark hair and lit up the planes of his face. He wasn't conventionally handsome, his nose was too long, his jaw too sharp. But his deep-set hazel eyes were striking. She imagined that any young woman who took the trouble to get to know him would find his looks compelling.

'See you next week! Come earlier if you like.'

It wasn't safe for him to keep coming here, but she enjoyed his company too much. Having resigned herself to ending her days alone and lonely, it had been a shock to feel her iron self-control softening into friendship with the troubled young man. She glimpsed aspects of her younger self in him, although their backgrounds were very different. His loyalty to his parents was touching. One day though, he would need to break free, and make his own way, for his talent for drawing was a driving force within him.

Oh, she did hope that Caleb would stay around a while longer and continue to visit her. But did she have the right to selfishly expose him to danger?

Ivy considered. Caleb respected her wishes about confining himself to the kitchen, apart from that one time when kindness had impelled him to bring a tea tray upstairs to her studio. He had not seen anything alarming, she had made sure of that. The charms she had placed outside her studio door had so far prevented the creatures from contaminating the rest of the house. Caleb ought to be safe enough. A sudden thought struck her. What about outside? He spent hours rambling about by himself, looking for things to draw. What if he ventured too deeply into the forest? She must speak to him. Make up some plausible story. Perhaps something about the dangers of coming upon marauding gangs of poachers, with fierce dogs and guns.

For Caleb wouldn't believe her if she told him the truth. A bitter laugh escaped her. What sane person would?

Ivy's eyes felt gritty and she pressed the heels of her palms into the sockets, enjoying the pressure and warm darkness. She found her thoughts drifting, the years unwinding. And there she was, a younger version of herself walking towards the forest, unaware that her life was about to changer forever…

Ivy swung her arms as she walked. Over one shoulder was a canvas bag containing her sketchpad, pencils and a well-used travelling case of watercolours. She had a commission for six illustrations for a children's book and was looking forward to a few hours of solitude, away from the demands of her two year old daughter, Joan. She smiled, thinking of how Ralph doted on their little girl. The two of them certainly wouldn't miss her company. They would be far too engrossed in each other.

At the forest's edge, shifting patterns of spring sunlight splashed the ground with washes of green, amber and gold. The beauty of it drew her in. A warm breeze stirred her hair, newly styled into a close fitting cap of fashionable curls. She became aware of an oppressive, heavy feeling. It was as if the forest, content in itself, shunned human intervention or perhaps it still bore a grudge from having been stripped of wood for the war effort, almost ten years since; although its rate of recovery was truly remarkable. Looking at the enormous trees and well-grown saplings, no one would guess at the former devastation. Shaking off her unease, Ivy pressed on.

Emerging shoots of bracken, curling like bishops' crooks,

brushed against her printed-cotton dirndl skirt. Ivy saw drifts of bluebells amongst the leaf litter and stopped to admire the contrast of sky blue against the faded gold of shrivelled winter aconites. Buds were already bursting on silver birches, so that the lacework of branches seemed clothed in pale green gauze. Ahead of her the thick undergrowth had made a kind of tunnel. She walked towards it, plunging more deeply into dappled shade.

The trees here had escaped any careless harvest. Vines clotted with pale buds wreathed their ancient trunks. All was still, as if even the birds were holding their breath. A tall, slender figure suddenly appeared between the trees. As it drew closer, She saw that it was a young man. He had shaggy dark-red hair and was dressed in forest colours; close-fitting trousers of light-brown leather tucked into darker brown boots, a leaf-green velvet frock-coat over a trailing shirt that looked as if it was made of cobwebs.

Ivy started, her step faltering.

He didn't look like a local man. Why was he wearing fancy dress? Her lips compressed as she made a probable connection. She had been shopping in the village when the fleet of garishly painted lorries, pulling huge trailers, had driven past. The seasonal circuses, which set up on the common, seemed to attract all kinds of layabouts. She felt uneasy. What was this man doing in her forest? Thoughts of being robbed or worse made her heart beat faster, but she wasn't going to be intimidated on her own land.

'I say! Do you realise that you are trespassing?'

'Forgive me. I had not realised.' The young man's smile was disarming. He was pale, sharp-featured, tall and over-thin. 'I was taking a stroll on this beautiful day and meant no harm. I did not mean to startle you.'

Ivy blinked at him. 'Well. I suppose there is no harm in you simply walking.'

He bowed his head. 'Indeed? A most pleasant season to be out and about, is it not?'

'Yes. Yes, it is.' What a polite young man. She smiled at him. 'I did not expect to meet anyone in here.'

'Then you are unwise to wander so deep into the forest. *Your* forest...' he said, with no change of tone, although she saw that his smile was now tinged with mockery. 'To those who live here, your intrusion might be seen as an... invitation.'

People living here? Invitation, to what? Ivy blinked in surprise. *What was he talking about?* She reassessed the young man's theatrical appearance. The old-fashioned way in which he spoke now seemed like an affectation. Really! She had no patience with someone acting the fool.

'I can assure you that no one lives here,' she said decisively. 'And if I found out that they *were* doing so, without my permission, I would alert the local constabulary and have them evicted, forthwith!'

'Would you indeed?' He looked openly amused now, but his lean, beautiful features had tightened with pride and anger. 'If you knew who you were addressing, you would rather bend your knee than speak so!'

Ivy had had enough. 'What on *earth* do you mea...' As the young man held up his hand, the words died on her lips.

There was an odd feeling like something twitching inside her head and a sense of paralysis. He came closer, moving in an alarmingly swift way. There was something wrong with his eyes. They seemed to have no whites or pupils, but each was flooded with a different colour. One moment, he seemed sharply in focus and the next his image was somehow obscured as if she was looking at him through glasses, smeared with Vaseline.

Ivy shuddered, gripped by terror. Her shoulder bag slid to the ground with a soft rustle.

The young man was speaking gently to her, but she couldn't follow. A mad swirl of words she couldn't catch hold of. On her tongue was a slick of honey.

He paused, studying her keenly, his head on one side. 'What is your name?'

'I...vy,' she murmured thickly.

'Your full name,' he wheedled. 'I am sure it is very pretty.'

Slowly she said her name as if she had just discovered it somewhere amongst her thoughts, 'Ivy... Elizabeth... Stark.'

He grinned, triumphantly, his mouth stretching wider than seemed natural to display a row of pointed teeth. 'Ivy. Elizabeth. Stark.' He licked his lips as if tasting each letter.

A chill ran down her spine. She felt a scream rising within her but her lips betrayed her with a loud honey-tasting burp and a panicked squeak.

The young man laughed. 'Manners. Ivy Elizabeth Stark,' he said, reprovingly. 'I command you by the power of your name. To beg my pardon. Most humbly.'

'I do most humbly beg your pardon.' She heard herself saying.

'Hmm. You were dreadfully rude to me, Ivy Elizabeth Stark. I think a pretty curtsy is in order.'

Ivy's knees bent, her fingers gripped handfuls of her full gathered skirt and her body thrust forward by itself, performing obediently like a puppet for its puppet master.

The young man laughed delightedly. 'Nicely done, Ivy Elizabeth Stark. You may rise.'

Ivy felt herself snapping to attention so smartly that her spine creaked. Dread resonated through every tingling nerve. It was as if she had no will of her own. She was compelled to do what he said. Too late, she understood, what power she had given away when she gave him her full name.

'Now, Ivy Elizabeth Stark. Listen well. This is what is going to happen…'

Her head was hurting . The taste of honey on her tongue was turning bitter with something rotten at its core. The forest seemed to be spinning around her…

'…I have spoken,' said the stranger, with an air of finality.

After that, everything became confused.

She could only recall stumbling back through the forest and bursting out of the trees. With no idea whether minutes or hours had passed, she headed towards the gardens and house, where she crawled upstairs grateful for solitude. Collapsing fully-dressed onto her bed, she fell deeply asleep, managing to rise just before Ralph and little Joan got back. Somehow she managed to behave normally, knowing she must say nothing about what had happened.

In the middle of that night Ivy woke and vomited bitter honey. An image of a thin white face haunted her thoughts. Up-tilted mismatched eyes, flooded with colour between long eyelids. One a startling green, the other a glowing amber – she could see them clearly now. A too-wide smile, crammed with teeth that seemed to grow in layers like a shark's. She could now recall some of what he had said, though at the time it had seemed a chaos of words.

Jack. He had told her she could call him, Jack. 'I'm not so foolish as to willingly give away my true name.' A mocking expression on his face.

Ivy reached shaking hands towards her bedside table. Grasping her diary, she wrote rapidly, as if in a dream, letters scrawling over the pages. And then exhausted, she slept again.

In the morning, while Ralph was in his dressing room, she opened the diary and read what she had written.

I met a strange young man in the forest today. More beautiful than any woman and as dangerous as a poisonous snake. He told me I will be famous and have untold wealth. He will see to it that I have beautiful, incredible creatures, such as few painters have ever seen, to pose for me. And for this privilege, he demanded something in exchange. I must give him... Here she had scribbled something illegible. *I have agreed to this bargain. I had no choice.*

Ivy trembled as she read, frozen in disbelief. It didn't even look like her writing. Agreed to what? God help me, I can't remember. What had Jack demanded of her? What must she give up, when he came to collect it?

Her mouth was dry. There was a terrible, raw gnawing in her belly as if she hadn't eaten for a week. This was madness. It couldn't be true. She must be ill. The imaginings of a sick brain.

Getting out of bed, Ivy looked down with horror at her bare ankles and calves, scratched, gouged and bleeding from where she had trudged through brambles and vines. Her skirt lay on the floor, torn and grass-stained. She remembered how her shoulder bag had slipped to the ground. It was lost, somewhere in the forest, close to where he, Jack, had appeared.

It was true. All of it. Dear God. What had she done?

Standing at her studio window, Ivy allowed the memories to sink and dissolve inside her. Caleb mounted his bike. At the place where the long grass lawn melted into the gravel driveway, he paused. She watched him grasp the hem of his T-shirt and bring it up to wipe his sweaty brow. Her trained eye registered the symmetry of his tanned limbs, the width of his shoulders and curve of his strong young back, before he disappeared into the woods leading to the lane. Perhaps she would ask him to sit for her. It had been so very, very long since she'd had a human subject to paint.

Behind her, in the shadows, a high-pitched whispering began. They were back. She heard a clatter of wings, a squeak of outrage. Then a loud crude fart. A bitter burning-leaf stench, followed by a hoarse titter. She had no choice now, but to start working again. *Yes, all right. Just a moment, you wretches!* She knew what to expect if she kept them waiting for much longer. After she had lingered over Caleb's drawings, that time, her arms had been black and blue for a week from their pinching fingers.

There would never be any rest for her; no comfort or serenity in old age. There was only the pressing need to keep working, the drain on her vitality, until she no longer had the strength to pick up brush or pen.

The chittering in the shadows became louder. Sharp little faces, some ugly, many breathtakingly beautiful poked forward into the light. Figures jostled and preened, taking up poses or rudely exposing themselves and wagging bare buttocks.

Ivy's head ached with exhaustion. A dozen small discomforts in her body fought for recognition against the relentless force that was driving her, like a ravenous hunger stirring its coils.

Gripping one of the newly cleaned brushes with trembling fingers, she loaded it with paint. A long susurration sounded in the studio. And then there was silence as Ivy settled down again to work.

CHAPTER 16

'YOU LOSE – again! Go on. Neck it down.'

He didn't need encouraging. Throwing back his head, he drained the glass. It was some kind of fruity soft drink, with an underlying kick. He was aware of the warmth already banked inside him. A pleasant numbness was beginning to spread through his limbs.

Sharon lost the next round. Whooping with laughter, she re-filled her glass. 'Down the hatch!' Wayward strands of long blonde hair were sticking to her damp forehead. She'd had short hair, earlier in the day, when she'd breezed into the shop. It was long now, extensions he supposed.

He'd been leaning on the counter, thinking about Mrs Stark before Sharon came in. The old lady was a strange old thing, bird-like and fierce. He liked her, though, and she seemed to like him. It suddenly struck him that the only significant woman in his life, apart from Mum, was old enough to be his great grandmother.

He was slow to look up when the bell over the door rang. He recognised the young woman at once. She worked at the hairdressers next to the flower shop.

'Hello, again,' he said, brightly. 'Not with your friend this time?'

She pulled a face. 'We're not joined at the hip, you know. I'm Sharon, by the way.'

'Hi Sharon. Caleb.'

'Nice name. So how come you never came into the salon for your freebie?' Planting her hands on her hips, she faced him in mock confrontation. She wore something purple and tight-fitting that showed off her curves and was pretty under the spray tan and pink lipstick. Against the dusty interior of the shop, she stood out like an exotic bird.

Caleb's lips twitched. 'I meant to. Just didn't get round to it. Sorry.' He felt flattered that she had come back into the shop to see him.

'A bunch of us are going out tonight. Fancy coming?'

The first attractive girl to show any interest in him for God-knew-how-long was waiting for an answer. He was in a state of panic. *Don't mess this up, you idiot!* Silence stretched, hanging heavy in the shop. Sharon looked amused.

'Erm...yeah. I'd like that,' he said all in a rush, a sudden surge of courage and defiance. He deserved a life of his own.

And now here he was in Sharon's small flat, playing drinking games with her and her mates. Now it was something called Ring-of-Fire. He couldn't work out the rules. But who cared. Apparently, he had lost again.

Grinning he raised his glass. His teeth clinked against the rim and he felt liquid dribble out of the corner of his mouth. He made a loud sucking noise as he tried not to waste any, which Sharon seemed to find hilarious. A candle on the coffee table flickered. Caleb screwed up his eyes wondering why it wouldn't stay in focus.

'Look at him. He's off his face,' a voice said from a distance.

'Do him good.' That was Sharon speaking. 'Stuck in that shop all the time. He's cute. Don't you think?'

'Nah. Not buff enough....'

Caleb didn't hear the rest of it. *Sharon thought he was cute.*

Well, Ditto. As she sat on the sofa beside him, the warm drift of her perfume made his head swim.

'All right?' she asked.

'Yeah. I'm good.' He couldn't stop the silly grin from plastering itself across his face.

A car horn sounded from the street. 'They're here!'

The room emptied rapidly as Sharon's friends poured from the flat.

'Better get tall, dark and pissed to his feet.'

Caleb found himself hustled outside and into a transit van, already crammed to bursting with people sitting on mattresses and cushions.

A young man wearing a leather jacket over a grey hooded top loomed over him. 'Who's this, sis?'

'Caleb,' Sharon told the man. 'Caleb, meet Si, my brother.'

'Aw right, Si.' He attempted to flap one hand in greeting.

'Where'd you find him, sis? At the school gates? Still up to your old tricks, eh?'

'Hey! I'm no baby snatcher!' Sharon answered indignantly. 'Caleb's older than he looks. He works in his dad's shop'

'Well he won't need I.D where we're going.'

As the van moved off, loud music with prominent drum and bass notes started-up. Caleb moved his body in time to the beat.

Sharon nudged him. 'Great, isn't it? You wait. We're really going to smash it up.'

He could barely hear her above the music, but he smiled, nodding. He was up for it, whatever *it* was.

The throat-catching smell of dope added to the heat in the cramped van. He'd tried it a couple of times, but the only effect of it had been to send him to sleep. Streetlights flashed by. At one point they were racing along a stretch of motorway and then navigating narrow roads along which trees formed living archways. Eventually the van turned onto a dirt track, bumping over ruts and potholes before finally coming to a halt.

Caleb was disgorged with everyone else onto a wide stretch of concrete. Cars, jeeps, and vans were parked at random. In the near distance, coloured lights pierced the darkness. He and Sharon linked arms, joining streams of people, heading towards a scaffold tower, hung with flags in fluorescent colours. Rotating search-lights were fixed to the platform on top of it. Swivelling, pin-beams of a laser, illuminated the DJ standing, arms raised, at a desk with a brightly flashing LED display. Projected onto large screens were multi-coloured images, pulsing and flashing in time with the music. A forest of arms and bodies moved in staccato rhythm, a vast crowd of shadowy figures gyrating to the deafening hypnotic beat.

'Wow!' He had never seen anything like it. He felt the music throbbing in his chest, like a second heartbeat.

'Time to get *really* messy!' Sharon's fished in her pocket, tossed a small screw of paper into her mouth, swilling it down with a can of cider. 'Open wide,' she ordered.

'What?'

'You need to get connected.' She was holding another fragment of paper between finger and thumb. 'Don't pussy out on me. OK?'

Connected sounded good. Why not? He had nothing to lose. Caleb opened his mouth, accepting the paper scrap. Sharon offered him the can and he washed it down.

'I need some dirty dub-step beats!' She pulled him into the centre of a group of dancers, her face vivid in the flashing lights.

Tossing her head from side to side, her long hair whipping

out, she raised her arms, jumping up and down in time to the music. Caleb moved stiffly at first, feeling self-conscious, until he realised no one was paying him any attention. Sharon was making jerky movements, doing an on-the-spot pogo. She looked totally out-of-it. Blissful. Wherever she was, he hoped he could get there, soon. He danced on, reaching for the connection she had promised. Whatever that stuff was it wasn't working.

Wait.

Woah! Oh, Yeah. It was now. Suddenly he was *inside* the heavy bass notes and insistent drumming. Thud. Thud. Thud. Repetitive electronic sounds, skittering back and forth in a hypnotic undertow, found an echo in his pulse. Music squirmed beneath his skin, itched in his head, forged pathways in his mind. He became aware of new levels; levels beyond levels. Which he could rise to and then plumb down into. A sense of belonging consumed him, blotting out everything else. He was part of the music, at one with every single person here. All around him people were smiling, ecstatic, dancing, connected to the group mind. Loving it. Colours flowered in his head, the colour of love. Love. Another word for connection. He felt himself swept along on wave after wave of powerful emotion, floating in space. He felt safe, cherished by this noisy, roiling mass of humanity. Everyone was on the same level, sharing the connection. The love. The music, all dancing, thrashing, synchronised.

And then the level – deepened. Impressions soaked into him as if by osmosis. Jagged angles, flashes of stark shapes between the writhing bodies, like the negatives of bones lying on damask. Tattoos on white skin, dark against pale, soot rubbed into scrimshaw. Hair all colours, rising and falling silk-like in the waves of sounds. Jewels flashing from ears, eyebrows, belly buttons. They were all so beautiful. And he loved them, simply, whole-heartedly. His heart squeezed painfully at the tenderness of them, the fragility.

If he could only capture these images. Draw them.

Someone was juggling with firebrands. The flames leapt, glowing plumes against the night. Thud. Thud. Thud. The beat thumping in his chest. Complicated riffs, rills of the undertow pulled him in and he went, willingly. Caleb closed his eyes, shuddered with pleasure. The sounds had colours, their vibrancy almost unbearable. It was mind-blowing.

Sharon reared closer, hair plastered to her wet face, streaks of make-up down her cheeks. Her eyes were wide, pupils huge and dark, her jaw clenched. In the intermittent flash of strobe lights, she appeared to be dancing in slow motion. Light snaked along her jaw, flickered over her hair, and sinuous limbs. Caleb could smell her perfume, the foxy tang of her sweat. He reached for her. Their mouths met. He groaned as the taste of her scorched his blood. He was speared on a needle of pleasure he had never imagined existed. Thud. Thud. Thud. Moving together. Wet, slippery, tongues meshing.

Living. This was *really* living...

* * * * *

Silence, which seemed more than the mere absence of sound, spread across the disused airfield like after a heavy snowfall. The weight of it pressed on his ear drums.

One arm round Sharon's waist, he trudged along the crumbling runway, its faded markers and numbers revealed by the grainy light. All around them other revellers were heading back to their vehicles.

Sharon swayed against him, swigging from a can of cider. She licked her lips. 'I am *so* bombed out.'

Incapable of speech, Caleb's brain was still buzzing, chasing light trails of bass and drum beats. The sense of having shared something unique lingered. He wasn't a loner. He belonged. If only this feeling could last forever.

On impulse, he dipped his head and kissed Sharon on her damp forehead. He tasted salt on his lips. 'You're beautiful,' he whispered. And she was, even with her hair hanging in sweaty strands, make-up smudged into panda rings round her eyes.

She smiled, mouth crooked. 'Still loved- up?'

'Yeah.' *Loved-up. That about described it.*

'Here.' Sharon passed him the can. 'Dehydration can make you feel really shit.'

'Thanks.' He swallowed deeply, passed the cider back to her.

They piled back into the transit, with the others, and headed home. They were dropped at Sharon's flat. Caleb saw Si, his pupils dilated hugely in his white face. *Is that how I look?*

Si was still moving to the sound of some invisible beat. 'Really cool night, huh guys? Am I right? Or am I right?'

A chorus of voices expressed agreement.

'Yeah. Good one, Si!'

'Beyond magic, man!'

'Group hug!'

It felt natural to join in. Caleb exchanged hugs with girls and guys. In normal life he would never had hugged a stranger or had one hug him back. This was how the world ought to be. Loved-up. It was amazing.

'I am so off my pickle!' Sharon's eyes were glazed beneath heavy lids, a blissful smile playing about her lips. 'Bye, guys! Love you!' She waved as a group of people began wandering off toward their cars.

Si turned to Caleb. 'My sister made sure you had a good time?'

'Oh, yeah. Totally. She's amazing.' Caleb lifted Sharon off her feet. Burying his head in her shoulder, he kissed her neck while making growling noises and spinning her around.

Sharon squealed in mock alarm.

'Oh man, he is *well* smitten. Poor sap.' Si threw Caleb a pitying look.

Caleb frowned, dimly aware of some subtext to the conversation between brother and sister. Some private joke. He gave a mental shrug.

'So. Where we off to?' someone asked.

'We can crash at mine,' suggested a girl wearing a camouflage print Trapper. 'Order in pizzas. Watch music vids on YouTube.'

'Cool!' More people peeled away, drifting off.

Caleb knew he should go home, try to slip into his bedroom, unnoticed. Fat chance. Dad was a notoriously light sleeper. He couldn't face the row that would ensue about how irresponsible he'd been, taking off without explanation. Besides, he was too hyped to sleep. He wanted this feeling of euphoria to last forever. Having Dad on his case was guaranteed to trash the whole unbelievably, amazing experience. Leave him feeling like a silly, useless kid.

Sharon yawned. 'Count me out, guys. I'm vegging out at mine.'

Caleb saw his chance. Summoning his courage, he whispered, 'Want some company?'

She shrugged. 'Why not?'

His heart leapt. She really did like him. A big rush of happiness lodged in his chest. This was what *normal* people his age did. People who had a life, friends, interests. The world, the shop, his parents faded into insignificance. Caleb rested his chin on Sharon's hair as they lurched unsteadily into her flat.

★   ★   ★   ★   ★

'Caleb! I've been frantic. Where have you been all weekend?' Sally Farmer's voice held a mixture of anxiety and anger.

'A party. All-nighter. Sorry, I should have phoned...' Caleb knew he owed Mum a proper explanation, but if he had to stand here talking he was going to be ill again. His bowels growled warningly and he hurried towards the bathroom. 'Talk to you later. OK? Got to get changed. Have to open the shop.'

'Is that all I'm going to get?' she called after him. 'This isn't like you, Caleb.'

'I know. It won't happen again. Promise...' He threw the words over his shoulder, already rushing through the flat.

Dashing into the bathroom, he locked the door and only just made it to the toilet, where he sat huddled, sweating and shaking while his body emptied itself. He ached all over, hurting in places where he didn't even know he *had* muscles. Even his tongue was sore from where he must have bitten it while dancing. His head throbbed dully. It was the come down, Sharon had explained. The price you paid for the gift of having your consciousness chemically expanded.

'You've been over the mountain. Now you're on the descent,' she said poetically.

At the moment, Caleb felt anything but poetic. He had begun feeling ill as he walked back to the shop and was rapidly feeling worse. Stripping off his clothes, he stood under the shower, letting needles of hot water play over his aching body. The incredible feeling of love and connection with everyone had morphed into a looming flatness that threatened to overwhelm him. It was like watching the slow build-up of massing storm-clouds in a summer sky.

To distract himself, he pictured them lying fully-dressed on her single bed, huddled under her purple-satin duvet, giggling like idiots at the fact that his feet hung over the end of the bed. She'd encouraged him to share a joint. It had seemed lame to refuse. So he took a drag, choking on the acrid smoke burning pathways into his lungs.

'You kill me!' Sharon spluttered laughing.

'Glad to oblige,' he said huffily, which only made her laugh more.

'Moody now, are we?' she teased.

He had grabbed her. Kissed her; hard. Her breathy groan against his lips was exciting. Encouraged, he slid a hand up to cup her breast. She pulled away, with a throaty giggle that inflamed him further. Sliding out of his embrace, she went to the kitchen, returning a short time later with a bag of Nachos and jars of salsa dip, which they ate under a tent made of the duvet. After eating, they dozed the day away. Once he awoke to find long shadows slanting across the room. She was kissing him and he responded hungrily. Slipping her hands inside his clothes, she pulled him close. His breath hitched as he remembered the feel of her soft skin, the incredible sensation of their bodies moving together, and then sleeping again, entwined and replete. It had been a shock to wake up and find it was Monday morning, almost time for the shop to open.

'Christ! Gotta go!' He'd stumbled out of bed, eyes gritty and mouth tasting like a gorilla's armpit.

Sharon sat up and lit a cigarette, smoking it while she watched him dragging on his jeans and shoes.

'Coming to see me off then?'

She nodded, yawning and shuffled to the door, still swathed in the duvet.

He kissed her cheek. 'Can I see you again?'

Holding the cigarette with scissored fingers, she blew a thread of smoke into the air. 'If you want. I'll call you.'

Caleb smiled as he finished towelling himself dry. Even feeling as ropey as he did right now, thinking of Sharon made him feel confident and desirable. She was gorgeous. Amazing to think that she fancied him, Caleb - the nerd from the hardware store. Padding into his bedroom, he dressed quickly, before going through to the shop. No time for breakfast. He was too queasy to eat anyway. To his relief, the place was empty. Mum must have gone shopping. He could hear Dad thumping and banging about in the back storeroom. *Probably picking his moment to have a go at me*, Caleb thought gloomily. *Bring it on. If that was the price he had to pay for his weekend of freedom. So be it.* He made a cup of strong coffee, stood drinking it at the counter.

'Good weekend?' Neil Farmer asked neutrally, coming out of the stockroom with some empty cardboard boxes, which he dumped on the floor.

Caleb tensed, trying to gauge his mood. The lines of discontent on either side of Dad's mouth seemed less pronounced than usual. He appeared calm, but that meant nothing. His usual style was to start in a low key, lulling Caleb into a false sense of security, before a row ratcheted to fever pitch. 'Um...yeah. Pretty good,' he said carefully. 'I've apologised to Mum for taking off straight after work...'

'Had a go at you, did she? Women. Always making a drama out of everything. Your mother wanted to call the police, but I stopped her. I told her you'd be out with some mates, chasing women, getting tanked-up. She wouldn't have it. Said her precious son, wasn't like that.' He laughed shortly, a sound of complicity as he stamped boxes flat, piling them up. '*All* men, are like that. You just took your time catching up! I've been wondering when you were going to grow a pair.' He clapped Caleb on the back. 'Looks like you have and not before time. Fill your boots, I say, lad. No harm in that, just as long as you know where your loyalties lie. The shop comes first. Never forget it.'

* * * * *

'Classy Cuts.' A bright, sing-song voice answered the phone after three rings. 'Tracy speaking. How can I help you?'

'Hi, Tracy. Can I speak to Sharon, please? It's Caleb.'

'Oh, right.' Her tone changed. 'I'll go and see if she's about. Hang on.'

It had taken him three days to get up the courage to phone the hairdressers. He waited, listening to the sounds of voices and hair dryers. He thought he heard Sharon's throaty laughter rise over the babble.

'She's on early lunch. Do you want to leave a message?'

'Erm…no. Maybe she can phone me when she gets back?'

He waited expectantly all afternoon, but she didn't phone. By the time he decided to phone her again, it was too late. An answerphone cut in, informing him that *Classy Cuts* was closed until 9am the following morning.

Sharon didn't phone on Thursday either. By the middle of the afternoon, Caleb's patience had worn thin. He was alone in the shop, so there was no one to eavesdrop as he phoned *Classy Cuts*. Tracy told him it was Sharon's day off and gave him her mobile number.

He had just dialled the number, when Neil Farmer walked in the front door, having arrived back from the wholesalers.

'Who are you calling?' he asked suspiciously.

'Wrong number.' Caleb put the phone down. He didn't want his dad offering advice about how to treat women.

Friday crawled by. The phone seemed to mock him with its silence. The shop was unusually busy, for once. He and Dad barely had a moment to themselves. While washing his hands, Caleb took the crumpled paper with Sharon's number out of his jeans pocket. If he'd had a mobile, he could have texted her. But Dad was dead against them, on the basis that they were a waste of money. The landlines in the shop and flat were perfectly adequate for their purpose. He managed to sneak upstairs, phone Sharon's mobile and leave her a message. She didn't phone back.

Just before bed, Caleb went into the shop and rang Sharon's mobile again, but it was turned off. He lay staring dejectedly into the dark for a long while. It was pretty obvious that she was avoiding him. *So, get over it.*

Mid-morning the following day, Caleb was standing in the shop doorway, staring blankly out at the street. The clock on the church spire opposite chimed the half-hour, mocking him as it ticked off the minutes of his life. *This is it for you*, it seemed to say, *all there will ever be.*

Caleb waited until his parents were engrossed in the TV, that evening before using the phone. Sharon answered. It was a shock to hear her voice.

'Who is this?'

She obviously didn't recognise the number. 'It's me. Caleb.'

'Caleb?' She sounded surprised.

'You said you'd call back.' It came out blunt and raw.

'I… did. I erm…left a message,' she lied, hardly bothering to sound like she meant it.

He wanted to believe her. 'Must have missed it. How have you been, anyway?'

'Busy. The salon's been mental.'

He could hear laughter. A male voice close to her, wheedling. 'Sharon. Come on…'

'Look. Caleb. I'm…with friends.'

'Sorry.' *Why was he apologising?* 'I thought…maybe we could meet sometime?'

'Hang on.' Her voice became muffled as she put her hand over the phone. 'Wait. There, don't move an inch,' she said to someone.

Caleb heard her husky laugh, which he had found so engaging. It seemed forced now, calculated. There was the sound of a door closing.

Her tone was cooler. 'Last weekend was fun, right?'

'It was fantastic. I thought we…You and me – '

'Caleb. Listen. When you're buzzing, you love everyone. Totally adore them. All loved-up. Hugs all round. Boys. Girls. You even love people you're never going to see again. No one takes it seriously. That's how it is. Get it?'

He did, now. *Finally. Thanks for the memory. But no thanks.* 'Yeah. I get it.' Hurt and humiliation trickled through him like runnels of ice water.

'Look, Caleb. You're a nice guy…'

Nice? One degree away from boring. The sound of a door opening again. The same male voice. Confident, assured.

'Sharon? You keeping me waiting?'

'I've got to go. You understand…'

Lying on his bed, he stared up at the ceiling. Who had he been kidding? She hadn't given him a second thought since the night of the rave. What a lame brain to fall in love with the first girl to pay him any real attention. Pathetic. How could he have gotten it so wrong? He could hear their laughter.

'Caleb! Get down here. Now!' Dad's voice with a note of panic

He sat up, knuckling his eyes. 'Coming!' he called, descending the stairs. A figure lay slumped in the doorway of the sitting room. He almost fell down the last few steps. 'Mum? What's happened?'

'She got up to make a drink and just keeled over. I've called an ambulance. You wait here with her. I'll go outside. Make sure it finds us.' White-faced, Neil wrenched open the flat door. Caleb heard his heavy footsteps hurrying downstairs.

Mum was resting against the door jamb, legs sprawled like a broken puppet. Her head was tucked in against her shoulder. One side of her face seemed to have slipped out of alignment.

CHAPTER 17

L EON REALLY HAD gone. He must have called one of his mates, probably one with a van, because he had taken all his clothes and other belongings and disappeared. There had been no sign of him at his usual haunts around the estate and no word from him. Jess hoped that he'd moved out of the area, but Leon was the kind who always had to have the final word.

Alice had taken his leaving badly. She was still curled up beneath the grimy duvet, refusing to get up, except to go to the bathroom. Her sobs and wails of self-pity echoed round the flat. It didn't help that her body was battling with the after-effects of her latest bout of heavy drinking.

'All men are bastards! They use you then they throw you away, as if you're a used tissue. You'll be leaving next. What is there to stay for? I'm a rotten mother and a pathetic human being. I can't even keep a loser like Leon. Why don't you just go? I wouldn't blame you.'

'I'm going nowhere. As soon as you're feeling better, we'll look for somewhere else to live. I want you to get some help. There's a drop-in centre in the town centre. They deal with all kinds of addictions.'

'You say that now. But you don't really want me dragging round with you. And I don't blame you. I'm such a hopeless mess. Look what I've brought us to...'

She had heard this before, self-pity masked as love. Words so worn that they had become a ritual. The sniffles coming through the walls were grating on her now.

Jess went into the bathroom, undressed and climbed into the bath to stand under the shower. She bowed her head, letting the water drum on her scalp and skin before cascading over her body. With a sigh of pleasure she turned round to let the pressurized water massage her shoulders. The area between her shoulder blades still felt sore and tender, although the bruises on her face were now hardly noticeable. It was while she was drying herself that she twisted to look at it in the bathroom mirror.

The raised ridge looked bigger, about ten centimetres or so now. The skin covering it was reddened and shiny. Frowning, she pressed it and gave a gasp of pain. The lump was hard and hot to the touch and seemed to move very slightly beneath her probing fingers. She must have grazed the skin while she was lying on her back struggling with Leon.

She was supposed to be meeting Lisa at the cinema in half an hour, but she couldn't leave Alice. The first few days without alcohol were always punishing, with tremors, sweats and cravings. She hated letting Lisa down, but she couldn't even phone her to explain. Their landline had been disconnected for months and Jess had never had, or wanted, a mobile phone. Just the thought of carrying a jangling metal object around, close enough for it to burn her through her clothes, was enough to set her teeth on edge.

Her damp hair secured into a messy bun low on her neck with two black chopsticks, she entered Alice's bedroom, throwing open the door. Alice blinked at her from the depths of the rumpled bedclothes on the floor mattress. The room was dark and smelt fusty. Sullen light, seeping in through the bent slats of the wonky blind, barely penetrated the gloom.

'It stinks in here!'

She tried to open the blind, but the mechanism resisted her efforts. As she pulled harder, the blind collapsed at her feet with a clatter. The room was flooded with light.

Alice threw her arms over her face. 'Leave me alone!'

Jess crouched beside her, knowing that she had to be strong and take charge.

'No chance. Time to move on,' she said firmly, folding back the duvet. Reaching out one hand, she gently stroked Alice's hair. It smelt sour and unwashed. 'We'll do this together. OK?'

Haltingly, Alice pushed herself into a sitting position. She blinked at Jess in slow motion, her head drooping like the bent stem of a faded flower. Her skin was the colour and consistency of dough, her lips were bloodless. After a long pause, she nodded slowly.

'I'll run you a bath. It'll make you feel better.' Jess cupped her mother's chin, lifted her face gently so that their eyes met. 'It's you and me now. The old team. We can do this. *You* can do this. One step at a time. Right?'

A tear rolled down Alice's puffy cheek. 'I'll try.' It was a hoarse whisper.

Jess felt a surge of hope, quickly suppressed as she thought of all the other times when hope had been drowned by a cheap bottle of vodka. This time it might be different. She had to believe that. Or what was the point of anything? She helped her mother to her feet and walked her to the bathroom. Alice sagged on the toilet seat while Jess ran water into the bath. There was no bath gel, so she added a few drops of essential oil and a squirt of washing-up liquid, before helping her mum to bathe and wash her hair. Half an hour later, Alice was curled up on the sofa in a clean track suit. Her damp dark hair was drying into a soft cloud around her face, making her look younger.

Jess plumped up the cushions and turned on the TV. She pressed the buttons on the remote, surfing through the channels until she found something Alice liked. 'There you go. An antiques programme.'

'Thanks, Love. I feel a bit better.' Alice smiled wanly.

Jess smiled, heartened. 'Could you eat something? A sandwich? Coffee?'

Alice grimaced. 'My stomach's hurting. I couldn't keep anything down. Maybe a glass of milk?'

Jess knew they didn't have any. There was nothing for Alice to eat or drink in the house; what there had been, Leon had taken with him. It didn't worry Jess. She'd been fine with just chemical-tasting tap water and the few packets of nuts and raisins she kept in her bedroom. There was no money for groceries either, so she'd have to go out and see what a trawl through the supermarket bins turned up.

'Will you be all right if I go out for milk? I'll be as quick as I can.'

Alice nodded. 'Don't worry about me. I'll stay right here. Promise.'

It crossed Jess's mind that Alice probably had a bottle or two secreted around the flat, but it would take too long to search the place and get rid of them. Besides, they needed to re-build the trust between them. Now was as good a time as any to start.

In the bedroom, she threw a crumpled, printed-cotton dress over her vest and leggings, then put on her hooded fleece, grabbed her shoulder bag and keys and went outside.

It was already getting dark. She jogged along the walkway and ran down the steps two at a time. Sodium street lights cast dismal pools of green-yellow light and left much of the pavement in shadow. One or two cars trawled slowly along the kerbs, where scantily clad working girls shivered as they waited to do business. Jess's breath steamed in the air as she hurried through the estate in the direction of the underpass. She ran through the concrete tunnel, where Mike's cardboard shelter seemed deserted. Perhaps he was passing the time with one of his friends at the allotments. Minutes later she was pounding past the garage and along the duel carriageway, trying to ignore the familiar discomfort of burning lungs and disordered senses from metal and exhaust fumes.

She reached the supermarket's delivery bay, climbed over the barrier and slipped through the narrow alleyway that led round the back to the bins. Frost glittered on the ground. There was a faint smell of spilled diesel from the delivery trucks and a waft of charred meat from a nearby takeaway. Jess rubbed her chilled hands together, lifted the heavy rubber lid of the nearest bin and began sorting through the contents. It didn't take long to fill her shoulder bag with milk, packs of sandwiches and ready meals for Alice and bagged salads, fruit and cartons of juice for herself.

She pulled up her hood as she retraced her steps and was striding away from the delivery bay, when she saw a familiar figure cross the road just ahead of her.

'Hey. Lisa. Wait for me!'

Lisa had her head down and showed no signs of slowing down. 'What's wrong…' She was reaching out to grab the girl's arm, when Lisa stopped dead.

'I waited for you for over an hour!' Her mouth twisted with distress. 'Stacey, Debs and a load of their mates were there. They thought it was hilarious that I'd been…stood up. They think we're a *couple*.' A red tide rose up her neck. 'Stacey said

I must be desperate to fancy you. And…and it's because no guy will ever want me. She called me a fat lard-arse and…'

Jess hadn't got time for this. She had to get back to Alice. 'So what? Who cares what they think?'

Lisa looked shocked. 'I do!' she wailed.

'Look. I can't do this now – '

A car pulled to a halt. Two men got out and moved towards them. One of them looked vaguely familiar. Jess thought he was one of the guys who played cards with Leon, in the flat. Before she could react, they had grabbed her arms, and were hustling her towards the car. She cried out as she dropped her bag and groceries spilled all over the pavement.

'Get off her! Leave her alone!' Lisa ran forward, pulling at one of the men. He swatted her away.

Jess heard Lisa's cry of pain. She dug in her heels and tried to pull free, but they were too strong. She kicked furiously. There was a grunt of pain.

'Bitch!' A rough hand grabbed her hair. 'You'll be sorry you did that!'

The air around her tingled and thickened. The latent power she had felt when Leon attacked her surfaced, forming a protective veil, silvery and shimmering…

'Christ! Just get her in the fucking car!'

A heavy blow made Jess's head ring. She felt a stabbing pain in her arm and gasped with pain as her vision darkened. *The subtle, inner sensation fizzled out like a damp firework.* What had they given her? She'd never done drugs, had no resistance to them. Her legs crumpled. She would have fallen if the men hadn't kept hold of her.

She couldn't speak, couldn't order her thoughts. Her hair had pulled free of the chopsticks. It tumbled over her face, half blinding her. *No! Help me!* She tried to focus, to call upon that newly-discovered source of power – to will it into being – but it was like trying to hold smoke in her hands.

Her wrists were seized, pulled behind her back, thin bands of some flexible material wrapped around them. A faint sound of rasping plastic as the bonds were slid tight enough to cut into her skin. Cable ties. Strong as metal. No chance of getting them off without help. She felt herself lifted and thrown sideways onto the back seat, her legs thrashing weakly and her boots scuffing against the kerb. Fingers that smelt strongly of stale tobacco plastered tape over her mouth. They had difficulty bundling her long legs in, but eventually managed it. The door slammed shut.

Jess's fury gave way to terror. Everything was becoming muffled as if she was deep under water. She tried to scream and her stomach rebelled. Bitterness flooded her mouth and scalded her nostrils. She choked, swallowed vomit.

From far away, someone was shouting.

'Help us – someone. Please. Help!' Lisa's voice?

The car sank on its suspension as the men slid into the front seats. Two more doors slammed in quick succession. The surface Jess lay on juddered. There was a screech of tyres, a sudden backwards movement that sent her pitching forward into the seat well where she lay crumpled, wedged with her legs angled painfully.

'No! Stop…'

She thought she heard a scream that was cut short, felt a bump as the car connected with something solid. And then everything went black and there was silence.

CHAPTER 18

NINKA HAD WOVEN a tiny boat and was now making a boatman out of an acorn. Rolling a ball of mud between her fingers, she used blobs of it to attach arms and legs made of twigs. Watching with a look of intense concentration on her little face, Aerith reached out and picked up another acorn. She scooped up mud with one finger and daubed it on as Ninka was doing. Jamming a twist of grass on top of the muddy acorn, she patted it with the flat of her hand.

'Oh, you're giving it hair, are you? Clever girl,'

The child's intelligence and willingness to learn amazed her. She was quick to copy everything Ninka did and was nimble with her fingers. Mortals were generally slow and clumsy creatures, which was ironic when their hearts beat so fast and their skins were warm from the racing of their blood. Poor things. They had such a short life span and were so easily broken. Ninka pitied them, while she feared for Aerith.

She hoped the child would benefit from living in Faery. It must surely have some kind of positive effect on her, though she had no idea what that effect would be. No mortal, brought into the Shadow Court, had been allowed to grow beyond childhood, although she had heard vague rumours of some of them reaching adulthood in far off, kinder courts. Under Catelysma's rule, foundlings usually faded away from being ignored and neglected, that is, if they weren't killed by accident or design.

But this foundling posed a threat to the Dark Lady. Oblique that threat might be, but could Catelysma afford to ignore it? She thought of the tiny, pink body-suit that Aerith had been wearing when Catelysma first brought her into the Shadow Court, and which she, Ninka, had placed inside an earthen-ware-pot and buried deep in the forest. It would remain there, protecting Aerith's secret, and acting as insurance, should Catelysma's ire ever ignite and take up arms against Ninka, or her beloved.

Aerith was rinsing her muddy fingers in the stream, before wiping them dry on her tunic. Ninka noticed that the tunic was halfway up the child's thighs. She would have to lengthen it soon, especially with the days already growing shorter and the nights colder. There were many preparations to make before winter. Things she usually did alone. She was looking forward to having Aerith with her, teaching the child to forage for dry berries and nuts and cure skins and furs. Later, as the child grew, there would be hunting skills to master and weapons practice.

But she was thinking too far ahead. At any time, Cate-lysma could order the child brought back to live at court. At the thought of Aerith surrounded by constant danger and uncertainty, Ninka felt an icy hand grip her heart. She could not sleep, her mind beset by nightmares of what could happen to a helpless little mortal at the hands of any flesh-loving fey.

Now, finally, her mind was made up. If Aerith was to prosper, she must remain in the forest, where Ninka could care for her. But how to ensure this? Useless to simply request that the child be allowed to remain in her care. Catelysma was deaf to pleas or entreaties. Besides, to declare herself openly would be a serious mistake. Any sign of affection for a mortal was seen as a weakness and quickly dealt with. Only Gentry, who were beyond reproach, were allowed such indulgences.

Perhaps she could make a bargain of some kind, Ninka mused. That could buy them time. But it would be risky. The fey only made bargains that were heavily weighted in their own favour. Gentry were worst of all. Gradually, a solution of sorts came to her. Yes, that could work...

Aerith's laughter broke into her thoughts. She turned to see that the child had picked up a wriggling pink worm that was half the length of her arm. The creature coiled against her tanned skin, leaving splatters of mud, but she did not flinch from the slimy feel of it. Instead, her little face was a mask of curiosity. After a moment, she gently placed the worm on the ground and covered it with a leaf. Aerith then picked up the little boat and boatmen and placed it into the stream, where it immediately snagged in a clump of water mint. With a sound of impatience, she splashed into the water which reached above her knees.

'Take care.'

'I fine, Mam. Not worry.'

Her long hair, the colour of bleached corn, spilled in a tangle over her shoulders. She would comb the leaves and twigs from the child's hair later. It was a bedtime ritual she loved; the way the golden strands flowed over her fingers like silk. She had taken to unthreading the hairs caught in the bone comb and then weaving them into the coarse lock on her own scalp, where they glimmered satisfyingly.

'Look, Mam! Look!' Aerith cried proudly, eyes glowing as the boat swirled in circles.

'Yes, sweeting. It is a fine boat.' She must stop Aerith calling her, Mam. It had seemed natural to teach her the word as she learned to speak, after all she felt like the child's mother. But now Ninka saw that had been a mistake. However much she insisted on being called by her given name, Aerith had other ideas.

'No, Ninka. Mam!' she would insist, wagging one finger for emphasis.

Truth be told, Ninka liked it. More than liked it. But she was fearful lest they were overheard by one of Catelysma's spies and news carried back to her. Some, like the fawning Tweeter, sought only to curry favour with his dark mistress.

Thoughts of Tweeter brought the court to mind again. It must soon be time for the oak ball, which celebrated the production of acorns, a symbol of plenty, when all the fey gathered together to feast and dance. It was the perfect time to put her plan into action.

Was she brave enough? Her heart faltered at what she must do, but there was no sense in putting it off.

Ninka hesitated for a second longer before unplaiting her scalp lock. She felt a pang of sadness as she combed her fingers through it, so that the golden hairs were released and blew away on the breeze. Taking her soft cap of woven rushes from her pocket, she tucked her few long coarse hairs out of sight beneath it and then pulled it well down over her eyebrows.

'Come, Aerith. No more time for play. Catch your boat now.'

'Want play!' Aerith complained, frowning. Planting her hands on her hips, she looked back at the boat and then at Ninka. She sighed. 'Coming, Mam!' she decided, clambering onto the bank.

Ninka gave a cry of dismay as the tiny boat went scudding downstream and out of sight. 'Oh, your boat!'

'Mam make 'nother one,' Aerith said equably. She half-turned again, waving. 'Bye, boat.'

'Come then.' Ninka smiled approvingly at this practical approach. Aerith never made a fuss or threw tantrums if she didn't get her own way. 'We are going on a journey to see a very beautiful lady. She may look kind, but she is not. If she speaks to you, you must say nothing. In fact, it would be best if you do not speak at all, unless I tell you to. Do you understand?' she said seriously.

Aerith looked at her with puzzled blue eyes beneath brows knitted in confusion. She seemed to be thinking hard.

Perhaps it was too much to expect of a child, even one as bright as Aerith, Ninka thought, her spirits sinking. But without her cooperation, the plan was doomed to failure. No one could help them. Not even Crowle, although she knew she could always rely on the ogre to do whatever he could.

She turned to Aerith bending down so their eyes were on a level.

'Listen well, sweeting,' she said gently. 'It is *very* important that you do exactly as I say. Can you do this for me? Can you keep quiet and say nothing, no matter what happens?'

'Yes, Ma...' Aerith blinked. Smiling, she nodded. Lifting one finger, she placed it against her pursed lips.

'Ah! You have it now!' Ninka beamed, extending her hand. There were still dangers. There ever would be, when visiting that terrible stage, which was the Shadow Court. But it must be done. Now. Before she lost her nerve. 'Come then. We have much to do before we set off.'

Aerith took her hand. Their enmeshed fingers were the same size.

CHAPTER 19

CALEB BRUSHED ASIDE a strand of dark hair that was blowing into his eyes as he worked his way along the outside of the kitchen wall, laying rat traps at intervals. It was early evening and a chill breeze was blowing, but he hardly noticed. He was glad to have a valid reason for making an extra visit to Windroth. Caleb had been deliberately vague about who the client with the rat problem was and had managed to escape, while his father was distracted by a customer. He didn't plan on disturbing Mrs Stark. She wouldn't be expecting him at this hour and he wasn't in the mood to make small talk. It was enough just to be here, his sanctuary, where he could put his worries about his mother to the back of his mind for a few hours.

He couldn't help thinking about it. The way the consultant had explained that there was a high possibility of another stroke. The tense hours of waiting for the results of tests and brains scans. And his father just sitting there, rock-like; brooding, with a scowl on his face. 'Great bloody timing,' he had grunted. 'She's gone and left me to carry the can. Never could rely on her. Your Gran said she was too bloody airy-fairy. And you're no blasted help.'

Now she had been moved to a specialist hospital in the Midlands. Caleb phoned every day. There'd been no change in her condition. He wanted desperately to visit her. But his father was adamant. 'I'm not forking out good money for petrol. Visiting your mother's a waste of time. She won't even know we're there.'

The atmosphere between the two of them in the shop, heavy with ill feeling, was worse than ever. He couldn't understand that his father could be so dense, so unfeeling that it didn't occur to him that the struggle to make end meets and his relentless bullying might have contributed to his wife's illness.

Caleb could hardly bear to look at him. His mouth seemed filled with the taste of hatred, dusty and bitter.

He made a decision as he cycled home after finishing setting the traps. He'd use some of the money Mrs Stark had paid him for the drawing, to buy train fare and visit Mum this coming Thursday. His father would know nothing about it, which suited Caleb just fine.

* * * * *

Jess heard someone moan from very far away. It was a few seconds before she realised, that *she* was making the sound. She fought her way painfully to the surface.

Her head was throbbing and her body protested as she changed position. She was lying on something that gave slightly with her movements. Her hands were still bound and her wrists felt raw from where the bonds had cut into them. She flexed her fingers. Pins and needles stabbed her numb flesh and she grunted with pain.

Thick grainy darkness surrounded her. Facing her, there was a square of lesser darkness, from which came a faint glimmer. It was barely enough to illuminate the room she found herself in. As her eyes adjusted, a dark hump against one wall resolved into the shape of a bulky old-fashioned wardrobe. She turned her head and found that she was lying close to a cheap black-vinyl covered headboard. It looked as if someone had taken a bite out of one corner. Wood and stuffing protruded through the ripped plastic.

Jess's ears strained for familiar sounds. Faintly, she could hear traffic and a dog barking in the distance. She tried to lift her head and the room seemed to pitch sideways. A starburst of light exploded in her head. The shifting patchwork of light, shadow and swift movement that followed, threatened to overwhelm her. For a while, she knew nothing. And then she was staring fixedly into the darkness again, with no recollection of having even closed her eyes. A door opened. Figures came and went. She was aware of someone bending over her. At some point, the bonds at her wrists were cut. She slept and woke again. The window was too bright. Turning her head, she pressed her face against the surface she lay on. By turns, she was helped to a bathroom, her legs like jelly so that she had to be half carried. Time passed in a haze. And then it was dark again.

She slept once more and in her dreams, she was standing *inside* Krast's *Royalty's Revenge*, looking down at the face of the sleeping figure in the dove-grey dress. With a start, she realised that the face she saw against the silken pillows was her own. She watched as a slender girl with silvery-blue hair and wings, approached the bed. The girl smiled, her pink eyes glowing as she leaned over to plump up the pillows. Jess saw that the girl's beautiful wings had been ripped, deliberately and cruelly, so that only the bloodied membranes remained. A tiny creature with a nut-brown face, eyes like sloes and arms and legs like twigs was perched on the girl's shoulder. As the girl reached out to pet it, it bared its teeth and a lizard tongue licked the air.

Jess woke with a start, panic rustling around somewhere deep inside her, but she couldn't seem to make herself care. There was only an odd feeling of suspension, as if she was occupying the space inside the eye of a hurricane. There came a low rumble of men's voices from somewhere below her. She heard coarse laughter, the sound of footsteps on a wooden staircase and feet passing close by, just outside the door of the bedroom.

At the window, there was a faint scratching sound and then a rush of cold air as it opened. She heard a flutter of movement. Something large, angular and vaguely human shaped entered silently, crouched to balance on the sill and waited with one steadying hand placed against the embrasure. Jess could make no sense of what she was seeing. The figure glowed with a soft radiance, as if lit from within. Were those folded wings at its shoulder? It must be a dream, another image from the Krast painting. No, she was definitely awake, because she felt cold and was shivering. But what she was looking at was impossible. The hairs on the back of her neck prickled. She blinked and the shape at the window disappeared. One moment there, then instantly gone.

Imagined then, after all. Her mind was playing tricks on her.

And then a scream of terror lodged in her throat, as a figure spun itself out of the shadows beside her. She hadn't seen it move, but it was right up close and crouching down to be on a level with her.

'Be still, Jess. Have no fear.' It was a hoarse whisper and somehow familiar.

She found herself looking into a face - pale and all sharp angles, and with a beauty that was far from human. A faint perfumed breeze and a soft whirring vibration came from the large silvery wings that stretched above its head. Slanted almond eyes, the irises silver, stared back at her. One overlong finger was placed against bloodless lips, and Jess understood that she was to remain silent.

She nodded, although her head swam again and her insides cramped painfully. She was going to vomit. She retched, but her stomach was empty.

Then everything happened at once.

The door opened and a man came in. Slightly built, with rounded shoulders bringing with him a rank body smell, overlaid by cheap aftershave. Jess felt a shock of recognition. Leon.

He laughed softly. 'Not so arrogant now.' Light glinted on the needle in his hand. He said something else, but there was something wrong with her ears and she couldn't make it out.

His speech sounded slow and heavy, like a vocal track played at the wrong speed. He appeared to be walking towards her in slow motion. The air in the room thickened, sliding against Jess's skin like oil. She realised that she was seeing Leon advancing *through* the tall other-worldly figure that stood beside the bed.

Before she could draw another breath, she felt herself lifted in strong arms and borne away. Leon's bellow of rage and confusion, echoing and then swiftly fading as time switched into fast forward. A jumbled impression of dizzying move-ment, too swift to encompass. Jess chanced a look behind her and wished she hadn't. Receding at the speed of light was a townscape of darkened toy-town houses, open spaces and dots of light moving along a necklace of roads.

Before she had fully taken this in, there was another quicksilver temporal adjustment. Her stomach turned over as they plummeted. She found herself held more closely against the thin hard body that cradled her. The creature's strong smell of earth and wet leaves surrounded her. Moments later, she felt it touch down and with another preternatural burst of speed, they entered a vaulted space. Jess knew it at once. The underpass.

She found herself placed gently down onto a pile of cardboard. The impossible creature hunkered down beside her, its vivid pale face close and the alarming silver eyes blinking in staccato rhythm as if in the beam of a strobe light. While Jess was still trying to catch her breath, the air around the being shimmered like a heat haze and it began to transform. Matted dreadlocks and a beard overlaid the sharp, otherworldly features. A filthy army greatcoat covered the wings and flowed down over the thin, fine limbs. The slanted almond eyes rounded, became dark-brown and twinkled at her.

'Mike!' Jess gasped, incredulous.

He grinned narrowly. 'It's called glamour. The ability to cloak your form in any disguise you choose.'

'How did...? What are...?' She stared at him, her mind whirling with questions.

'All in good time, Jess.' He placed a gloved hand gently on her arm. 'The main thing is that you are safe. There are things you should know.' He produced a plastic bottle of water from his coat pocket and handed it to her. 'Drink this. It will counter the effects of anything Leon has been giving you.' Mike snorted, a sound grimly humorous. 'He did not know that it is impossible to harm us... you,' he corrected quickly. 'But the drugs did have the temporary effect of disorientating you. That is why you could not use your powers to help yourself and why I could not hear you calling me clearly. It took me longer to find you than I would have wished. And for this, I blame myself.'

My powers? What can he know of them? Jess frowned, trying to make sense of what he was saying; to fit all the bits together. She looked down - saw the needle marks in the crook of her left arm. She looked back up at Mike, unseeing, for a moment.

'I am sorry. This is partly my fault,' he said, regretfully. 'I knew what Leon was like. I should not have underestimated him. But I did not expect he would go this far.'

Jess hardly heard him. She had begun to tremble with rage

'He arranged to have me kidnapped. He must have been planning to get me hooked on drugs, so he could put me to work on the streets. Some of the girls round here will do anything to get their next fix. I could kill him! Just you wait until ... '

'You must listen to me,' Mike interrupted. He gripped her thin shoulders and shook her gently. 'Put thoughts of revenge aside for the moment. You need to harness your wits for what is to come. Drink this now,' he encouraged, cupping her hands within his own and raising the water to her lips. 'It will clear your thoughts and restore you.'

It flashed through Jess's thoughts that Mike's speech was different, the rhythm of it more archaic, as if he was no longer bothered about shielding his true self from her.

She drank deeply from the plastic bottle. The water had a clean, peaty taste. Instantly, she was clear-headed and alert. Her skin tingled with well-being and her entire body felt as if she had just woken from a deep, cleansing sleep.

She took a long, calming breath. 'How long?'

Mike held her gaze, his eyes steady. 'Almost four days.'

'Shit! Alice must be half out of her mind with worry. I told her I was going out to get milk! I have to go!' She thrust the drink at him and made to move away.

His hand detained her. 'Of course. But there is something more. It is Lisa.'

'Lisa? What about her?' Jess looked at him as she searched her thoughts. She hadn't thought of her friend in days, but now with her mind clear again, a memory surfaced. 'I was talking to her that night, when the men bundled me into the car. I heard her yelling for help...' *and felt a sickening bump as the car collided with...*

A chill hand clutched at her heart. 'Tell me,' she said.

CHAPTER 20

'Now, do not be afraid,' Ninka said as they walked towards the steep, tree-lined slope. 'Stay close to me.' Aerith looked up at her trustingly and nodded.

As they moved nearer to the foot of the hill, the glamour dissolved to reveal an opening framed by stout wooden pillars, carved all over with spirals and curlicues. A small wing-less being became visible. It was sweeping up leaves with a birch broom. Ninka nodded shortly to it as she and the child stepped inside the fey knoll.

They were in a tunnel with walls of smooth-packed earth. A twisting network of roots protruded from the domed roof, tiny greenish lights glimmering amongst them. A complex smell of earth, stone and sweetish, aromatic smoke drifted towards them. Ninka saw that Aerith was looking around with wide eyes as they progressed downwards, the tunnel sloping slightly. They passed passages that led off at intervals, which she knew led to sleeping quarters, kitchen and storerooms.

'See there?' Pausing, she pointed out the carved and gilded entrance to the great chamber where Catelysma held court and presided over the balls, markets and seasonal gatherings which were also held there. 'But we're not going there today. The lady we have come to see will be elsewhere.'

They were almost there now. She could see the light flooding into the tunnel from the chamber Catelysma used as her withdrawing room.

As they reached the entrance, a tall, elegant figure swept out. By its height and general air of superiority, Ninka guessed it was one of the higher-ranking solitary fey. She occasionally glimpsed them riding their fierce mounts in the forest and took care to avoid them. Although of lower rank than Gentry, they were usually called upon and pressed into their service. Haughty and cavalier, they demanded respect from anyone they considered beneath them.

Ninka was one of the solitary fey herself, but of lower class and therefore fair game, as she knew only too well. Instinctively, she pushed Aerith into the shadows behind her as the man approached.

He wore a dark-green jerkin and trousers. A purple breast-plate, that resembled an insect's carapace, covered his torso. The greenish tunnel-lights picked out the dark red glints in his shaggy, shoulder-length hair. Ninka just had time to register the displeasure on the lean, pale features, before he gave her a dismissive glance from mismatched eyes, and swept past her.

She knew him then. Jackryn Fleet. One of Catelysma's more recently discarded lovers. Fiercely handsome almost beautiful, with his one glowing amber eye and the other of emerald green. No doubt he had come here expecting special favours and, from the look of him, had been summarily dismissed. Her lips curved in a grin. Well, he wasn't the first of the high-ranking solitaries to have his plans of advancement crumble to dust. Catelysma had never shown any desire to take a consort. The Dark Lady seemed content to rule alone, unlike the rulers in some of the more distant Faery courts.

Ninka waited until the faery lord had disappeared round a bend in the tunnel, before bringing Aerith forward.

'Now. Remember what I said?' she whispered, urgently. 'No matter what happens. You must be silent. And all will be well. Do you understand, sweeting?'

Aerith nodded solemnly.

Ninka took a small rush cap from her pocket and jammed it down onto the child's head. She then twitched the rough, nettle hemp tunic into place, pulling it down over the bony little knees and gave her a final check. Aerith was barefoot, her toenails still rimmed with mud. The dirt she had smeared on the child's face and limbs and the slug slime smeared around her nose and mouth was still in place. Aerith blinked; her eyes red and crusted from the herb Ninka had rubbed into them. They looked sore, but she knew that the herb did not sting, and the effect would soon wear off.

Had she done enough? Well, it was too late to worry about it now. She gave Aerith's hand a reassuring squeeze. 'Ready? You are my brave girl. Never forget that.'

'Who is there?' a harsh voice demanded. 'Declare yourself!'

Ninka almost jumped out of her skin. She caught her breath as she heard the uneven patter of Tweeter's hooves on the stone floor.

Squaring her shoulders, she stepped forward into the doorway. 'If it please you, Master Tweeter. It is Ninka Minka, solitary hudskin. And the hot-blood child, come to beg audience with your mistress.'

'Hmmph!' Tweeter's barrel chest swelled as he looked her up and down, but she could see that he was pleased by her deference and the formal greeting. 'For what purpose?'

'I wish to discuss the matter of Catelysma's gown for the oak ball.'

Tweeter's glance flickered over her and lingered on Aerith for a second. He gave a loud sniff and bared his mud-coloured teeth. 'I will see if my lady deigns to speak with such a common little personage. Wait here.'

'Thank you.' Ninka humbly inclined her head.

She moved to stand in the doorway, as he made his shambling way across the room to the shimmering curtains, strung in many layers across the width of the room hiding the occupants from view. Two pixies hurried forward and drew the curtains aside to admit him.

Ninka waited in silence, acutely aware that Aerith was taking everything in. Her mind was sharp as a tack. It pained her to see the child looking such a fright, but it was to good purpose and would not be for long, if all went to plan.

Eventually, Tweeter reappeared and made his way back to her. 'Ladyship will see you. Follow me,' he said abruptly.

Ninka suppressed her nerves as she and Aerith moved forward. Once again, the billowing folds of the curtains were parted, so they could walk through.

The chamber they entered was illuminated by many glowing globes and carved pillars, strung with more lights, supported the ceiling. At the far end of the chamber, Catelysma lounged on a dais beneath a large tapestry depicting the night sky. A slender pixie, of lavender hue, paused in the act of weaving dragonfly wings and spider-silk ribbons into her ladyship's waterfall of silver-green hair to stare at the visitors. Catelysma slapped it and the pixie gave a yelp of pain before re-doubling its efforts.

The Dark Lady seemed out of temper, Ninka thought, trembling inwardly, wondering whether it was Jack Fleet's visit that had displeased her. It did not bode well. She bowed low, at the same time nudging Aerith who did the same.

'I do not recall commanding you to attend me. Nor to bring this…this graceless scrap of mortality to bruise my eyes.'

Catelysma grimaced with distaste as she glanced at Aerith. 'What a pity. She had such a promising beginning.'

There were titters from the fey clustered in groups around the chamber. Three hags sat at a table sipping something dark red from small hollow skulls. A Brownie popped out one of its eyes, licked it lovingly and then replaced it in its socket.

'She did indeed, Majesty,' Ninka agreed. 'I too am disappointed to find her so slow and sickly.'

Catelysma was surrounded by silken cushions in jewel shades. On a table beside her, there was a crystal jug and goblets. Honeyed fruits were heaped in rainbow gleaming dishes. She looked more closely at Aerith. 'Does it please you to dwell in the wild forest, child?'

Ninka tensed, but Aerith just blinked and said nothing.

'Come now. Speak up. I shall not bite,' Catelysma snapped. She swatted the lavender pixie, which flew off and landed sulkily next to a group of boggarts. The tip of one pointed ear showed through the Dark Lady's hair as she leant forward.

Mutely, Aerith regarded her with red-rimmed blue eyes.

Catelysma made a sound of impatience. 'Is something wrong with the child?'

'Unfortunately she has not learned to speak,' Ninka replied. 'I think her mind may be somewhat damaged. It is so easy for a mortal to break, is it not?'

'You *broke* my mortal?' Catelysma's voice rose.

'No, no,' Ninka replied hastily, cursing herself for her error. 'I have taken the most tender care of her. She is naturally...rather burdensome. That is her way.' She dared not risk a glance at Aerith and prayed that the child would remember to keep silent.

'Indeed? Are you complaining about having been given the care of her?'

'Perish the thought, Majesty,' Ninka said smoothly. 'I am honoured to do your bidding. I was simply reporting Aerith's progress. I know how you value the little hot-blood, as a pet. And thought you would wish to know.'

'Hmm. Take off that dreadful shapeless hat. Let me look at her properly.'

Ninka stepped in front of Aerith. She blinked encouragingly, putting all the love she felt for the child in that one short glance. And then she removed the rush cap to reveal the child's patchily shaven head and remaining tufts of dull, brownish hair, which appeared to be glued together in sticky clumps.

There was a collective indrawn breath. Someone sniggered.

A hoarse voice rang out. 'What a horrid little bug!'

'Whoo-hoo. It is turd ugly!' another chortled.

Catelysma flashed a warning look in the speakers' direction. Silence fell. '*What* happened to Aerith's golden hair?'

'It fell out. Some mortal weakness, I imagine. So far it has not responded to any of my simples. I am sure it will grow back...one day. See how her eyes are afflicted with some malady too? I only hope the sickness will not be passed to any fey.' She hoped she had not gone too far.

'Quite.' Catelysma shuddered. 'Put the hat back on.'

Ninka did so. *Good girl*, she mouthed silently. Aerith's little mouth twitched into a tiny smile. Ninka turned back round to face Catelysma.

The Dark Lady made a gesture and two pixies rushed forward to reposition her silken cushions. A tiny grass hob flew over, green wings flashing, wielding a fan of glossy black corax feathers.

'Well, hudskin. I hope you had good reason for begging an audience. Enlighten me.'

Ninka drew herself up to her full height as she began her carefully rehearsed speech. 'I entertain the fervent hope that you will judge my reason kindly, Majesty. I fear that I have been remiss in not presenting myself earlier. I expect that you will require my humble services to make your gown for the oak ball, my sewing skills being of the kind that would grace a queen's apparel. I would not wish to fail you. Only the very finest gown would do justice to your singular beauty. But...I...fear that...' she paused, deliberately.

'Yes?' Catelysma said, impatiently. She reached out to pet a feathery red-cap, which had drifted down to perch on one of cushions. It was poking its bloody teeth with a long bone needle.

'...I fear I have been so taken up with caring for Aerith, that I have neglected my other duties,' Ninka went on. 'I beg your forgiveness.'

'Ah.' An expression of understanding disturbed the perfect Gentry features. 'So, if I were to relieve you of the task of caring for the hot-blood, you would be free to make such a gown?'

'Just so, Majesty.' Ninka smiled, with feigned delight. 'As always your understanding is illuminated by wisdom.'

'What would you have me do with Aerith?'

'Well,' Ninka pretended to consider. 'Could not your pet stay at court?'

'Mayhap. And if I were to give her to the scrags?' Catelysma purred.

One of the creatures was lolling on the floor beside the dais. Ninka could smell the loathsome thing from across the room. She swallowed hard, steeling herself to remain silent as it scrambled to its feet.

Bloated belly wobbling, the scrag's raw nostrils were aimed

in the child's direction. A string of drool leaked from its wide mouth. 'Yes! Yes! Yes!'

Scenting more interesting entertainment, some of the fey began clapping and stamping in unison. The scrag was beside itself. It began heaving its seal-like bulk towards Aerith.

Catelysma let it get halfway, by which time Ninka's nerves were stretched to breaking point, before pointing a finger and sending out a stream of sparks. There was a sizzling noise and a black streak appeared between the creature's stumpy ears. A thread of smoke rose from the burn as it shrank back with a whimper and humped itself sullenly beneath the dais.

There were howls of laughter from the watching fey.

Run, Run. Before it is too late. It was all she could do to resist grasping the child's hand and fleeing back through the tunnels as fast as she could.

'What about the redcaps? They might appreciate a tender morsel?' Catelysma gave Ninka a measuring look.

Somehow, she managed to shrug. Her lips felt frozen. 'As it please you, Ladyship. I bow to your will.'

'Dear, little hudskin. So obedient.' Catelysma smiled sweetly. She swung herself from the dais, her red gown swirling around her, hair streaming out like a cloak. Her wings sprang up, whirring angrily as they beat the air. 'Wretch! To come here, pretending to offer your services as seamstress when your intention is to rid yourself of the hot-blood. You dared not harm her, because of my wrath. So instead you try to trick me into disposing of her for you. I should have you shod in shoes of heated iron and make you dance until you faint from agony!'

Ninka blanched. She knew the Dark Lady might well carry out her threat. Terror burned within her, but not just for herself. What would become of Aerith?

'I will kindle the fire,' one of the fey offered.

'And fetch a blacksmith,' said another. At the dais, the little green hob hovered in the air, its face hidden behind the black fan.

'Silence!' Catelysma gave Aerith a pitying glance. 'The child will live, but not as *my* pet. I do not play with nasty toys. She is yours, for always, Ninka. Attend to her. I have spoken. Be gone.'

Tears of relief pricked Ninka's eyes. *I have spoken.* Catelysma had voiced the words of binding. They could never be taken back. She bowed her head, fearful that her triumph would show.

'One other thing, hudskin! Your skills as a seamstress will no longer be required. You are a stranger to my court. Seek another audience, at your peril.'

Banishment! It was a terrible punishment. Ninka blanched, unsure of what the future might hold. But her plan had come into fruition. The child was hers. Aerith was safe. As safe as any mortal ever could be in Faery.

'I shall comply with your wishes, Majesty. Thank you for your gracious indulgence.'

At Catelysma's gesture of dismissal, she reached for the child's hand and slowly backed away.

Catelysma began admiring the glistening embroidery on the sleeve of her dress. She called for the lavender pixie to finish dressing her hair. 'Aerith. Such a waste of a pretty name,' she murmured.

CHAPTER 21

RACING ALONG THE path between litter-strewn grass banks, Jess passed the rusting mattress springs on her way up the incline towards Limefields. Her breath caught in her throat, the usual sting of vibrating metal and residual chemicals making her cough. She ignored it, pressing on to where the block of flats reared above the houses directly ahead of her. Dawn shades of peach and silver-grey tinted the sky. The street was deserted except for a couple of shift workers returning home. At this hour, even the ever-present hum of traffic from the dual-carriageway was muted.

At the entrance to the run-down gardens that bordered the flats, she paused looking around cautiously. Leon was probably still zoned-out on whatever chemical mix was spiking his bloodstream, but it wouldn't be long before he came looking for her. This time, it would be a more equal battle. The tips of her fingers tingled in readiness. She located that internal pulse of ignition, which was starting to feel as a natural part of her as the texture of her own skin, and felt it subtly click onto standby.

Suddenly something caught her eye. A figure had rounded the corner. A woman, stringy-haired, hunched over plodding along like a sleep-walker. She was coatless and her shabby pink track suit hung on her thin frame.

'Mum?'

Alice's head jerked up. Shock then joy chased across her

features. She stumbled forward and grasped her as if she'd never let go. 'Where the hell have you been? I woke up and you'd gone. I waited and waited for you to come back, but then I fell asleep. And it got dark and you still hadn't come home. I thought...you weren't coming back....' words spilled out of her.

'I know. I'm sorry.' Jess pulled away, gently. 'But I... '

'I went next door. Got them to phone the police. They sent someone round. But they just asked if we'd had an argument. And anyway it wasn't like you were a little kid. You'd probably gone to stay with a friend and you'd come back when you were ready. I tried to tell them, that you wouldn't run off without telling me. Anyway, you don't have any friends. They wouldn't listen. I waited and waited, but you didn't come back. I haven't been drinking. Not a drop. I've really tried this time. But I felt so bad, sweating and shaking and sleeping for hours on end. I lost track of the days. Then I went out looking, hoping to find you.' Her voice sounded odd without the usual blurred tone lent to it by alcohol.

'It's barely light. Have you been out all night?' Jess glanced over her with concern.

'I...I must have been. Feels like I've walked miles.'

Her mum's feet were bare inside the old threadbare slippers. Despite the sheen of sweat on her face, her lips were blue and she was shivering with cold. She had probably not eaten in days. 'Come on. Let's get you inside.'

Jess put her arm round her, supporting her as they climbed the stairs. As they stepped onto the walkway, she frowned. What was all that stuff outside their flat? It looked like someone had dumped a load of rubbish. As she drew closer, saw the front door hanging off its hinges, the broken front window, she understood. Leon's spite was not just centred on her. His mates had paid Alice a visit. Finding the flat empty and with nothing worth stealing, they had taken out their frustration by trashing the place.

'Oh no...' Alice murmured brokenly, as she bent down to pick up a slashed cushion with the stuffing hanging out of it like entrails. She cuddled the ruined thing close, stroking it sadly.

Jess's senses were alert for any sound, but she could hear nothing. The place had the hollow feel of an empty building.

Broken glass crunched beneath her boots as she went through into the sitting room. Splintered wood and ripped fabric littered the floor, the debris of their battered sofa, car-boot coffee table, bookshelf and curtains. It looked like someone had put a boot through the ancient TV.

They went through to the kitchen, where rubbish from the bin was strewn everywhere. Their cheap mugs and plates lay in fragments. The kitchen table and chairs and wall cupboards were in bits and the fridge lay face down on top of everything, leaking water everywhere.

It was the same in her bedroom. Her wooden bed frame had been hacked into pieces and the mattress ripped into strips, with such viciousness that Jess was put in mind of someone plunging a knife into a carcass. The room stank like a sewer. Flies rose from a pile of shit on a heap of CDs, torn magazines and T-shirts. *The vile, filthy...* Shuddering with revulsion, she went out and closed the door behind her.

Alice was standing in her wreck of a bedroom as if in a trance. Jess went inside.

'My room's a write off. Let's find somewhere to sit in here.' She kicked the debris aside, until she uncovered the bottom half of the bare mattress on which Alice and Leon had used to sleep and which was still partially intact, unlike hers. She sank on it and pulled Alice down to sit beside her. It was icy in the room, even with the door closed.

'We didn't have much in the first place. Now we've got nothing. What are we going to do?' Her thin frame was wracked with sobs.

Jess slid her arm around her. 'Hey! We've got each other. And that's all that counts. We'll survive somehow. We always have. Right?'

Alice looked up, her face bleak. 'Not this time.'

'Don't say that!' Jess said more sharply than she'd intended. After all she had been through, she couldn't bear it if Mum cracked up now. 'We're not giving up. Because, if we do. Leon's won.'

'Leon?' Alice wiped her eyes on the back of her hands. 'You think he was behind this?'

'I know it.'

She began at the beginning. How Leon had attacked her in the laundry room and how she'd fought him off. 'I've still got the lumps and bumps to prove it. Don't worry, it's nothing major.' The hard ridge between her shoulder blades gave a twinge as if on cue. She rubbed at it absently. 'I threatened to go to the police and tell them he had tried to rape me, unless he cleared out of the flat. He's already been done for dealing drugs. Zac Simpson, a girl in my class's brother, told me about it. Can't say it was a surprise. So, anyway, that's why Leon did a bunk.'

Alice listened in silence, a numb look on her face. Jess told her what had happened.

'The night I went out to get milk, two of his scumbag mates grabbed me, bundled me into a car and drugged me. When I came to, I was in a locked room. Leon was injecting something into my arm. I think he planned to get me hooked on the stuff, so that I'd do anything to get the next fix. But he got careless. You know what he's like. He's out of it himself, half the time. Anyway, the effects started to wear off. Once I realised what was happening, I played along. Soon as I was left by myself, I broke a window, climbed out and got away. I was coming back to the flat when I saw you.' It was a plausible version of events. More plausible than *I was rescued by some kind of winged creature, disguised as a ragged homeless guy.*

'How could all this have happened? I should have been there for you.'

'You're sick. You couldn't help it.'

'But I'm your mum, for God's sake. It's my *job* to take care of you.' Wincing a little as if her stomach was sore, she sat up straight. 'We have to leave. Tonight. Before Leon finds out that you're back at the flat. He's got a vicious streak. I should know. You've hurt his pride. He's never going to let this go.'

They were no longer safe here. They had no money, no possessions, no one they could call upon to put them up for a few days.

Sudden tremors shook Alice's body and her limbs were jerking uncontrollably. Her eyes had rolled back to show the whites, a chilling sound came from between her tightly clenched teeth.

'Mum?' Jess threw herself down beside her. 'On no! Don't do this to me!'

CHAPTER 22

A TIRED-LOOKING YOUNG DOCTOR with dishevelled hair came into the cubicle. They had been in A and E for hours.

'How are you feeling, Mrs Morgan? Any pain?'

'Where…where am I…' Alice's voice was muffled. 'Jess? Where's Jess?'

'I'm here,' Jess said.

'Can someone please find my daughter?' Alice batted at the oxygen mask with one hand, dislodging it. 'You have to let me go to her.' She groaned softly. 'My head hurts. What's wrong with me?'

'Try and stay calm, Mrs Morgan. You collapsed. You're in hospital. I'm Dr Benson.' His voice was calm, reassuring as he repositioned the oxygen mask.

'Jess? Where's Jess…'

'What's happened to her?' Jess asked worried. 'Why doesn't she recognise me?'

'She's very dehydrated. The confusion and headache are symptoms of that. It's usually temporary,' the doctor explained, turning pages. 'I see that your mother is long-term, alcohol dependent.'

'But she's really trying this time. She hasn't had a drink in three or four days. That's good, isn't it?'

The doctor looked at her kindly. It wasn't that simple, not with her level of dependence. To stop suddenly was dangerous. She needed to be supervised, a programme of gradual reduction. Suddenly reducing the level of alcohol in her blood had given her a seizure. She would probably make a full recovery but for the moment she needed to stay in hospital. They had to do more tests; blood, liver function. She was in safe hands

He left the cubicle. The nurse began swabbing the back of Alice's hand. The hot tang of some chemical substance assaulted Jess's throat. She turned away and covered her mouth with her hand.

'Sharp scratch,' the nurse said to Alice, as she inserted a needle and then attached a tube leading to a plastic bag of fluid hanging from a metal stand. 'There. All done, my love. You'll be a lot more comfortable now.'

Alice seemed to have understood. She was no longer picking feebly at the oxygen mask, but had relaxed back onto the pillow and closed her eyes. The nurse turned to Jess. She smiled. 'It might be a while before Mum's taken to a ward. We're waiting for a bed. Are you hungry? You can get coffee and a sandwich from the machine in the corridor.'

Jess wasn't listening. With Alice attended to and out of danger, she allowed herself to think of Lisa. *That sickening bump and the scream, cut short...* 'How would I find out about a friend of mine who was admitted to hospital a few days ago?'

'You'd have to ask at the Reception desk,' the nurse said, placing a cotton blanket over Alice and tucking it in around her. 'I'm afraid we don't deal with general enquiries. Too busy, as you can see. Sorry.'

'Please,' Jess said in her best persuasive voice. 'I'm really worried about her. She's my best friend and I think she could have been badly hurt. It's...it's partly my fault.'

The nurse hesitated. Her expression softened as she searched Jess's face. 'What's her name?'

'Lisa Simpson.'

'I'll see what I can do.' She left the cubicle heading towards the nearby nurse station.

Alice flexed her shoulders to ease out the tension, feeling another twinge from the lump between her shoulders. It felt different, softer and partially collapsed, like a large blister. She sank onto the hard red plastic chair beside the trolley where Alice lay, looking peaceful but with a pinched look about her mouth and eyes. Strangely, she looked younger. Over the years, her features must have been ravaged by sadness and grief as much as the alcohol.

A memory stirred and it was a moment before it was fully formed in Jess's mind. That woman in *Royalty's Revenge,* wearing a dove-grey dress lying on the four poster bed. Right now, Alice looked so much like the woman, it was uncanny.

Jess felt a stir of tenderness. She reached across to gently stroke the hair back from her mum's clammy forehead. 'You just get better. Right? I'll sort things for us, like I always do. Don't worry.'

Alice's eyes fluttered open. 'Windroth,' she whispered. 'Go back there. Only option...'

'Windroth?' Jess, whispered, leaning closer. 'Where's that?' She was certain that she'd never heard Alice mention any place called Windroth. Was it a village a small town? Something about the name sent a frisson through her, like a half-forgotten memory.

From outside in the corridor, she heard a voice call the next patient. 'Mr Curtis? This way please.' Footsteps approached.

There came the swish of curtains in the adjacent cubicle, the soft squeak of a trolley's wheels. Moments later, their nurse popped her head into the cubicle. She smiled at Jess. 'Your friend's in HDU.'

'HDU?'

'High Dependency Unit. Go up to the main corridor. You'll see a colour-coded map of all the wards and departments. HDU is in Area C, along with the Stroke Unit. It's out of visiting hours at the moment, but you might be able to have a word with the ward sister.'

At the entrance to the ward, Jess covered the metal door handle with a fold of her long sleeved T-shirt, so that she needn't touch it. But the door appeared to be locked anyway. There was a button on the wall to one side. She pressed it and heard the faint echo of a buzzer from inside the ward.

After a few moments a nurse appeared. 'Yes. How can I help?'

'Um...Hi. My friend, Lisa Simpson's in this ward. I...I wondered if I could see her.'

'I'm sorry, but visiting on HDU is restricted to immediate family only,' the nurse said, with a sympathetic smile.

'But I really need to see her. Please, I won't stay long.'

'There's no way...' the nurse began.

Jess felt a hand encircle her upper arm. 'It's OK. You can let her in,' a familiar voice behind her said. 'She's with me.'

She turned and found herself looking into Zac Simpson's hostile face.

CHAPTER 23

ZAC DROPPED HIS hand so that it fell to his side. He unconsciously wiped it on his jeans. He found even that slight touch of the girl repellent. He threw Jess a sideways glance, not trusting himself to speak. Not yet.

He'd been out with one of the tagging crew, Ben, an old school mate. They'd planned on starting a new piece on the virgin wall of an empty factory; letters over a metre high, with a figure bursting out of the centre of them. It was *well* risky, doing this in the daylight, but the buzz was something else. Up and over the wire fence, like cats. No problem. He liked it best when it was only him and Ben. Although it was risky without a third person as a look-out, it was easier to split and run in different directions if there was any trouble. Which was just what they had done, when the Panda car cruised past. He and Ben were slick. Ben sprinted towards the multi-storey car park, while he'd legged it down an alleyway, stopping only long enough to stash his stencils and spray cans behind a waste bin until he came back for them. As soon he was certain no one was pursuing him, he'd ducked into a doorway while he considered his next move. With a Panda car on the prowl it was best to avoid the crew's usual haunts. And home wasn't a good place to be, not with Mum and Dad in pieces over Lisa and both off work. On balance, hospital was the best option.

And just look who he had bumped into. Jess Morgan. The

last person he'd expected to see trying to get into the ward.

He couldn't stand the sickly-looking bitch with her sullen face and sly, brooding expressions. Her bony hands and feet and mass of unruly black hair, which looked as if it hadn't seen a brush in about ten years, repelled him. There was nothing feminine about her. His insides ached with anger. This was all her fault. Why couldn't she have listened when he warned her off Lisa? What the hell had his sister seen in her? Couldn't she have found a more suitable friend? There were enough students to choose from. But he didn't blame Lisa. She was just too soft, had always been too naïve for her own good. All this was down to Jess.

He and Jess walked on, their footsteps sounding on the tiled floor. The corridor ran alongside a series of small open wards. Apart from the hum of low voices at the nurse stations and the mechanical blips of various machines, it was very quiet. Zac paused at the end of the corridor, beside some rooms with swing doors. A familiar nurse came out of one of them, carrying something on a tray. She was small and blonde, with a curvy figure and good legs. He had seen a lot of her during the time he had spent here in the past few days and felt a quickening of heat in his belly as he smiled at her. She gave him an answering nod, a knowing look in her eyes. He was well in there. Definitely one to follow up.

Zac dragged his attention back to Jess. It was a renewed shock to see the contrast between the two young women. One so soft rounded and appealing, while the other was angular, sharp and cold.

'Lisa's in the room at the far end,' he said tonelessly, not bothering to hide his dislike.

She noted it, he saw that by the slight tightening of her jaw, but she simply nodded and then looked straight at him. 'Look.

Thanks,' she said, stiffly. 'I wouldn't have been allowed in, if you hadn't...'

'Save it. OK?'

He had always found it off-putting, that she was able to meet him eye to eye. Girls usually had to look up to him. He preferred it that way. It made him feel strong and protective. He liked looking after his girlfriends, giving them a good time, so they would give him what he wanted. Trade off. That's how it worked the world over. But Jess didn't seem to get that. Maybe she was a lesbian or an Emo, even one of those saddos who'd sworn off sex. Straight Edge, he thought they called themselves. The directness in her slanting, greenish-eyes, unnerved him. It felt as if she was looking *into* him, not just at him.

'Whatever.' She shrugged now, a spot of hectic colour standing out on each pale, high cheek-bone.

Her breathing was rapid and oddly uneven. Zac remembered Lisa telling him that Jess suffered from asthma. He was glad. Maybe she'd have a really bad attack and die in agony, her lungs struggling to drag in air. He imagined standing over her, watching the light go out of her eyes. It would be poetic justice.

Thrusting her hands into her pockets, she looked down, scuffing at the floor with the toe of one of her ridiculous, scruffy paint-splashed boots. 'How...how's she doing, any-way? I hope she isn't hurt too seriously.'

He stared at her in disbelief. Did she think Lisa was in HDU on a whim? Another shard of anger flickered through him. He noticed for the first time that her clothes were crumpled as if she'd been sleeping in them. Her dark hair was worse than usual, hanging in tangled rat's tails. She smelt unpleasant, sharp and sour and with a faint undertow of something sickly chemical. Christ, what was she on? It reminded him of something a tom cat had once sprayed in their kitchen doorway.

His lips thinned with disgust. 'Oh I get it. You've been on planet Jess for the past few days! So you don't know that my sister's spine was crushed when those hit-and-run bastards ran her over. Or that, as she fell, her head smashed into the kerb. Her skull cracked open like an egg. Double whammy. Paralysis and brain damage.' His voice broke and he swallowed hard, abruptly choked by grief. He still hadn't cried. Somehow he'd managed to hold it together for his parents' sake. But he was so wired he felt that he might just shatter into fragments.

He wouldn't have believed that Jess could look any paler, but her skin now had a greenish cast.

'God. Oh, God.' She had cupped her face in her hands and was swaying slightly. He almost felt sorry for her.

'Lisa's been on a life-support machine for three days,' he went on. 'They've done tests. There's no brain activity. Her pupils have blown. Mum and Dad have gone home to rest. Tomorrow we have to decide whether to…to turn off the machine.'

'Turn it off? Why?' Her brows drew together in puzzlement.

She really didn't seem to get it. 'Are you thick or something?' He shook his head slowly, his lip curling in derision.

Her face crumpled as realisation slowly dawned. 'She's…Oh, no! No! Lisa can't be… ' she gasped. 'I never imagined… Oh, Zac. I'm so, so sorry.' Reaching out, she placed a hand on his denim sleeve.

He looked down to see it crouching there like a long-legged white spider. 'Don't!' He jerked backwards, shuddering with disgust.

He saw it register with her. But she didn't look surprised, just resigned, as if his reaction was nothing new. She dropped her hand. There was a set look to her face now and her lips were trembling. 'Have they caught whoever did it?'

He gave her a pitying look. 'Despite repeated requests by the police for witnesses, no one has come forward,' he said in a mock newsreader's voice. 'I'm willing to bet that you know something about it. Why didn't you go to the police? Mum said Lisa was meeting some girl from college at the multiplex. That was you, wasn't it?'

'I was supposed to be meeting her, yes. But something came up. I didn't make it.'

'Let her down, did you? No surprise there then. But you know what happened to her. You're mixed up in some dirty little business with those pimps and druggies you hang out with. Lisa just got caught in the fall-out!'

The pretty blonde nurse glanced their way as she passed en route to another of the side rooms. 'Keep it down. OK?'

'Yeah. Sorry.' He winked at her automatically, noting the way her uniform strained across her tight round arse as she moved away.

He turned back to Jess. All at once he felt bone tired. He dragged a hand through his hair, allowed his shoulders to slump. 'What's the fucking point? It doesn't matter now. None of it matters, because it won't bring Lisa back. Go on in. See what you've done.'

A spasm crossed her face. 'What *I've* done? It wasn't my fault... I didn't *do* anything...'

'Oh, you *so* did!' he interrupted, coldly. 'Whether you meant to, or not. So deal with it! You say Lisa was your friend? Bullshit. You never really cared about her. You were just using her as a way of getting back at me. Because I saw through you and told you so.'

Her expression hardened. For a moment it was so loaded

with contempt that it made him shiver. He didn't scare easily, but he had to stop himself taking a step back.

'Think what you like about me,' she said, quietly. 'I don't give a shit.' Turning away, she walked rapidly towards Lisa's room.

He hesitated, and then started forward, grabbing the swing door just before it closed. He didn't go in after her, straightaway, but slouched in the open doorway.

Jess's strangled cry of horror gave him a bleak satisfaction. He remembered his first glimpse of Lisa, the swelling and discolouration of her head and body so terrible that he thought they had made a mistake. The pumpkin-headed, crash-test dummy couldn't be his little sister. They had identified her from her smashed glasses and a small gold necklace she had been wearing.

The bank of machines and monitors, to which Lisa was connected, emitted regular blips. Jagged lines forming peaks and troughs passed at regular intervals across their screens. Jess had gone over to stand beside the bed. She was looking down at the stranger who lay there. She began speaking in a low voice, but he could hear every word.

'Oh, Lisa. I'm so sorry I couldn't be here for you. It was Leon. You know what he's like. He kept me locked in a room. It was days before I got away. And now Mum's sick. I came as soon as I could. Zac's right. It was a *really* bad idea for you to be my friend. I tried not to get you mixed up in my shitty life. Hell, *I* don't want to be living it! But look at you. You got hurt anyway. I want you to know how much your friendship meant to me. You're the only one who's ever had time for me. The only one who cared enough to get close…'

Her genuine distress seemed to kill his anger. It took too much energy to hate her. He'd seen too many tears from

Mum and Dad and he'd been holding his emotions back for so long that his chest felt tight as a drum. Seeing Jess crumple, when he'd thought her so tough and uncaring, it was too much. A wave of emptiness swept through him. He walked slowly into the room and sank down on a chair placed on the opposite side of the bed.

* * * * *

Zac came to, with a jerk. He didn't know how much time had passed. Jess was still standing beside the bed. She was leaning over Lisa, holding both of her hands.

And then he knew he must still be asleep and dreaming, because there was a faint greenish-silver glow around the tall skinny form. Around the region of Jess's upper back, the glow was more concentrated. Light streamed outwards, flashing, stranding and wavering in ragged purple-green fronds, like the display of Northern Lights he'd seen on a TV documentary. The glow around her grew brighter and spread outwards and downwards, drifting like mist over water until it obscured the figure on the bed.

She was still talking in a low voice that vibrated like the deep note of some musical instrument. He could feel it like something physical, spreading tendrils through his mind. But he couldn't move a muscle.

'Lisa. Listen. I'm going now. I probably won't see you again. Goodbye. I…I love you.'

It really was over. Lisa had gone. Even Jess seemed to have accepted that now. A new wave of distress began low in his belly, pushing upwards to fill his throat. He jerked upright, staggered to his feet and lurched over to the wash basin, where he was violently sick. Wiping his mouth, he straightened up and ran the taps to rinse the basin. The back of his throat stung. He filled a plastic cup, rinsed and spat. Groaning he dampened a paper towel and pressed it to his face. He was straightening up, when he caught a swift movement in the mirror above the basin.

Jess. She was leaving.

It was a fleeting impression, but he registered that there was something different about her. She looked somehow bulkier about her shoulders, but it could have been because she was hunched over as if in pain.

No point in going after her. What was there to say?

He binned the wet towel. Something had changed in the room. It felt…wrong. It was another moment before he worked it out. The dim room was silent. No blips sounded, no lights flashed. All the machines were off.

Shocked he approached the foot of the bed to look at the stranger that was Lisa. Only she wasn't a stranger any more. Her round face was pale and only slightly marked by bruises. Without the terrible swelling and discolouration, his sister was now perfectly recognisable. It was another moment before he realised something else.

Her chest was rising and falling gently.

She lay there in her checked hospital gown, arms outside the sheets, her reddish blonde hair spread out on the white pillow. As he leaned closer, he actually *saw* the colour flooding back into her cheeks and lips, just as if they were being painted by an invisible brush.

Slowly, she opened her eyes focusing on his face.

'Zac? I'm so thirsty. Can you get me a drink?'

Obediently he filled a cup and brought it back to the bed. He slid his arm around her, gently supported her while she sat up and took a sip. She told him she wasn't in any pain and waggled her arms and legs to show him that she really was fine. He couldn't understand. But he didn't care.

'Jess was here, wasn't she?'

'Yeah. But she's gone now. Good riddance. You don't need her sort. She's poison.'

'It wasn't her fault, Zac.'

'Whatever. It's you I care about. Listen, I'm going to phone Mum and Dad. OK? I'll go get a nurse to come and sit with…'

They both jumped as there was a loud crash. His pretty blonde nurse stood in the doorway, a look of shock on her face. The contents of the tray she was carrying were strewn on the floor.

CHAPTER 24

JESS STUMBLED AS she threw herself headlong down the last few stairs leading to the ground floor. She felt as if all her energy had been drained, like floodwater rushing away in a conduit. Grabbing the banister to stop herself from falling, she stood still for a moment until the dizziness passed.

I brought Lisa back. I really did it.

She was scared. Really scared.

And not only because of what she had somehow just done in the hospital room. Something terrible was happening to her. She could feel a slight weight in the region between her shoulders, where a soft mass was now straining against the fabric of her vest and cotton-print dress. Warm fluid was trickling down her back and soaking into the waistband of her black leggings.

She didn't dare investigate, for fear of what she would find. Jess moaned softly as there was another twitching movement between her shoulder blades, which found an echo in the muscles of her back. The soft, pulpy mass slid around as if trying to escape. Trembling with revulsion, she took a deep breath, pushed herself away from the banister and hurried towards a door she could see ahead of her. It opened directly onto a large car park. She sped across the concrete, her feet barely touching the ground.

There was a guy walking towards the hospital entrance. As she swerved to run past him, he suddenly changed direction and she careened straight into him. She had a brief impression of a tall, strong body and the smell of fresh air captured by his skin and hair.

'Sorry. My fault. I wasn't looking where I was going,' he said. 'Are you OK?' His gripped her arms to steady her.

She nodded, took a breath. Feeling herself swaying towards him, she steadied herself with an effort. She glanced up and for the briefest moment locked eyes with him, saw the concern on his face. He wasn't much older than her, maybe a year or so, and he had kind eyes and shoulder-length dark hair, blown across his cheek by the wind. Something flared between them, taking her by surprise. A connection made in an instant. And then her stomach cramped again with terror and panic, and she was pulling away from him, hurtling past rows of parked cars.

She thought he called after her, but the sound of his voice was lost in the air rushing past her ears. She found herself already at the exit. Without her being aware of the transition, a kind of super-charged energy had kicked in. She didn't understand how or why and she was too hyped to care right now. She ran on, moving more swiftly than she had ever thought possible. Streets, shops, parks flashed by in a blur of muted colour as she headed on, not stopping. Moving, moving. Keep going. It didn't matter where. She pumped her arms, moved her legs in a clean, effortless rhythm that channelled all thought into a moving meditation. Opening-up a space. Safety. It was where she wanted to be – just for now. In the total absence of thought.

★　★　★　★　★

Caleb stood in the hospital car park, staring at the place where a fraction of a second before the girl had been standing. One moment he'd been gripping her thin arms to steady her, because she looked as if she was about to collapse, and the next she'd torn away and just…gone. Blinked-out, like a light snuffed from a candle. He still had a clear impression of her face, twisted with emotion.

She'd looked up at him. For the briefest moment their eyes had met and…*something* happened. A spark had ignited, arcing between them like an electrical charge from a machine in some miniature Frankenstein's laboratory. Every detail of her unusual face was committed to his memory. He could see them as vividly, as if she stood before him now. The silky-sweep of delicate eyebrows that winged away from luminous, upwardly-tilting eyes. The fine bones beneath unusually pale, smooth-textured skin. The wild tangle of dark hair that cast shadows on the hollows and planes of a face that any artist would want to paint, over and over again.

Good old fusiform-gyrus. Reliable, as always, whatever else was falling apart around him.

A particularly enlightened teacher had informed him during a discussion about anatomy that his *fusiform gyrus,* the part of the brain that identifies and stores human faces must be particularly sensitive and well developed. Caleb remembered the laughter in class, when the teacher had suggested that a career in the police force might be a smart move for him.

This unique ability was the only thing stopping him from believing that he had conjured that brief interchange from his imagination. Because, no one moved that fast. It was impossible. Maybe she was a ghost? An echo of something that had already happened? His didn't know if he believed in that stuff, but he accepted that not everything could be explained.

And he wasn't exactly in his right mind, was he? He'd been

thinking of nothing but Mum, for the entire journey here; first by train, then bus and finally on foot. Amazingly Dad had accepted his excuse about having to visit the customer and set more rat traps, so he'd been able to leave first thing that morning. Now that he was finally at the hospital, his courage had almost failed. Would Mum be recognisable, with her face all twisted out of shape? Would she be conscious? And if so, could he keep a lid on his distress, so that he didn't add to hers? He was trying to decide whether to go straight to the Stroke Unit or to sit outside on a bench and collect his thoughts first.

So he'd changed direction, almost without thinking. And collided with the girl. Where had she come from? He would have sworn that a second ago, he'd been the only person on the path leading to the main entrance, the only sound the scuffing of his trainers on concrete.

Well, wherever the troubled girl had gone, he hoped she would overcome her demons. She had made a lasting impression on him. He didn't expect her to have had a similar reaction. Another time. Another place. Who knew what might have happened?

He smiled wryly. Seemed like he was making a habit of bumping into people. First Mrs Stark and now *her*. At least he was feeling calmer about seeing Mum. The mystery girl had done that for him. Why put it off any longer? Turning up his collar against the chill wind, he ignored the bench and headed for the door to reception.

CHAPTER 25

CALEB WAS CHECKING the traps he'd set along the outside wall of the kitchen. Most of them had been sprung by rats. After dumping the bodies into a bin-bag, he re-set the traps with peanut butter, as he'd once heard Dad advising a customer.

'Far more effective than cheese. They can't grab a chunk and run off. So they lick at the peanut butter. Gives the trap time to work. Snap!' Neil Farmer clapped his hands together. 'No more rat!'

There were some plusses to working in a hardware store, Caleb conceded wryly, although very few. It was now afternoon. He felt he'd done the right thing, holding Mum's hand, kissing her, telling her how much loved her. It amounted to something, something to hold onto in the face of the fact that she was seriously ill. Her stroke-contorted face on the pillow, the consultant's words that he shouldn't 'expect too much.' He was trying not to think of that. Keeping busy, that was the thing.

He reached the ancient drain, where he had hidden the last two traps. The cast-iron, kitchen down-pipe, emerged a metre or so above the base of the wall, and sloped down to a rusted grill. Windroth Hall appeared to have its original plumbing. No wonder rats got into the house. With a stick he had found for the purpose, he probed about in the long grass around the drain, found the trap and dealt with it. Only one left now. The grass parted beneath the stick to reveal that the last trap had been sprung, too.

But what was caught in it, wasn't a rat. It didn't look like a mouse either.

Frowning, Caleb got down onto his knees for a closer look. He could see blood, innards and mostly mashed fur; although a tiny bit of it was still intact. There was also something that looked like part of a delicate wing. Was it a large beetle, a hawk moth perhaps? He had glimpsed some pretty odd-looking things flying about in the long grass.

Exerting pressure on the metal spring, he freed the broken little body and placed it in the palm of his hand. The remaining fragment of fur was reddish, silky with a purple sheen. He brushed at it with the tip of one finger. Something pale in the mess became stuck to his glove. A bone probably, he thought with a twist of revulsion. He went to wipe it off, but stopped dead at what he saw.

Clinging to the latex was a tiny limb. It ended in a ragged stump at one end, but at the other end was a hand. A perfect hand, in miniature, with four fingers and a thumb, each tipped with a pearly nail. *An actual arm? In miniature?*

Caleb felt his jaw drop in shock as tried to make sense of what he was seeing. He shook his head slowly, looked again at his gloved finger. The tiny arm had gone, blown away on the breeze. 'Oh, crap!'

He poked around in the grass with the stick, but there was no sign of it. Had it been an arm, after all? Rat's paws were pink and hand-like. That must have been it. It was a baby rat in the trap. A particularly fluffy one, with unusual colouring. It could happen. And the scrap of wing? A bit of internal organ or something. He didn't know. Didn't want to know.

It was too weird. He was starting to get the creeps.

'Yuck!' With a shudder, he scraped the mess off his palm, and then wiped the glove in the grass. He still felt shaken.

However much he tried to make himself believe that he had been mistaken about that tiny, human looking arm, he couldn't get it out of his mind.

Should he mention the thing in the trap to Mrs Stark? Best not. She'd think he was losing it. Well, maybe he was.

There had been that episode with the mystery girl in the hospital car park. Had *she* been real either? He still couldn't make sense of what had happened. All he knew was that every tiny detail of her unusual face was imprinted on his brain, nagging at his artistic sensibilities, so that he couldn't wait to pick up pen and paper and start drawing her from memory. He shrugged. Maybe some things in life weren't supposed to be understood, only accepted.

Stripping off his gloves, he stuffed them in the bin-bag before securing it with a double knot. Moments later he was heading back toward the kitchen door. He just had time to check on Mrs Stark and apologise for the shortness of his visit, and then he'd better head for home.

* * * * *

The first stars were glinting in the grey-violet sky as Caleb peddled through the back streets of town. He passed the hair salon beside the florists and felt a pang at the thought of how things had panned-out with Sharon – or rather, how they hadn't. What a muppet he'd been to misread the signs so badly. He'd never make that mistake again. The pavements and buildings reflected a little of the day's heat. It was generally warmer here than at Windroth, due to the close-packed buildings.

Mrs Stark had had a heavy cold. It hadn't slowed her down, though; nothing did. She had come down from her studio to greet him in the kitchen, still wearing that splattered old smock, looking even more tired and drawn than usual. He had persuaded her to stop working for just long enough to eat the pack of prepared fruit salad he'd bought on the way there. And then she'd gone back up to her studio, while he gave the usual mountain of dirty crocks in the kitchen sink a cursory rinse. 'I'm off now! Bye, Mrs Stark,' he called from the foot of the staircase. 'Take care of that cold. There's a lemon and honey, for drinks in the fridge. See you next week.'

'Go home, Caleb!' she shouted, huskily. But he could tell she was smiling.

Unlocking the flat door to the side of the shop, he stowed the bike in the walk-in cupboard. His stomach growled as he climbed the stairs, reminding him that he hadn't eaten for hours. Dad's voice from the hall, on the phone, to Pa Farmer, by the sound of it.

'A few minutes ago. Another stroke. Fatal, this time. Just had the phone call. Yeah, I'm sorry too. As beautiful on the inside as on the outside. Never speak ill of the dead, eh?' his voice tripped coldly, quickly along. 'Sally and me we didn't ...' a pause containing what everyone knew. 'No. I haven't told Caleb yet. You know how he and his mum were. Thick as bloody thieves. He'll have to man-up, now that it's just him and me...'

Realisation crashed in on Caleb with numbing force. He felt sick. Mum was dead. No. *No.* There must be some mistake. He'd been with her only a few short hours ago. But although he didn't want to believe it, he knew it was true.

'Well, I have arrangements to make,' Neil Farmer was saying. 'A funeral's going to cost an arm and a leg...'.

The hall door opened. Neil came into the room, head

down. He was threading his fingers through his hair. 'Christ! Why now?' he groaned. 'As if I didn't have enough on my plate!' Suddenly, he slammed the door shut so hard that Caleb felt the reverberation in his chest. Catching sight of Caleb, Neil gave a start. 'You're back then.'

'Yeah.' Caleb couldn't meet his eyes.

'You heard what I was saying to Pa Farmer? About your mother? She died a short while ago.'

Caleb nodded. 'I know. It was another stroke,.' he said, tonelessly. *And I heard how you spoke about her. You cold-blooded sod.* Bitter words rose to his lips, but he swallowed them. What was the point? Mum was free now. Dad could never hurt her again with his meanness and cruel jibes.

'Nothing else to say?' Neil challenged, chin jutting. 'Your sainted mother is dead. Go on. Why don't you say what you're thinking? It has to be my fault, doesn't it? Like everything else around here.'

Caleb recognised the signs. Dad was looking for a fight. Well, he wasn't going to give him the satisfaction. He didn't have the energy for it. Besides, it wouldn't bring Mum back. He felt light-headed with hunger, but the thought of food brought bile rushing into his throat. 'I'm going to bed,' he said wearily, wanting nothing more than to close his bedroom door, throw himself face-down and give vent to his grief.

'No you're not!' Neil's expression sharpened. He moved quickly, standing deliberately in Caleb's path. 'Not before you tell me who she is.'

Caleb frowned in confusion. 'Who's who?'

'The girl you've been spending all this time with.'

'Girl? There isn't any girl.' Was Dad insane? For one single moment, an image of the mystery girl in the hospital car park flooded his thoughts. Of course, Dad couldn't mean *her*.

Caleb wasn't even sure she existed, outside of his imagination. He gave a hollow laugh.

Neil's eyes were cold. 'Don't lie to me, boy. Or you'll be laughing on the other side of your face.'

Caleb could feel himself tensing up. 'How would I get time to meet anyone? I'm always working in the shop.'

'Except on Thursday afternoons,' Neil said pointedly. 'And today, you've had the whole *day* to yourself. So, where have you been?'

No wonder Dad hadn't raised any objection, when he'd left this morning - he'd been hoping to catch Caleb out in some subterfuge. A trickle of fear ran down his spine. Had Dad followed him to the railway station? He quickly dismissed that possibility. That would have meant closing the shop. Nothing short of an earthquake would make him do that. And Caleb had been ultra-careful as he'd smuggled his bike from the flat, before cycling to Windroth.

Momentarily, he considered telling the truth, but then he'd have to explain how he'd been able to afford the train fare to the hospital. More important, was the fact that those precious, last moments shared with Mum, were *his* alone, to treasure and re-live whenever he wanted to. Hopefully, they would bring him some small comfort. It was little enough to hang on to. He wasn't going to give Dad the chance of rubbishing that.

'I had those rat traps to sort out, didn't I? And then I was on free time. So I went for a bike ride to...' Caleb thought quickly. '...the country park.' He named a place Neil wasn't likely to know about. 'It's about ten miles away. They've got a lakeside nature trail, a cycle track and a café.' *It was pretty good, on the spur of the moment.* For a moment, he thought he'd gotten away with it.

Neil took a step closer. 'You've been gone since eight a.m. That's one hell of a bloody bike ride! I've seen how you dash off the moment we close on Thursdays. It's been going on for weeks.' His voice was heavy with mockery. 'Don't tell me there isn't a girl involved.'

Despite the grief he was just about managing to hold at bay, Caleb felt his temper rising. Did they have to do this *now*? Dad was unbelievable. 'There is no girl. Get it? So what if there was? I've got a right to a life of my own.' As soon as he said it, he knew it was a mistake.

'You're still eighteen, boy. That makes you answerable to me.' Neil stared at Caleb, his mouth twisted. Unexpectedly, he chuckled. 'I expect she's some tarty little piece, eh? I remember what I was like at your age. Couldn't think of anything but getting my end away. Think I haven't seen the signs? You're heavy-eyed in the mornings. Hardly a civil word to anyone. I can read you like a book, you randy little sod. We all have to sow our wild oats. I've no problem with that. But I won't have you lying to my face. D'you hear?'

Caleb's face was burning. Didn't he have any respect? Mum was hardly cold in her hospital bed. He nodded silently.

Neil hadn't finished. 'If you've started seeing some decent girl who won't let you into her knickers, it's time you brought her home. So I can suss her out. Make sure she's not just after your money. I wouldn't trust *your* judgement on anything. It's all you can do to wipe your own arse!'

Caleb could feel his insides churning. 'For the last time,' he burst out. 'I haven't *got* a girlfriend!'

A sly look crossed Neil's face. He slipped a hand into his trouser pocket and brought out a fistful of notes. 'So what's this then? Now try telling me you haven't been splashing out on some bit of skirt!'

Caleb gaped in disbelief. Dad had searched his room and found the money under his mattress. He couldn't believe it. How dare he? 'That's my money,' he said through gritted teeth.

'Yeah? How did you get it? Been stealing stuff from the shop and flogging it? Dealing drugs? You tell me.' Neil was rocking forward onto the balls of his feet and back onto his heels, like a boxer.

'Is that really what you think of me?' Caleb's temper finally snapped. 'I *earned* that money,' he shouted. 'If you must know, I've been visiting an old lady. She paid me for one of my drawings!'

Neil snorted. There was a triumphant twist to his mouth. 'That's so bloody pathetic that you couldn't have made it up. You should have told me then, shouldn't you? You know full well, how tight money is. This'll come in useful. We'll say no more about it.' He began stuffing the money back into his jeans pocket.

'No!' Caleb looked at him, incredulous, seeing his plans crumbling. 'No! You can't do this!'

'I just have.'

Caleb was trembling with frustration. 'I want my money. Give it back to me!'

'Pathetic.' Neil wagged his head and gave a sneering laugh.

Something seemed to explode in Caleb's head. He sprang forwards, arms flailing.

Taken by surprise Neil took a step back. 'You little...' He swung back his arm, clenched his fist.

The punch caught Caleb full in the face. The heavy blow was numbing. He reeled in shock and disbelief.

His ears were ringing. He could hear Dad shouting, but it sounded like he was under water and he couldn't make out the words. The pain was kicking in now, making his eyes water. His nose hurt like hell and there was a throbbing soreness in his mouth where he'd bitten his tongue. Blood was pouring down his chin. With a sob, he wheeled round and headed for the front door. Dragging it open, he flew down the stairs and grabbed his bike and backpack.

There was a cry behind him. Neil was coming down the stairs. Heavy booted footsteps thudded on the concrete treads. But Caleb had the street door open and was outside now. The night air cleared his head, but his teeth and the whole of his jaw were on fire. Gulping back blood and tears, he threw himself onto his bike and began peddling away for all he was worth.

Behind him, a door banged. Neil ran out onto the street. 'Caleb! You get back here!' he thundered. 'I'm warning you!'

Caleb wobbled and almost fell off the bike, before quickly regaining his balance. Leaning forward over the handlebars, he raced towards the back streets. He had no idea where he was going. But he wasn't coming back. Ever.

CHAPTER 26

JESS WAS ON her way to find Mike. Because she couldn't do this by herself any more. After hours of roaming the streets, followed by an uncomfortable, sleepless night spent huddled beneath a wooden climbing frame in a deserted children's playground, she felt hollowed-out. Her eyes were gritty. Chills crept over the entire surface of her skin, scraping gently like the tiny feet of soldier ants on the prowl.

Just as she feared her legs were about to give out, she made it to the underpass. Mike was there. She could have wept with relief.

'I…I didn't know where else to go.'

He nodded, smiling a welcome as if he'd expected her. Jess stumbled forward and sank gratefully onto an upturned cardboard box.

Producing his make-shift stove and clean jam jars, Mike set about calmly making tea. 'What has happened? Is it Leon again? I could put an end to him, if you wish it.'

'What?' Jess looked up at him sharply. He looked fierce, feral. There was an icy glint in his dark eyes. She had never thought of him as dangerous before now. 'No. Not Leon. It's…it's something else…'

'Tell me then. You have my full attention.'

'OK.' She took a deep, steadying breath. 'This is going to sound totally insane. I went to visit Lisa, right? I was standing there, looking down at her lying in that hospital bed. She was so broken up and bruised. I hardly recognised her. There were all these wires coming out of her arms, a mask over her face. They had her connected to some machines.' Jess's voice caught on a sob. She swallowed hard and forced herself to continue. 'You should have seen her. She was so badly hurt. And all because of me. Everyone, the doctors, Zac, her parents, they all thought she was dying. Zac blames me. He *really* hates me now, more than he did already. I…I couldn't bear to see her lying there. It wasn't fair, was it? I mean, Lisa never hurt anybody in her life. I wanted to *do* something. Make a difference, somehow. Repay her for being sweet and trusting. And the only kid at college to give a shit about me. And then - I can't explain how - but I started to do this…thing.'

Mike's eyes had narrowed. 'I am listening. Go on.'

'OK. This is where it gets uber-weird. I…I've been having these strange experiences – even before what happened with Leon. It's like there's an energy in me that I can sometimes control. I get tingles around me and then…something kicks-in and things…happen. It started-up again - right there while I stood beside Lisa's bed. The tingling, the energy-surge. But it was so much stronger than anything I'd felt up until then. Some inner part of me seemed to peel away, like it was separating and moving forward. I…I kind of stepped outside of myself. I could feel that I was still standing beside Lisa's bed, still looking out of my own eyes. But that *other* part of me was moving away, so I was in two places at once.' She glanced at Mike to see his reaction. He was watching her closely and gave a small nod.

'The other me – or whatever it was - was standing in a thick mist. I could hear wind swirling round me and there was some kind of regular noise. Thump, thump, thump. Like a drum-beat, you know?'

'Your heart?'

'No. It was the sound of marching. I was part of this enormous crowd. There were thousands and thousands of figures. Not just people, but animals too. And…and shapeless, shadowy things I didn't recognise. They were all moving slowly towards a bright glow in the distance. I could see enormous rays of golden light, reaching up into the black sky, but all around the marching figures it was dark and gloomy. Horrible.'

'Those figures. How did they look?' Mike asked.

'Pale grey and wispy, as if they were made of the same stuff as the mist. They were pressing up against me, jostling me as if they knew I shouldn't be there. It was gross. No one spoke. Their faces looked as if they were made of clay that was smudged out of shape. Some of them were almost transparent. There was one with just black holes for eyes. I saw another one with a face like hot wax. His nose and chin were slowly dripping down onto his chest. Some of the figures moaned and others sobbed.' She gave a shudder, remembering.

Mike looked thoughtful. 'It sounds terrifying.'

'Yeah! And then something happened. I thought I knew what shit-scared was, but I didn't. Not until then.' She took another breath. 'The worst thing was this awful feeling – like…like a big hole had swallowed all hope. Then I looked at Lisa. She was grey all over too, her eyes not fixed on anything, but they didn't seem drained of consciousness. Those were the blue eyes I knew. There was faint colour in her lips, too. It gave me hope that she hadn't been there for long.'

Mike nodded.

'So I called out to her, tried to get to her, but the others grabbed hold of me and…and I couldn't get free. That place didn't want to let us go.' She fell silent, feeling again that cloying mist that had rushed at her, swirling round her, getting thicker until she started to feel cold. She had looked down, seen that her legs were turning grey, and known that she couldn't stay there much longer. But she couldn't leave Lisa. She glanced at Mike, who was now listening with a kind of awe mixed with horror. 'I started yelling Lisa's name. The mist filled my mouth, rushed down my throat, filling me up with all these feelings. It was like all those grey figures were dumping their emotions *into* me. Huge waves of stuff, sadness, hatred, regret – and…and worse things that I never want to think about again. I could taste it in my mouth. God…it tasted so foul, I almost threw up. I panicked and was about to run, when Lisa suddenly fully conscious saw me. She started struggling to get one arm free, so she could reach out to me. And I got my second wind – you know, like at school sports day? When you're running the hundred and fifty metres and you think you can't run any faster, but the girl you hate most in class is about to streak past you and somehow you find the extra energy to move your legs and you nail the bitch, right at the finishing line.'

Mike raised an eyebrow. 'I have no knowledge of such matters. But please go on.'

'So then… I just went mad and began fighting to get close to Lisa. The others grabbed at us, trying to drag us back. But I shoved them aside. I…I hit out at them. Punched and kicked them. It was like slamming memory foam. I couldn't get anywhere near Lisa. Then…our fingertips touched. There was this flash of light. So bright, that I couldn't see for a moment. The whole place, all the grey figures, started melting, dissolving. I felt like my body was being shaken – as if a dog was holding me in its teeth, tossing its head. Shaking, shaking me, so hard that I thought I was going to break apart. I think I screamed. And then, somehow, I was back inside my body, standing looking down at the bed. Lisa lay there, as if she hadn't moved. But the bruising and swelling from the accident had completely gone. She was asleep, peaceful, and I knew she wasn't going to die. I…I had brought her back.' Jess looked across at Mike.

He was staring at her in shock. And something else. Something she had not expected to see. It looked like…fear?

'You went in search of a mortal's damaged life-force and called it into full vitality? That is deep magic. Forbidden to all but a few. And beyond most. You should not have been able to do this, Jess.'

'No shit, Sherlock? That's not exactly helpful,' Jess murmured, unable to hide her disappointment. Is that all he had to say? She bit back a grimace of irritation as she felt more of the sticky stuff running down her back. Some of it had dried, leaving her skin feeling tight and uncomfortable. She felt too ashamed to mention this to Mike. It was too intimate, too disgusting.

'Sherlock?'

'Forget it. This whole thing's freaked me out. It's not every day you get to give your dying friend a second chance at a life.'

Mike raised his eyebrows. 'Why are you not delighted by what you achieved? You were fond of Lisa, were you not? Without your intervention she would be lost to this world. She and her family are greatly in your debt.'

'Yeah? I don't think they'd see it that way. I'm not expecting Zac Simpson to become my number one fan any time soon! Look. I'm sorry for being a pain. I always get like that when I'm angry or scared. I just don't get why all this stuff's happening to me. I didn't ask for any of it.'

Mike looked thoughtful, but still oddly wary. He handed her some tea. 'Drink it. It will help,' he said.

He was right. Jess felt herself becoming calmer as she raised the jam jar and sipped the herbal brew. Sage this time and something flowery, with another flavour she couldn't identify. The warmth of the glass against her hands was comforting, but the sanctuary she had sought here seemed spiked with yet more uncertainty. What was wrong with Mike?

His robin-bright eyes gleamed above his beard as he drank his tea. His matted dreadlocks hung down over the scarf muffled around his neck, and his filthy army greatcoat brushed the floor as he hunched on his improvised seat. Jess still had a vivid mental image of how he had looked when he appeared at the open window of the high-rise flat where she was being kept prisoner. That rapid, jerky way he had moved; a creature glimpsed in the missing beats between the pulsing of a strobe light, the crackle of static around him, like an out-of-tune TV channel. As he bore her to safety, she'd had a close-up view of sharp, blade-like features, slanted silver eyes and large silvery wings.

It was mad, all of it. Her life had gone totally haywire. Mike shouldn't exist. What was he, a rogue guardian angel? Something from a Marvel comic or a nightmare? An impossible figure. Yet here she was, sitting talking to him. At this moment, he was the one constant in her shifting world. The only person she could rely on. He ought to have all the answers. His brooding look, his reaction to what he'd heard, told her he didn't. Unnerving.

She shook her head slowly. 'I don't think I understand anything.'

He frowned slightly. 'I am not sure that I do either.'

'But you know more than I do, don't you? Just give it to me straight, Mike. OK? What's going on with me?'

He looked at her closely, as if he was judging how much to tell her. Silence stretched between them. 'Very well,' he said at length. 'It is time you knew the truth. Sixteen or so years ago, at least, in mortal time. Someone whose friendship I value highly asked me to watch over you.'

'Why?'

'I did not ask her.'

'Why not?'

'My friend's reasons were her own. Besides, I needed no explanations. It was plain to me that you bore the mark of the fey.'

Jess stiffened. The mark of the what? Some kind of rare illness? That must be it. She was sick. Really sick. That thing that was going on with her back. A tumour or something. Oh, God. She was dying. 'How…how long have I got?'

'Sorry, I'm used to mortal speech, but my parlance might be confusing at certain times. I should have explained. Fey is the name we call ourselves. We are known by many others. Faeries, The Fair Folk, The Sidhe, The Old Ones, to name but a few.'

'You're telling me…you're a faery? A fey?' Relief warred with Jess's shock. She wasn't going to die. She felt her mouth twitching, the urge to laugh hysterically bubbling in her chest. A faery? It sounded so… whimsical. 'But aren't they little fluttery things that dress in flower petals and stuff and eat honey dew?'

'Some are,' he said seriously. 'But the host of fey is infinitely varied in form and size. Depending somewhat on where we dwell. Some wear glamour to live and walk amongst mortals undetected. As I am doing, presently.' He paused. 'And so are you, Jess.'

'Me?' *I'm wearing glamour.* 'Is that like a disguise?'

'In essence. Although there is much more to glamour.'

Jess shook her head, puzzled. 'Your long coat and dread-locks and stuff cover your true form. I get that. But I'm just...me. Boring Jess Morgan. Local no-hoper. What you see is what you get. Right? I don't need a disguise. You've got this all wrong.'

Mike made a steeple of his long fingers. They were slow to settle into shape and bent in an odd way. For the first time she noticed that he seemed to have extra joints. Although elegant, there was something horrific about his hands. And something oddly familiar.

'There is no mistake,' he said gently. 'The glamour you wear is the strongest and most cunningly woven I have ever seen. A powerful faery set it upon you. It was fashioned to last.'

Jess felt new panic. *Glamour. I'm wearing faery glamour.* The concept still wouldn't take root. She imagined it as some kind of invisible, flexible shell attached to her skin with the equivalent of magical super-glue. Did it even cover her eyes, like soft contacts? Snakes sloughed their clear eye coverings, along with their skins, didn't they? A repellent thought.

'As far as I know, I've never taken a bite from a poisoned apple or pricked my finger and collapsed! I think I should go!' As she jumped to her feet, the jam jar slipped from her fingers, the sound of breaking glass echoing in the underpass.

'Wait!' Quicker than blinking, Mike's hand shot out and gripped her arm. 'You must listen to me!'

Her breath left her in a long sigh. She sank slowly down onto the cardboard box. All her life, she had faced challenges head-on. Hit out first, before you were attacked. Don't get close to people; they always let you down. It was the only way she knew how to act. She needed facts. Something to fasten on to so she could begin to deal with it. 'I'm listening.'

'You think you are mortal, Jess. But you are not. You are one of us. A faery.'

She was suddenly finding it hard to breathe.

'Do you know what a changeling is?' he continued ignoring her distress. 'Sometimes *stock* – made of wood or wicker and enchanted to look like a mortal babe – is left in a cot and the living babe killed or taken into Faery for a pet or for…other reasons.'

For other reasons? Again she sensed that he was censoring his words, but she let it pass for the moment. *Because he was wrong, wasn't he? He had to be. She'd had human parents. Alice and Rob Morgan. And a twin baby sister, Stella, who had died in her cot.* 'Go on,' she said, her mouth dry.

'Very rarely, an actual fey child may be left behind. It was a common occurrence in the old days, when the veil between the mortal world and Faery was thinner. But such exchanges almost never happen any more. One reason being, that specific intervention is required for us to survive in these drear lands of once-apes who have shaped the world for their use and pleasure. The mortal world becomes ever more complex, with concrete, metal and glass structures covering the earth.'

Us? Jess didn't like the inclusive term. 'Intervention?' she echoed. She had a bad feeling about where this was going. 'Like spells or magic?'

Mike nodded. 'In essence. Although 'spell' is not a term we use. Fey do not *use* magic. We *are* magic. Glamour is inherent within us all, to a greater or lesser extent, and can be manipulated in many ways. In the mortal world, glamour is used like a cloak for concealment and protection. Many things here act upon us like poisons. Iron burns our flesh and sickens us. Chemicals in the air, water and food eat away at our vitality.' He glanced towards the entrance to the underpass, where the sound of morning traffic was increasing. His voice deepened with a note of warning. 'Even with glamour, living mortal-wise is never a comfortable experience for us.'

How well she knew the feeling of burning lungs and the discomfort of scorched, metal-kissed flesh. She was scared now. Her reluctance to believe him was crumbling to nothing, like a skeleton leaf dissolving under a rime of frost.

'A glamour would have been put onto the faery babe, before exchanging it for the mortal babe. For, make no mistake, you are a true-changeling, Jess, fey-born and not formed of stock. As to why you, a faery babe, were secretly left for mortal parents to bring up in place of their own child – who can say?'

A shadow passed over his face. There were still things he wasn't telling her, but she'd have to let that go for now. There was enough to take on board. More than enough.

'This faery babe. The changeling. It's…it's…' She was cringing inwardly, still unable to actually say it aloud. *I'm a true changeling. One of the fey. Like Mike. That's why I'm able to do all this weird stuff.* Memories rose unbidden. The bright, semi-visible amorphous forms she had glimpsed hovering around the fruit and vegetable displays in supermarkets. Green leaves sprouting from the dead tree in the albino peacock's pen in the park. Leon. Lisa. Other stuff. If she was this thing… this fey-born, changeling, it would all make sense.

Where was this fey form lurking? Was it inside her, masked by the glamour placed upon her before the exchange, melded to blood and bone or did it overlay her human shape, like some kind of armoured suit of fey flesh? Did she even have a heart, lungs, normal internal workings? *Normal.* She bit back a hollow laugh. That was a word she could never again apply to herself.

'Jess?' Mike prompted gently. 'Do you understand now?'

She lifted her chin. *Hell no! I don't understand anything. But I'm trying to. I'm really trying.* She felt numb from information overload. But she had asked for the truth and got it, so she could hardly complain. 'I...I need to think.'

'That is only natural. You will have many more questions. I will answer them, if I can, and help you in any way within my power.' Mike inclined his head in a graceful bow like a courtier in some TV costume drama. Straightening up again, he removed his scarf and adjusted his grubby collar with the horribly elegant fingers of one hand.

A fresh jolt of recognition pierced her. *His hands are like mine. More extreme, but the design is the same.*

Another damp slithering movement beneath her vest demanded her attention. Sudden heat prickled Jess's skin as a new suspicion blossomed.

Here goes nothing.

'I've got something I need to show you.' She hung her head, couldn't meet Mike's eyes. 'It's...pretty gross. Try not to freak-out. OK?'

'You have my word,' Mike said softly.

Gritting her teeth, Jess turned her back on him. Quickly, before she could change her mind, she grasped the hem of her dress and dragged it up to lie in concertina folds across her shoulders. The vest was pulled up with it. As the cold air played across her bare back, she felt a sensation of gentle ripping; like after the only time she had lain in the sun, in an attempt to get a tan like the other kids, ending up having to peel away long, papery panels of reddened skin to reveal an unharmed pale layer below.

Something rose for a moment before flopping back to lie against her back like a cloak of warm, damp silk.

Mike laughed delightedly. 'You *really* need to renew your glamour. Before someone notices those wings! I can teach you how...'

The word hardly registered, seemed unreal. She closed her eyes briefly. Let the word sink in. *Wings.* Yes. Then it must be true. All of it. A thrill of horror swept through her. *I'm not human, at all. I'm a monster.*

CHAPTER 27

CALEB WOKE TO feel warmth on his upturned face. Sunshine was threading down through the branches of the tree he lay beneath, spreading a diffuse glow of greenish-gold over him. A strand of grass tickled his cheek. He could smell the clean, damp soil beneath him.

With a groan he turned over and lay huddled on his side. The whole of his face was tender and one side of his jaw was stiff and sore. There was a metallic taste in his mouth. He probed the side of his raw tongue experimentally and then hawked and spat clotted blood into the long grass, almost crying out as fresh agony lanced through his damaged nose.

It would serve Dad right if he did him for assault. The hateful bastard deserved it. Caleb cringed inwardly as he recalled Dad's crude language, when he accused him of secretly meeting some girl for casual sex. There was an element of truth in it, he thought, his skin prickling with shame as he recalled what had happened with Sharon. Best not dwell on what a total loser he'd been, falling for the first girl to show him any proper attention.

Mum. Mum was dead. The pain of it slammed into him with more force than Dad's fist had done. He rocked back and forth as tears scalded his throat. He wept for the way Mum had died and because it was so painful to lose her; he wept with fury and bitterness for what Dad was, and what he had just done, and he wept because he felt scared, helpless and adrift. Eventually, he stopped crying. His breath was still hitching spasmodically as he sat up, drew up his legs and encircled his knees with his arms. The throbbing in his nose and jaw was worse now, but he welcomed the pain as a distraction from grief.

Dad had pulled some mean stunts, but stealing his money, that was really low. The train fare and the cost of the bicycle he'd bought from the local recycling centre had eaten into the money Mrs Stark had paid him for the drawing. There was about half of it left in the envelope hidden beneath his mattress, but he'd had plans for that. Mrs Stark had promised to show him how to cut mounts and frame some of his drawings. If he could find a gallery owner who would take them, he would make a small profit. It wasn't a career, but it was a start. He could perhaps forgive Dad for the assault, accepted the grudging apology that, no doubt, would have been forthcoming after Dad weighed everything up and decided that it was necessary, if only to persuade him to carry on as usual. But taking the money made all the difference. He couldn't get past that.

There was still Mum's funeral to get through. But he wasn't going back. Sighing deeply, he stood and stretched his cramped limbs. He was aware of a sensation of emptiness, which seemed centred more in his head than his body. It made him feel oddly adrift. Through a gap in the bush, he could see the weathered red brick of Windroth hall in the near distance. It looked impressive in the early morning light, like an extension of Mrs Stark, ancient, worn and a bit shabby, but still proud and indomitable. Maybe he could let himself into the kitchen. Mrs Stark never bothered to lock the outside door. She would be working in her studio and was unlikely to come down, as he had visited only yesterday. He would get himself something to eat from her fridge, clean himself up.

Caleb shouldered the back pack which contained his faded

denim jacket, two drawing books, his tin of pencils, pens and other drawing tools, an empty plastic water bottle and a handful of crumpled paper napkins, taken from a café when he bought a takeaway coffee a few days ago. He wished he'd had the presence of mind to pack a few more things before rushing off in the heat of the moment. He shrugged. *No time for regrets. Deal with it.* His bike lay on its side in the long grass. It should be safe enough but, just in case, he dragged it towards a rose bush and pulled a few thorny branches to cover it.

He began walking through the meadow, veering off at an angle so that he approached the house from the side, just in case Mrs Stark happened to glance out of her studio window and spot him. He had almost reached a knee-high patch of some dense, ferny-leaved plant, when a sudden rapid move-ment from deep within the plant set the entire thing shaking and bobbing like a ship in a storm. A high-pitched sound rang out, curiously like a human scream. The leaves were thrust aside as something brightly coloured shot away and disap-peared into the long grass. Caleb glimpsed what looked like a jaunty little cap, stuck with an iridescent blue feather. *What?* He did a double take, grinning with amusement. It had obviously been a cock pheasant. Their colourful heads were topped by little feathery crests. They often dashed across his path, when he was cycling down the lane or through the woods.

He continued heading round to the back of the house. Small trees bordered the little-used path; their blurred outlines a fading ghost of once manicured shapes. There was a small orchard in front of an overgrown hedge. Hundreds of windfall apples dotted the grass, mostly brown and dented like bloated puffballs, but a few still hung from the branches. He reached up to the nearest tree, picked one and bit into it without thinking.

'Ah! Jee-sus! Shit!' Renewed pain stabbed along his jaw as he bit down on the hard flesh of the fruit.

He dropped the apple and kicked it viciously against the nearest tree, feeling a bleak satisfaction when it shattered into pieces. The pain had subsided to a dull throbbing by the time he reached the kitchen door. It was unlocked, as he'd hoped. All was quiet as he slipped inside. It smelt faintly of lemon-scented, cleaning fluid with which he'd hurriedly wiped the sink the previous day. A mug with a slice of lemon and a centimetre of cold cloudy water in it, stood beside the sink. He smiled, glad that Mrs Stark had remembered his instructions to make a drink to ease her cold. Movement sounded from the studio overhead. Good. Mrs Stark was up there working.

He caught a glance of his face in the cracked and grease-spotted mirror hung on a nail above the sink. He looked like the loser in a bare-knuckle cage fight. *You should see the other bloke! OK. Maybe not.* One eye was puffy and bloodshot. The bridge of his nose and one side of his jaw were bruised and swollen, giving him a lop-sided appearance. But it was the dried blood that made it worse. It streaked his nose and chin; while a great smear from where his nose must have started bleeding again as he slept was plastered across one cheek and caked around his ear. Gritting his teeth, he sluiced his face with cold water, gently patting it dry with kitchen roll. His reflection showed a marked improvement.

After re-filling the sink with clean water, he stripped off his T-shirt and attacked the bloodstains with cold water and an ancient bar of soap, so cracked and dried out it looked more like a slab of greyish stone. 'Cold water for blood stains. Hot water just bakes them into the fabric.' Mum's practical voice rang in his head. Bless her. She ought to have left Dad years ago. Mum had stayed for his sake, he knew that, and, even though he also knew it was irrational, he couldn't help feeling some responsibility for that.

Caleb made a sound of irritation as he squeezed water from the T-shirt. Despite the care he'd taken to wash only the blood-stained area, he'd somehow managed to soak the entire front. It was going to take ages to dry. He was so absorbed, that it was a moment before he caught a small movement from the corner of his eye. He turned round to see a slight black-clad figure standing near the kitchen table.

'Mrs Stark!' *How long had she been standing there?*

'I hope you are not planning to put that wet garment back on,' she said, without preamble.

'It's no problem. Really…' Caleb stood facing her. He tensed, expecting her to ask him about his injuries. Weariness ran through him just at the thought of having to talk about it. Her sharp eyes flickered over his bruised and swollen face, but she gave no reaction beyond a slight tightening of her mouth. Caleb felt relief, followed swiftly by the sudden realisation that he was naked from the waist up. Cheeks burning, he held the wet T-shirt up to cover himself. 'Sorry. I…I shouldn't have come. I'll get going…'

'You will not. Wait there,' she ordered. 'Do not move, until I come back.'

'OK.' He nodded, too dispirited to argue. Besides, it wasn't like he had anywhere to rush off to.

He watched Mrs Stark pad out of the kitchen, her battered old trainers making hardly any sound. She left the door into the house open, giving him a partial view of the large entrance hall; the side of a dark cabinet and a sweep of ornately carved stair rail. He heard the creak of the wooden treads as she ascended and then came the faint sounds of doors opening and closing somewhere on the upper floor. Minutes ticked by, while Caleb stood there waiting. What the heck could she be doing up there?

The sun had gone behind a cloud and without its warmth the gloomy kitchen was cooling rapidly. He shivered. How long could he reasonably wait, before ignoring the rule about never venturing into the main body of the house and dashing upstairs to check she was all right? He heard the creak of wood again. Mrs Stark reappeared a few moments later. To Caleb's surprise, her arms were full of men's clothes.

'Here. Take these,' she said. 'You look about my late husband's size. Ralph was tall and wiry too.'

Caleb laid the clothes on the table. Somehow, he had never considered whether she had been married. Of course, Mrs Stark must have family and relatives, everyone did. But she never spoke of them and, as far as he knew, he was the only person who ever visited her.

'Will they do? The clothes?' she asked.

'Um…yeah. Think so.' Caleb began sorting through them. There were two white dress shirts, with pleated front panels and long shirt tails. They had real pearl buttons and no collars at the round necks. The linen was a little yellowed, but of excellent quality, and with deep creases as if the shirts had just been taken from their packets. There was also a dark-grey, pin-striped waistcoat, single-breasted and with tab pockets, and a V-necked knitted pullover, with a label that read 'Cashmere'. It was sleeveless and banded with stripes of muted greys, blues and purples. The pair of obviously brand new, black tailored trousers, had a monogrammed leather belt. He knew quality when he saw it. Every one of the garments shouted money.

'This stuff's much too good. I can't take it.'

'Nonsense. Of course you can. 'There are stacks of Ralph's clothes in his old dressing room. Much of it is still in its original packaging. I never got around to clearing out his things.' She gave a faint smile. 'He was considered quite a sharp dresser, in his day. Ralph had his own tailor who used to come to the house.'

'I'm sorry. About your husband dying, I mean,' Caleb said.

'Oh, he's been gone a long time,' she said coolly.

'Did you have any children?'

'One. A girl. Joan. Ralph would have liked more…' she tailed off. 'Well. That's enough about that. I am not one to visit the past more than is necessary.' She gave him a long look. 'I hope you are not going to bombard me with tedious questions about my family affairs.'

'Course not. Whatever you say.'

'Good. Then we understand each other. The clothes are yours if you want them.' Her eyes in their deeply wrinkled pouches gleamed with a sudden flash of humour. 'Unless, that is, you're too fussy or too proud to wear them.'

Caleb shook his head. 'I'm neither. Can't afford to be.' *It wasn't as if poor old Ralph had actually died wearing the stuff, was it?*

She looked pleased. 'What size shoes do you wear?' He told her and she nodded. 'Slightly smaller than Ralph. There are some brand new boots upstairs. They should fit if you pad them out with thick socks.'

'No really. I couldn't…' Caleb began to object. He was grateful for her generosity, but she had given him enough, especially as he had no way of repaying her.

Mrs Stark held up one arthritic finger to forestall him. 'I am glad the clothes will be put to good use. Who else would want them, after all?' As usual, her tone brooked no argument. 'Now, get dressed before you catch your death. I shall make tea.' Lifting the electric kettle from its cradle, she moved towards the sink.

Caleb hastily scooted aside to allow her access. While she

had her back turned and was filling the kettle, he pulled one of the shirts over his head and thrust the long shirt tails into his jeans. The expensive linen felt cool and soft against his bare skin. The shirt had deep floppy cuffs, of the sort meant to be folded in two and secured with cuff-links. He had never owned a pair in his life. Quickly, before Mrs Stark noticed and felt obliged to go and ferret through her late husband's dressing table for some embarrassingly expensive cuff links, he folded up the sleeves until they rested just below his elbows. He still felt chilled to the bone, so he pulled the pullover on over the shirt and added the waistcoat too. He rolled up the smart black trousers and belt, deciding to keep them for another time. His jeans were fine for now. Looking down at himself in amusement, he decided that he looked like a reject from the nineteen seventies. All he needed was a tight perm and stacked heels.

Mrs Stark finished pouring water onto tea bags in a china tea pot. She looked up from stirring the tea with a silver spoon. 'The clothes suit you. You look rather raffish, with your dark hair. Very Heathcliff.'

'Wuthering Heights. We had to read Emily Bronte for English Lit. That book's too depressing for words. Never could see what all the fuss was about. The girls in the class really went for it, though.'

She chuckled then, the sound of it rusty, as if from lack of use. Her shoulders shook and her white hair, lying loose about the shoulders of her black dress, like a threadbare shawl, moved slightly. 'I expect they liked the idea of a dark, brooding hero. Most young women do, you know. Including myself, at one time.'

Caleb didn't know what to say. This was territory he definitely did not want to stray into. It was hard enough to imagine Mrs Stark ever being young, let alone fancying anyone.

She looked amused, as if she could read his thoughts. 'Well don't stand there like a goose. Sit down. Drink your tea.'

Gratefully, Caleb took a seat at the table. She moved around fetching milk and sugar, before sitting opposite him. Her scratchy, matter-of-fact way of dealing with things had been just what he had needed. Softness and kind words would have broken his resolve, had him choking back tears.

Mrs Stark poured the tea. 'Well. I think we have avoided the thorny subject of your damaged face for quite long enough.' She nodded towards the wet T-shirt, he had draped over the end of the table and which was dripping onto the stone floor. 'Soaked with blood, was it? What happened? And do not insult my intelligence by saying that you walked into a door.'

Caleb sighed, knowing he owed her the truth. She would accept nothing less. But he couldn't talk about Mum. Not yet. The pain was too raw. 'It was Dad,' he began, as Mrs Stark added milk to delicate, flowered-china cups. 'He accused me of sneaking off to meet a girl on my afternoons off. I told him it was total crap. But it made no difference. God, he was vile! So crude. But glad to have caught me out, actually pleased that I'd acted like a man for once. As if I'd *ever* want to be *anything* like him. And ...and he had this sly look, as if he knew something, but wasn't about to let me in on the secret.' Caleb swallowed hard.

'Go on,' she prompted, after a moment.

Caleb pressed his thumb against a small chip on the cup's delicate rim. His hand was trembling so much that he didn't trust himself to pick it up. 'He'd found the money I'd hidden under the mattress and accused me of stealing stuff from the shop. Selling it, or dealing drugs. That's what Dad thinks of me. I'm a thief and a waster.'

Mrs Stark's lined face was impassive. 'Did you tell him, that I paid you for the drawing?'

'Yeah, I did. But my scribbles, as he calls them, are a waste of time, aren't they?' Caleb said bitterly. 'Who's going to buy one?'

'The man is a complete idiot!' She shook her head slowly, while drumming her fingers on the table. 'I suppose he refused to give the money back?'

Caleb nodded. 'I told him I'd earned it, fair and square and I wanted it back. But he stuffed it in his pocket. I…I suppose I lost it for a second. I went for him. We sort of grappled. That's when he…he punched me.' Caleb's throat burned. He felt a muscle tighten in his cheek. 'I managed to dash outside, grab my bike and take off. Dad came after me, but he was too late. Last time I saw him he was standing on the pavement, roaring after me. I'm finished with him. Finished with the bloody shop and everything..'

'Are you sure?' Mrs Stark asked. 'Things are often said in the heat of the moment. Cruel, hurtful things. Your father will have calmed down by now. No doubt he's regretting his outburst. Perhaps if you were to go back, talk things over calmly?'

'No way! I'm never going back there. Dad can kiss my arse! Sorry,' he said.

'No matter. I have heard worse. I can see that you are adamant. What will you do? Is there a friend or relative you can stay with?'

'I'm working on it.' He didn't meet her gaze. '

'You are not a good liar, Caleb. I have the perfect solution. You must stay here.'

His jaw slackened and he bit back a stab of pain. 'Here? In the house? But I…'

'No, not in the house!' she broke in, sharply. 'I could not

abide having a great boy lumbering around, getting under my feet. Besides, I need solitude to work. I have an idea.' She rose stiffly, bracing herself on her arthritic hands with their ragged and permanently discoloured nails. 'Come with me.'

Puzzled, Caleb followed her outside, matching his steps to hers, as she made her way past the new vegetable patch he'd dug and down the path he had walked along earlier. At a break in the hedge beyond the small orchard, there was a stretch of red brick wall, so covered in ivy that Caleb had not noticed it earlier.

'There is a gate here.' Mrs Stark began pulling at some of the trailing strands.

Caleb stepped forward. 'Here. Let me.'

A few minutes of clearance work, revealed a wooden gate, which opened stiffly after he applied his shoulder to it and gave it a couple of hard shoves. Mrs Stark led the way into a walled rectangular garden, with brick paths and raised beds. Trained trees grew against the walls. There was a central bed, circular and with a sundial in the centre. As elsewhere in Windroth, weeds carpeted every centimetre of bare soil. In one corner, he could see a glasshouse, constructed of brick and cast iron; most of the panes were intact, although obscured by green mould. Through them, the vague shapes of flower pots, wooden trays, and garden paraphernalia showed like the ghosts of gardeners past.

'The old kitchen garden,' Mrs Stark informed him. 'A team of gardeners used to provide us with all the fruit and vegetables we needed.'

She moved on, heading towards an archway in one of the walls. Stepping through it, Caleb found himself in another roughly rectangular garden. Three sides were bordered by tall hedges. The fourth wall had open archways in the brickwork.

Through them could be seen a vista of gently sloping hills, and a forested valley. Dominating this garden was a formal pond, its surface almost entirely covered with leathery, green leaves, amongst which the buds of white water lilies showed like candle flames. A lichen-spotted, stone fountain, in the form of three water nymphs reared up at one end. Caleb guessed that it hadn't been in use for many years.

'Well. Here we are. What do you think?' Mrs Stark gestured to the far end of the pond.

Caleb had not noticed the small building which merged into the mixed green background. As he studied it, it resolved into a dilapidated little house, with shuttered windows on either side of a panelled front door. Its paint was so sun-bleached that only faint traces of its original bright-green remained in the angles of window frames and door panels. It had a pitched roof, trimmed with ornate wooden carving. A veranda complete with carved handrail and pillars, jutted out over the pond.

He was totally charmed. 'It's a summer house!'

'It has not been used in a very long time and will need some work before it is habitable. But you are welcome to stay here for as long as you wish.'

Caleb was undaunted by the idea of fixing the place up. He had a somewhere to stay. 'This is *so* brilliant of you, Mrs Stark. I'll think of a way to repay you.'

'That is not necessary.' She seemed amused by his enthusiasm. 'There is no electricity, but you will find a wood-burning stove and candles inside. There is a water tap at the rear. Feel free to use my kitchen, and the old washhouse next to it. And help yourself to food.'

'You've saved my life. But I'm not a sponger. Maybe I could do jobs around the place to earn my keep.'

'We'll talk more about that...' Mrs Stark paused, a spasm

crossing her face. Caleb thought he saw panic in her flickering glance back towards the house. Her head was poised, as if she was listening to something.

'What is it?'

She shook her head. 'I…I've been too long. I must return to work. Can you sort yourself out? The summer house is unlocked. You ought to be fairly safe from them here…' she said distractedly.

Safe? From whom? Was she worried that Dad would come out here looking for him? If so, why had she spoken in the plural? It must have been a mistake. He noticed that beads of sweat had broken out on her lined forehead. She turned without another word and began hurrying down the side of the pond towards the brick archway.

Caleb stared after Mrs Stark. She was flaky at the best of times. Perhaps due to having lived alone for so long. He was worried that she was unwell, but she was moving quickly enough. As she disappeared into the old kitchen garden, he shrugged. There was work to do here. He might as well get started.

His heart lightened, as he turned and went towards the wooden steps leading up to the summer house's veranda.

CHAPTER 28

JESS UNCURLED HERSELF slowly and threw off the blanket, before crawling out from the tunnel of the cardboard shelter. It had been surprisingly warm and comfortable on Mike's bed of moss and heaped twigs. She stood shivering slightly in the chilly dim light of the underpass.

A thin, cross-legged figure, little more than a darker smudge in the gloom, sat with its back hunched against the curved brickwork. Mike was as motionless as a statue. He had been keeping watch over her.

His face was in shadow. As he turned to look at her, a flash of silver glinted from the region of his unseen eyes. 'You are awake. Did you rest well?'

'Yeah. Though I didn't think I would.' Jess was still reeling from all that had happened over the past few hours. Despite her exhaustion after the wakeful night roaming the streets and playground, she'd felt certain that she'd never be able to unwind enough to sleep. But the moment she rolled herself in the blanket, she had known nothing, until now. She glanced towards the vaulted entrance to the underpass and was shocked to see the glimmer of the first stars in a grey-purple sky. 'It's almost evening again! I've been asleep for the whole day. Why didn't you wake me?'

'You did not ask me to,' Mike said simply. 'Added to which it was obvious that you needed a place of shelter for a few hours. I decided that you were safer here, with me.'

'You decided?' Jess flared at him. She was used to making all the decisions, both for herself and Mum. Trusting anyone else was a big issue with her. Realising that she was being unnecessarily rude, she softened and gave Mike an apologetic grin. 'I didn't fancy going back to the hospital's relatives' room, anyway. Not with the chance of bumping into Zac or his parents.' She had a sudden thought. 'What if Mum's been discharged? I have to go.'

'She is still in hospital. I made certain of it.' Mike unfolded his long figure and rose to his feet. 'Well then. Come. We have much work to do.'

'Work?' As Jess swivelled slightly to look at him, she felt an upwards swooping movement. Her dress immediately shot into folds at the back and tightened across her front, leaving her midriff bare. Warm, vaguely flower-scented air fanned either side of her face as her wings vibrated gently. Oh, God. Her wings. She had been hoping that she had dreamt that part of her last conversation with Mike.

'Your wings are very beautiful, Jess,' Mike said reverently. 'Such luminous colours. Fair are they, indeed. Even amongst the winged Fey.'

'Don't touch them!' she snapped, feeling an unexpected burst of protectiveness.

Mike frowned. He spread his hands. 'I would not so presume. It would be the greatest discourtesy. Only a lover would caress another's wings. It is considered to be a most intimate act.'

Jess felt the heat rush into her face. *An intimate act? She didn't even want to go there. The details of faery sex were way too shocking to even imagine.* A thrill of renewed horror pierced her. She could feel the new sensation at her upper back - it couldn't really be called a weight. Her wings. What was she supposed to do with the stupid things? Did they even work? They seemed to have a life of their own. She tried to jerk her clothes down to cover them, but since they had sprung free and begun flexing, they seemed bulkier and unwilling to fold up small again. It was like grappling with an umbrella that wouldn't close. She battled to squash them down, only to find that half their flimsy length drooped over the backside of her leggings. Reaching behind her, she felt their trailing edges sticking out foolishly below the hem of her dress, like a little kid's fancy dress skirt.

Mike said nothing. He looked away politely, but not before she had noticed his expression. What was he keeping to himself? It wasn't the first time she had seen that look on his face.

She grunted with bad temper, still trying to tuck the wings into the back of her leggings. It was a moment before she realised that sensations were building beneath her fingers. The fabric of the wings had grown warm and the raised veins in their surface seemed ultra-sensitive. Feelings she could not describe were beginning to spread outwards, flowing down her backbone. Suddenly, a tiny explosion of pleasure rippled through her lower body. She bit back a gasp and jerked her hands away.

Her cheeks burning, Jess folded her arms. The wings were an extension of her body, with a blood supply, nerves, everything. She could no longer shy away from the truth. The wings – *her wings* - were a part of her, in the same way as her arms, legs and inner workings. Time to shelve the panic. Get a grip and get on with it.

I'm a faery changeling. An actual real *one – not one made of sticks.* Whatever that meant, in all its strangeness and complexity, she must now begin to discover. Either that or she'd go totally mad.

Scowling, she pirouetted to present Mike with a view of her back. 'So, what do I do now? I can't walk about like this!'

'That is true,' he agreed, solemnly, a grin stealing across his face. 'You must restore your glamour.'

'Oh, is that all?' she grunted, with heavy sarcasm. 'Are you going to stand there then, grinning at me like an idiot or tell me how I friggin' do that?'

He laughed outright. 'Graceless creature! Well, then. To begin. You must know your true form before you seek to re-shape it and bind it to your will.'

'You mean…?'

'Yes. Remove the old glamour.'

'But how?' She felt a prickle of trepidation. Mike had said her glamour was very strong, very powerful. She had worn it, like armour, almost her whole life.

'I'm…I'm not sure if I'm ready for that.'

'Be not afraid, Jess. You are safe here. And I am here to aid you.'

She chewed at her lip. 'I'm still bricking it. But I don't seem to have any choice. So - how do I do it?'

'There are many ways. Looking at your reflection in water, through a rock with a natural hole. Rubbing your body all over with a handful of four-leaved clover. Bathing in the dew under a full moon. To name but a few. In your case, I would favour drinking a tea of rowan berries.'

She had expected him to at least suggest that she scrub herself all over with the skin of a warty newt and suck the juice out of a spider, or something equally disgusting. She had no idea what rowan berries looked like.

'Do you have some?' she asked.

'I collected some last autumn from a tree on the allot-ments.'

He snapped his fingers, conjured a small bluish flame that danced on his palm, and made a small fire. In a short time, he had set a cleaned soup-can of water to boil. Extracting a twist of paper from his greatcoat pocket, he tipped some wrinkled dark-red berries into his palm and added them to the can.

He swirled the brew, before tipping the reddish-amber liquid into a jam jar. Her fingers trembled against the glass as he handed it to her. She blew on the hot liquid, hesitating before raising it to her lips.

'What will happen? Will…will it hurt?'

'In truth, I do not know,' he said. 'I know only how this might be done. I have never witnessed it. I told you that changelings are rare in these times, remember? And one such as you…'

'Great. Looks like it's the blind, leading the blind. Here goes.'

She threw back her head and swallowed the rowan tea in two gulps before she could change her mind. It tasted of nothing much, just faintly musty. Nothing happened. Maybe Mike was mistaken and what was needed was the equivalent of a faery mallet and chisel or something more hard-core. Like some heavy-duty power tools.

No, wait. Something was happening. A faint tingling all over followed by a feeling of energy swirling around her. The swirling intensified, spiralling outwards. Thousands, millions of microscopic points of light, like shards of ice glinting in moonlight. Like standing inside a child's snow dome. Suddenly, a silent explosion of light burst into the underpass. Total white-out, blotting everything in its glare. Then just as suddenly, the gloom of early twilight was re-established.

A moment of stillness, as if time was held in suspension.

Mike was standing a few paces away, watching her closely. Waiting. His expression gave nothing away.

She swayed gently, taking stock. Everything around her was the same. The dim and grimy underpass with its litter blown in by the wind. The dirty raindrops that dripped from a crack in the roof and plinked into a spreading puddle. The familiar stink of stale piss, dust, traffic fumes and iron.

Then a swift change.

Before her eyes, colours danced with a life of their own. The grubby concrete vault shimmered with many-hued creams, browns and specks of glittering minerals. The shadows were velvety, darkly glittering, as if sewn with subtle jewels. A crumpled crisp packet looked as rich and textured as embroidery. Jess coughed to clear her throat as she breathed in deeply of newly unfiltered smells. The reek of iron was uppermost, its cruel bite almost making her retch, but she was aware of many other faintly chemical smells. Levels of smells, layers of them. The smoke of a bonfire somewhere on the allotments, green things growing, dank brown earth, water coursing through pipes deep underground.

Sounds too were magnified. The rumble of traffic was like thunder, but beneath that she could hear the dusty drift of leaves scudding along pavements, insects toiling inside bark and amongst roots. A sensory cacophony threatening to overwhelm her. She clapped her hands to her ears and discovered that they now ended in points. She took a step back, lowered a hand to brush it against Mike's familiar cardboard house. Steadier now, she glanced towards the half-circle of sky beyond the underpass. And cried out at the flaming glory of stars crowding the sky in infinite layers. Seen through her new eyes everything was more beautiful and more terrible than she could ever have imagined.

Mike's mouth was moving. A sound, like the high-pitched cry of a bird, pierced her ears. Jess cried out. Frowning in consternation, as he made another screeching noise. She could feel herself making some kind of inner adjustment. The bird sounds were still fast, running together, but they gradually decreased to a bearable level. Now she was able to pick out the individual words from the babble.

'Are...you...all right?' he was asking her.

Mike grasped her arms lifting her easily as if she weighed nothing. The tips of her toes brushed the ground. He shook her gently. 'Listen to me! Unprotected, we become a conduit for every sensory impression. Do you understand? It is startling, at first, to slough the glamour which shields us when living mortalwise.'

As he set her back on her feet, Jess angled her head to look at him. 'Startling? Do you realise how inadequate that word is? This is... totally mental! It's like being part of an on-screen movie with, total kick-arse CGI and *I'm* one of the special effects! What am I? Na'vi, with wings?'

She had lost him, again. It was becoming a frequent occurrence.

'Your fey form possesses its own wisdom,' he said patiently. 'Trust it, Jess. It will make the necessary adjustments for you.'

'Are you telling me... I should try to relax?'

'Indeed. It may help to close your eyes.'

Jess did so. With her eyes shut, she could ignore the jewelled splendour of her surroundings. She forced herself to take deep breaths without thinking what they tasted like. And fought the urge to picture how she looked; how monstrous. Gradually, she was aware of a change happening within her. It felt like a kind of *lessening*, but without any true sense of loss. She felt everything just as keenly, was still bound by the intensity of the impressions flooding her senses, but gradually, they ceased to terrify and overwhelm her. It was as if everything had taken root within her and some essential part of her had somehow expanded to encompass it.

She opened her eyes. It was still all there, waiting. The new reality of beauty. 'I feel…totally different. Like, I'm at ease with…this.' She smiled bleakly because she knew that her physical adjustment from human to fey was just the beginning. 'Mike. I need to see what I…how I…'

He was ahead of her and already ducking into his cardboard shelter. She heard him rummaging about inside it and when he emerged he was holding an object. An old hand mirror, the glass cracked and spotted.

'Traditionally, your first glimpse should be in the surface of a moonlit pool or a lake. But I imagine you would prefer not to wait.'

Jess snatched at the mirror's rusted metal handle and noticed her twig-like fingers, each with an extra joint, so that her hand curled slowly into a tight spiral, like a sideways view of a snail shell. Her nails gleamed as if she wore silver nail varnish, sparkling like a holograph.

Mike blew onto his palms, producing twin flames of cold, blue fire. 'You may wish to see yourself more clearly.'

'Neat trick that. Must save a fortune in candles…' Jess croaked. Her throat felt as dry as if she'd been licking stone.

She lifted the mirror, slowly. And saw that…

Always thin, she was now even thinner, as if pared to her essence. All of her exposed flesh was pale and softly glowing with rainbow-tinted glimmers, like a pearl. Her face was all sharp angles, pointed nose and chin and high cheek-bones. Her hair a wild nimbus of green strands, in shades from almost black to a silvery green, tumbled around her shoulders. The tall tips of her pointed ears stuck up through it. She tried to take in the strangeness of elongated, upturned eyes. She had no pupils or irises. The entire area between her lids was flooded by the palest jade green, which glinted like polished metal.

She would certainly stand out in a crowd. Trembling, she lowered the mirror and looked at Mike who was studying her in silence. There it was again. That carefully guarded expression.

'So what flavour of faery am I? Seeing as how you're the expert. Pixie? Elf? Something I've never heard of?'

'From your form and height you are solitary fey.'

'Solitary fey?'

'High ranking faeries. In appearance loosely like tall mortals. But there are exceptions.'

'Solitary fey. A faery alone?' She tried the words on her tongue, looking to Mike for confirmation. 'Is that what it means?'

'The host of fey are many. Some live in groups or are connected to trees or streams of water, like the oak women and dryads. Solitary fey have an individual existence. Some live alone, hunting in forests or wild places. Others glamour themselves and dwell mortalwise. The majority of them choose to swear allegiance to Gentry and do their bidding or live as subjects in their courts.'

'Gentry?'

'Our rulers. High-born fey. The ruling families are small in number and mostly related to each other. Only Gentry are permitted to form courts and bind other fey to their will. Gentry, both male and female, are long-lived. They are beautiful, proud and jealous of their lineage.'

'Rulers? As in kings and queens, with courtiers? Oh, per-lease! Don't tell me. You're ruled by Titania and Oberon!'

He looked puzzled. 'I know of no fey, so named,' he said

with perfect seriousness, a hint of annoyance creeping into his voice. 'But listen well. You mock Gentry at your peril! They can be fickle, autocratic and given to cruel whims. Murders, and worse, are committed out of sheer boredom. I advise you to avoid the courts completely, until you are more familiar with our ways. For in Faery, innocence is a delicacy to be torn piecemeal, shredded by sharp teeth and savoured like honey on the tongue!'

Something inward-looking in his eyes caught her attention. 'Why are you still looking at me like that? Is something wrong?'

'There is a certain density to your bodily structure, as if the imprint of mortality is still upon you. I am surprised it is visible, now that you are unglamoured.'

'Maybe the rowan tea didn't work properly?'

Mike shook his head. 'It worked. You are clearly fey, Jess. But you are also - somehow…other.'

'Other? What's that supposed to mean?' Why did he always speak in riddles? It was infuriating.

'I am not sure. You would pass amongst the fey host unnoticed. It is only because I am looking at you closely that I can see a certain difference about you.'

'Difference? How?'

'It is very… subtle. Nothing to be concerned about. Living mortalwise for your entire life may… have left an imprint on your essential being. Yes, that must be it. Forgive me, Jess. I can see that you are worried. I should not have voiced my thoughts.'

His halting explanation made no sense. He was concealing something.

'There will be time without measure for you to learn the ways of the fey. The night advances. What of your mortal parent? Alice Morgan is still sick and alone. She is in need of your help.'

Jess felt a stir of guilt. She needed to get back to the hospital, find out when her mum would be fit to travel. Get her to a place of safety, somewhere far away from Leon. Questions were tumbling through her mind. Who was her *real* mother? Did faeries give birth like humans? Why hadn't her faery mother wanted her? And, more troubling, of all, what had happened to Alice's baby – the human baby Jess, who *she* had replaced, like a cuckoo in a nest?

A flexing of the new muscles between her shoulders brought Jess up short. Lifting the mirror, she positioned it so as to examine her wings in profile. The delicate structures were overlaid with a pattern resembling fine silver lace. Their edges were not rounded like a butterfly's wings, but ended in fine, gauzy streamers, which wafted gently about as if floating underwater. Patches of pale green, blue and violet pulsed all over their surface, the colours varying in intensity to the movement of some unknown rhythm. *Her heartbeat? Her breathing?* She wondered again if the wings actually worked. They looked too flimsy for their purpose, but she wasn't going to test them out now. She had enough to deal with, without the complication of blundering about like a moth drunk on moonlight.

As she lowered the mirror, there was a movement at her waist. 'Oh!' She just managed to grab her leggings, before they slid down over her newly slender hips and pooled at her ankles. She felt a stir of very human irritation as she pulled them up, and then folded the waistband over a couple of times to keep them in place. Practical things needed attending to. For that she needed to be plain old Jess Morgan again.

'OK. I need a crash-course in how to use glamour. Will you teach me?

'You know how already. You have just forgotten. Hold in your mind, the image of that which you wish to happen. The more clearly you can picture it, the more convincing the glamour. Watch me.'

There was a slight disturbance in the air, like a heat haze. For the first time, since he had rescued her from the flat where Leon had imprisoned her, Mike appeared in his true form. Then he had seemed terrifying with his silver eyes, powerful wings and sharply-angled face. Now he seemed incredibly beautiful, his skin gleaming with a soft radiance. He turned towards her, over-long, thin limbs no longer moving in that alarming, staccato way.

Maybe because she was now fey, they inhabited the same time-zone, or dimension or whatever. It was a mind maze, she didn't begin to understand.

In a single smooth transition, he changed into a stag, which then shrank to become a rabbit and was suddenly a man with dreadlocks, dressed in a filthy greatcoat. A blink of an eye later and he again stood before her in his winged fey form.

Jess blinked, impressed. Even with her newly sharpened senses, she was unable to glimpse the precise moment when he changed. One moment he was one thing, and the next another.

'Now you try,' Mike said. 'Look into the mirror. Build the glamour. Fill your mind with the image of how you look when human.'

She attempted to picture every detail, watching her narrow sharp face and slanting jade-green eyes becoming overlaid, as if with a clear plastic face mask such as bank robbers some-times wore. Her human features seemed painted on it. The image wavered, dissolved. She began again, concentrating hard. And the same thing happened. She tried again and again, without success.

'Shit! I can't do this! The glamour feels…clunky and sticky. Why won't it work?'

'You are trying too hard. Do not force it. Let the glamour have its way.' Jess closed her eyes, let out her breath on a sigh. *Hold the image clear. Think of nothing else. Trust the change to happen.*

Better. This time, the overlay of human features was more convincing. Encouraged, she built on her success, until she was able to glamour herself into an image of Lisa, Zac and Leon. She couldn't resist growing dreads and allowing a filthy greatcoat to flow downwards from her shoulders.

Mike laughed, nodding approval. 'You learn quickly!'

By the time a bright crescent moon was rising in the sky outside the underpass, she was standing there with her wings tightly furled, glamour-cloaked as sixteen-year old Jess Morgan.

'How's that?'

He nodded, smiling. 'Very good, Jess. The glamour is strongly woven. No mortal will see through it.'

'What about faeries? Will they know what I am?'

'Most will not. You will appear to them to be mortal. A powerful Gentry might see through to your fey form. But by the time you meet one, if you ever do, you will be infinitely stronger and so will your glamour.'

'Cool! Then I can stay glamoured. Carry on being plain old Jess Morgan.'

'If that is what you so desire. But you are no longer mortal, in hiding. You are fey, living mortalwise. There is a world of difference in that.'

'I'm not sure what that means. But I guess I'll deal with that as best I can. I need to get Mum away from here.'

'Where will you go?'

'Somewhere called Windroth apparently. She mentioned it in the hospital. I've never heard of it, but it has one thing in its favour.

Something showed in his gaze, and then was gone. 'What is that?'

'It's a million miles away from here.' She laughed, grimly. 'I'll come back and see you before we leave. OK?'

Mike nodded.

He wore an unreadable expression, but she had no time to dwell on it. Her thoughts were all for her mum. Alice would need clean clothes, a warm coat, boots, washing things, food, money for train or bus fare. The list was endless. How was she going to get all that? A sudden idea came to her. She had new powers now, didn't she? Bending down, she scooped up a handful of dried leaves. Closing her fingers around them, she built a mental image. When she opened her hand, she was holding a fistful of notes. 'Cool!' Jess tucked the money into the folded waistband of her leggings 'How long does glamour last on…things?'

Mike laughed. 'Until the heat from your hand fades. Or until you move far enough away that your influence is weakened.'

'Long enough then!' Jess wheeled around and found herself at the vaulted exit in one swift movement. It was going to be a challenge to slow down and walk at her old speed, so as not to attract attention.

She looked over her shoulder to wave at Mike. 'Mike's not your real name, is it?'

He shook his head. 'To have possession of one's true name is to hold power over them. You may call me, Taryn.'

'Taryn. It suits you.' She smiled. 'Thank y…'

'No!' He held up a hand to stop her. 'Do not say it. When you thank a faery you give them a gift, which places them in your debt, binding them to you until that debt is paid. The laws of Faery dictate that any gift must be returned threefold. Having an angry faery bound to you, can be a very unpleasant! Be extremely careful who you thank from now on.'

Jess clicked her tongue. How was she ever going to get to grips with all this? There was so much she didn't know, so many pitfalls to tumble into. 'So, what *do* I say, to you?'

He grinned, eyes flashing silver. 'Say only that you are grateful.'

'I am grateful to you, Mike... Taryn,' she corrected.

He spread his arms wide, bowing gracefully. 'You are most welcome. Until we meet again, Lady Jess. Farewell.'

Lady Jess? It had a ring to it. 'Um...yeah. You too. Take care.' *That seemed safe enough.*

She emerged from the underpass, walking slowly and deliberately, measuring her stride. The night air was tainted with iron and complex chemicals, but beneath her newly restored glamour, shining and strong, she was better protected from the familiar burning discomfort. Sounds of traffic, the hubbub from the 24 hour garage, voices of a gang of kids up near the dual carriageway, all reached her clearly.

She wished she could have spoken to Lisa, told her about the unbelievable things that had happened during the past few hours. But that part of her life was over. She would miss Lisa, but at least her friend was safe.

In a few hours, she and Mum would be gone, never to return to the grubby flat on the run-down estate. A new life awaited them, maybe at some place called Windroth.

CHAPTER 29

CALEB WAS CHECKING out the old wash house, a large lean-to tacked onto the side of the kitchen. Its brick walls were coated with patchy whitewash that resembled scuffed suede. The only illumination came from a bare bulb, hanging from a length of old-fashioned twisted flex.

In one corner there was a tiny room, little more than a cubicle, with a toilet, washbasin and hot and cold running water, which would suit him fine as bathroom and laundry-room. He set to, ridding the place of trailing spiders' webs, mopping the flagstone floor with hot water and the bleach he'd brought with him, and wiping down surfaces and paintwork. He finished quickly. He was drying his hands, when he heard a faint cry. It seemed to have come from deep inside the house.

He found her in the hall, slumped on the bottom of the staircase, one shoulder resting against the wooden banister.

Her lined face was shiny with sweat. Colour stained both her cheeks. She was trembling.

'Looks like you're running a temperature. I'll call an ambulance. Where's your phone? Hall or sitting room?'

'Not…working.' Her voice was little more than a whisper. 'I'm not…ill. Just… annoying…cold.'

Caleb hesitated. No phone. And he didn't remember seeing any phone boxes on the way here. He would have to cycle to the village to get help. 'Who's your doctor? I'll call at the surgery, ask for someone to come out and see you.'

'No... doctor,' she gasped, her eyes glittering feverishly. She took a deep breath, tried to hide a wince. 'Need...rest. Upstairs. Help me...'

He was really worried now. Mrs Stark had never allowed him upstairs. She was near collapse. There was no way he could leave her alone. What should he do? There was no one to ask for help. It was up to him.

He tried to quell his panic, think clearly. 'All right. Let's get you up to your bedroom.' Caleb took her arm, feeling the soft, loose old flesh and the fragile bones beneath. Revulsion tempered by pity rose in him. 'Easy now. Lean on me.'

She tried to struggle to her feet, but her legs buckled. She sagged against him, her head lolling on her stringy neck. Caleb put one arm around her back, slipped the other beneath her bent legs and lifted her carefully.

She weighed very little. The smell of her washed over him, a mixture of dirty clothes, oil paint and dry skin. Something faintly chemical on her breath, he noted. Like acetone. *The smell from an open bottle of red nail polish on Sharon's messy bedside table.* Why was it that a smell could immediately transport you back to an instant in time? He felt a twinge of renewed humiliation at the thought of Sharon.

At the top of the staircase, a corridor led off at an angle. The first door they came to would be her studio. It was closed as usual, probably locked. There were a number of identical panelled wooden doors on either side of the corridor. 'Which one's your bedroom?'

'There.' Mrs Stark moved her head in a small gesture.

As the door opened, a close fusty smell hit him and he wrinkled his nose. It was a large pleasant room, overlooking the back of the house. Dust motes were dancing in the sunshine pouring into the room from the large bay window and pooling onto a richly patterned oriental rug covering the oak floorboards.

Bookcases dominated one wall. A table and two comfortable armchairs stood near the window. He glanced towards the large double bed with its carved wooden headboard. It was draped with some kind of velvet fringed bedspread, so thick with dust and cobwebs that its original colour could no longer be determined.

He had always suspected that Mrs Stark slept on the battered couch in her studio. He was about to lay her on the top of the bed but decided that it was a bad idea. All that dust would only weaken her already congested lungs. She was limp in his arms now, her breathing shallow. He knew that she needed to rest properly between clean sheets.

She stirred. He carried her over to the window and lowered her gently into the less dusty of the capacious armchairs. The seat cushion was dented and he supposed that she must occasionally come in here to read, if not sleep. Draped across the back of the chair was a woollen blanket. Caleb opened the windows wide and shook the blanket vigorously outside. The warm breeze blowing in was rich with the scents of falling leaves and dried grass.

He tucked the blanket around her. Swathed in its folds, she looked smaller than ever. She would be warm enough while he sorted out the bed. He went through into what appeared to be her dressing room. Layers of clothes littered the floor and hung out of an over-flowing laundry bin. Through another open door he glimpsed a small bathroom with built-in cupboards. On the shelves were pillowcases, and blankets. All neatly folded, wrapped in yellowing tissue paper and tied with faded blue ribbon. There was also a pile of long-sleeved, white cotton nightdresses. He gathered all the bed linen he needed. On his way out he picked up a nightdress on impulse.

To his relief she was awake and watching him from her nest of blankets.

'I found this. You'll feel more comfortable if you put it on. Do you need me to help you?'

Her eyebrows dipped in a brief flash of outrage. 'I do... not!' One thin hand emerged to snatch the nightdress.

It was a good sign that she was able to snap at him. He turned the mattress, plumped the pillows and began re-making the bed. Behind him, he heard the rustle of movement beneath the blanket as Mrs Stark changed into the nightdress. She seemed to take forever, but eventually she was covered from neck to ankles in clean white cotton. She had twisted her loose white hair into a single plait.

He helped her to climb into bed, asked whether she needed anything. She didn't reply, but lay there, overcome with weariness and a curious contentment. With her sunken face and hollow cheeks, she reminded him of his dying grand-mother, who has also looked as small as a child in her large bed. But unlike Gran, the old lady was awkward, stubborn and indomitable. And would fight her illness with every fibre of her being. Beneath the bed clothes her chest rose and fell.

Caleb was about to go downstairs, when he had a thought. Gathering armfuls of clothes from the dressing room, he dumped them in the corridor, ready to be relayed to the old wash house. Time to see whether that ancient washing machine still worked.

She slept for twelve hours solid, waking only briefly, to gulp the water Caleb brought her and to allow him to help her to the bathroom. He kept a close watch over her, now and then checking that she was still breathing, paranoid that she might take a turn for the worse if he left her alone. So he made himself comfortable in one of the armchairs and sat through the night, dozing to the accompaniment of her fevered murmuring. In the early hours, he woke cramped and cold, the blanket on the floor beside him. Mrs Stark was speaking, her voice, although weak and hesitant was light and carefree.

'Oh Mummy. Another party for the officers.... We have hardly enough to eat for ourselves. Yes, I know we all have to help the war effort... How can I not? Green canvas outside, as far as the eye can see. Men tramping about on the front lawns at all hours. Well I suppose if we are lucky one of them might bring us a tin of fruit or condensed milk.' She gave a girlish giggle. 'It isn't all bad. I was talking to that charming Captain Stark yesterday. Ralph is a lawyer in civvy street, you know. I might save a dance for him.... Hope the band will play some Glen Miller ...My favourite. In the Mood...'

In a shaft of moonlight he could see she was smiling. The shadows cast by the heavy carved headboard softened her sharp features and gave the impression that her pale oval face was surrounded by a thick mass of hair. Her wrinkles seemed smoothed out and the imprint of a startling faded beauty was overlaid on the fine bones.

For a moment the illusion was so marked that he felt a touch of fear. And then the moon slipped behind a cloud and in the grey half-light, Mrs Stark was once again a sick old woman, her deeply lined face drawn and sunken. Her head moved slightly from side to side, as if to a tune playing in her mind. It seemed to soothe her, for her breathing deepened and she slept again.

Touched and saddened by what he had seen and heard, Caleb went back to his chair. He was wide awake now and knew he wouldn't be able to get back to sleep. He switched on the reading light and noticed the small hardback book on the table. It was entitled, *Protection against Faeries*. The covers were stained and the pages spotted with brown marks, the edges crisped and slightly ragged. He laid it aside and went over to the bookshelves. The light here was dim, but he was surprised to see that almost every book was about faeries or related subjects. The titles on the spines of some were in bolder type. *A Dictionary of Faeries*, *English Folk Lore*, *Faeries in Tradition and Literature*, *British Faery Origins*. There must be hundreds of books. Mrs Stark must be a student of folk-lore.

He knew nothing about faeries, nor had he ever given them much thought. But he did know that it was going to be a long boring night, sitting alone and staring into the darkness. He went back to his chair, made himself comfortable and picked up *Protection against Faeries*. He began flipping through the pages.

Before long he was engrossed in tales of encounters between humans and faeries. There were tales of people stumbling across faery funerals, being led away by pixies, or spirited away to a watery death by water spirits, called kelpies. Others had been terrified in woods and forests by the wild hunt – fierce faery knights, streaking past on their sleek ruby-eyed mounts. Apparently there were things you could do to protect yourself against faeries. Strewing bread or salt across their path would bar their way, carrying something made of elder-wood would deter them. And turning clothes inside out could confuse them. There were other things that might work too, but here Caleb's interest began to wane. He turned the pages and began reading about faeries who took human lovers.

Sandwiched between the yellow pages he found an old piece of piece of paper cut out from a magazine. The Tatler 1947 it said in fine but faded writing:

A Delightful Summer Wedding. Mr Ralph Stark aged 23 and Miss Ivy Windroth aged 20 were married at the church of St Peter and St Paul in Windroth Village. The bride looked elegant in ecru satin. Her veil of hand-embroidered Brussels lace was held in place by a circlet of orange blossom. Her bouquet was a trailing teardrop of orange blossom, stephanotis and peach roses. The bridesmaids looked enchanting in peach satin gowns, with cream lace gloves, and held sprays of cream roses. The wedding breakfast was held at Windroth Hall. The happy couple are to honeymoon in Rome. On their return they will take up residence in Windroth Hall, in newly refurbished apartments with every modern convenience.

Caleb tried to picture the wedding but he couldn't. The *Tatler* was clearly a society magazine. She had kept the wedding notice, presumably proud to have been featured in it.

Suddenly she stirred moaning as if in in pain. Then he could make out what she said. Her voice was dark.

'We cannot have *another* baby. Not now. Darling Joan is safe. Born before it happened, before I made that promise, that terrible promise. ... A new baby will be in terrible danger...Oh, God. What to do. So tired... Day and night, the urge to paint consumes me...' Mrs Stark trailed off, her breath whistling in a long low note. 'Thank Heaven.' She sounded relieved. 'There is to be no baby. My body...taken care of things. Cannot risk becoming pregnant again. Danger to...any child born here...too great. Tired, so tired. No energy left in me for anything but painting. Must keep on. Nothing else matters. Thank God. Joan has got Ralph. He loves her. He must continue to be both mother and father to her...'

She drifted back to sleep. It was all so strange. Her becoming so obsessed with painting that she couldn't, or wouldn't, take care of her child, Joan. Although she seemed to care deeply for her. Something had happened after Joan was born. A new baby would be in danger. She had made some kind of promise...

*   *   *   *   *

He spent the next two days, while Mrs Stark's health gradually improved, making a number of drawings from memory of the mystery girl in the car park, who haunted his thoughts and dreams. But every one of the portraits was awful, leaden and lifeless. He became increasingly frustrated by his inability to translate onto the page the details of her pale, stricken face so vivid in his memory. How could this be? It was as if his pencils and ink washes deliberately conspired to smudge and blur her likeness so that it eluded him. He had never experienced anything like it. Had he lost his touch?

Panicked by the notion, he began frantically drawing anything *but* the girl; a bedroom chair, the view from the window, Mrs Stark herself, as she lay asleep. To his relief, these drawings were as successful and accomplished as his very best work.

If he lost his talent for drawing, he had nothing. His art was what defined him.

He took Mrs Stark mugs of hot water laced with honey and lemon, gave her aspirin he found in her bathroom cupboard and placed cool cloths on her burning forehead. She seemed content to lie in a half-doze. On the third day he decided to leave her for as long as it would take him to go to the village and do some shopping.

As he made his way down the stairs, he heard a sound from the studio, as if something was scratching at the wooden panelling on the inside of the door. A low angry sounding gibbering accompanied the sound. He moved closer. Was that buzzing? Perhaps wasps had found their way into the room. It was the time of year when they quit their nests. Something crunched beneath his feet. He bent down and threaded curious fingertips across the dusty carpet. Fine grains of some white powdery substance had been trodden in the pile. It looked like salt. Perhaps Mrs Stark had sprinkled carpet freshener there, but never got around to vacuuming it up. It would be just like her. Caleb stood up slowly, ears straining, but all was silent in the studio now.

The autumn breeze riffled Caleb's hair as he headed into the lane. There was a chill in the air, a smell like wood ash which heralded the first morning frosts. Drifts of fallen leaves scurried across his path as he cycled past hedgerows heavy with clusters of wine-coloured berries. Leggy toadstools, the colour of the strong tea Mrs Stark drank, poked from damp recesses beneath bushes and at the foot of trees.

Heading into the village he passed a small café, which had a bed & breakfast sign jutting out from above the door. The smell of fresh coffee drifted enticingly out of the open door and he slowed his steps. If he hadn't had to hurry back, he would have been tempted to go inside. A glance in the window revealed an old-fashioned wooden counter with a coffee machine and home-made cakes, arrayed beneath clear plastic domes. The day's specials were chalked on a blackboard. A few people were sitting at wooden tables with mismatched chairs.

There were two women sitting at the table nearest the door. The one facing him looked to be in her thirties. Her shoulders were hunched and her head drooped. Fragments of her conversation reached him. 'What's the hurry? We're safe enough here...'

'I don't get it. *You* wanted to come to Windroth village. Here we are. So what do we do now?' Her companion had her back to Caleb. The mass of her loose, dark hair spilled down the back of a red, figured-velvet jacket.

'It's not the village. It's a big house, near here,' the woman said, tucking a strand of lank hair behind one ear.

'OK. Let's find it then...' The voice was soft, persuasive.

There was something about that figure with its back to him. A suspicion arose in Caleb's mind. No. It couldn't be *her*. Could it? Coincidences like that, just didn't happen. Still, he found himself holding his breath, unable to move.

'We will. Soon...' The woman facing him sighed deeply. As she turned her head, Caleb saw her gaunt profile. Her skin was slack, with a yellowish tinge and there were deep creases around her mouth. She looked ill and strained. He felt another lesser jolt of recognition, although he was certain that he'd never seen her before.

'Look. What happened back there; it was a warning. OK? We have to take it seriously. You might not survive another bout like that.' The dark-haired woman's voice held concern, but also an edge of impatience. 'We have to get you some help. But for that, we need to be settled. Have a proper address...' Suddenly, as if she felt his gaze on her, she turned her head. And looked at Caleb.

It was her. The girl from the hospital car park.

She looked steadily at him, pinning him with fierce, slanting eyes, hazel-green beneath black brows screwed together into a frown. For a second he thought her eyes were lit with a pale-green flame, but it must have been a trick of the sunlight. Even so, her gaze was disconcertingly penetrating. And totally hostile. Of course, she must be angry that he had been eavesdropping. He blushed deep-red at being caught and spread his hands in apology to signify that he was harmless.

Didn't she recognise him? Obviously not. Why would she? Their eyes had met for only the briefest moment, before she had disappeared. And he'd already gained the impression that she was in deep shock at the time of that all too brief encounter.

He attempted a grin, but the girl's expression didn't change. Glowering at him, she half-rose from her seat and seemed about to march out of the café and give him a piece of her mind.

The older woman was reaching out now, grabbing her young companion's arm, urging her to sit down. *Yeah. Chill out, why don't you?* Caleb was already gripping the handlebars, wheeling past the café. The area between his shoulder-blades prickled faintly as if his body had distilled and then retained something tangible from the glare of those piercing green eyes.

He was deeply rattled by having seen the girl in the café. She was even more striking than when he'd first glimpsed her. This time, he'd had a sustained few seconds to absorb extra details of her pale angular face. Her looks were reminiscent of the chisel-featured women in the paintings of the pre-Raphaelite artists. She wore something black and layered beneath the sumptuous red jacket. Brown-leather boots, patterned in splashes of red and white, covered her rather long, narrow feet. She ought to have looked messy, but she somehow looked uniquely stylish. He couldn't tell her age. She could be anything from fifteen to eighteen years old.

What was he to do? He couldn't let her get away again. In his mind's eye he was already imagining capturing the planes and hollows of her face. Charcoal, with touches of white crayon for highlights. Harder black crayon for the line of her blade-like jaw, the swirl of her wild tangled hair. His fingers were itching to be at work.

By the time he'd bought cough medicine and a decongestant from the chemist, he'd plucked up courage to ask the girl if she would sit for him. What could she do, but refuse? But a quick glance through the café window revealed that the table where the two of them had been sitting was empty. Their conversation seemed to have implied that they might be saying there. 'We'll be safe enough here,' the dark haired one had said. He scribbled a note. *Hi. I'm Caleb Farmer. An artist. I'd really, really like to draw you. It was me looking in the window at you today. By the way, I'm not a perv or a stalker!* Shyly he spoke to a friendly middle aged woman behind the counter about the dark haired girl and woman who had been sitting near the door.

'That would be the Morgans. No problem. Leave it with me. I'll be seeing them later. They're staying here.'

His thoughts were full of the girl as he cycled back to Windroth. How would she respond to his note? Would she agree to sit for him or just tear it up? She was no pushover; that was clear. Should he arrange to meet her in the village or should he invite her to Windroth Hall?

Dumping the groceries on the kitchen table, he realised that he had left no contact details with the note. He could have kicked himself. *Shit. Shit. Shit.* Disappointment snagged him like a thorn, surprising him with its intensity.

He trudged upstairs to check on Mrs Stark. She was sitting propped up against the pillows. There were deep shadows beneath her eyes and her jutting cheekbones looked ready to break through her wrinkled skin, but the hands resting on the sheets were steady.

'How are you feeling?' he asked.

'Like a steam roller... has run over me.' Her voice was almost back to normal. 'But I shall be back...at work again before too long.'

'Never doubted it,' Caleb lied cheerfully. 'But you ought to take it easy for a while.'

A movement seemed to catch her eye. Sitting up straighter, she craned her neck and peered towards the window. 'Is that *washing* on the line?'

'It needed doing.'

'You are a remarkable... young man, Caleb. Resourceful, kind, practical. Rare qualities in...the youth of today, most of which seem passionately devoted to themselves.'

'What? You think everyone wearing a hoodie's a mugger?' he teased. 'You shouldn't believe everything you read in the papers.'

'Obviously.' Her lips twitched. 'Do you know, I think I could drink a... cup of tea. Perhaps some toast? And would you kindly...bring me a pen, some paper and an envelope? You will find them in a kitchen drawer.'

Caleb hid his surprise. Who could she be writing to? 'Coming right up, ma'am!' he said, performing a mock salute.

She gave a rusty laugh. 'Cheek!'

He was about to turn and leave the bedroom, when Mrs Stark turned to the side and began rearranging her pillows. Presented with a view of her sharp profile, a realisation struck him forcibly. That woman with the girl in the café – Mrs Morgan, he remembered - the one who had looked frail and ill and who he thought had seemed somehow familiar.

He knew now why that had been.

CHAPTER 30

JESS STOOD BESIDE the bed, looking down at her mum's sleeping figure. She hesitated, as she had done many times since they had left the hospital. Every time she thought of using glamour on her mum to make her well, her courage failed her. Turning leaves into money was easy as winking, but she lacked confidence in using her power for deeper, more important things.

She recognised now that she'd had latent abilities her entire life, but without the knowledge to direct them properly the results had been random, hit-and-miss. What had happened with Lisa had been a fluke. A lucky break. It could so easily have gone wrong. Time then, to take charge and gain control of her powers. And to stop feeling like a little kid, surrounded by unsteady towers built from plastic building blocks.

Thanks, in part, to Taryn, she knew the truth about herself. As horrifying as they were, the facts were bedding in; partly because she found herself unable to sustain the initial, dizzy-ing levels of shock and disbelief. You could get used to anything, if you had to, it seemed.

Taryn had intimated that there was a whole new world of glamour to bind to her will. It had to be worth trying to set her mum free from the addictions which had blighted her life for so many long years. But I'm still such a glamour rookie. What if something goes badly wrong? Jess felt a stir of irritation at herself. Stop being so feeble. Since when had she bucked a challenge? It was her own fear holding her back. She closed her eyes for a moment, took a deep calming breath. Gathering her courage, she reached for the folds of her glamour, drew it around her and immediately felt the thrum of power rioting through her body. Leaning over the bed she splayed her fingers, allowing the power to stream out of them until it effervesced into milky light that floated down to cover Alice like mist. So far, so good. Her mum was in a deep sleep, her mind and body in equilibrium. Jess could sense the subtle flickering energy body, like a finely woven net which was her mum's life force. She pressed deeper, exploring and touching the shimmering fabric with her mind. As her inner sight strengthened, everything expanded into sharp relief. The fabric of the energy body had texture, like a rich and complex tapestry. That tapestry was fretted with uneven dark patches, like parasitic growths on a sick plant.

Jess's mouth thinned with revulsion. She willed a small internal shift, distilling the glamour into a sunburst of sharp, cauterising points, each of which sought out one of the dark patches. For a moment, nothing happened. And then one of the tar-like masses began moving, sluggishly. Twisting into ropes of mucus, the dark matter rose upwards. A spasm passed over her mum's face. She gave a moan of pain and began thrashing about on the bed. As the dark matter seethed and writhed, waves flowed from Alice, her twisted feelings and suffering made tangible, the bitter stink of it washing over Jess, penetrating her lungs. It was all she could do to stand her ground against the onslaught of emotional fall-out. To her horror, she saw that the dark matter only dissolved to leave raw, seeping wounds on the subtle fabric beneath it.

Blood began trickling from the corners of Alice's closed

273

eyes and from her nostrils. Alice coughed and drops sprayed the pillowcase, poppy bright.

I'm killing her. Oh, God. How do I undo this? Forcing herself to remain calm, Jess withdrew her mind-touch, softening and reshaping the glamour into a wash of milky light. She watched trembling, as new masses spread like dark treacle over the open wounds on the complex tapestry of her mum's life force. Alice sighed, turned her face into the pillow and drifted back into a deep sleep. Bitter disappointment filled Jess as she withdrew the glamour.

She had failed. But she thought she understood why. Alice's addiction went so deep that it had become intimately welded to both her physical *and* essential being. She could not be healed by simply chopping out the patches like weeds; they were only a symptom of her deeper sickness. Alice must conquer the root causes of her addiction for complete healing, on all levels, to take place.

With a flick of her hand, Jess used a tiny thread of power to clear the blood from her mother's face and pillowcase.

'OK. I get it now.' She bent over and gently kissed her ravaged cheek. 'But I'll be here to help. You're not alone.'

It was still dark in the street, although the first seep of dawn was tinting the horizon. Although unobserved, she had clothed herself in a strong glamour to appear mortal. She probably had an hour or two before Alice woke up and missed her.

The street was empty, the village sleepy and silent. With no danger of being seen, Jess allowed herself to run full tilt, enjoying the rapid blur of movement, the slick passage through the air as she streaked towards the trees and fields on the outskirts. It was an enormous relief not to have to pretend that she was the same old Jess, the entirely *human* Jess. The strain of staying in the B&B was beginning to wear her down. There wasn't even a separate sitting room to relax in. For days now she and Alice had been either sitting in their cramped bedroom or the café or trailing endlessly around the small village.

'We really need to move on,' Jess had spoken into the darkness a few hours earlier, before her abortive attempt to heal her mum. She and Alice were lying in their twin beds in the tiny room. *Before the café owner discovers that the money I've paid her turns back into a handful of leaves.* Alice believed that the money came from the sale of items salvaged from their old flat, an unconvincing lie. It wouldn't be long before she questioned it. 'I know you're still exhausted from the journey down here,' she had said to her. 'But we have to find somewhere to live. You need medication, counselling, regular support meetings, like the doctor at the hospital said.'

'I'm just so tired. I don't think I can face any of it.'

'Not an option,' Jess insisted. How many false starts would there be before her mum faced up to the fact that her drinking was controlling her? 'Look what happened when you tried just quitting. You really scared me.' She gentled her voice. 'It's nice around here. Clean air, nice walks. If you've gone off this Windroth place, we could rent a bedsit.'

'How would we afford that? No, Jess. Windroth is our only option. It's time anyway…' Alice took a breath which seemed to cost her an effort. 'I'm just not quite ready.'

Jess felt a stir of tenderness, but she resisted the urge to give in, to agree to just stay on at the café until her mum felt stronger. That would be foolhardy. They were already on borrowed time. 'Two days, max. Then we're leaving here.'

Jess had lain in the dark, looking up at the ceiling and listening to the sound of her mother's breathing, before she gave up on sleep. What was it with Windroth? The morning's first light began stranding through the trees, hedgerows and fields, mimicking a Magic Lantern show she'd once seen in a museum of Victorian curiosities. Alice seemed fixated about the place, but the details were all a bit vague and perhaps shaped by an alcohol-fuelled imagination that muddled the facts and linked unrelated events. It wouldn't be the first time. Yet it made sense to go check out Windroth since they had come this far.

She passed the last house in the village and plunged into the countryside. Stopping at a gate, she looked out over the sepia-toned patchwork of fields, hedgerows and woods, as clear with her enhanced vision as if they had been lit by sodium street lights. She removed her boots and socks, thrusting them beneath a hedge, before she ran on. Her feet barely brushed the ground. She was enveloped by complex scents, flashes of jewel bright colours. There was no sound of traffic, just the myriad tiny noises of small animals and insects going about their business.

She stopped suddenly, aware of a subtle new presence. A deep grinding rumble and penetrating humming noise. She stood stock still, sensations seeming to vibrate through her bones, coming from above. Puzzled, she looked up, realising with a shiver of awe that she was hearing the sound of unseen, celestial bodies. The music of the spheres. Beneath her feet, the vital, embracing presence of the earth. Fearful joy swelled in her chest. She knew herself to be a speck in the living universe, insignificant, but at one and the same time, she was a universe in herself. And the world turned around her. Spreading her arms, she spun round in slow circles, bathed in the cold ancient light of the stars. *We are stardust. We are golden...* The Joni Mitchell song, a favourite of her mum's threaded through her mind. Corny, but annoyingly catchy, it seemed entirely appropriate.

After a few moments, Jess lowered her arms and stood still, trying to absorb the enormity of it all. Was this what Taryn meant when he had warned her that she would find life very different, now that she was fey living mortal-wise? She had a nagging feeling that he knew more about her origins, than he was letting on, but it was too late to ask him now. She had gone to the underpass to say goodbye to him and discovered his cardboard shelter already stamped flat, the area around it scattered with empty cans, broken glass and the used syringes of whoever had made a home there. Detecting the faint trail of his presence, like oil on water, she had tracked it to the allotments, where it had petered out amongst the grass.

Another friend lost. Was she cursed to lose everyone she allowed to get too close?

Jess climbed over a stile and padded through the dewy grass towards a small wood. The air filling her lungs was green-scented, only faintly spiked with iron and chemicals. Bracken clotted the ground beneath the canopy of birch trees. She walked through thigh-high ferns, her trailing fingertips brushing the coarse green fronds. At a place where the trees thinned out, brambles, heavy with fruit, formed sprawling impenetrable humps. Her belly rumbled. She couldn't remember when she had last eaten. Picking handfuls of juicy blackberries, she crammed them into her mouth. The most delicious things she had ever tasted. At the edge of the clearing she picked dangling clumps of purple-black elderberries, stripping the tiny berries from their reddish stalks with her teeth. She could hear trickling water and headed in that direction. Upon reaching a stream, she bent to scoop up handfuls of water, which slipped down her throat like liquid silk. As she straightened slowly, wiping the water from her chin, a movement caught her eye.

A hare. Leaping, out on an open field. Its brown coat blending with the long lines of stubble, which from this distance resembled textured embroidery. Once she would have needed binoculars to even see it, now she could clearly see the black and white patterns on the hare's long ears, the sleek body fretted with ginger-tipped hairs, long sinewy legs and large amber eyes. A beautiful animal. It was coming her way.

She stood in the shadow of the elder tree to watch its approach. There was a soft rustle as it entered the long grass. Moments later it broke cover. Jess smiled delightedly as it rose up onto hind legs and began washing its face with its front paws. She waited for it to come closer and drink from the stream.

Suddenly, the outline of the hare wavered, as if overlaid by a heat haze. It disappeared and in its place stood a small creature, about the size of an eight year old child.

Jess's hand flew to her mouth to stifle her cry of surprise. She caught the shape-changing creature's smell. It was something she had never encountered but at the same time seemed oddly familiar; warm fur mixed with wet leaves and newly dug earth, all spiced with a pleasant animal muskiness.

She gazed in fascination at the little being's reddish-brown skin. It had a broad face in which sharp black eyes glittered. Pointed ears stuck up through sparse strands of coarse hair, woven with plumed grasses and feathers. Its knee-length tunic was of patched leather, decorated with strings of small pebbles, and topped by a fur waistcoat. A leather bag was looped over one shoulder and there was a knife tucked into the belt at its waist. As the faery moved its head from side to side, bright eyes unblinking, Jess saw the twitching nostrils and parted lips, the blue-toned tongue partly extended. It was tasting the air. Seeking out subtle scents, like a cat. This, more than anything else, convinced Jess that the creature was no semi-tame town dweller. It was totally wild.

Excitement coiled inside her. Her first instinct was to call out to the faery. She hesitated. How should she approach the nervous creature, impress upon it that she meant it no harm? What was the accepted greeting? Taryn had given her a brief glimpse into the complexities of good manners amongst the fey, but everything he'd told her had totally fled her mind.

The faery seemed convinced that it was safe. It fell to its knees and began digging in the earth with the point of its knife. As it worked it hummed softly to itself, the sound as breathy as wind soughing through rushes. Jess watched unmoving as it dug up a number of knobbly roots. It was turning to stow the roots in its shoulder bag, when Jess made a slight movement.

The little creature caught sight of her. It froze instantly, black eyes widening in alarm. One of the roots dropped from its earth-stained fingers and rolled across the grass towards Jess.

Jess held her hand palms up, signifying that she meant no harm. The creature didn't move. Only its bead-bright eyes flickered over her, in a manner that suggested it was measuring and assessing her. After a moment, Jess sank slowly to her knees. Her fingers closed on the root and she rolled it back towards the faery. It didn't attempt to pick it up. She saw confusion and disbelief chasing across its broad features. Turning its head to one side, it blinked at her rapidly from the corner of its eyes, giving her jerky little looks.

'Not see me. Not see me...' it murmured agitatedly, making a sign in the air with one small hand.

Jess remained on her knees. She smiled to show she meant no harm. 'Don't be scared,' she whispered. 'I won't hurt you. I just want to be friends.'

The faery gave a cry of dismay. Its reddish-brown face paled with horror. Baring sharp little teeth, it hissed at her. An instant later it changed back into a hare and melted into the trees.

'Wait!' Jess rose swiftly to her feet. But it was gone. The first wild faery she had ever met had fled from her in complete terror. What had she done wrong?

It had murmured something. *'Not see me'* Yes. That was it. She had been able to understand it, so presumably it had understood that she meant it no harm. Why then had it seemed so terrified of her? It was only then that she remembered she wore a powerful glamour. She could see the little faery in its true-form, but what could it see of her?

The sky was now a wash of grey-toned peach and the topmost leaves of the elder tree gleamed red-gold. Mum would be waking soon. She had to get back to the café, but she felt reluctant to leave while there remained the slightest possibility that the faery would return, if only out of curiosity. Maybe she could leave it a message. But how? Storybook images from her childhood came to mind, of words woven into spider's webs, or linking to form the branches of trees.

She spotted a tree stump, with a flat top. She went over to the stream, gathered handfuls of gravel and wrote *Hello. My name is Jess. What is your name?* on the stump. She would come back late tonight to see if there was any response.

After a final glance around, just in case the glamoured hare was hiding somewhere nearby, Jess retraced her steps through the trees. She was still thinking of the little faery as she retrieved her boots and socks from beneath the hedge and sat in the grass to pull them on. Would it return to the clearing? Could it even read? By way of an introduction, the pebble message was almost as lame as the folded piece of paper she had in her pocket.

She smiled as she recalled being handed the scribbled note by the café owner. Caleb Farmer. That was the name of the intense-looking, dark-haired cyclist who had been staring in the café window at them. *I'm an artist. I'd really, really like to draw you. By the way, I'm not a perv or a stalker!*

There had been something familiar about him. Had she seen him somewhere? She couldn't recall. Poor guy. He had looked so startled when she glared at him. It was just his bad luck to be looking in the café window when her patience with Alice's stubborn refusal to move on from the B&B, coupled with her fear that her mother would have a relapse at any moment, was stretched to its limit. She hadn't meant to react to him like that. Maybe he really was an artist. But what sort of idiot forgot to leave an address or a phone number? *The same kind who was stupid enough to scare off the first faery to cross her path when it was right under her nose?*

Annoyed and frustrated with her own stupidity, Jess headed back towards the village. For some reason it was Caleb's face that stubbornly remained in her mind, and not that of the little red-brown faery.

CHAPTER 31

NINKA LEAPED ACROSS the fields, dashing between clumps of long grass, using the scrubby growth at the bottom of hedgerows for cover. She flattened her long ears, felt her eyes bulging with exertion. She was panting, her furry brown sides working like bellows, her leg muscles taut and aching as if one of the bad-tempered trolls who lived under the bridge had doused them with rusty water from its metal cooking pot.

She dared not shrug off the glamour. Not until she was certain that the mortal was far behind her. She ran as if a pack of scarlet-eared gentry hounds were snapping at her heels, as they had done to her ancestors, and didn't stop until she reached the cover of the wild wood that bordered the grounds of the big house where the aged female mortal lived. Heart pounding wildly in the hare's narrow ribcage, Ninka sagged against the bole of an ancient hazel trying to catch her breath. With a final glance around to make sure that she was alone, she sloughed her glamour and dumped her forage bag onto the grass. The few roots she had managed to stuff into it before fleeing in terror spilled out and rolled in all directions, but she was still trembling too hard to reach for them.

A mortal with true sight. It was almost unbelievable.

Ninka had heard tell of such a thing. Faery mothers sometimes regaled their children with stories about those rare mortals who were able to see through glamour. It was said that one with *true sight* was able to hunt faeries, luring them with sweet words and then capturing them, before locking them in iron cages and forcing them to do their will, or worse. Far worse. Ninka had never really believed such tales, until now.

Her red-brown skin was prickling with cold sweat at the memory of how that tall, dark-haired figure had stepped silently from the shadow of the tree. Amazing that she had not detected its smell or sensed the quicksilver rush of its hot blood beneath its thin skin. She, who so prided herself on her hunting skills! Yet, all at once, there it was, standing exposed in the clearing, looking at her with a penetrating greenish gaze. It was even smiling slightly, as if revelling in its power over her. And despite all Ninka's efforts to confound it or mask her form with trickery, it kept looking at her with its hungry piercing expression. *Truly seeing her.*

Ninka shuddered. There had been such urgency, almost desperation, about it. She felt that it would have liked to lay hands on her, pet her like a small animal, and gentle her into a sense of false security. Every instinct had been screaming at her to run, run! Even then, in her stupidity, she had remained rooted by shock and disbelief.

And then. Horror of horrors. It had spoken to her! Smooth words, meant to beguile her and entice her into lowering her guard. Her very bones flinched from the imaginary bite of the mortal's knife. The hectic pace of her breathing had slowed now. At least the mortal had not pursued her. It must be far behind now. What could have brought it here? She wondered. Perhaps it was seeking something? Or someone…

Aerith. Her Beloved. Ah, Gentry save us. No! A cold hand seemed to grip her heart.

Time moved to a different tune in Faery. It slowed down

or sped up at Catelysma's will, so it was entirely possible that Aerith, now grown tall, strong and striking as one of Gentry's own, although without the demarcation of wings, was still being sought by a grieving mortal parent or parents. Ninka trembled at the thought. She was the *only* one, excepting the Dark Queen, who knew that Aerith was more than a forest foundling. But she had tricked Catelysma into believing Aerith to be sickly and, by now, probably dead. Ninka was determined to keep her knowledge about Aerith's true origins close to her heart. It was known that mortals, as disgustingly fecund as sap-suckers clustered on a stem, were curiously attached to even a single lost offspring. And they could be most tenacious in their efforts to recover such a one.

Ninka remembered laughing until tears ran down her cheeks, when, at one of the berry festivals, Tweeter had entertained the revellers with a tale of a mortal woman he had come upon stumbling through the forest weeping and wailing as she searched for an infant that had apparently been led away, months since, by someone who she suspected wished it harm. How the gathered fey had whooped and capered, clapping each other on pale skinny backs or scaly hides, as Tweeter recounted how he made a sound like a crying child and tricked the anguished mother into falling over a cliff where she dashed out her brains on the rocks below to the delight of hungry, fishtailed nixies.

It did not seem funny now. She would willingly walk on hot coals, swallow pellets of iron, or drive thorns deep into her flesh, to prevent her beloved coming to harm. Urgency awakening within her, she grabbed her bag, gathered the spilled roots and stuffed them into it. She must warn Aerith, tell her to beware; although it would take a keen eye indeed, maybe even more than true sight, to discern the remnants of

Aerith's cumbersome mortality. The willing recipient of Ninka's secret and arcane skills, her beloved was now more than nine parts ninety faery and could pass unnoticed amongst all but the most powerful fey. But there was always the risk of discovery. Ninka lived in fear that Catelysma would recognise the golden-haired child she had procured as a pet and once bounced on her knee while it toyed with a golden ball. She had thought that the worst that could happen was that the Bright Lady would discover that she had been tricked and Aerith was not the sick, ugly, lack-wit mortal she believed her to be.

But with this new dangerous mortal abroad in the region, there was a deadly threat to Aerith's well-being. Ninka needed to get back to their dwelling to warn her beloved of the danger and then to take steps to ensure Aerith's continued safety. Assuming the form of a hare once again, she sped away through the trees.

CHAPTER 32

JESS TOOK THE stairs to the bedroom above the cafe two at a time. She opened the door to find her mum holding a piece of paper.

'Where did you get this?' Alice demanded, white-faced, flapping the page in the air as if she was fanning flies away from food.

'What? Oh, that. It's from an art exhibition catalogue. Where did you find it?'

'It was sticking out from under your bed.'

'I must have dropped it. I kept the picture of *Royalty's Revenge*. It was my favourite painting from the exhibition in London.'

Alice knuckles showed white through her skin as she clutched the page. 'I didn't know this painting existed. God, it gives me the creeps to see that room again. Why did she paint me lying on the bed? And what is that *thing* lying beside me? It's like some kind of revolting chrysalis!'

'I thought it looked a *bit* like you. But I never imagined…'

'It must have been not long after I'd given birth to you and Stella. A few months probably…I was barely eighteen.' Alice shook her head distractedly, holding the page at arm's length. 'Who's that red-haired figure leering from the shadows? And what are all those other vile creatures? The whole thing's twisted! Like something from a nightmare!' Scrunching up the page, she threw it to the floor

'Hey! I want that!' Jess swooped down to pick up the page

trying to smooth out the creases. 'You might hate it. But you have to admit that it's an amazing painting. You should be proud that you posed for Krast. She's really famous.'

'Don't I know it! Krast is my bloody grandmother,' Alice said through gritted teeth. 'Ivy Stark was obsessed with painting, didn't give a fuck about anything else. She always signed them, Krast. Her only daughter, Joan Stark, is my mum. And I never posed for that painting. That old bitch must have done it from memory.'

Jess blinked. 'Whoah! This is way beyond freaky! How come you never told me I was related to a brilliant artist?'

'Because I hate her! She was selfish, remote – a real cold fish. Nothing mattered to her except painting, certainly not family. She was obsessed with daubing all manner of horrors on her precious canvasses. Sick in the head, if you ask me. Had to be... I need a cigarette.'

'Thanks.' Her fingers trembling, Alice lit it and dragged the smoke deeply into her lungs. She blew out a stream of smoke. 'I didn't even know that my grandmother was still alive until my early teens. Mum told me that both her parents, Ivy and Ralph Stark, were dead. Her childhood wasn't happy, with Ivy being such a workaholic, and with no time for her. Mum thought she was jealous of her, too, because she and her dad were really close. Apparently, Ralph virtually brought her up. But he'd never hear a word against Ivy, who he said had adored Joan as a young child. I don't think my mum believed that. It was Ralph who drove Mum to school, took her shopping for clothes, or to the cinema. When she got older, they'd have dinner in smart restaurants. Ralph sounded like a lovely man. Wish I'd known him.' She paused to take another pull on her cigarette. 'But he got cancer. A brain tumour, Mum thought. Six months after he was diagnosed, he was dead. Mum was devastated. But Ivy didn't seem to care about Ralph dying, or that Mum was grieving and in a terrible state. She'd shut herself away for days on end in the bedroom she used as a studio.

'My mum was just going on seventeen. I don't know how she coped without Ralph and with Ivy as obsessed as ever with painting, and virtually ignoring her. She stuck it out for a year or so, before getting an office job in a shoe factory. Having money gave her some independence. But she could never ask any boyfriends home. Ivy was paranoid about having strangers in the house. The second she was eighteen, Mum upped and left. Didn't leave Ivy a note or anything.'

'You can't really blame her, can you?'

Krast, the brilliant artist, was not only her great grandmother, but also a mean-spirited and emotionally defunct human being. Ivy Stark was a far cry from the glamorous Bohemian woman she had imagined Krast to be. Had wanted her to be, if she was totally honest. 'Maybe weird goes with the territory. Talented people can be a nightmare to live with. Look at all the artists, poets, musicians who ended up being casualties of one kind or another. It's like...the passion to create great art is a curse. It takes you over, twists you out of shape.' Carelessly, she had spoken her thoughts out loud. Alice looked angry and confused.

'Oh, Ivy was twisted all right!' Two high spots of colour burned on Alice's ravaged yellow-toned face. 'Why are you sticking up for her? Do you think my mother was *lying* about how coldly Ivy treated her and Ralph?'

'Of course not. Why would I?' Jess said hastily. 'I'm just trying to get some perspective. People have reasons for acting the way they do. Maybe Ivy was bipolar or something. Like some of the celebs in the trashy gossip mags.'

Alice shoulders slumped tiredly. 'It's possible, I suppose. I could never work Ivy out. Not even after I discovered for myself that a lot of what my mother said about her was true.'

'You knew Ivy?' Jess's pulses quickened, in anticipation of any fragment, however vague about Ivy's alter-go. What made Krast tick? She wanted to know everything about the woman with such an amazing talent.

'I lived with her for around two years.'

'You *lived* with Ivy? So she and your mum, managed to make things up between them?'

'No. They never did. My mother never saw Ivy again. At least, not face to face. It's a long story. Are you sure you want to hear all this?'

Jess nodded, fascinated. Alice had never volunteered this information before.

'OK. Well, to backtrack a little. My mother, Joan, gradually worked her way out to Australia, where she met my father. He was a decent man, but no mover and shaker. He sold insurance. I was born in a village called Newport. Dad was my hero. He'd come in, exhausted from work, but he'd always pick me up, swing me around and then crush me to his chest in a big warm hug. He did that until I grew too big, but I'd still get a hug and a kiss on the cheek. They were so happy. Mum was always singing and laughing.'

'Newport was a great place to grow up in the eighties. I'd run wild with the neighbourhood kids, swim in the nearby creek, climb trees, play in their back yards. When we got older we'd go to town, hang around at the cinema, chat up the local boys, make a pest of ourselves in the stores. Normal stuff.' Alice took another drag of her cigarette and slowly blew smoke into the room. Her hand was trembling. 'I...I was waiting to be picked up from upper school when a neighbour brought the news. Mum and Dad had been driving back from the supermarket. A car ran into them. It was a head-on collision. They were both killed instantly.'

'Oh, God. No! That's terrible.'

'It was stupid and mundane!' Alice cried, her voice raw. 'Death by shopping. It was such a waste. How could they have been so careless? They left me all alone. I was furious with them. I tore up all our photographs. Threw them all away. I was sixteen. After the funeral and everything, there I was all alone in our rented bungalow with everything reminding me of Mum and Dad. I couldn't stop crying, couldn't eat or sleep. Friends of my parents brought me food and stayed over with me, but no one really knew what to do with me. I was going to have to move out of the bungalow pretty soon. Eventually, one of the neighbours offered me a home. But everyone knew that her husband was handy with his fists. And she had three hulking great sons who were always arguing. Living with them would have been like being in a war zone.'

Alice had finished her cigarette. She lit another from the glowing tip, pinching out the stub with saliva moistened fingers. 'One night...I was sick of lying awake, staring into the dark. I decided to sort out some of Mum and Dad's things. That's when I found a letter addressed to Ivy Stark. Mum had been trying to get up the courage to make amends. Maybe she lost her nerve. I don't know. But it was clear that she wanted Ivy to know about me, her only granddaughter. I thought that I could at least do that one thing for her. So I wrote to Ivy, explaining about the car crash and I put Mum's letter in the envelope.'

'And Ivy wrote back?'

'Her letter was short and to the point. She was moved by

Mum's letter and shocked to learn of her death. Reading between the lines, I thought she regretted all the years they'd been apart. How wrong can you be, eh? She said I must come to England, to live with her. She'd make all the arrangements. Pay for everything.'

Alice continued, her tone bleak. 'So I came halfway around the world to live with Grandma Ivy in her draughty old barn of a house.

She was true to her word though. She gave me a home. I was grateful for that. I had a huge bedroom and the run of the rest of the house. She opened a bank account in my name, too. I had a generous allowance, more than enough to live on and buy anything I wanted. And then, she made it pretty plain that I was expected to keep quiet and stay out of her way.' A thoughtful silence.

'To be fair, I think she did try. She listened while I talked endlessly about Mum and Dad. Our life in Australia. She even spoke about my mum. What Joan was like as a small child, you know. Told me that she wished she and Joan could have been closer. I saw a softer side to her and hoped we might eventually get along together. But after a few days, Ivy changed. She started to get edgy. Restless. I remember the exact turning point. I was talking about Mum's phobia about black widow spiders, how we all had to check inside our shoes and lift up the loo seat before using it, when Ivy suddenly jumped up and excused herself. I thought she'd gone to get a drink or something. I waited and waited, but she didn't come back. She'd gone up to her studio and locked herself in. I thought she might be ill. I knocked on the door, to ask if she was all right. She shouted angrily at me to go away. I didn't see her for two days, that first time. But I thought I heard her, muttering to herself, on my way to my bedroom. There were scratching noises too, as if she was scrubbing frantically at canvases. Another time, I heard crashes and sounds of things being dragged across the floor. I knocked on her door again, told her I was worried about her. She shouted at me to go away. That's how it went on. I might see Ivy for a half an hour a day, if I was lucky. Otherwise, she spent every waking moment in her studio. I had no choice but to accept that that's how things would be from now on. Didn't take her long to get bored with me, did it? She was the same old Ivy. Cold, remote, obsessed with her painting, just as Mum had described. She wasn't interested in being a mother to Joan and she wasn't interested in being a grandmother to me. She'd done her duty by letting me live at Windroth. I was expected to take care of myself.

I didn't go to school. I couldn't have faced it. All those curious faces. The probing questions. I don't think the subject of school even occurred to Ivy, which was fine by me. It was a cold wet spring, I remember. Rained constantly for weeks on end. I mostly stayed in my room or wandered round the grounds on good days. I longed for heat. Huge, open blue skies, warm breezes that smelled of red dust and eucalyptus. Even the birds here seemed so dull. I missed the flocks of brightly coloured lorikeets in our garden.

I began staying in bed for days on end. Didn't bother to wash or get dressed. I hadn't the energy. I hardly ate anything. My birthday came and went and I didn't bother telling the old cow. Anyway, she went away for a couple of weeks. She said an important client had insisted that she personally deliver a painting they'd commissioned. The weather turned hot. Finally it was summer and I was feeling a bit better with myself. I used to lie and sunbathe in the grounds.. And then... I met Rob Morgan.'

'My father? I mean, our father. Mine and...Stella's?'

Poor Stella, the long-dead, but never forgotten twin. *The true human baby.* Jess felt a quickening of apprehension as Alice's narrative approached that part of her life which concerned Jess directly. *Had she, the monstrous cuckoo child, instinctively hauled that other innocent chick from its nest, ensuring that her adoptive parents showered the usurper with all of their attention?*

'Yes, your father.' Alice's face had softened. 'When I say I met Rob, I mean that I got to know him properly. I'd already seen him working around the estate, gardening, doing odd jobs. We just got talking about Australia. He'd always wanted to go there. He was far too handsome for a man. Beautiful, actually. Hazel eyes – like yours, although yours are greener.' Remembered happiness brought a faint flush to her cheeks. She looked younger, prettier. 'Rob wasn't vain or full of himself, like most good-looking men. He was gentle, understanding.

We fell in love over that hot summer. Ivy didn't even notice us. She'd be shut away in her studio for days on end. We just left her to it. Rob and I had our own secret place. An old summer house, near the kitchen garden. He was holding down three jobs and saving hard. Then, a few months before my eighteenth birthday, the inevitable happened.'

'You got pregnant?'

'I was *so* happy. I wanted Rob's baby. And when I found out I was expecting twins – well, we were both over the moon.' Reaching for Jess's hand, she squeezed it hard. 'I know things haven't always been easy for us. I've made rubbish choices. Messed up and been a crap mother. But you've *always* been loved Jess. Rob and I loved you and your sister before you were born.'

'And Ivy?'

Alice rolled her eyes. 'She went ballistic! Said Rob had betrayed her trust. She called him a grubby, money-grabbing social climber. Well - I totally lost it. I told Ivy she had no right to take the moral high ground. She'd never cared what I did, as long as I kept out of her way. So she could keep it buttoned now! I told her that Rob and I were in love and going to get married. If she gave us her blessing, fine. But we didn't need her permission!'

'You really told her!'

'It had been a long time coming. Once Ivy accepted that Rob wanted to provide for me and our babies, she calmed down. Even said we could stay in the house, as long as we didn't disturb her. But she was adamant that she didn't want crying babies about the place. They'd have to be born at a private clinic, which she'd pay for. I could bring the babies home after a few weeks. Presumably after they'd settled into a routine. Rob and I agreed, but it didn't work out that way.' Alice paused, her eyes, inward-looking. 'You and Stella were born two weeks early. My labour was short and intense. There was no time to go anywhere. I had you in our bedroom at Windroth. Rob was such a proud dad. We ought to have been so happy... But it all unravelled...' she whispered, moving her head slowly as if the weight of it was too much for her thin neck and narrow shoulders. 'It was after we lost poor little Stella... I thought I was the fragile one. But it was Rob who went to pieces. Blamed himself for Stella dying. He became a different person. He had terrible nightmares. He'd wake screaming, saying that monsters were after him. He seemed to sink more and more into himself. I tried *so* hard, but I couldn't reach him...'

Monsters? What kind of monsters?

CHAPTER 33

FROST HAD RIMED the fallen leaves on the path that morning, so that they crunched underfoot when Caleb came outside; the smell of impending winter on the air as sharp as diluted vinegar. On the pond, lily leaves were fretted with brown spots.

He chopped logs, before stacking them neatly and washing his hands at the outside tap. As homes went, the summer house was sparse, but warm enough with the wood burning stove and few bits of furniture. He'd rescued a decent rug from rubbish piled into a corner, amongst it, incongruously a faded Mother and Baby magazine.

The solitude suited him. Allowed him to build up new personal reserves. Nothing here to jar his spirits, interrupt his thoughts or stem the tide of any creative impulse. *I'm happy here, Mum. You don't have to worry about me.* Why did no one ever tell you that grief felt so much like fear? There was still the funeral. Dad and Pa Farmer to face. But not yet.

The sketchbook pages pinned to the wall above a rickety table caught Caleb's eye. They were more drawings of the girl. They were competent, he could see that. A couple of them were very good, but he was still dissatisfied. Some vital element was missing, something was evading him.

Why was it such a struggle to capture the sharp angles of her face, her expressive eyes, long slender neck and unruly mass of dark hair? Given his special gift for remembering faces it was surprising and as annoying as hell. Come on *fusiform gyrus* – do your stuff. But it wasn't listening. What he *really* needed was to have the girl from the cafe sit for him, so that he could study the underlying bone structure and peculiar muscular arrangement that informed her singular face. He didn't expect to ever see her again. Still, he felt compelled to keep producing new drawings in the hope that, with repetition, he would capture the essence of her.

Caleb fetched sketchbook and pencils and began working. Selecting a medium hard pencil, he drew quickly, delineating the girl's hair and general face shape with bold strokes. He used a softer lead for mapping out shadows and hollows. So far, so good. Her eyebrows were a straight line on either side of the narrow bridge of her straight, slightly long nose; the two features forming a definite T-shape that gave definition to the rest of her face. Encouraged by his progress so far, he picked up another pencil, began the more detailed work of eyes, ears, mouth.

Gradually the girl's face appeared on the page. Lost in his work, he used his fingertips to smudge and soften the line of her neck. No that was wrong. Her neck was longer, more slender. A small grunt of annoyance escaped him. Scrubbing at the drawing, he adjusted the angle of her jaw, but that threw out the other proportions. Her face was narrower than that, her chin smaller. A line here and there only made things worse. With a sinking feeling, he began re-working parts of the drawing, attempting to bring the whole thing back into balance. But succeeded only in making the girl's expression wooden and lifeless. The drawing was now over-worked, beyond saving.

He threw himself onto the old metal-framed bed and slumped there, arms linked behind his head. He stared gloomily up at the ceiling, aware that his armpits smelt musky. His hair needed a wash too. The enamel bowl was fine for a daily wash-down, but it couldn't compare with a long hot soak in a bath. Maybe that was what he needed to jolt himself out of his black mood.

Grabbing a towel and clean underwear, more of Ralph's unworn items, he headed towards the archway in the brick wall. The crumbling paths crunched underfoot as he navigated the old kitchen garden. Once through the ivy-covered gate, it was a short walk across the overgrown lawn to the old washhouse, where he lifted the tin bath down from the wall and filled it with hot water from the tap. When the bath was full, he squirted in shower gel, stripped off and lowered himself in. With a sigh of pleasure, he lay back.

Closing his eyes, Caleb allowed his thoughts to drift.

Almost immediately images seeped into his mind. First there was movement and colour, as if a torn silk scarf the colour of a rainbow straned across his vision. As the colours dissolved a scene formed. He saw a glade, grass wreathed with mist and lit by sunlight streaming through leafy branches. Three naked women appeared; all lithe, with slender limbs and small, high breasts. Caleb felt a tightening at his groin.

Two of the women were caressing the third, kissing her hands and feet, stroking her. They spoke softly, between caresses, calling her My Lady, praising the beauty of her form, professing their desire only to serve her. My Lady stood up and walked across the glade. She was very tall and slender, her movements fluid and beautiful. Her lips curved in amusement as she looked over her shoulder to watch her companions crawling after her on their hands and knees. He could see their white buttocks swaying and glimpse the shadowy places between their slender thighs.

My Lady leaned back against the deeply ridged bark of a fallen tree. Her laugh, soft and breathy as her companions resumed their ministrations.

Caleb was transfixed. The sounds of pleasure in the glade were louder now. His body tensed, breath quickening. *Don't stop. Don't stop now.*

And then. My Lady's smiling mouth stretched impossibly wide, until it opened up into a slash that reached from ear to ear. Within that red maw, needle-sharp teeth gleamed like milky glass. Her slanting eyes flooded black, between raw-looking rims and green scales stained her skin from neck to toe. She roared triumphantly reared up, her neck growing in length. Swooping over in a graceful movement, she swallowed the head of one of her companions within those wide-spread jaws.

There was a strange beauty to the creature. Its scales gleamed like an opal he'd once seen. Claws like curved swords tipped each of the long thin fingers. As if in slow-motion the creature made a single, one-handed sweep downwards towards her other companion.

'No! Don't…' Caleb gasped.

He thought at first that it had misjudged the blow, either deliberately or to prolong its moment of enjoyment. And then the separate halves of the woman's body slipped sideways. Limbs buckling, she slid to the ground.

A tide of red spattered the grass. 'Oh, you… You murdering…' Caleb felt vomit rush into his mouth, stinging the back of his throat and nose.

The creature lifted its scaly head, nostrils questing in the air. And then it looked across the glade. Straight at him.

Caleb looked back, unable to lower his gaze. He felt those reptilian black eyes raking his face, worming inside his skin, tasting and assessing. Time stopped. Seemed to stretch endlessly. He felt his skin shrinking back from his skull in terror. He knew himself to be a prey.

The creature smiled; its glass-like teeth wet and red. The spell was broken. A silver waterfall seemed to clothe the green scaly skin changing it into that of a radiant woman. He couldn't find words for what he saw. How to describe such beauty? A cold bluish flame flickered around her outline. Rising up from behind, he could see shimmering wings. An angel? Hardly. Tossing back pale-green hair that streamed out behind her as if blown by a hidden wind, she was walking towards him, her smile tender. He felt bathed in the glory of it.

Tears ran down his face, but he didn't notice. Somehow, he could see the glade, *through* the figure of the advancing woman. There was no blood on the grass, no remnants of the carnage he had witnessed; only the fallen log and two mounds of twigs and leaves. Had the whole scenario been an elaborate trick? An illusion? As she glided closer on bare feet, she held out her hand. Soft words reached him.

Would you know me, Mortal?

Unbidden Caleb's hand rose to meet hers. A fearful heat was washing towards him. Their fingers were about to touch. He shrank from that contact, but at the same time he had never wanted anything so much...

Coughing and spluttering, Caleb broke the surface of the water. He pushed back his streaming hair and wiped the water from his eyes. The bath was stone cold. He must have dropped off to sleep and slid under the water. Holy crap! What was that dream about? It was heavy, weird stuff. He wasn't in to slash horror movies or the pervy stuff some guys downloaded onto their mobile phones and paraded around school. Shivering, he got out and briskly rubbed himself dry with the towel. He must be a bit unhinged.

Shivering, he dragged on his clothes. He emptied the bath, throwing the buckets of water onto the small vegetable patch. The dream, or whatever it had been, was already starting to fade. He couldn't recall any detail of the face of the strangely luminous woman face. Strange that. Had his famous fusiform gyrus totally shut down? There was just the lingering echo of those few puzzling words, *Would you know me, Mortal?* And then, even they were gone, beyond recall. He felt relieved. That stuff wasn't the kind of thing he wanted cluttering up his mind.

Mrs Stark had left earlier for town, her white hair neatly pinned up, diamond studs in her ears, a small enamel brooch in the shape of a butterfly on the lapel of the smart jacket she was wearing over one of her black dresses. To his surprise she had been wearing black stout boots instead of her usual trainers. A few days earlier she'd been in bed, almost dying he had thought. She was remarkable.

Standing in the doorway at the entrance to the hall he called her name. There was no reply. Turning back into the kitchen, he noticed a used cup and saucer on the work surface beside the sink. A crumpled tea bag sat next to it in the middle of a damp orange-brown stain. He touched the kettle. It was cold. She couldn't be home yet. He might as well take the washing upstairs, or it could lie there for weeks.

He reached Mrs Stark's bedroom and pushed open the door with one foot. It smelled close and musty. He frowned. It was strange that Mrs Stark should keep the windows firmly latched, now that she was well again, when she so valued the health-giving properties of fresh air. He was about to go back downstairs when something on the table near the window caught his eye.

A navy and white marbled fountain pen with a gold nib lay next to a pad of writing paper and a small pile of neatly addressed envelopes. To his surprise, the topmost envelope bore his name. Caleb Farmer. There it was, written in Mrs Stark's elegant old-fashioned hand. He picked up the envelope and turned it over. It was unsealed. He felt torn between curiosity and his natural inclination to respect Mrs Stark's privacy. But the letter *was* meant for him. At some point he assumed that she wished him to read it. What harm could it do to have a quick look and then put it back? Lifting the flap, he could see that it contained a single folded sheet of paper, covered with the same neat handwriting. He examined the other two letters. They were addressed to an Alice Morgan and a Jess Morgan. *Morgan.* It seemed vaguely familiar. But it was a common enough name. Quickly, before he could change his mind, he put all three letters back in place and turned to leave the room.

Mrs Stark's black boots were lying on the floor beside one of the armchairs. In his mind's eye he saw her sitting there and changing back into her comfortable old trainers. She must have returned and gone straight to her studio, probably sorting out paints and canvases, ready for when she started work again. To his knowledge, she hadn't been anywhere near the place for well over a week. She must be desperate to get back to it.

Just then he heard a strangled cry from the direction of the studio. He was out of the room in an instant, running along the corridor. He grasped the studio door handle and twisted it, but it was locked.

'Mrs Stark? Are you all right in there?'

'Go away, Caleb!' Mrs Stark called, her voice sounded weak, but it might just be that it was muffled by the stout panelled door.

Caleb pressed one ear against the door. He heard rustling sounds, thought he heard her give a low moan. And then her voice again, faint and tremulous. 'Leave me alone you wretches! Stop that. Ah, no. No!'

He knew it. The journey to and from town had been too much for her. She sounded feverish and confused, which meant she was running a temperature again. What if she was to collapse in there? 'Mrs Stark! Open the door!' he cried, concern roughening his voice. 'Can you hear me? You need help. Let me in!'

He heard a crash as if a window had banged open. A gust of wind was swirling around the room and there came a scraping sound as if the walls were being lashed with bundles of twigs. Something heavy was thrown against the door, the reverberation making it shake.

Caleb leaped backwards in shock, his ears ringing. 'What's going on in there? Mrs Stark. Let me in! Now,' he roared. 'Or I'll break this door down!'

'No! Caleb. Don't...' her voice was barely audible.

At a loss as to what to do, he listened at the door again. He held his breath to quieten his breathing, straining to hear. And thought he could hear whispers, little yips of delight and odd snorking laughter. Had Mrs Stark lost her mind? Whatever the hell was going on, it didn't sound good.

'I'm coming in. Stand back!' he warned.

He threw his weight against the wood, again and again, but succeeded only in almost dislocating his shoulder. The door was solid oak, unmoving. Hurtling downstairs, two steps at a time he cast around for something sturdy with a bit of weight to it. His eyes fell on a cast iron umbrella stand. Tipping the umbrellas and walking sticks onto the floor, he staggered back upstairs with the heavy stand. He reached the studio and slammed the umbrella stand against the lock again and again until he was breathing hard and his arms were aching with exertion. Finally, the glass door handle shattered and fell in pieces at his feet. Caleb continued raining blows onto the lock until with a metallic groan and a splintering of wood the door swung open. He dropped the heavy stand and half-fell into the room.

The sight that met his eyes was so bizarre, so unexpected, that he came to a full stop and stood with his hands at his sides.

Mrs Stark lay on the floor. Her eyes were wide open, her mouth stretched in a silent scream. Her white hair was loose and waving gently in the air as if she was floating in deep water. Blood streaked her face. She was batting weakly at something that was perched on her chest. It looked like one of the big cockchafer beetles he had seen hovering around the light streaming from the open summer house door. He could see the glint of a blue-grey carapace and hear the whir of its gleaming wings. The thing was probing at her mouth and nose, with a black front leg that ended in a tiny wedge-shape that resembled a hand. Caleb caught a movement from the tail of his eyes. Another of the things was trailing through the air on skeletal-looking wings. Suddenly the huge beetle made a sharp right turn looming towards him. He lifted an arm to fend it off. For an instant, he glimpsed a dark triangular head with silver feelers and slanting red eyes that blinked at him malevolently, before the thing swooped down to land on one of Mrs Stark's wrists. It lowered its head and a small trickle of blood snaked across her hand.

Mrs Stark moaned faintly, trying to shake off the thing, but with no success. Even while Caleb was struggling to find a rational explanation for why the things were attacking her, his legs were propelling him towards a nearby table. He scattered paintbrushes and felt his fingers skid on wet paint as he grabbed one of Mrs Stark's palettes. Brandishing it like a table tennis bat, he rushed towards her and swiped at the creatures. The one on her chest gave a muffled shriek and rose into the air. Caleb wielded the palette again and felt it connect with the thing. He swatted it across the room. There was a wet splat as it hit the side of a cupboard dropping to the floor, leaving a smear like lumpy yellow porridge behind.

Caleb felt a clutch of revulsion. He swallowed hard and gave his attention to the thing biting Mrs Stark's hand. It was quickly dispatched on to the floor, where he crushed it beneath his foot. But to his horror he saw that more of the things were emerging from corners and crawling out from beneath furniture. He ducked as an even larger insect with purple and gold wings buzzed close to his ear. There was a clattering of collective wings, an angry murmuring like an undertone. He had the mad impression that the purple and gold creature was ushering its troupes like a general in a battle. And then the whole army of nightmare creatures streamed towards Mrs Stark.

'Get away from her!' Caleb swivelled placing himself squarely between them and Mrs Stark and laid about him with the palette.

He felt bodies, wings and legs crunching against the improvised weapon. The pungent smell of oil paint sur-rounded him. Another winged creature with a furry body smashed to the floor and limped away on broken wings. A round-eyed creature with a body like a crumpled brown bag burst with a foul smell. Caleb's gorge rose, but he fought it down as he battled with the cloud of skittering, fluttering creatures.

His arms were beginning to burn with exertion. Crushed and crumpled bodies littered the wooden floor boards, but still they came. He was sobbing for breath. He felt something tangled in his hair, a burning sensation, as if he was being whipped by stinging nettles. Something warm trickled down his neck. Another of the creatures landed on his back. It felt far too heavy to be an insect. Something pierced his skin beside his shoulder blade and he cried out with the sudden pain as the thing clung to his T-shirt as it scrabbled upwards.

Hunching over he shook himself, trying to dislodge whatever was on his back, while still swatting away the others that were trying to get past him to Mrs Stark. But they were too many and he was tiring. Fear rioted through him as he imagined what would inevitably happen to her when he was too weak to fight them.

A sound rang through the room, like the tolling of an invisible bell. His nerves jangled at the noise. He felt it in his teeth and his bones. The creature on his back chittered with rage and then fell away. There was a subtle shift within the cloud of insects. He heard mutters, buzzes, low rumblings. The things hovered, circling him and then began skittering and fluttering towards the open window. As the final creatures disappeared through the window, it slammed shut behind them.

Caleb's arms felt like lead as he lowered the palette. A steady drip of blood and filth pooled on the floorboards at his feet. It was only then that he realised that his T-shirt was splattered with the stuff. Gasping for breath, he rocked back onto his heels. The bell-like noise has ceased, but it had left something behind, like a sharp and penetrating perfume hanging in the air, disorientating him, making it hard to think clearly. Blinking sweat from his eyes, fearing what he might see, he turned slowly to look at Mrs Stark. To his astonishment, he saw a woman kneeling on the floor beside her.

He was too exhausted to wonder where she had come from and felt only a deep relief that there was someone here to help him as he had no idea what to do next.

'Mrs Stark. Is...is she... She's not...' he stammered.

'She's still breathing,' the woman said in a toneless voice, turning her head to look up at him.

She had a thin face beneath stringy dark hair and looked very worn and tired. The last time he had seen her had been in the café, sitting opposite the mystery girl he was obsessed with drawing.

'We need to get her out of here. Let's carry her into her bedroom. Which one is it?' Her voice was stronger now, with a different timbre that seemed to itch in his mind.

Caleb frowned, gaping at the woman in confusion. How come she was speaking, when her lips didn't appear to be moving?

'Hey! I'm talking to you. I assume you know your way around?' A second voice, coming from somewhere near the doorway. It seemed to take a super-human effort to turn and look towards it. He saw a tall slender figure with a wild mass of hair regarding him with suspicious slanting greenish eyes.

Her. The girl was here too?

The vision darkened, a shutter seemed to slam into place in his mind, the girl was transformed into a stick-thin figure with sharply pointed features and elongated limbs silhouetted against a corona of light streaming upwards, pulsating with pale blue, violet and green flames. Caleb felt a laugh bubbling up in his chest. He must have totally lost it.

CHAPTER 34

BETWEEN THEM JESS and Alice managed to propel a semi-conscious Ivy Stark past the young man who stood gaping at them, out of the studio and along the corridor until they came to an open door.

'In here! This looks like her bedroom,' Jess said. Ivy Stark weighed hardly anything, but as they lifted her onto the bed Jess saw that Alice was breathing hard with exertion. 'Leave her to me now.' She cradled the slight figure, taking her weight. Released from the burden, Alice nodded gratefully, while Jess reached for a pillow and slipped it beneath the old lady's head.

Ivy's eyes shot open suddenly. She struggled to sit up. 'I'll thank you to take your hands off me, young woman!' she snapped, glaring. Her claw-like hands, the backs of them fretted with veins resembling bruise-coloured cords, brushed agitatedly over her loose black dress as if removing imaginary crumbs. 'Who are...you anyway? And what are you doing...in my house?'

Jess was taken aback. The old lady's recovery was remarkable. Her emaciated, heavily-wrinkled face still had a ghastly pallor, but the bead-like dark eyes were alert and, Jess noticed with some surprise, radiating hostility. They had just rescued her, you'd think she might be a tad grateful. Some of the scratches on her skin looked deep, but she didn't appear to be in any great discomfort.

'Well! Speak up, one of you!' Ivy rapped, looking from one to the other.

Alice was standing rigidly beside the bed. 'Don't you recognise me?' she asked in a curiously flattened voice. 'Have I changed that much?'

'Am I supposed to know you?' Ivy blinked at her, grizzled brows drawn together in a frown. For a long, uninterrupted moment, she stared hard at Alice, her narrow shoulders taut with irritation. Then her expression slowly changed. Jess thought she saw a softening of the deep wrinkles around the old woman's mouth, but she might have imagined it.

'It can't be....' Ivy said. 'Joan's daughter...Alice? It is really you? I never expected...You came back.'

'I didn't plan to. But well – I ran out of choices. So here I am, like a bad penny,' Alice said with a thin smile.

Ivy's mouth worked as if she were moistening her throat. 'Foolish of me to expect that this might be a social call.' She turned her head slowly. Jess found herself snagged by a penetrating gaze. 'This young woman, she must be...'

'Jess. Yeah, that's me.' Hunching her shoulders, Jess gave Ivy an open-palmed wave. 'Hi...um great grandma.'

'Jessica.' Ivy's flinty eyes were hooded. 'I deplore this modern trend of shortening names. You have your father's height, I see. And his colouring.' She made it sound like an accusation.

That's it? That's all she was to get? Jess thought, suppressing her disappointment. OK. She hadn't expected a fanfare or a red carpet, but "pleased to meet you" wouldn't have gone amiss. *Could this difficult old woman, really be Krast?*

After barely acknowledging Jess, Ivy ignored her completely. She looked sideways at Alice. 'You should never have come back here. It is not safe. Especially now....' she said as if to herself, and then broke off abruptly. 'Where is Caleb?'

Her voice rose querulously. 'You have not left him in the studio?'

Jess thought of Caleb, standing there with that stunned look on his face. She'd expected him to follow them into the corridor. It was only now that she realised he hadn't. His concern for the injured old lady ought to have brought him running. What exactly was his relationship with Ivy anyway? Did he work for her? She was glad that Caleb had missed that touching family reunion. Having another person witness it would have multiplied the cringe factor. To her annoyance she found that she was still smarting from the fall-out of Ivy's glacial regard. Prickles of embarrassment heated the back of her neck.

'I'll go and check on him,' she decided, relieved to have a reason to leave the room. She tossed her hair back over one shoulder. 'You two stay here. Mum will look after you.' Turning on her heel, she strode towards the door.

'Come back here, girl!' Ivy called imperiously.

Jess felt a flicker of irritation. Where did the frosty old relic get off, ordering her about? She turned to see Ivy Stark trying to shuffle towards the edge of the bed. When Alice reached out a restraining arm, the old lady shook it off impatiently.

'Get out of my way, can't you! Those wretches are dangerous. The girl does not understand what they are...'

Ivy Stark clearly knew more about the creatures that had attacked her than she was willing to let on. Did she know they were glamoured fey? If so, was Ivy able to detect something of faery about her? Her invisible, tightly-rolled wings prickled with panic, but she dismissed the thought at once. Ivy's reaction to meeting her had been coolly understated. Besides, her glamour was unusually powerful and impervious to all but the most powerful fey.

She gave Ivy a level look. 'I'll be fine. I can deal

with…who…Whatever's been going on in there,' she said with careful emphasis. 'Chill, OK? Trust me.'

'How can you possibly…You are no match for…' Ivy tailed off, looking perplexed as if she read something unexpected in Jess's direct gaze. Her mouth opened and closed but no sound emerged.

As Jess left the room, she heard Ivy's renewed protests and Alice's calm voice, which took on a firmer edge as she took charge. 'Relax, Ivy. Jess doesn't panic easily. She'll sort things with Caleb. Now. Some of those scratches look deep. They need cleaning or they'll become infected. Do you have antiseptic? Dressings…'

Their voices faded as Jess went down the corridor. In the studio she found Caleb crumpled on the floor. He was lying on his side, facing her. She noted the leaden colour of his skin, the pinched look to his nostrils and the bluish cast to his lips.

His breathing was so shallow that each breath barely stirred the surface of the old-fashioned white top he was wearing. Had he missed his step or blacked out for some reason, maybe hitting his head on the way down? She threw herself down beside him, searching for evidence of a head injury. Why was he still unconscious?

She had a flash of insight. The fey, the hoard of attacking faeries. Had they done something to him? She chewed at her lip in impotent frustration. *I'm way out of my depth here. What to do? Think. Think.* She had failed to heal Alice, but she had to try and help Caleb.

A spasm of pain crossed his face and he moaned softly.

Jess leaned closer. She needed to discover what had been done to him. And quickly.

Think. Come on. Clear your mind. Had the faeries used spells on him? No, it didn't work like that. Faeries don't have magic, they are magic. Faeries – like me. I'm the same. I can do whatever they can. Maybe more.

'Taryn! Where are you when I need you?' she murmured and seemed to hear his calm steady voice. *It's all about the glamour. Use it. Trust yourself, Jess. The answer will reveal itself.*

'OK. Here goes nothing.'

Drawing in a deep breath, she held it for a moment or two and then let it out slowly. As she had done with Alice, she envisioned her glamour flowing outwards, as if she was casting a large net over a shoal of fish. She sensed it settling like a veil over the lanky figure on the floor. Immediately she was aware of a vibration, a thrumming resonance encapsulated within a faint glow. And she knew it to be something outside of, and yet still connected to Caleb's physical body. His life force was still connected to him. It was a kind of amorphous bridge between the worlds of the seen and the unseen. Jess understood this to be the vehicle through which the physical body interacted with the more subtle levels of being.

She touched it with her mind, probing the fragile cage of this energy body, somehow knowing instinctively not to intrude in too intimate a manner. *Too much and you'll drain him. Leave him as no more than a husk. Not enough and you'll read nothing. Reach out with your senses, not your intellect.*

'Ah, yes. There,' she breathed softly.

Within the light of his being, two small areas of dark matter which did not belong. Versicolour on his essential self.

Jess wasted no time. Reaching out, she gripped Caleb's shoulders. It was no effort for her to flip him gently over onto his stomach. Now he lay with his face in profile, his long limbs relaxed. In this position, Jess could see the two alien shadows, floating in the air just above him as if smudges had been left on his aura by fingers coated with coal dust. There was one in the region of his head and another larger one, just to the edge of his left shoulder-blade. She plunged her fingers into his dark hair and began exploring his scalp. The warmth of his skin beneath her fingertips, the heavy silkiness of his hair and the smell of him enveloped her.

It was the first time she had been this close to a guy. The intimacy of it was startling. He smelled faintly of almonds and something intangible like freshly air-dried cotton. Jess shook her head, clearing her mind and concentrating on the task before her. Suddenly a sensation like an electric shock shot through the fingertips of one hand as she located what appeared to be the end of a tiny splinter protruding from his scalp. Gripping the object between her finger and thumb nail, she pulled gently. There was some resistance as if the thing was reluctant to quit Caleb's skin, and then it gave to the relentless pressure.

Caleb gasped with pain as Jess extracted and then scraped the object onto her palm to examine it. It seemed to be a barb, like the points on fishing spears used by Amazonian Indians in Rain Forest documentaries, small and finely worked. She couldn't tell what material it was made from. Seconds later, the tiny barb crumbled to dust. Just to be certain that there was no lasting damage, Jess swiftly probed Caleb's scalp again, but could find no other wounds. Satisfied, she sat back on heels.

OK. One to go.

From Caleb's profile she could see a muscle in his cheek jerking in spasm, as if he was in pain or trapped in a nightmare. The large sooty mark that floated in the air just above his left shoulder blade pulsed black and blacker. Grasping the hem of his white cotton top, Jess dragged it up to lay bare his

312

shoulder-blades. The small, horizontal black mark beneath his olive-toned skin was easily visible. This barb was in deep, stitching down a blood vessel. Was it continuing to pump venom, like a sting torn from a dying bee? As she watched, the mark grew fainter and appeared to be fading. She felt a moment's hope.

And then Caleb groaned loudly. The skin across his shoulders flushed the colour of a storm cloud. With a thrill of horror, Jess understood. The poisoned barb was working its way inwards, seeking to bury itself in some vital organ. She reached out, laid her palm flat against his skin and willed the vile thing to come forth. There was a second's pause that stretched for just long enough for doubt to quicken her pulse. And then she sensed the barb slowly backtracking along the path it had forged in Caleb's flesh until, finally, the tiny blunt end of it nudged against her skin. She grasped it, plucked it out and laid it on her palm as before. It appeared to be a sliver of quill, perhaps from a hedgehog, wickedly sharpened and carved with impossibly tiny intricate designs. Shuddering, she crushed the thing between her thumb nails. There was a tiny cracking sound as it crumbled to dust.

The exit wound on Caleb's shoulder blade was now leaking a dark, tarry substance. Jess bent forward, placed her lips to the wound and sucked hard. She tasted sickly sweetness with an underlying bitterness, along with the copper tang of his blood and suppressed the urge to vomit. Turning her head aside she spat a watery substance streaked black. She forced herself to repeat the action, although her gorge rose and she gagged at each new mouthful of poisoned blood. Finally, she sensed that the wound was clean. As she wiped her mouth on her sleeve, she saw that the skin across Caleb's shoulders was beginning to lose its dark-grey tinge. Scant seconds later, it turned a normal colour. His breathing assumed a natural rhythm, as if he were sleeping.

Jess loosed a long sigh of relief. He was out of danger. She made no move to get up, but remained sitting there, regarding him curiously. Suddenly, she knew him.

The guy from the hospital car park! Their eyes had met for a fraction of a second, before she had fled in panic and horror of what had happened with Lisa. She had been so mixed-up, so adrift and confused, at the time, that she had hardly registered him. But it *was* him. She was certain now. She remembered his kind eyes and the way he had steadied her when she would have collapsed.

He was the same guy who had left that note for her in the café. How could he possibly be here, in her great grandmother's house? They needed to have a serious talk – if he survived, with all his wits intact.

She could see that he had unusually smooth skin, so fine that the pores were almost invisible. The strands of his dark hair lying against it gleamed like a crow's wing. She recalled the sensation of warmth beneath her fingers as she had explored his scalp. Hardly aware of what she was doing, she bent closer, reaching out one hand to hover, palm down, just above his muscled left shoulder. She let it rest in the air, barely a centimetre above his flesh. How would it feel to lay her hand on him now, to trail her fingertips down one strong bare forearm? There were streaks of blue and yellow oil paint on one wrist. It was an elegant wrist with a prominent rounded bone. She could easily encircle it with the too-long fingers of one hand. The thought that he would find her hands ugly, made her draw back. Even glamoured, they retained something of her feyness and were the one feature she was most self-conscious about.

She had never thought of guys as being vulnerable before - arrogant, annoyingly confrontational and with a certainty that they owned the world, yes, but never vulnerable. And yet, that was how he looked lying there. Jess's breath hitched. She gave a start and self-consciously curled her fingers into a fist. The impression of his warm skin remained on her lips. While the aftertaste of his tainted blood lingered on her tongue and roughened her throat, bitter as an unripe walnut.

She had the odd feeling that, having tasted his blood, she had forged some kind of intimate connection with him. What might that mean for him? She knew so little of how this fey thing worked or the implications of her actions.

She shook her head slowly. What was she thinking? Trying to rationalise her confused feelings? *Face it. This is the first guy you've found attractive. Since when? Since forever.* Although she would have died rather than admit it aloud. Thank God, he was still unconscious. Because she had just come perilously close to making a complete and utter *arse* of herself. Thankfully, Caleb would never have the faintest idea about his effect on her. She'd make sure of that. Relationships were for other people. Normal people. Why would any guy want to get involved with a freak like her? Better to stay aloof, than risk getting hurt.

Still crouching, Jess rocked back onto her heels. He was snoring softly. She thought it best to leave him to sleep on for a while and wake naturally. How much did he know about the plague of hostile faeries, she wondered. Faeries bold enough to mount an attack *inside* Windroth hall, which was pretty weird when you actually thought about it. Weren't there some kind of rules about trespassing? She had a vague hunch that you had to invite a faery into your home, otherwise they couldn't cross the threshold, or maybe that was something she'd read in the books of faery stories she'd loved as a young child. According to Taryn, the fey took pains to keep out of sight of humans, have as little to do with them as possible. She heaved a sigh, she had so much to learn. Each time she was beginning to accept that she could, just maybe, have a *normal* life, relatively speaking, as long as she continued to mask herself with glamour, something happened to confound her all over again.

Odd things appeared to have been going on at Windroth Hall. What part did Caleb play in all this? From the little she had seen of Ivy Stark, she felt certain that the prickly old lady didn't encourage visitors. Well, it was futile to sit here trying to puzzle it all out. Things would no doubt become clear in their own time. Right now, she needed to go and see how her mum was getting on with tending Ivy's wounds. The fact that Ivy was still conscious, and being generally obnoxious, probably meant she'd escaped any real harm.

She was reluctant to leave Caleb lying on the hard floor and contemplated picking him up and carrying him into one of the bedrooms. But what if he woke and saw her face, up close, looking down on him? She imagined the shock on his face, his panicked struggles to get free. So many guys had looked at her with thinly disguised disgust that she had come to expect it. Lisa's brother, Zac Simpson, had treated her as if she were something that he had just scraped off his shoe. She didn't possess the kind of model-girl looks that most guys went for. That's just how things were. Nothing would change.

But Caleb had taken the trouble to write that note about wanting to draw her. Lame OK, but kind of cute, too. He obviously saw something attractive about her. *Yeah, right. Maybe he had a thing about gargoyles!*

'Oh, come on! Get over yourself!' she murmured in

self-disgust, moving into a crouch beside him. 'What do I care what he thinks of me, anyway.'

She slipped her arms beneath him. He was as tall as her, but it was easy enough with her preternatural strength to manoeuvre him so that he lay over one shoulder like a heavy coat. Deciding against taking him along the corridor to one of the so far unexplored bedrooms, she carried him to the battered old sofa in the corner of the studio and covered him with the crumpled blanket thrown over the back of it. His head had fallen back. He was sleeping like a child, his cheeks flushed and his mouth soft. It was a nice mouth. Well-shaped and sensitive.

Schooling herself not to look back at him, she turned and left the studio. The door with its shattered lock, she left ajar.

CHAPTER 35

CALEB WOKE SLOWLY from another impossible dream, peopled by nightmare figures, some crawling towards him like bats scaling a church's spire; others cat-faced and winged, beautiful in a strange way. Creatures had flashed close to his face, blinking curiously and then zipping away into nothingness. One of them, a pale spider with wide blue eyes had perched on his shoulder and lovingly stroked his hair. Reaching out an appendage, it snagged a strand of his dark hair and nibbled along the length of it, biting it off when it reached his scalp.

These and other troubling images remained. The dreams were getting to be a habit he could do without, but at least, this time, there had been no murderous lizard-woman.

Opening his eyes, he discovered that someone seemed to have been at work on his eyeballs with an electric sander. He palmed his eyes, blinked hard a few times, and then tried to make sense of the unfamiliar shapes surrounding him in the gloom. The small amount of light seeping through the panes of a window across the room illuminated the surfaces of cluttered tables, shelves, chests of drawers. He could see stacks of square objects leaning against a nearby wall, something angular with three legs, which, on closer inspection, resolved itself into an easel. Mrs Stark's studio then. Her sanctuary. The holy of holies. What was he doing in here, asleep on her couch? She'd be furious at his imposition.

Caleb struggled to sit up and groaned in pain. His temples were throbbing with the mother of all headaches. The same person who'd been busy sanding his eyeballs, now appeared to be tightening a vice-like band around his forehead. His left shoulder was sore and tender and a rat appeared to have sicked-up its breakfast in his mouth. This was even worse than the fall-out after his excesses at the rave. He had no idea how he had got into this state. Oh, God, he hoped he hadn't made a complete idiot of himself before collapsing.

He wanted nothing more than to flop back against the cushions and attempt to sleep off whatever excesses had brought on a hangover of such epic proportions, but his bladder was full and the need to pee was urgent.

'Never again. Whatever I drank. Never again,' he moaned. Moving slowly and carefully, he pushed himself to his feet. A shaft of sunlight, slanted into the studio. The door was ajar. Some kind of an iron-stand was lying on its side, the floor next to it peppered by shards of glass.

As Caleb made his way gingerly across the room, dry husk-like things rustled and crackled beneath his trainers. He winced, the crisp sound assaulting his ears like the crashing of cymbals. Chancing a glance downwards, he saw things crumbling to dust, spiralling away into dark smoke and dissipating.

'Ow! Jee-sus!' Even that slight movement of his head brought pain stabbing through him. He was leaning on the edge of a table, waiting for the pain to subside, when he noticed trails of scratch-like marks, like birds' footprints in snow, leading from a pool of oil paint from a burst tube. On the edge of the desk, a single bright blue smudge like a handprint, impossibly small, with five fingers and a thumb. *That tiny arm he thought he'd glimpsed in the rat trap?*

There had been some sort of commotion in the studio. Mrs Stark calling out for help. It was beginning to come back. An infestation of insects, attacking the old lady. The car park girl from the café had been here. Her mother, too. Or had he imagined that?

He stumbled into the corridor. He wouldn't make it downstairs to the old washhouse. He heard voices floating up the stairwell, as he hurried towards Mrs Stark's bathroom unzipping his jeans in the nick of time and, groaning with relief, peed noisily and luxuriously. He stripped off his top, sluiced his face and upper body running his wet hands through his hair. His reflection in the mirror above the basin, showed him looking a bit pale and with shadows beneath his eyes, but all in all, looking better than he had any right to expect.

About to put his top back on, he noticed a dark stain on the collar band that looked as if someone had smudged a stick of charcoal across it. A larger patch of the same substance was covering one shoulder. A smell like burnt caramel rose from the stains with an undertow of something rotten or long dead. His already queasy stomach rebelled at the thought of putting the soiled garment back on. There were more granddad-style T-shirts in Ralph Stark's dressing room. He found a cellophane-wrapped package and was smoothing the new top down over his torso, when he heard the door open in the bedroom next door.

'Mrs Stark? I was just....' he said, turning. *She* was standing there, framed by the doorway. The girl he couldn't get out of his mind and who haunted his thoughts. The girl he was having such trouble drawing. 'Oh! It's you,' he said inadequately. 'You really are here.'

'Yeah, I'm here,' she said, coldly. 'And just in time, by the look of it.'

'Just in time? For what?'

'To stop you helping yourself to Mrs Stark's property while her back's turned.'

She was glowering at him, hands on hips, booted feet planted firmly on the carpet. Her clothes were another odd mix; a dark, close-fitting top that accentuated her long arms and narrow shoulders, a knee-length skirt of some stiff, layered fabric over black tights printed with red roses. The light behind her was having an odd effect; for an instant it looked as if her outline was moving very slightly, almost vibrating, like the wings of newly emerged dragonflies he'd seen clinging to reeds at the edge of the overgrown lily pond.

Caleb blinked hard and the impression faded. 'It's her late husband's stuff. She said I can help myself.'

'Got none of your own?' she challenged, eyes narrowing. 'Shouldn't you be looking for a job, instead of hanging around here sponging off a wealthy old woman?'

'Oh, so I'm a sponger as well as a thief? Thanks for the vote of confidence!' He was starting to feel irritated. 'You can believe what you like. But if you're going to throw insults at me, you can at least tell me your name.'

Her taut shoulders relaxed a fraction, the ghost of a reluctant smile softening her mouth. 'Jessica Morgan. Jess.'

'Hi Jess. I'm - '

'Caleb Farmer. Yeah. I already know who you are.'

Of course. The note he had left for her at the café. Heat rose up his neck and he groaned inwardly. What a dork he'd been. No wonder she didn't have a very high opinion of him.

She had turned away and was looking towards the open wardrobe and chest of drawers. He noticed her interest quickening. With a rustling of skirt layers, she brushed past him and stuck her head in the wardrobe. She had seemed taller in the doorway, mainly because she was reed thin and held herself very straight and upright, but he still topped her by half a head. He caught the smell of her and had to suppress an indrawn breath. What was that perfume she was wearing? It was something deep and sweet, like cinnamon, with a strong grassy or woody undertone. He wasn't sure whether he liked it or not, but it was doing odd things to his already delicate equilibrium.

He watched her flipping through the racks of garments. Extracting a pale scarf with a creamy fringe, she stroked the fabric. 'Opera scarf. Feels like silk. You'd pay a mint for one like this, even in a charity shop,' she commented. 'I wonder when he last wore it.'

'Ralph,' he said.

'What?' She murmured, examining a dark tail coat with satin lapels.

'Ralph Stark. That was her husband's name.'

She gave him a level look. 'You seem to know a lot about her. Looks like Ralph had expensive taste. Classic stuff like this doesn't date.'

'Help yourself, why don't you?' he said sarcastically, nodding towards the opera scarf she was rolling up before pocketing.

'Thanks, I will,' she said, unabashed. Taking the coat off the wooden hanger she slipped it on, before examining herself in the floor mirror in the corner of the room. 'Not bad, if I fold the cuffs back.' A faint smile was pulling at the corners of her pale mouth. 'Mrs Stark's got no use for this stuff, you already said. I'm collecting early on my inheritance.'

He wasn't sure whether she was joking. 'Inheritance?'

'My mum's Mrs Stark's granddaughter. Which makes me her…great granddaughter – well, kind of,' she said, screwing up her face. 'I'm still getting used to the idea. Looks like we'll be house guests, for a while at least.'

'Er...right.' He couldn't hide his surprise. Her hesitancy about her blood connection to Mrs Stark was puzzling. Either she was the old lady's great granddaughter or she wasn't.

'The idea of us staying here bother you, does it?'

'Why would it? It's none of my business. It's just that Mrs Stark has lived alone for so long. Never heard her speak of any family.'

'It must be quite a shock then, us arriving out of the blue! Didn't expect anyone to come crashing in on whatever it is you've got going on with great granny, eh.' Shrugging off the tail coat she slung it towards a chair. It slid to the floor. She ignored it.

'Nothing's *going on*, as you put it,' he said, nettled by this prickly girl who seemed intent on thinking the worst of him. He resisted the urge to snap at her as he picked up the discarded coat and put it back on its hanger. If he alienated her he could kiss goodbye to any chance of getting her to pose for him. Which would seriously piss him off. Now that he could see her close up and really appreciate her startlingly unusual looks, the impetus to draw her was burning with a new insistence. It was all he could do to contain his excitement. In an attempt at diplomacy, he gave what he hoped was a disarming smile. 'Look. Can we start again? There's no mystery about why I'm here. I left home because I don't get on with my dad. Mrs Stark lets me use a small place in the grounds as a live-in studio. In return I do shopping, gardening, cook her something now and then. That's all. Ask her. She'll tell you it's the truth.'

'Oh, I will,' she said evenly. 'I want to know everything about the mad old bat. Particularly why she turned her back

323

on a career as a successful artist. She's been rattling round by herself inside this incredible pile for years on end. I've only had a glimpse of the place, but it's like something out of Dickens.'

He found himself grinning. 'I thought that when I first saw it. Feels like time's stood still, doesn't it? Wait until you've seen the grounds. They're something else. The trees in that tangled bit of forest beyond the old formal garden look ancient. There's an amazing oak tree here. I was planning to draw it but got…distracted. I could show it you if you …' he tailed off as she stiffened, glancing into the bedroom beyond.

Her narrow green eyes slid towards a window, partly in view through the open door of the dressing room, and came to rest. She was staring fixedly at the glass, her head tilted, a look of astonishment on her pale face.

Caleb looked in the same direction, but could see nothing to account for her expression. 'What? Can you see some more of those insects that got into Mrs Stark's studio?' He shuddered. 'They were huge. I think they might be some kind of hornet or mutant beetle. Maybe they've made a nest under the rafters.'

'Insects?' She shook her head. 'No. It was erm a… bird pecking at the windowsill. It's gone now.' She walked rapidly into the bedroom and across to the window.

Caleb frowned, following more slowly. Odd. He'd been standing right beside her, hadn't seen a bird, or anything else. She was being evasive. But why? What had *really* brought Jess and her mother to Windroth after so many years? Maybe they were safeguarding their inheritance, Mrs Stark was very old and frail, not likely to live for much longer. But he had the feeling there was more to it than that.

And the incredible coincidence of it - he and Jess - being

here, sharing the same space. First the car-park, then the café, and then here, at Windroth? What were the chances? A million to one? Had to be fate, didn't it?

Enveloped in Jess's spice and moss perfume, he looked down at the overgrown lawn with its nodding wild flowers, trying to see the place through her eyes. Here and there a slender sapling protruded through the grass as the land began its gradual metamorphosis back into native woodland. He remembered when he had discovered the estate, what painterly possibilities he had seen in the blurring and softening of its classical borders from so many years of neglect.

'See there, beyond the old front lawn that borders the drive,' he said pointing. 'That bit of scrubby woodland beyond the old gravel path leads to a sort of alley way at the back of some houses. It's so thick with brambles you can hardly get through it. People dump their garden waste there. I don't think anyone has any idea this house exists.' How long ago it seemed since he had worked in the hardware shop and spent secret afternoons at Windroth. It felt like another lifetime.

Jess didn't reply. Opening the window, she leaned out, looking towards the eastern side of the house, where the window to Mrs Stark's studio was tight shut. With an almost imperceptible shake of her head, she turned her attention to the more formal grounds in the near distance. And then her gaze travelled to the deep green shade of the forest beyond. She was rigid, intent; seemingly lost in thought, unaware of the fact that he was there.

He was put in mind of a cat, watching its prey, poised for the moment when it would strike and deal a death blow with razor-edged claws and pitiless teeth.

When she closed the window and turned back towards

him, he noted a slight flaring of her nostrils and the determined set of her jaw. He was taken aback by the flooded milky-greenness of her eyes, which appeared to have no pupils. And then she blinked. The illusion was gone, leaving him thinking that he must have imagined it. In fact, he wasn't feeling too good. There was a pressure in his stomach, as if he'd swallowed a stone. Renewed pain stabbed at his temples, so intense that he could not help expelling a long halting, almost silent breath. He had tried really hard not to make any noise, but Jess's eyes were on him in an instant.

The fierce frown, the concern shadowing her face was the last thing he expected. 'Caleb!' Somehow, without seeming to move, she was next to him and grasping his bare forearm. 'What is it? Are you OK?'

'It's my head. It's banging something fierce.' He forced a grin. 'I need a coffee and a painkiller. Don't worry. I'm not going to pass out or anything.'

She didn't look convinced, but she let go of his arm. 'Well, you don't look too good. Come on. I'm coming down to the kitchen with you.' Jess went on ahead of him down the stairs, turning to look over her shoulder to make sure he didn't miss his step.

Caleb headed after her, rubbing absently at his arm. Where she had touched him, all the hairs were standing on end, as if they retained the imprint of her long, cool fingers. Jess was the strangest girl, full of contradictions with her mercurial changes of mood. He couldn't work her out at all, which was partly why his fascination with her was deepening by the second.

CHAPTER 36

'BUT *WHY* MUST I stay hidden?' Aerith grumbled shaving strips from the peg she was carving. 'It makes no sense when there is much to do during leaf fall.' She tossed the finished peg into a nearby basket, already stuffed to bursting with pegs and hanks of newly-plaited nettle twine. The sappy smell of fresh-cut wood and strewn rushes filled the dwelling.

Ninka chewed at her lip. Aerith was right. Her skills were being wasted, yet she hesitated to allow her to roam the forest freely, as she did usually while hunting and gathering roots and berries. Was she being too cautious? The mortal with true sight had not reappeared in the woods bordering the large open fields near the small township. Ninka had returned there in the dark of the moon, on the same day the mortal female had accosted her. But there had been no sign of it, even though she searched until star-strings threaded silver streaks across the deep-blue vault of the sky. She *had* glimpsed a flat tree stump, on which a complex design made up of pebbles had been set out, but had not dared to approach it too closely, lest it be a trap. Having convinced herself that the mortal had gone, she left as silently as she arrived and, although she had stolen back there, twice since, she had not seen it again.

A sound interrupted Ninka's thoughts as Aerith gave an explosive hiss of frustration, thrust the flint knife aside and jumped to her feet. 'Mam! You do not answer! Have you set me to simple tasks, because…' she gulped before continuing in a rush, '… you have lost faith in my hunting skills!'

'Never think that!' Ninka blinked in surprise. 'Was it not I, who taught you all I know of hunting? If there is any question about your skills, then I must doubt my own!' she said with an attempt at humour.

Aerith did not laugh. She continued to glower at Ninka from beneath tangled, sun-bleached hair, so densely woven with plumed grasses and fern leaves that it appeared that she was wearing a festival hat. The girl's vivid cornflower blue eyes, usually glinting with good humour, were the colour of a thunder-cloud.

How tall she was now, almost as tall as Gentry. Although still as slender as a reed, her hips were softly rounded and her tunic was stretched taut across small, high breasts. Ninka had been aware that Aerith was a child no longer, but the fact struck her forcibly at this moment. How could she expect her to sit here any longer, when she was free to do as she wished, go where she pleased? It was only out of respect for her, Ninka, that Aerith had agreed to remain hidden.

Aerith strode across the dwelling, the green rushes creaking beneath her leather boots. Her golden-brown limbs were marked with half-healed scratches. One knee bore a crusty scab. A jagged scar, the legacy of an encounter with a wild boar, showed white on one of her sleek, muscular thighs. 'If I have to sit here for even one day more … '

'You will not have to.' Ninka decided that enough was enough. 'At darkfall, we shall hunt together. Scorid and corax young are plentiful this season. The yield of meat, fur and feather should be excellent. By dawn's first light, we will use those new-made pegs and twine to string our cache from one side of the cave to the other.' She grinned. 'Your work is not wasted.' Barely had the words left her lips, when she was surrounded by a whirlwind of movement. Thin whip-cord strong arms scooped her up, wrapped her in a tight embrace. 'Aerith! Put me down. Now!' Ninka ordered, legs dangling in mid-air.

Aerith planted a kiss on her cheek before complying. 'As you command!' She swooped down, and set Ninka on her feet. Hurrying to the back of the dwelling, she plunged through the leather curtain that screened the dwelling of wattle and daub panels from the cave beyond. The space there served as storeroom and living quarters during the wettest and coldest months of the year.

Ninka was still dusting herself down in an effort to regain her dignity, when Aerith reappeared, her arms full of bulky objects and dangling straps. Dumping them on the floor, she hunkered down and sorted them into two newly-made quivers, two bundles of arrows and two hunting belts. She rose to her feet and held out a set of hunting tools to Ninka.

'For me?' Ninka felt her eyes growing wide with surprise, which quickly turned to delight as she examined the hunting tools. The soft leather had been pieced together with fine scorid-gut stitches, before being decorated. Wondering, she ran her fingers over the intricate whorls and curlicues, hammered into the soft leather with a fire-hardened thorn and then highlighted with dark pigment. The work was exquisite. *Hudskin craftsmanship, lost along with her dead kin, except that it lived on in Ninka. And now in Aerith, too.*

'Any of my once proud tribe would have been honoured to wear these,' she said, her voice rough with emotion.

'My mind was numb with making pegs and twine. So I made these,' Aerith told her. 'I am pleased they find favour with you.'

Ninka strapped on the quiver, perfectly shaped and balanced for her body size, and packed the arrows into it; the flights were golden-brown, the arrows smaller than those Aerith had made for herself. Ninka saw that her belt also had a sheath for her knife. Thin straps trailed from it, ready for securing it to her thigh.

Aerith had also donned her equipment. The arrows she was slotting into her quiver had black and white flights. 'Come, Mam. Why wait for dark?' she said, eagerly. 'Let us put these to good use!'

The girl - young woman, Ninka corrected, was fairly fizzing with repressed energy. How could she refuse her, after the gift of the wonderful hunting gear? 'Why not? But you'd best stop calling me *Mam* now, even when we are alone,' she said, unable to suppress a fleeting moment of sadness. 'If overheard by any court fey, it will draw unwanted attention.'

Aerith nodded. 'As you wish...Ninka.' She went to stand in the doorway, peering sharp-eyed up the short track and past the huge bulk of the fallen oak, whose tangled branches effectively concealed the dwelling. 'I am thinking that scorid and corax offer scant pickings, when it is the start of the cervid rut,' she said, looking back over her shoulder. 'Might it not be more of a challenge to bring down a fine buck?'

Ninka considered. A well-grown cervid would provide meat, hide, antlers for carving and other riches for many months. 'Very well...'

'Then what are we waiting for?' Aerith spun round, ready to plunge into the forest.

'Wait!' Ninka called urgently. Reaching up, she took a small earthenware bottle from a wooden shelf.

Aerith threw her a look of impatience. 'Can I not leave *that*, just this once?'

'You could. But answer me this. What do you think

happens to a fledgling that insists on rooting for grubs, even though it clearly detects the reek of nearby brush-tails?'

Aerith looked chastened. She poured a few drops of the golden, herbal-smelling oil into her palm. The masking minerals in the oil glittered briefly, fading as she smoothed it over her exposed skin and hair.

Ninka watched her; still shaken that Aerith could even think of going bare-skinned into the forest. It was reckless and foolish. She had indulged her too much. Lately she had begun to wonder whether she had also protected Aerith *too* well. Even after she made the masking oil, Ninka had never dared to let Aerith attend any of the seasonal revels, especially as her own banishment from court still held. She could have used some of the masking oil herself, but on balance had decided it was safer for her and her Beloved to keep to the forest. By now it was widely believed that Catelysma's little gold-haired foundling mortal had sickened and died. Ninka was happy to go along with that, grateful that none of the Dark Lady's spies had bothered to pay her a visit. But the consequence of growing up in the forest, avoiding even solitary fey, most of whom had been pressed into Catelysma's service, was that Aerith had no first-hand knowledge of what could happen to an unwary mortal that stumbled upon the denizens of the Shadow Court.

Ninka shivered, remembering what had made up the centrepiece of one notable Hawthorn feast. Catelysma's delighted laughter, as Tweeter presented his Queen with cutlets of still quivering red flesh, had rung in her ears for days. Echoes of that remembered horror prompted her to grasp Aerith's arm.

'Promise me that you will never, ever, stray from the dwelling without using the masking oil! Say it!'

Aerith glanced at the small red-brown hand on her bare arm and seemed about to shake it off. But at the look on Ninka's face, she patted it instead. 'Very well. I vow it. Will it make you feel better, if I carry some with me?'

'An excellent idea.' Why hadn't she thought of it? Ninka reached for a woven basket hanging from one of the supporting roof poles. She sorted through coils of gut thread, horn buttons, birch bark pouches, bone tubes of needles, until she found a tiny leather bottle. She decanted a measure of the precious oil into the bottle, secured its horn-stopper with twine. 'There. Carry this inside your tunic. It will be on hand at all times.' Aerith slipped the bottle inside an inner pocket.

Satisfied that Aerith's mortality was now as securely cloaked as if she wore the strongest faery glamour, Ninka could relax. But almost at once a new worry pricked at her mind. What if they encountered the mortal with true-sight? She could still recall its hungry eyes, softly pleading voice and its hand outstretched in a way meant to inspire trust. Yet she knew that the mortal yearned to grasp her. To such a one, her beloved's humanity would be as plain as the warts on a troll's face. There was nothing she could do about it, but hope that the stranger had gone on its way and never came back.

'Let us hunt!' Aerith urged, already halfway out of the door.

Ninka hurried to catch her up.

* * * * *

In the deepest, deep of the forest, beneath the natural temple formed by a spreading canopy of living colour, spiked, dark green leaves of holly showed against the russet and mustard underskirts of ancient ash, oak, beech.

Ninka and Aerith moved swiftly but softly across the deep

leaf litter. Down a slope and into a gulley that sliced deep into the earth, where water gushed from an unseen spring and tumbled over slab-like rocks. Sure-footed they crossed the wet stones, filed along grassy paths with fast-flowing rapids below them, until the ground flattened out and they were able to climb the gentle slopes and emerge onto a ridge. After a while they dropped down again into a shallow wooded valley, where the trees were stooped and stunted and the ground beneath was pleated into moss-covered hummocks. Ninka knew that beneath the bright green moss were the boles of trees so ancient that even the fey could not remember when they had stood straight and tall. After a moment's pause to murmur a few words of respect, she and Aerith pressed on.

Gradually the ground evened out. They found themselves passing beneath younger trees that emerged from the ground-cover of bracken, brambles and vines. Cervid tracks could be seen snaking away through the undergrowth in all directions. Ninka and Aerith slowed, careful now where they trod, alert to the slightest sound or subtle movement. There was a clearing ahead. As one, they sank down to crouch in the undergrowth.

Beyond the screen of bracken, a number of does were nibbling the grass. Sunlight slanting through the branches overhead illuminated the forest floor. As a series of harsh barks rang out, Ninka and Aerith exchanged knowing glances. The grazing does looked up, ears swivelling and noses twitching.

Ninka held her breath, her fingers itching to string her bow. Moments later, a large buck emerged from the trees on the far side of the clearing. Its nose was scarred from many encounters. Two of the tines on one antler ended in jagged stumps. There were bald patches on its flanks. Head thrown back, it strutted about emitting guttural sounds.

Not this one. Unspoken agreement passed between Ninka and Aerith. The old buck's meat would be tough, the pelt rank and pest-damaged, not worth curing. They waited in silence, knowing that it would not be long, before a pretender to broken antler's throne answered the challenge. Up ahead the does flicked their tails in excitement as the buck ran back and forth. His head was thrown back on his powerful neck, his harsh cries continuing to echo in the still air. The salty stench of his potent musk blew towards them on the breeze. Ninka parted her lips, tasted it.

A large cervid had stepped into the clearing. Broken antler immediately leaped forward to meet it. The bone-jarring clashes of their antlers filled the air. Aerith and Ninka remained hidden, neither moving a muscle. Ahead of them, flashing hooves churned up the ground, foam flecking powerful shoulders as the bucks toiled for supremacy. Broken antler rolled his eyes, blood from a deep slash wound colouring his neck.

A faint rustle in the trees to one side of them. A new challenger, approaching from a different direction. The flash of the new buck's red coat was visible through low branches. Ninka absorbed its scent; healthy, full of vitality. A young beast in its prime. *This one!* Aerith had sensed it too. With swift, economical movements, she strung her bow, selected and notched an arrow. Ninka did the same, but she had already decided this buck was Aerith's. She would only fire if a back-up volley was needed.

Aerith rose up silently, drew back the bowstring, sighted the kill and let the arrow fly. Even before it had found its target, she had drawn another arrow, notched it and loosed it. Her aim was sure. Whoosh! Whoosh! Thud! Thud! Both arrows entered behind the cervid's left ear. The buck's momentum carried it forward, even as its knees were starting to buckle, Aerith was on her feet, hurtling forward, her face vivid with triumph.

Ninka felt a wild excitement as she leaped up and ran after her. She had drawn her knife ready to help despatch the animal if it was not already in its death throes. By the time she reached the wounded cervid, Aerith was there, solemn words on her lips. 'For the gift of your life, which will nourish my own. I thank you, most humbly. All honour to you and fair speed on your journey…'

…to your brother and sister herd-kind, in the Land of the Light. Ninka completed silently. Aerith had not needed her help, she thought proudly. It had been a clean kill. She was about to sheathe her knife when a shrill voice rang out.

'Hoy! You two! Get away from my master's kill!'

Ninka whipped round to see a little fellow sitting astride a large rangy dog that resembled a lurcher. He had sharp features and a rather pointed face, topped by ears which ended in tufts of red-brown hair, giving him a fox-like appearance. The bare arms protruding from his patched jerkin were well-muscled.

'This is *my* kill!' Aerith said, bridling.

'No, it ain't then. And if you talk to my master like that, he'll slit ya tongue,' the creature sneered, revealing over-sized canine teeth.

Before Ninka could ask who the creature was and what business he had ordering them about, a number of sleek white horses burst silently from the trees, their silver hooves brushing just the very tips of the grass. They had red ears and their eyes gleamed like rubies. More of the smaller beings, riding a variety of dogs, brought up the rear. Ninka groaned inwardly at the rich clothes and refined features of the male and female horse riders. A hunting party of solitary fey. It was just their luck to cross paths with nobles.

Aerith had straightened up and turned to face the riders. Regarding them with keen interest, she stood with hands at her sides as the leading rider approached on a magnificent horse. Its plaited silver mane, woven with red feathers and gems, sparkled like fire.

Ninka's blood ran cold. There was no mistaking the lean, coldly beautiful white face from which blazed one emerald and one amber eye. The dark hair, stranded with all shades of red, from watered-down blood to almost purple, was tied back. Jackryn Fleet: one of Catelysma's discarded lovers. And who was always seeking to get back into her favour.

'Aerith. Have a care,' she hissed from the corner of her mouth. If Aerith had heard, she did not show it. *Gentry, love us. Give her the sense to be afraid.*

Jackryn Fleet leaned forward, resting one elegant arm on the high pommel of his chased-silver saddle. He ran a contemptuous gaze over Aerith and Ninka, but quickly seemed to lose interest. Good. He had decided they were not worth bothering with. Ninka's frayed nerves loosened a notch.

'Grint!' Jackryn addressed the foxy creature. 'Have wood cut to build a travois. Get that cervid ready for transportation. And arrange for refreshments to be set out beneath those trees.' He gestured to the edge of the clearing. 'My companions and I shall rest there, in the shade.'

'As you command, my Lord.' Grint gave Aerith a told-you-so grin.

There was a burst of voices and laughter behind Jackryn, as some of the hunting party dismounted. Others rode their horses into the shade.

'Come. Best that we leave now,' Ninka whispered. 'While they are distracted.'

Frowning in a way Ninka recognised, Aerith looked down at the cervid. But she still might have abandoned the kill, if Grint hadn't chosen that moment to urge his dog forward and deliberately jostle her. 'Outa my way! You too, Hudskin scum! Lucky my master dint seek rarer sport! Or we'd av 'ad *your* mangy hide! Be gone now. Lest ya feel Greymarl's teeth.'

Seeing Aerith stiffen, Ninka groaned inwardly. Grint might as well have just poked a nest of snakes with a very short stick. 'What that creature said. It matters not …'

But it was too late. Aerith moved like lightening. She grasped the dog's bridle, one hand either side of its jaws, and hung on tight. It snarled and tried to twist sideways to bite her. 'Oh, would you, eh? Unschooled puppy!' Tightening her grip, she lifted the dog up onto its back legs and held it at arms' length while it writhed and tried to savage her.

'Oof!' Sliding off his mount, Grint landed in a heap. Face flaming, he leaped to his feet. 'Get the bitch Greymarl!' he urged. 'Goo on! Tear 'er fingers orf! Chew 'er nose inta bloody rags!'

Aerith gave a sound of disgust. She lifted the heavy dog even higher, waited until it closed its jaws for a second and then reared up and head-butted it smartly between the eyes. It gave a startled yelp and went limp. Aerith dropped the dog to the ground, where it scrambled up onto all four paws, shaking its head as if its ears were ringing. Moments later it recovered and tottered off with its tail between its legs.

'Greymarl! Come back 'ere, boy!' Grint bawled. But the dog had disappeared into the bushes. He turned back to Aerith, a poisonous look on his face, and drew a large knife. 'Hurt my dog. Hurt me. See?'

'That is your second mistake.' Ninka wagged a finger. She knew what Aerith could do, with or without a weapon.

'Shut it! Filth!' Grint began circling Aerith, feinting with the curved blade.

'Best save your breath. It could be your last.' Aerith was watching, calmly, measuring his every move, choosing her moment.

The noise had drawn interested looks from the hunting parting. Scenting unexpected entertainment, some of the fey showed signs of drifting back towards them.

'Listen to me, Grint.' Ninka affected a reasonable tone. 'Blood need not be spilt. We can settle this simply. Tell Jac....your master, that Aerith's arrow took the cervid's life. We will leave with the animal and have an end to it.'

'Bog it! I told ya already.' Grint advanced on Aerith, his curved knife extended.

'Grint! Stand down,' ordered a curt voice. Jackryn Fleet had approached, unseen on his swift silent horse.

'Master.' Grint backed away immediately. He lowered his knife, but stood watchful, the long canines protruding from his upper lip.

Aerith faced the faery lord. 'If you mean to stop the fight to save me from harm, there is no need. I have the creature's measure!'

'I don't doubt it.' Jackryn Fleet's mouth twitched. His gaze slid towards Aerith with a quickening of interest. 'You dealt swiftly with the dog. It was well done. I would have killed it, but you did not. Curious.' He paused and rubbed at his chin with one long pale finger. 'Does the Hudskin speak the truth? You brought down the cervid?'

Aerith raised her head looking him in the eyes. 'I did.'

'Where is the proof?'

'Turn the animal over,' she replied, coolly. 'You will see that my arrows found their mark.'

'Indeed?' Jackryn raised one eyebrow. He turned to Grint. 'Put that toy knife away and get to it. You there, aid him,' he said, motioning to a number of similar creatures mounted on large dogs.

Grint ran to do his master's bidding. In a short time, he and his companions had cut and stripped some sturdy branches. With a lot of huffing and puffing they managed to lever the heavy animal onto its side.

Ninka noticed an arrow buried in the animal's flank, silver with red flights that glittered in the sun. So Jackryn Fleet and the others *had* been hunting this animal. Aerith was frowning. She too had noticed the silver arrow.

'What say you now, huntress?' asked Jackryn.

Aerith walked forward, stood beside the cervid's head. Reaching down, she grasped the shafts of her arrows and twisted them. There was a slushy grating sound as the movement enlarged the entry wounds. Gritting her teeth, she pulled hard to extract the bloody arrows from the skull and then held them up to display the black and white flights. 'I say again. I dealt the killing blow.'

For a moment, no one spoke. Grint drew in his breath sharply, shocked by such brazenness.

Ninka was stunned by this turn of events. Too late now to explain to Aerith that Jackryn's arrow had marked out the cervid as his own. It mattered not that they hadn't seen it before shooting the animal. There it was for all to see. They were expected to acknowledge the high-born, solitary fey's prior right. She chewed at the inside of her mouth. It was her fault that her beloved knew nothing of the ways of courtiers and their pastimes. Any hunting transgressions were severely dealt with; the docking of ears, fingers and slitting of nostrils being some of the milder punishments.

They were going to have to fight their way out of this. Instinctively, she weighed the odds. With luck she and Aerith could probably fire off enough arrows to overpower Grint and any nearby dog men. Maybe even wound one or two of the hunting party as they were sure to plunge towards the fray, once it broke out. But Jackryn Fleet's prowess as a warrior was legendary. He could overpower her in an instant and that would leave Aerith, accomplished weapon-smith though she was, vulnerable and outnumbered. Still, Ninka was determined that their lives would be not easily won. It would be a bloody battle.

She caught Aerith's eye, saw that they were in accord. Very slowly, she began inching her hand towards her bow. And then froze as Jackryn laughed.

'And I say that such pretty boldness wins the day. Take the cervid, huntress. It is yours.'

Ninka blinked. Why this sudden turnaround? In another moment she realised what Jackryn was about. Her insides clenched tight with alarm. If Aerith accepted the cervid as his gift, it would put her in his debt until she had given him a gift of equal value. If she was unable to produce anything suitable, he could name his price.

But Aerith was no fool. 'An elegant gesture. What must I do to repay you for this favour?'

Jackyrn looked at her with new respect. 'Nothing too arduous. Hunt with me. We shall match our skills, you and I.'

'But I have no mount.'

'You may have the pick of my stable.'

'More gifts?'

He grinned. 'A loan only. No repayment is necessary. Will you accept?'

'And if I do? We are even?'

'Certainly.' Jackyrn shrugged his elegant shoulders. 'I will claim nothing from you. Unless you wish it otherwise, huntress,' he said, his voice deepening.

Ninka saw the way his bold gaze raked Aerith's slender form. Against the elegant fey women, with their gleaming, carapace-like breastplates, flower circlets strewn with gems and graceful flowing skirts, her beloved looked like a half-wild creature of the elements. *She intrigues him. He sees her as a challenge. A new plaything.* She wanted to scream aloud, to say to Aerith, 'Do not trust him. You endanger yourself. Stay here with me. Where I can keep you safe.' But surely her words were not needed. Aerith was too level-headed to be impressed by Jackryn Fleet's affected courtly manners. She waited for her to refuse him.

'Very well,' Aerith said, unflinching beneath his regard. 'We shall hunt together.'

Jackryn grinned. 'Excellent! The Hudskin knows the way to my stables. I will expect you on the morrow.'

Ninka saw how Aerith stiffened. 'Her name is Ninka.'

'What?' Jackryn's face bore a look of incomprehension.

Do not draw attention, Ninka thought, though pride burned in her breast that Aerith should speak up on her behalf. *If he knows that you care for me. He will use it against you.*

'Oh, the Hudskin,' Jackryn said, with a narrow grin. 'Very well. Ninka, if it please you, will you show...' he paused. 'What should I call you, huntress?'

'Aerith.'

'Will you show Aerith the way to my stable?' he said, courteously enough, to Ninka, although his odd jewelled eyes mocked her.

There was nothing she could do. 'As you wish.'

Shifting in the saddle, Jackryn turned towards Grint. 'Butcher the cervid, parcel it up. You and some of your dog men shall transport it for Lady Aerith. And...before you do, you'd best go and search for Greymarl.'

Grint ran the tip of a warty tongue across his enlarged canines looking daggers at Aerith, but he nodded and ran to do his master's bidding.

Ninka did not trust herself to speak. This was more than generosity. She knew the tricksy ways of courtiers. *Jackryn Fleet was set on discovering where she and Aerith lived!* She hated the very thought of his sly dog men sullying the ground around their dwelling with their presence, but it was impossible to refuse Jackryn's offer of help without causing offence. They had narrowly avoided bringing down his anger upon their heads. In the circumstances it was best to cut their losses. By the sentinel oak, how had this happened? As Ninka moved to stand beside Aerith, she felt as if everything was spinning away out of control; the very fabric of their previous existence, fraying into shreds. There must be something she could do, but right now her mind felt full of thistledown.

Jackryn wheeled his mount and rode the short distance towards the party of colourfully dressed fey men and women taking their ease on silken cushions beneath the trees. A number of dog men, moved amongst them offering trays of food and drink. As Jackryn drew close, a woman, dressed all in glittering bronze with sprigs of copper beech woven into her knee-length white hair, rose to her feet and came forward to meet him. Reining in his horse, he bent low in his saddle to take her outstretched hand and bring it to his lips. The women smiled as he placed a kiss on her palm, another on her wrist and finally pressed his mouth into the crook of her elbow. Aerith looked away, flushing.

Ninka's heart sank.

The moment she had been dreading for so long was upon them. Aerith had drawn the attention of the proud solitary fey. And not just any one. Jackryn Fleet, who was high-born, as full of himself as Gentry, and handsome enough to have once stirred even the proud Dark Lady's passions. She knew without a doubt that the time of living together in their forest dwelling, undisturbed by the machinations of the Dark Court and the far reaching implications of Catelysma's rule, was over forever.

CHAPTER 37

JESS COULDN'T FORGET the sight of the tiny, wing-less faery perched on the studio windowsill. She'd had a clear view of its pointed face, narrow-lipped mouth and jagged teeth gleaming against its cloud-grey skin as it pounded on the glass with a clenched fist. A look of panicked horror had crept over its sharp features when it realised that Jess could see it. It took to the air, somehow arrowing towards the direction of the forest beyond the old formal garden.

It was the first wild faery she'd seen since the glamoured hare she had encountered on her pre-dawn walk along the field edges near the village. Every detail of the child-sized being the hare had morphed into was carved on her memory; the broad, red-brown face, sharp black eyes and the pointed ears that stuck up through sparse strands of coarse hair. The two fey creatures could not have been more different in size and looks, but Jess knew instinctively that they were of a totally different order from the hoard of tiny fey that had attacked Ivy Stark.

She would have leapt out of the window and pursued the grey faery but Caleb had been there. Now she heard him moaning in pain. She couldn't leave Caleb alone. What if traces of fey poison remained in his system?

Jess watched him closely for any sign of sickness, but he was moving normally and his colour remained good as he filled the kettle and set about gathering things to make coffee.

Probably just a severe headache then, understandable after what he'd suffered. She felt annoyed with herself for panicking and throwing away her chance of discovering more about Faery. Sighing with frustration, she rested her elbows on the table and propped her chin on her knuckles.

'Something wrong?' Caleb asked.

She shook her head. *Nothing you can help me with, anyway.*

'This kitchen's pretty basic by modern standards,' he said, with an obvious attempt at conversation. 'I don't think it's had anything done to it for about a hundred years.'

'I've seen worse,'

'Really?'

She nodded. 'When our flat got trashed.'

'God, that's awful!' His eyes widened. 'Weren't you terrified?'

She shrugged. 'Shit happens. We lived in a rough area.'

'Lived? In the past tense? Is that why you came here? Because you don't have anywhere else to live?'

'Maybe. But it's not that simple.' Deciding that she'd said enough, she fell silent. Rocking back so that the kitchen chair tilted at a sharp angle, she twirled a long strand of hair between the fingers of one hand as the wood creaked loudly.

'You'll break it, doing that.'

'What? So?' She rolled her eyes, irritated by his air of ownership, and carried on rocking. 'What do you care?'

'I was just saying. The chair's hand-made. Over a hundred years old. I respect craftsmanship. Don't you?'

'Never thought about it.' Now she felt guilty about the damn chair. Annoyed that he could influence her in even that small way, she sat down abruptly. The chair legs clunked satisfyingly on the stone floor. Stretching her legs beneath the table she glanced idly around the room. He wasn't kidding about the state of the kitchen. It was cluttered and gloomy and due a serious paint job. But it was stacked with the kind of stuff that belonged in a museum or an antique shop. 'People with too much money would pay a fortune for some of this stuff. Kitchenalia's big right now. I don't suppose Ivy would notice if a silver teaspoon or two or copper saucepan went missing,' she said slyly.

Caleb gave her a sharp look. 'I wouldn't know!'

'Oh, come on. Don't tell me you couldn't use some easy money.'

'Maybe I could, but I'd never do that to Ivy. She's been good to me, letting me stay here after...'

'After what?' *So he had secrets too.*

'Doesn't matter.' He shook his head slowly. 'Do you always think the worst of people?'

'Pretty much. Until they prove otherwise. Works for me.'

He gave her another of those searching looks, which she couldn't quite decipher, but which made her feel oddly uncomfortable. And, if she were honest, were doing something not altogether unpleasant to the pit of her stomach.

'What?' she challenged, squaring her shoulders. 'If you're expecting me to spill a load of gory details about my deprived upbringing, you'll have a long wait!'

'None of my business.' he said evenly. 'But I'm a good listener. If you ever do... Just want to talk, I mean.'

How did he do that? Stay so damned *nice*, when she couldn't resist having a dig at him? It didn't seem like an act either. He didn't come across as slick or street-smart. Even his slight shyness appeared genuine. She swallowed the comments that rose to her lips. To be mean to him, would be like kicking a puppy. There was no fun in that. It was totally infuriating.

She settled for folding her arms, pressing her lips together and looking at him with studied blankness.

Caleb looked away first. She saw a red flush spreading upwards from his neck before he turned his back to her. There came the clink of the metal on china as he spooned instant coffee powder into a mug.

The kitchen door opened. Alice came into the kitchen with Ivy. Jess caught the residual smell of antiseptic cream. The smaller scratches on the old lady's face had dried to thin lines and the deeper ones were already scabbing over. She was pale, slightly stooped and moving with faltering steps, but Jess was struck again by Ivy's strength of character. After the ferocity of the fey attack, she wouldn't have been surprised if her great grandmother had taken to her bed for a day or two. She'd heard her mum trying to persuade Ivy to do just that, but without success.

Suddenly, Ivy stumbled. Instinctively, Jess was out of her chair, in a blur of speed, catching Ivy even as she began to topple sideways. As if from far away, she heard Alice cry out in alarm. From the corner of her eye, she saw Caleb seeming to move forward in slow motion. She had set Ivy back on her feet and was helping her towards a chair, before either of them had fully gathered their wits.

Looking shaken, Caleb rushed towards the now seated Ivy. 'Are you all right?'

'Yes, yes. It is these uneven floor tiles.' Ivy clicked her tongue in irritation. She pushed Jess away. 'Don't *fuss*, girl. There was really no need for you to manhandle me like that!' she complained, adjusting the folds of her black dress.

Biting her tongue against the sharp comment that rose in response, Jess moved away to the further corner of the kitchen, watching Caleb crouch down so that he was on a level with Ivy. She wished now that she'd let the ungrateful old thing fall over.

'You gave us quite a fright.' Caleb reached for one of Ivy's hands. 'Maybe you should take it easy. Rest more, after what you've been through.'

'Oh, I am as tough as old boots,' Ivy countered, the beady eyes in their pouches of wrinkled flesh markedly less fierce, the emaciated features softening. 'You know that better than most.'

Jess saw that her mum had noticed the warmth of their exchange. She recalled the longing in her voice, thinly masked by anger, whenever she spoke of Ivy's complete lack of ability to show affection towards any of her own family.

'Shall I get you a glass of water?' Alice offered helpfully.

'No thank you.' Ivy didn't bother turning her head. 'But I would like a hot drink, Caleb.'

'Coffee coming right up,' he said.

As he moved towards the work surface, Alice went and stood beside Ivy. She patted her shoulder awkwardly. 'You'll feel better after you've sat down for a while.'

The old lady twitched with annoyance and shook off Alice's hand. 'Please do not patronise me!'

'Sorry. I....I didn't mean...'

Seeing how her mum's face fell, Jess burned with anger on her behalf. She could see the signs of alcohol withdrawal in the slight trembling of her hands, the almost imperceptible slick of sweat on her top lip. She was proud of her for sticking with her regime of medication and reduced alcohol intake. Ivy had no idea of the battle her granddaughter was fighting. Would she care a toss if she did?

Caleb made coffee and passed cups to Alice and Ivy. Jess poured fruit juice, which tasted strongly of chemical sweetener and the plastic coating on the inside of the paper carton. She tipped most of it down the sink.

'Jess, love. Come and sit with us.' Alice motioned towards an empty chair.

She shook her head. 'I'm fine here.'

Ivy glanced at Jess, tight-lipped. 'You're being very rude,' she said in a clipped voice. She turned to Alice. 'It costs nothing to teach good manners. Could you not even manage that?'

Jess's self control snapped. 'You've got a nerve, talking to *me* about manners! I've never met a more self-centred, ignorant, nasty, ungrateful, mean-spirited old...' Words failed her.

Caleb looked scandalised by her outburst. Too bad. She couldn't care less what he, or the frosty old fossil at the table, thought of her.

'Oh, dear. I'm sorry about Je...' Alice began.

'Don't! Don't you dare apologise for me,' Jess burst out, pointing a trembling finger at Ivy. 'We don't owe *her* anything.'

There was an awkward silence, in which the ancient kitchen clock ticked loudly. Caleb shuffled his feet beneath the table, his trainers squeaking on the kitchen tiles.

At length, Ivy said calmly, 'Jessica's right, Alice. You do not owe me anything.' She took a deep, calming breath. 'I am very much afraid that the same cannot be said of me.' Lifting her cup to her mouth, she drained it. Some of the coffee slopped onto the bodice of her dress, but she didn't appear to notice.

Alice did. She leapt up and grabbed a kitchen roll. Tearing off a sheet, she leaned over Ivy and mopped up the wet patch on her dress. This time Ivy didn't protest. She even managed a thin smile. 'Thank you, my dear.' There was a pinched look to her wrinkled features and she drooped forward in the chair.

She seemed drained of vitality. Her hands were visibly trembling.

'Mrs Stark?' Caleb said, alarmed, rising from his seat.

'No. Stay where you are.' Ivy raised a hand to him wearily. 'Alice? Would you kindly help me into the sitting room? I wish to talk to you. Alone.'

'How did you do that?' Caleb asked, frowning.

'Do what?'

'Catch Mrs Stark like that. You were…Wow! Beyond fast.'

'Good reflexes. I keep in shape,' Jess lied. 'I need some fresh air. Laters.'

She bit back a smile. It was fun verbally sparring with him, and a novelty to have a guy colouring up like that when he met her eyes.

CHAPTER 38

WINDROTH ESTATE WAS even bigger and more wild-looking than had been evident from the upstairs window of the house. Jess wandered down overgrown paths and weedy borders backed by rambling hedges. She glimpsed a wooden gate set in a wall, half-hidden by the ivy that covered it and guessed at the walled gardens beyond it. But it wasn't those, or the rest of the grounds she was interested in. She made her way across lawns and an open field until she came to the remains of a decaying fence. Beyond it there was a stretch of woodland, sombre and dim, even in the bright autumn sunlight. There was little undergrowth; even the few remaining brambles and nettles were weak and stunted. As Jess entered the forest, a thick layer of dry twigs and leaf litter crunched beneath her feet, releasing a pungent smell like old leather.

There it was. The oak.

Caleb had been right. It was magnificent, with deeply ridged bark and a massive trunk that bore the scars and damage of countless seasons. The wide, spreading branches and sheer bulk of the tree put her in mind of a cathedral. Deep within it, she could sense the beating heart of the ancient being that inhabited it.

She walked forwards, aware of a subtle shift in the air as she approached the tree. It was as if the oak-being was curious about her. She felt it probing her, with an intelligent but neutral curiosity. It was not unpleasant. *Fair enough. I'd be suspicious of me.* She stopped a short distance from the trunk and stood looking up through the branches, as she attempted to transmit a silent greeting.

There was a long pause. Nothing happened and she began to feel foolish for her wild imaginings. *Talking to trees. What next?* She was about to leave when something changed. Gradually, at first, a deep musical note filled her head, sweetly penetrating and accompanied by a light, flowery perfume. Tiny lights appeared all over the tree. They glittered, amber, gold, and silver amongst the branches. With a soft rustling sound, a thick shower of leaves floated downwards confetti-like around her.

Jess smiled, holding up cupped hands, which filled to overflowing with leaves. She tossed them into the air, where they hovered briefly before turning into glittering dust and disappearing. The tree-spirit had given her its blessing.

'Thank you,' she felt moved to whisper into the silence as she backed away.

'Jess?'

'Who's there?' She spun around, but could see no one.

'Over here.'

She peered into a grove of trees that were in shadow. Nothing. There was a shift in her vision. Imprinted on the pattern of trees, there was now a figure, backlit by faint light as if a door was partly open behind it. Without appearing to move, the figure was standing directly in front of her; a spun-glass form of swirling grey light, that glinted with movement, like motes of dust in a shaft of sunlight. The movement slowed as the form thickened, resolving rapidly into the shape of a tall, slender being. Its pale face, all sharp angles, was dominated by slanted, almond-shaped eyes.

Streams of silver extended upwards from behind its shoulders.

'Jess?' it said again, more softly.

How could this creature know her? Jess was poised to run, but something about the figure gave her pause.

'Do not fear me. Not you. Never, you.' Disappointment tinged the voice. 'Do you not know me?'

'Mike? I mean, Taryn?' Jess felt her jaw drop. It couldn't be. Could it? 'Taryn! I thought I'd never see you again!'

'Then we are well met, Jess.' She saw the gleam of white teeth in his narrow smile.

'What are you doing here? How did you find me?'

'Word of a human with true sight has spread amongst the fey,' he informed her. 'The description fitted you. And I dared to hope... Well, it seems I was right. Also, you may recall telling me that Alice spoke of coming to Windroth,' he finished with a smile. 'I needed only to wait.'

'Oh, right. No mystery then!' She was grinning like an idiot, more pleased to see him than he would ever know. 'The old woman who owns the place is Alice's grandmother and *my* great grandmother. How amazing is that?'

'Ah, that is the connection. I had wondered.'

'Can you believe it? All those years living in shitty squats and flats. Mixing with low-lifes, having no money. When all the time, this place was here.'

'Indeed. And now you are returned. So then. It is time, Jess.'

'Time for what?'

'To complete your education. Since you are here, we had best make haste,' he said, gravely.

Jess couldn't tear her eyes off him. He appeared completely solid now, beautiful, but otherworldly, even more so than when she had first seen him in his true form; when he had rescued her from Leon's clutches. Then he had looked fierce, even feral. Now he had an added quality. He looked... noble. Yes, that was the word that came to mind. He wore some kind of tightly-fitting outfit, finely woven from grass or rushes. It resembled Samurai armour, moulded to his slender frame by buckled straps. The tips of his pointed ears showed through his flowing straight hair. Blade-like folded wings jutted above his shoulders.

She felt self-conscious, like a tattered urchin in her charity shop clothes and paint-splattered boots. If she'd known, she was going to be in such elegant company, she'd have made more effort.

'Do you understand me?' Taryn asked with a touch of impatience.

She nodded. 'Yeah. I'm supposed to enrol in faery college or something.'

He ignored her attempt at humour. 'This will not be easy for you. Do you trust me?' he asked, silver eyes glinting.

'Of course,' she said at once. It was true. He was the only person who had never lied to her and who she could rely on completely. She owed him her life.

'Then come.'

'Where are we going?'

'Into Faery. To the Apple feast. But first, you must re-weave a strong glamour and change form. In these woods, it is unsafe for mortals to roam abroad.'

Wearing her human disguise had become a habit, with which she was comfortable. Now, appearing to be human could, apparently, expose her to harm, so she must appear in her true form. *I must become a monster, to walk amongst monsters.* Jess took a deep breath. Hadn't she been looking for answers? This was the best chance she was ever going to get. *Here goes nothing.* She concentrated for a few moments, willing that internal shift and feeling the tingling in her fingertips as she manipulated the glamour.

'Woah!' She gasped, rocking back on her heels. She had forgotten how it felt to be stripped of the heavy restriction of glamour. The world was so much brighter, more intense, so wonderfully... alive, through unfiltered fey senses.

She stood before Taryn, suddenly gripped by shyness. It was all she could do to keep still as he ran his eyes over her. Looking at him was like holding up a mirror, except that he was a living patchwork of silver and she a symphony of leaf-shadow. She knew her hair to be a wild, spun-sugar halo in all shades of willow, emerald and lime. Her eyes were entirely jade-green, with no pupils or irises. The muscles at her shoulder blades flexed as her wings unfurled. Their soft warmth against her back, more than anything else, left her feeling more exposed than if she had been standing there completely naked. A soft perfume wafted from them as the delicate strands and streamers moved of their own accord.

'Exquisite.' Taryn swallowed hard, lowered his eyes.

'Erm. Can we go now?' Jess murmured, uncomfortably, shuffling her feet.

'Not quite.' He looked up, his expression neutral again. 'Remember that you are a true-changeling. Some fey here knows who you are. Why you were left with human parents. He or she will not have expected you to survive. Even less, to find your way back to Faery. Caution must be our watch-word, until we know more.'

'Oh, great. So now I'm a target for whichever psycho faery parents dumped me? I'm guessing that mummy and daddy won't exactly be throwing a welcome home party, since the baby-shower was a no-go?'

Puzzled, he looked at her in silence. She remembered how he had sometimes struggled to understand the way she spoke. It seemed even more difficult for him, now that he must be spending all of his time back in Faery.

'I'm in danger? Right?'

'Ah, yes. That is so,' he said, his face clearing. 'For that reason, I think it most unwise to enter Faery in your true form.'

'I need *another* disguise? How about a hairy troll? Or a warty ogre?'

His lips twitched. 'Either glamour would be most charming on you. But some subtle detail to your true form will suffice. There will be many high-born, solitary fey at the feast, roughly mortal in shape. It will seem natural for you to blend with your own kind. May I suggest shades of brown for your hair and eyes? Dull garments. A muddy tint to your skin and wings?'

'Sounds boring.' Jess screwed up her face, but she could see the sense in what he suggested. Again, she willed glamour to flow over her body. It was done, instantly. Plucking at her mouldy-straw skirts with twig-like fingers, she noticed that her nails still sparkled with pale green glitter and quickly turned them dull and brown, too.

'There. Every detail sorted,' she looked up at Taryn. 'Will I do?'

'You are perfect,' he said, seriously.

'First time I've ever been called that! OK. I'm as ready, as I'll ever be. Let's do this.'

They moved forward together into the canopy of trees. After a few paces the air shimmered as if in a heat haze. Everything changed.

The forest was transformed into a rich multi-coloured

landscape, so ancient and untouched that she wouldn't have been surprised if a herd of dinosaurs had appeared. The trees were enormous, some of them so tall their tops were shrouded in mist. Bracket fungi, as big as dinner plates, jutted from trunks. The ground was mossy underfoot and she could hear running water. Ferns and pale-flowered plants grew on sloping banks and half-covered the giant trunks of fallen trees. Over everything hung a glittering, pale-green light, with bars of gold where shafts of sunlight pierced the lacework of leaves.

Taryn went ahead, following a trail that only he appeared to be able to see. Soft grass brushed against Jess's bare ankles. At one point the trees thinned out and she could see the glint of a vast lake. On the far shore she could see dim, tree-lined slopes and purple hills. In the distance, the tips of snow-capped mountains.

'Wow! This place is beyond huge. How can it be here, hidden in Ivy Stark's forest?'

Taryn slowed his steps, so that they walked side by side. 'Faery and the world of humankind occupy the same space. Made of different fabrics, they overlay each other. The barriers between them can only be crossed by those who know how.'

'Has Faery always been here?'

'Indeed. For time out of time. Where better to hide a jewel than in plain sight?' Taryn spread his arms wide and lifted his face, so that a shaft of sunlight gilded his sharply angled features. 'This is my homeland, Jess. It gladdens my heart to be here again, after living in that drear, soul-less otherworld of stone and iron. Not,' he said, with another of his narrow grins, 'That I regret one single moment of it.'

'I'm glad you were there,' she said, smiling in return. 'I don't know what I would have done without you.'

'I have a feeling that you would have made your own way.'

'Maybe. But I didn't have to, did I? You made things a lot easier. Th…' She stopped herself and settled instead for, 'I'll always be grateful to you.'

'You learn quickly.'

'Never thank a faery or accept a gift, or you put it in debt to you, right? Or you become in debt to it. Whichever way around, you'll have a heck of a time trying to get rid of it.'

'As you say.'

They pressed on along the banks of a river and then turned inland until they were once more engulfed in deep green forest. Birdsong filled the air and emerald fireflies winked from the dim shadows. Further on, in an open glade, sunlight flashed on the wings of clouds of golden dragonflies that flitted around hanging vines with flowers in shades of violet, old-rose and pearl-grey.

No. Not fireflies or dragonflies. They were tiny faeries.

Jess completely lost track of time. She had no idea of how far they had travelled.

At length, Taryn paused. 'We are approaching the Dark Court. Stay close to me and keep your wits about you. That way you should be safe. Whatever you see, do not react. That is important. You must give me your word.'

Jess nodded, amused by his serious expression. Had he forgotten she was in disguise? And it was only a party, wasn't it? How wild could it get? She'd seen her fair share of alcohol-fuelled fights, legless people staggering about. Girls covered in vomit with their underwear on show, lying in gutters or being carried home by friends. Intoxicated faeries couldn't be all that different. 'OK. Hey, discretion's my middle name.'

They walked down a long, gentle slope. After sometime it

flattened out and a steep hill reared up before them. The top of it was choked with brambles and thorny bushes. Taryn drew a symbol on the air and a gateway framed by complexly carved wooden pillars appeared in the hill. At the same time a line of fey, filing slowly, into the hill was revealed.

It was so different from what Jess had expected that she stifled a laugh. Taryn had obviously over-played the danger element. Getting into the oh-so-dangerous Dark Court appeared to be similar to gaining admission to a popular nightclub in any human town on any Saturday night! All that was missing was a couple of bouncers in shiny-black bomber jackets.

And then she took a closer look at the fey.

The queue had nothing of humanity about it. There were creatures of all shapes and sizes; some tall with sharp, cat-like faces, others short and squat with gnarled hands and feet, whiskered snouts or humped backs. Tiny beings hovered in the air above the queue, zipping back and forth and chattering amongst themselves. Here and there Jess glimpsed slender, winged faeries, richly dressed in vibrant colours. The women were fine-featured and coldly beautiful with their flowing hair, high cheekbones and glittering eyes. Walking beside them were their equally beautiful consorts, wearing what looked like leather armour, studded with jewels, and sweeping cloaks. A stunning woman with a complicated up-do of vivid, purple hair, woven with red feathers, caught Jess's eye and smiled revealing piranha teeth. She blew Jess a kiss, twitching her long skirts flirtatiously. Slim ankles ending in hairy goat feet were revealed before the long skirts covered them again.

Jess was still staring at the goat-woman, when a lumpy, dough-coloured being lumbered past her and pushed into the queue. It was dragging a rat-like creature on a lead. The little creature stumbled along on its back legs, whimpering with pain and pawing at the thick metal ring around its middle. Beneath the iron, its fur was completely burned away, to reveal raw flesh.

Horrified, she grasped Taryn's arm. 'Someone should teach that bully a lesson!'

He turned a mildly quizzical gaze on her. 'Oh that. Some commonplace dispute. It is not our affair.'

'But it's cruel! Haven't they heard of animal rights here?'

Alerted by her raised voice, the goat-woman and one or two other fey threw Jess interested looks. There was a stirring and muttering in the crowd. One or two creatures bared their teeth.

Taryn threw back his head and laughed loudly. 'So amusing!' he said, pointing at the wretched little rat. Other fey joined in the laughter, pointing and jeering, while the rat's captor puffed itself up and grinned proudly.

Taken by surprise, Jess struggled not to object. Taryn took advantage of the diversion to grasp her arm and quickly steer her into line behind an elegant couple with blue fur instead of hair.

'I can't believe you think torture is funny!'

'On my oath, I do not! But it is unwise to show public disapproval. The small creature will be freed and soon recover, but slights, real or imagined, amongst the fey, fester longer than iron-burn. Feuds have been sparked over less.' He wore a set look she had not seen before. 'You gave me *your word* that you would not draw attention to yourself. If that is beyond you, then declare it. And we shall leave, forthwith.'

Jess swallowed realising she had put them both in danger.

He had warned her that the rules here were different, but she hadn't taken him seriously. 'I've been an idiot. I'm sorry,' she said in a small voice. 'I get it now, OK?'

'Very well.' Taryn nodded, tightly, as they moved forward.

He said nothing as they neared the entrance to the hill. Ahead of them a group of fey were talking animatedly as they went inside. And then it was their turn. Jess tensed as she saw a domed tunnel stretching ahead. The ceiling was constructed of twisted roofs, amongst which glimmered tiny greenish lights. A complex smell, smoky and heavy, like incense, floated towards her.

'Shall we, my Lady?' Taryn bowed slightly, extended an arm, courtier-like.

'Why not?' Forcing a smile, Jess placed her hand on his wrist.

He winked at her and she knew she was forgiven. She made a promise to herself to stay close to him. *And to keep my mouth shut,* which, she thought wryly, would be a first. Even so, as the tunnel engulfed them, she could not suppress a shudder of apprehension.

There was no going back now.

CHAPTER 39

THE FUNERAL SERVICE was held at the County Cremato-
rium. Caleb sat through it with an odd sense of detach-
ment. Mum wasn't in that coffin. There was nothing of her,
here.

He had made his own way to the chapel. Slipping in the
back door unnoticed he'd taken a seat just inside, so that he
could leave the moment the service was over. There were
not many people present. Dad and Pa Farmer sat in the front
row of pews. A smattering of long-standing customers, come
to pay their last respects, were dotted around the small chapel.

Caleb rose to his feet and stood woodenly as hymns were
sung. Pa Farmer's and Dad's deep voices rose above the
muted, polite singing of the other people.

Hypocrites; both of them.

The vicar's address and formal prayers swept over, and past
him. The words, meant to offer comfort, were impersonal.
Mum had believed in actions being louder than words. She'd
been spiritual, in her own way, but she'd had no time for
organised religion.

As the service drew to a close and everyone rose to their
feet, he stood up. With his hands clenched by his sides, he
stared ahead as the curtains closed around the coffin and it
trundled silently away on rollers.

As if feeling Caleb's eyes on him, Dad turned around. Caleb
almost didn't recognise him, clean-shaven and with his wiry,

grey-hair brushed flat. His dad's face twisted with grief, or perhaps anger. There were tears on his cheeks. Caleb hoped Dad felt regret, but he doubted it.

Too little. Too late.

Their eyes locked, held. Father and son. Caleb felt no emotion. He remained still, unblinking, stony-faced.

Dad looked away first. He was fingering his shirt collar, as if uncomfortable in his best suit. And then he seemed to come to a decision. He made a move as if to walk into the aisle. Caleb tensed. *Bring it on then. Why don't you? Show everyone what you're like.*

Dad paused, hesitated. Abruptly, he turned to face the closed curtains that screened the now-empty platform. As he sat down, Pa Farmer reached out a hand and squeezed his son's shoulder.

Two-of-a-kind. Old school, survivors.

Caleb was done with them. Nothing connected him to them any longer. He had a life of his own. He knew Mum would be pleased. She had wanted that for him. Turning on his heel, he walked out of the chapel and kept on going.

* * * * *

Alice sat alone on the edge of the bed, staring into the gloom of the wood-panelled room, wondering about Jess. She hadn't seen her since that awkward scene in the kitchen. She'd assumed that Jess had gone off to explore the estate and on returning, had gone straight up to her room. Which wasn't unusual. Jess liked to keep her own company. But on checking this morning, Alice had discovered that Jess's bed hadn't been slept in.

Now it was beginning to get dark again and still Jess hadn't returned. Perhaps she was spending time getting to know that boy, Caleb. Ivy had mentioned that she allowed him to use the old summer house as a live-in studio. (The irony of which was not lost on Alice, Jess and Stella having been conceived in that place.) That aside, she thought Caleb seemed pretty decent, if a bit of an oddball. But knowing of Jess's wariness around most guys, Alice thought it highly unlikely that her daughter had spent the night with him.

No, Alice's fears were beginning to move in another direction. What if Jess had finally had enough of being nurse maid for her useless excuse of a mother?

But she couldn't quite believe that Jess would leave without a word of explanation. She was too up-front for that, not to mention loyal and caring. Alice comforted herself with the thought that her daughter would reappear when she was good and ready. All she had to do was sit here and wait. Which was easier said than done.

Being back here was painful. Everything about Windroth conjured up memories. It seemed as if Rob would walk through the door at any moment. She might turn and see him, slouching against a wall, that lazy smile pulling at the corners of his mouth. Or come upon him sitting cross-legged on a carpet with a newspaper spread out before him. This was the same bed where they had spent so many stolen afternoons. If she drew back the bedcovers, she might, even now, glimpse the imprint of his body on the rumpled sheets.

Impossible that the space around her did not contain him.

From the window, Alice studied the blurred patchwork of grounds, long left to the elements. How Rob would hate to see things looking that way. He'd been so proud of the neat, weed-free flowerbeds and close-mown lawns; even sweeping the gravel free of leaves, with a besom he'd made of birch branches – silly word, besom, it had made her laugh and he had laughed too, at her. Apparently a besom disturbed the small stones less than a yard brush. She had teased him for his neatness and attention to detail, telling him that his efforts were wasted on Ivy Stark who was oblivious to anything but her painting. Laughing, he'd chased her down to where the manicured grounds gave way to fields. One of which, left to lie fallow, was a glory of nodding, purplish grass heads and wild flowers the colours of foil-wrapped sweets. Here too, were hedgerows, thick with lacy elder flowers.

'My wild, beautiful girl,' Rob had called her between kisses. They lay naked in the long grass so often that their bodies turned honey gold.

Coming back to Windroth, after so many years, she had thought, must offer some possibility of closure. Alice imagined uncoiling her happy memories, like a lock of a lover's hair, captured behind glass, and feeling them slide against her fingers. Walking down the path that led to the kitchen she had caught the scent of sun-warmed grass on the breeze. And been transported straight back into Rob's embrace, felt his hair brush against her face. And that had made her sense of loss too tangible. So much hope, all of it fallen to dust. As her eyes blurred with tears and she fell to her knees, a stone scraped her skin drawing blood. She was glad. There was release in physical pain.

Alice reached for the bottle of whisky which stood open on the bedside table. She had found it along with other unopened bottles of spirits in a cabinet in Ivy's disused dining room.

If only Jess would hurry up. She really needed to talk to her about Ivy. Because it was obvious that her grandmother was suffering from dementia. There was no other explanation for the weird stuff she had told her, after they left the kitchen. That meeting with a mysterious, strangely-dressed man in the woods who had promised her fame and riches. She had made a pact with him, promising to give him something in return. It was complete nonsense, of course. But Ivy hadn't seemed confused. If anything, she was completely calm, her sharp black eyes like chips of jet in their web of wrinkles. Apparently, otherworldly creatures had bullied Ivy into working on her paintings to the exclusion of all else. Oh, yes, she did get rich and famous, as the stranger had promised, but the impulse to paint became a curse, an addiction, draining her until she was little more than a dry husk. Leaving her with no energy, or will for anything else; even Ralph and their young daughter, Joan.

The most pathetic excuse for coldly neglecting Alice's grandfather, her mother, and Alice herself, she had ever heard! She drank more whisky. Addictions? Oh, she knew all about those. But an addiction to painting, spurred on by faeries? It was mad.

Ivy insisted that the monstrous things had hounded her mercilessly for half her life, threatening and punishing her if she stopped painting for more than a few hours at a time. She'd barely even had time to sleep between their torments, so had taken to napping on the couch in her studio. Apparently it had been a hoard of the tiny creatures that were attacking her and Caleb, when she and Jess arrived. The reason being that Ivy's recent illness had kept her from her studio for over a week. This was their revenge for her supposed desertion.

What a load of rubbish. She'd seen the swarm of bugs attacking Ivy.

And yet? There were things that nagged at Alice. Unexplained things she had buried deep and would rather not think about. Brief glimpses of movements from the corners of her eyes. Shifting shadows on dull days, in this very bedroom, where there ought not to have been any shadows. Then there was the time soon after the twins were born unexpectedly early, when she woke in the middle of the night, drowsy and exhausted from sleep-deprivation. And thought she saw a column of light near Jess's cot.

Alice's head was spinning with exhaustion as she tried to reason it all out. Her tongue felt swollen, her spit was thick and bitter, drying instead of moistening her throat. She needed Jess. Jess was strong, fearless and practical and faced the world head-on. She'd had to, because of me, Alice thought without emotion.

It was slipping into twilight outside the window. The bedroom was filled with grainy darkness, the bulky wooden furniture transformed into nightmare shapes, but Alice didn't switch on the light. She gulped more whisky, ignoring the raw burn of it in her sore stomach. Climbing onto the bed, she sat cradling the bottle. The house's presence was all around her, silent, oppressive. It was like having been swallowed by some enormous animal made of wood and bricks.

So much of her life was wrapped up in this room. There was the cast-iron radiator where the twins' cots had stood. Jess with her sharp, creased up little face and shock of black hair, so like Rob, but somehow completely herself too, even though she was so tiny. And Stella with her creamy skin and golden curls, like herself as a baby. A baby each, Rob had said, proudly.

Alice stretched out fully-clothed and closed her eyes, let the numbing haze of alcohol steal her soul. Slip into oblivion. Jess would be back soon. Jess would sort things. She always did.

But Ivy's voice, as if at a distance, intruded on her disordered thoughts. There was a letter, Alice recalled dimly. To be opened in the event of her death. Which, Ivy said would fill in the gaps. Something about a debt which still had to be paid to the faery stranger in the woods. But Alice could no longer harness the thoughts fleeing her mind, along with all pain, all care, and eventually consciousness.

CHAPTER 40

THE GREAT CHAMBER under the hill was brightly lit by glowing globes, suspended from complicated structures strung net-like across the vaulted ceiling. Rows of market stalls were set out around a large central area, where musicians were gathered on the broad stone steps of a well. Laughter and raised voices rang out as all manner of fey twirled, leaped and high-stepped to the music. All was colour and flashes of movement. Garlands of leaves, dotted with bright red crab apples, dried apple rings and berries were draped around the walls. More of the same decorated the stalls.

Apart from the flashes of gorgeous faces and nightmarish figures in the crowd, it might have been some kind of charming village fete. But Jess was already learning not to take anything to do with the fey at face value.

She and Taryn wandered amongst stalls displaying delicious-looking pies and tarts in moss-lined baskets. They stopped to admire some cakes topped by a complex lacework of spun-sugar. Taryn selected two and held one out to Jess. She watched as he bit into his cake that instantly became an apple.

He smiled at the expression on her face. 'Glamoured. What else did you expect? Look more closely.'

Jess did so and the glamour shredded before her eyes. The delicious food was just piles of mushrooms, nuts and apples.

Was nothing here as it seemed? She nibbled her apple, as they walked on. A slender faery drifted towards them, holding a tray of tiny wooden cups. She had an unruly froth of pink hair, topped by a circlet of apple rings. The tips of her long toes dangled just above the cobbled floor as she hovered in mid-air.

'Fabe.' Taryn greeted her with a shallow bow. 'I did not expect to see you at the feast. I trust that I find you well?'

'Well indeed.' Two rosy spots of colour stood out on the faery's pale cheeks. 'I am no longer a scullery fey. Crowle has given me charge of the still-room. I helped make the apple wine. He agreed that I may bring it to the feast,' she said proudly. 'Of course, you would not know that. It is some while since we have had the pleasure of your company at court.'

'Might I flatter myself, that you have missed me?'

Fabe waggled a finger at him. 'I would not pander to your vanity, by admitting or denying that fact!'

Taryn clasped his hands over his heart. 'You wound me sorely, pretty pixie.'

'I think not, my Lord. For you are in fine company.' She smiled at Jess. 'Welcome, Lady... Forgive me. We have not met. What name do you prefer to use?'

'Jess,' Jess supplied.

'Lady Jess. An honour to meet you.' Fabe spread her hands and performed an elegant mid-air curtsy. Straightening, she held out two of the acorn-sized cups. 'Wine. To bless the gift of apples,' she said dimpling prettily.

Taryn took a swallow and rolled the liquid around his mouth. 'Pure nectar. My compliments to you. I expect Crowle is hard at work in the kitchens. He is well, I trust?

'Dear Crowle is well indeed. I shall convey your comments.' She shifted her gaze to Jess and her brow furrowed. 'Your lady finds no pleasure in the draught?'

Jess blinked, as they both looked at her expectantly. She'd had no intention of drinking the wine. Painful stomach cramps and vomiting had always followed any ingestion of alcohol or cooked food. She hesitated, remembering the cake that had been an apple. The wine was probably only glamoured water. Besides, what might happen if she refused to try it? For all she knew, this innocent-looking little pixie would lay a curse on her.

Lifting the cup to her lips she took the tiniest taste. 'Delicious,' she said, automatically. To her surprise it was. Light, honey-sweet and scented with a flowery perfume. What was more, the effect was instant. Warmth spread through her limbs and pooled in her belly, while a pleasant lightness swirled in her head. She took another tentative sip of wine and then drained the cup. '*Really,* delicious!'

'More?' Fabe offered.

'That would be unwise,' Taryn sounded a warning note.

Jess heard his voice, but it registered only faintly. Her hand seemed to have developed a life of its own and was already reaching for another cup. She tossed back the wine in a single swallow. It really was amazing. Faery wine obviously agreed with her. She could drink this stuff all night. Before she knew what she was doing, she was reaching out for more.

Taryn captured her hand. 'Enough.'

'Hey! What are doing?' Jess protested as Taryn slipped a strong arm around her waist, began steering her away. She craned her neck, straining back towards the hovering faery.

'Come, my lady. There is much to see,' Taryn said, a smile in his voice which contrasted sharply with his implacable grip on her. 'My regards to you, Fabe. Enjoy the revels.'

'And you, Lord Taryn.' The pixie beamed at him in return. She nodded at Jess. 'Lady Jess.'

'Er...Pixie.' Jess's head felt full of cotton-wool. She couldn't seem to think straight. A golden haze flickered at the edge of her vision. She struggled to get free as she found herself being marched down the aisle at the back of some stalls. 'Thash...that's the second time you've man-handled me! Or should that be fey-handled? It's getting to be a habit!' She felt a giggle bubbling up in her chest, which turned into a loud burp. 'Ooops, pardon!' She clapped her hands over her mouth.

As Taryn turned to look at her, the corners of his mouth twitched. 'Faery wine is best taken in very small measures, if one is unused to it. Too much of it will steal one's wits away, forever.'

'That right? How mush is too mush...much?' she asked, trying to care, but failing. The taste of apples danced on her tongue.

'You are safe enough. I stopped you drinking in time. The effects will soon wear off. The fault is mine. I should have realised what might happen. Come. We shall find a place to sit until you are yourself again.'

'Sounds cosy.' Jess yawned. Her limbs felt heavy and she would have liked to sleep. She laid her head against Taryn's broad shoulder, feeling the fine weave of his grass jacket against her cheek. He had relaxed his tight grip and the arm encircling her waist felt companionable. 'Just don't keep dragging me about. OK? Ish...it's kind of humiliating.'

He grinned. 'You have my word.'

They wove through the stalls and past a sort of pit in the ground where a motley collection of fey appeared to be betting on the outcome of some kind of animal fight. Taryn led her to a clearing, where groups of fey were reclining on wide couches, set around stone tables. A group of grey creatures with smoke-like limbs drifted past. Further back, candles that smelled of cloves spread discreet pools of light over tangles of naked limbs.

'Are they…oh!' Jess blushed as she saw what was going on, but Taryn paid no attention. 'Awkward,' she murmured, as she hurried past.

A fresh breeze blew from somewhere, stirring black and silver veils fastened to screens of woven twigs. She threw herself down onto an empty couch. Swinging her legs up, she rested her head against the deep silken pillows and crossed her ankles. The visual displacement was fading now. Her head was slowly beginning to clear, but the pleasant warmth in her limbs remained.

Across the chamber, lights were being lit in sconces on the wooden pillars of a structure that rose into arched points above a dais of shiny black stone. It put Jess in mind of Gothic church architecture and was made of some dull substance, so perfectly black that it seemed to absorb light. A high-backed chair, heavily carved and glittering with diamond-like jewels became visible in the torch-light. The sides and top of the chair were covered with sharp black thorns.

Taryn perched stiff-backed on the edge of the couch, his face in three-quarter profile. Jess blinked at him through heavy lids. He was starkly beautiful. More so than any androgynous cat-walk model. She wondered how many faery hearts he'd broken. On impulse she patted the space beside her.

'Sit here. It's more comfortable,' she invited. 'Would it kill you to relax for a change?'

He raised one silver eyebrow. 'Not at all. But it would be most unwise. Remember where we are. It behoves one of us to keep their wits about them.'

'Well pardon me for being such a disappointment. Maybe you're expecting too much of me?'

'I think not. Why do you say such things?'

'Don't know. Always been my own worst enemy, I 'spose. Rubbish at being human,' she found herself saying. 'Couldn't hack it at all. Now I'll probably be a crap faery.' She clamped her lips together before she embarrassed herself with any more revelations. *Serious note to self. Faery wine is a no go area from now on.* 'That pixie was pretty,' she said, quickly.

'Fabe?' Taryn looked bemused by this complete change of subject. 'A sweet creature.'

'She seems fond of that cook. Crowle, was it?'

'Indeed. A good fellow, for an ogre. Big as a cart horse. Ever ready to do a good turn for any fey. More than can be said for many of his kind. He is devoted to Fabe.'

'An *ogre*? With that delicate little pixie?' Jess rolled her eyes. 'The mind boggles.'

Taryn did not reply. He was watching a slender woman who was moving haltingly towards the dais, her steps slow as if she was bone-tired. Glistening red hair, moulded to her small head, streamed down her back and appeared to blend seamlessly with her clinging red robe. Jess noted with surprise that the faery woman's exposed arms and bare feet were also red. The woman sank to the floor and sat leaning against the base of the thorny throne, seeming not to notice if the sharp points pierced her skin.

A stricken look flickered briefly across Taryn's face, before he resumed his mask-like expression. Jess noticed that his hands were linked so tightly that the bones of his knuckles showed through the skin. She would have asked him about the red faery, but her attention was captured by a movement at the far end of the chamber. A channel was being cleared to admit some kind of a parade. A general hush settled over the revellers. In the silence, music rose on a more sombre note.

All around Jess, faeries were on their feet, rearing up on back legs or crawling forward for a better view.

Taryn stood up, motioning to Jess to do the same. As she took her place beside him, the crowd parted briefly. She glimpsed a group of fey men, with lean, haughty faces. One of them met her eyes briefly before looking away. She felt a stab of recognition. There was no mistaking that face, framed by dark-red, shoulder-length hair. Or the penetrating, mismatched eyes, one emerald and one gold.

The shadowy figure from *Royalty's Revenge*. She would have known it anywhere. How amazing was that? Her interest quickened.

'Who's that?' she whispered, plucking at Taryn's sleeve. 'The one with different coloured eyes.'

Looking up, he saw where she was pointing. His lips thinned. 'You do not want to know. He is dangerous.'

'What's his name?' she insisted.

'He answers to Jackryn Fleet.'

Jess's thoughts were reeling. Ivy Stark had painted Jackryn Fleet. When had she encountered him? It was another piece of the puzzle that surrounded her great grandmother. She was trying to get a clearer glimpse of Jackryn, when with a sweeping, forward movement, the faeries around her, including Taryn, bowed. Jess quickly followed suit. Turning her head sideways, she watched a number of richly dressed courtiers sweep past. Behind them, came the most stunning woman she had ever seen. Her hair and clothes blazed with jewels. It was hard to look at her through the burning, rapturous aura of power that surrounded her. So this was faery royalty. Jess could not stop staring.

The woman paused in front of Taryn. 'Lord Taryn. You have returned to us,' she said gesturing for him to stand up straight.

The woman's sweet voice rang bell-like in Jess's ears.

'Catelysma. Dark Majesty.' He took her outstretched hand and pressed his lips to the ring of spiked black crystal she wore. 'I trust I find you well.'

Catelysma' lips curved, but her glowing turquoise eyes were expressionless. 'You find me ever hopeful of your compliance.'

Taryn still held her slim white hand. 'I am humbled by the honour you do me with your indulgence. And would not wish to cause you even a moment's distress,' he answered smoothly.

'Indeed?' Catelysma turned her hand to expose her wrist. Jess could see the blue veins beneath the milk-white skin. Taryn placed an open-mouthed kiss on her wrist. The queen gasped and her eyes darkened with desire. 'I would that you remained at court, at my pleasure,' she said huskily. 'Is there… truly no way I can persuade you to it, my lord?' She glanced towards the thorny throne and the red faery who slumped there with her head drooping like a wilted flower.

A muscle twitched in Taryn's taut cheek. 'I cannot help but wonder whether when a thing is beyond possibility, it is not better to accept the fact,' he said coolly.

The queen's eyes glittered. 'You dare!' She snatched her hand away and slapped his cheek, hard. Jess suppressed a gasp as she saw that her spiked ring had left a deep cut on Taryn's cheekbone. Blood flowed down his face and pooled at the neck of his jacket, but he made no move to stem the flow.

The queen flashed an appraising glance at Jess, but her eyes slid away almost immediately. Jess knew a moment's fear. It felt as though a flame had warmed her and been abruptly withdrawn.

Capturing a drop of Taryn's blood on one fingertip, the

queen smeared it across her lips. 'Beyond possibility, say you?' she hissed, leaning forward. 'Beware lest you presume too much! The patience, with which I favour you, wears thin.'

Taryn's face was like stone. 'Majesty.' He bowed stiffly as the queen glided away and headed towards the dais, leaving a cloud of intoxicating perfume in her wake.

As Catelysma took her place on the jewelled thorn throne, two willowy fey women glided forward and arranged the folds of her sumptuous gown. No one paid any attention to the red-faery. Her eyes were closed, Jess wondered if she was dead, but thought she could see her breast moving slightly in time with her breathing.

'Are you OK?' she whispered to Taryn.

'Perfectly.' His pale cheekbone was already swelling and turning purple. She could tell by the set of his shoulders that he was holding himself tightly in check. 'Although I would prefer you had not witnessed that.'

Presumably he was embarrassed by the openly sexual display she had just witnessed. 'Why did you play hard to get? It's obvious you've both got the hots for each other?'

His eyes were like flint. 'You understand nothing!'

Jess bit back a reply as an odd-looking creature scuttled forward and stood at the foot of the steps. Its bulky yellowish body was balanced on skinny legs ending in tiny hooves. It glanced around and gave an ingratiating smile revealing mud-coloured teeth.

'We are honoured by the presence of her peerless Majesty,' it announced, spreading its arms. 'Who, by her very presence, sheds blessing on the apple trees, which we honour at our feast. Hail, Dark Lady. Ruler of the Shadow Court. Most illustrious and beloved, Night Queen. Gentry of pure blood, whom we are sworn to serve. Whose beauty inspires devotion and makes lesser beauties weep. Whose word is Law. Whose every whim, must be indulged. Most glorious and of the highest order ...'

The praise was unstinting. Not one of the fey moved a hair while the creature continued to list Catelysma's titles and praise her attributes. Its voice droned on until some of the fey around Jess began stifling yawns.

Catalysma gave a sound of impatience. 'Enough Tweeter. You will have the entire court famished by boredom.'

Tweeter fell silent. He bent low, his head retreating, turtle-like, into the wrinkled folds between his shoulders. 'Your pardon, Majesty. I do most humbly beg your indulgence. The glory of your personage stole my wits for a space.'

'I tire of your endless flattery. Methinks it time I chose a new steward,' she said, examining her long glassy nails. Butterflies flew up from the silver-green hair, which was arranged in complicated coils over a jewelled frame that stretched far beyond the width of her shoulders.

Tweeter blanched. 'If that is your wish. I will present a number of suitable candidates for the position, before slowly roasting myself to death on the kitchen spit. For without I am in your service, my life has no purpose,'

'Do not tempt me to take you at your word!' Catelysma placed her hands in her lap. 'You may redeem yourself, if the spectacle you have arranged is entertaining.'

Tweeter jumped to attention and motioned to two beings standing in the shadows. A young girl and boy came forward. Their eyes were glazed and they moved mechanically, as if sleep-walking.

Jess felt a clutch of dread. *Human. They're human children.* No, she told herself, they're glamoured fey. She remembered the gorgeous food that was really apples, nuts and berries. All was illusion here. She willed the glamour to drop from the children and reveal their true forms. Nothing happened.

Catelysma yawned. 'I trust this is not to be a commonplace display of innocence destroyed. I grow weary of such spectacles.'

'No, Majesty,' Tweeter said, hurriedly. 'I had something other in mind. These are brother and sister. Devoted to each other, I am informed by their procuress.'

'Ah,' the Dark Lady leaned forward. 'Then it is to be a test of love?'

'As your Majesty predicts.' Tweeter produced a curved bone blade. He approached the children and handed the blade to the boy. 'One of you may leave this place alive.' He bent close and said in a whisper, which somehow penetrated the chamber. 'Is it to be you, lad? Yes? Then use the knife on your sister.'

Jess heard the boy's moan of distress. Although his face was still blank, tears gathered in his eyes. 'I…I can't. I won't…'

'Poor sweet thing,' Catelysma purred in a voice like velvet. 'But you must. If you would live.'

Yells and screams of bloodlust rose from the fey packed into the chamber.

'Yes! Yes! Slay the little hot-blood!'

'Carve up our fresh meat for us!' This from a bloated-bellied creature that dripped drool from bared teeth.

The crowd had become a melee, all manner of beings pressed so closely together that Jess was hemmed in, hardly able to move or to see anything beyond the seething bodies. She was rooted by horror. This must some trick. A staged performance. But the look on Taryn's face told her otherwise.

A high-pitched scream rang out. It was met by cheers and more calls for blood. Another scream, prompting howls from the crowd. Jess weighed the possibilities of shoving forward, grabbing the children and hustling them to safety.

Taryn seemed to know what she was thinking. 'You think that course has not occurred to me on numerous occasions?' He sounded sorrowful, bone weary. 'You cannot save them. Every fey here is sworn to do Catelysma's bidding without question. You would be torn to pieces, before you had taken a dozen steps.'

Jess knew he was right, but she hated herself for doing nothing.

'See how the hot-blood cuts his self!' crowed a voice in the crowd.

'Oo-ooo, he's bleedin' like a stuck swine!'

'Such loyalty. Delightful!' Catelysma clapped her slim white hands. There was an avid look on her face.

Jess was shaking. 'Stop. Please stop it,' she whispered, but her voice was swallowed up by the noise.

As the crowd suddenly surged forward in a wave, she caught a glimpse over their heads. Tweeter was on his knees before the queen holding up something wet that dripped dark liquid down both arms. Behind him lay the crumpled form of the boy. The reddened knife lay on the ground. White to the lips, the girl stood with tears dripping from her chin. In a swift movement, she bent, picked up the knife and drew the blade across her throat.

The cheers and roars re-doubled. Faeries poured forward to caper around the still-warm bodies, before attacking them with claws and teeth. Jess saw one break free and scurry off with its bloody prize. Her stomach suddenly twisted so violently that bile rose into her throat and blackness crowded the edge of her vision.

'Get me out of here!' she hissed at Taryn.

Taryn too looked sick with disgust. 'Come then. No one will notice us now.'

As they wove their way across the chamber Jess stared ahead, blind to the smeared faces and bloody hands of the feasting faeries. The music struck up again and wild dancing resumed. At the exit tunnel Jess could not resist a final look at Catelysma. The queen was giving her fingers a final lick clean before wiping her hands on the hair of her nearest courtier. The red fairy had collapsed at her feet. Throwing back her head so that gouts of silver butterflies clouded the air, Catelysma laughed mockingly and kicked the faery down the steps. She rose, swishing her trailing skirt aside, she walked past the lifeless body.

As the crowd parted to make a way for their queen, Jess spun round and ducked into the tunnel. Taryn was waiting for her, his head bowed and his tall slender form slumped against a wall. In the half-light, it looked as if his shoulders were trembling.

At her approach he straightened instantly. 'Why did you tarry? Come. We must go,' he urged, stretching a hand towards her.

Jess wasn't about to argue. She rushed towards him and meshed her fingers with his, surprised at the implacable strength of his grip. Together, they lurched through the tunnel, navigating the twists and turns at breakneck speed. Even that wasn't quick enough for Jess. She couldn't wait to get out of this place.

CHAPTER 41

WHERE WAS SHE? If it hadn't been for his churning thoughts about Jess, Caleb would have been content. There'd been a skin of ice on the pond this morning. Frost rimed the fruit trees in the old kitchen garden. Days had passed. But Jess had still not returned.

He'd seen Alice gathering salad leaves one morning. She'd answered his enquiries about her daughter's whereabouts. 'No she didn't know where Jess was. Or when – if – she'd be back.'

Of course she'd come back. The alternative didn't bear thinking about. Keeping busy, that was the thing.

He gathered the best of his drawings into a folder, having decided to cycle into town and risk approaching a couple of gift shops. Normally he'd have checked with Mrs Stark if she needed any shopping before setting off. She had Alice to take care of her now, but she was unreliable.

Caleb rapped on the kitchen door with his knuckles. There was no answer, so he knocked again, louder, waited, and finally opened the door and went in, calling out, 'Hi! It's me, Caleb!'

No one answered. The house was silent, with that imperceptible stillness in the air that signified emptiness. Used crockery stood on the kitchen table. Frowning, Caleb peered into a mug, from which a faint smell of stale coffee rose. There was a centimetre of dark liquid, filmed with stale milk at the bottom. On the work surface, an open jar of instant coffee and some used spoons.

Where was everyone? He went into the hall and peered into the sitting room. It was shuttered and gloomy. Puzzled, he went deeper into the house than he'd ever been before, opening doors leading off the hall, to reveal a dining room, a study, and a number of other downstairs rooms, all of them with closed curtains, fusty with the smell of disuse. He caught glimpses of wooden panelling, richly patterned carpets and dark furniture. Carefully closing doors behind him, he retraced his steps.

'Hello? Is anyone here?' he called, at the bottom of the staircase.

A figure appeared above him, causing him to stop in his tracks. Jess. Joy flared in his breast, his pulses raced.

But it was Alice, hair hanging in limp strands around her puffy face. She seemed to have trouble focusing and was swaying very slightly, steadying herself by gripping the banisters. Caleb felt a stirring of alarm.

'Oh, it's you. Thought...was Jess.' Alice drooped with apparent disappointment.

'She isn't back, then?'

'Don't *you* know where she is?'

'Me? Why would I?'

Alice shrugged. She held her hands palms up for emphasis. 'Just thought... you would. Likes you. Can tell. You... find her. Bring her back.'

Jess liked him? She had a very funny way of showing it. But then Alice was obviously tanked up on something and not making much sense.

'Where's Mrs Stark...' he began.

But Alice had turned, and was making her way unsteadily along the upstairs landing. Fingers of one hand splayed against the wall, she placed each step with exaggerated care.

Caleb shook his head, exasperated. It was a miracle that she'd made it to the stairs. He deliberated about whether to follow Alice, make sure she didn't collapse. Shouldn't you make sure someone who was drunk was lying on their side, in case they were sick and choked on their own vomit?

But Mrs Stark was his priority. Alice would have to take her chances. He lurched forward, took the stairs, two at a time and went straight to the studio. The damaged door was pulled to, but unlatched.

'Mrs Stark?' he called, knocking on one of the panels. 'Are you in there?'

There was no answer. He pushed the door open slowly. The studio was the same as always, a total clutter of painting materials covering every surface, canvasses, three or four deep, leaning their faces against the walls. At first glance, Caleb thought the room was empty. It was a second or two before he caught sight of the small, crumpled figure on the old couch, a dusty threadbare blanket pulled up to its chin.

'Mrs Stark!' He was across the studio in an instant and on his knees beside her. She was so still. Her skin had a slight yellow-grey sheen like marble. Oh, no, she couldn't be... 'Hey.' His heart in his mouth, he reached out and shook her gently. After a moment, she stirred and her head emerged from the blanket.

She blinked at him, like some small burrowing creature awakening from hibernation. 'Caleb?' she said, voice hoarse with sleep.

Relief washed over him. 'Who else?'

'Where have you been? I missed you.'

'Did you?' He felt touched by this admission. It wasn't like her to say such things. 'I thought I should keep away. You, Jess and Alice had a lot to talk about.'

'Hmph! We talked, Alice and I. For all the good that did. I do not know why I expected her to believe me. She thinks my mind is going. I could see it in her face. No matter. Not much longer now.' She paused. 'She and Jess have kept to themselves for the most part. Perhaps Alice told the girl what I said and she came to the same conclusion as her mother. Not that I blame them for keeping their distance. In their position I would probably have reacted in the same way. So much for blood being thicker than water. More fool me, for expecting things to be different. All...this. It has gone on for far too long.' She shook her head slowly. 'Was it all worth it? I do not know any more. I ought to have fought against it. Been stronger...'

Caleb could hardly concentrate on what she was saying for the anger boiling up inside him at the way Mrs Stark had been neglected. Alice seemed to have gone on a serious bender and was as useless as he'd suspected. But she ought to have had the common decency to at least make sure Mrs Stark was comfortable and had something to eat. He'd expected more of her, of Jess too. Just wait until he saw her again. He'd have a few choice things to say to her.

'Well, I'm here now.' He slipped a careful arm around her, helped her to sit up. He wondered whether to tell her about Alice. But there seemed little point in telling her that her granddaughter was totally plastered. 'I suppose you've been painting. I know what a terrible workaholic you are,' he teased gently. 'How long have you been in here?'

'I really don't know. It might be quite a while.' Mrs Stark relaxed against him. He caught her smell of linseed, unwashed clothes and elderly sleep-warmed skin. Her brow furrowed. She looked perplexed. 'I did *try* to work, but somehow I could not concentrate. So I laid down my palette and brush and decided to take a cat nap. It is very odd, you know, but everything is different, since *they* left.'

'Since who left?' asked Caleb.

Mrs Stark patted his hand. 'No one *you* need worry about,' she said, enigmatically, smiling at him so that her deep wrinkles softened. 'At least, I dearly hope that is the case. I have tried so hard to keep you from them.'

Them? He nodded, humouring her, although he hadn't the slightest idea what she was going on about. 'Right. That's...er great.'

She seemed confused, rambling. He wondered how long she had spent on this couch without so much as a glass of water. Gran Farmer had once become so disoriented that she hadn't recognised Mum. It turned out she was badly dehydrated.

'It is peaceful in here now, is it not?' Mrs Stark commented. 'You must be able to feel it too, Caleb? Can you? Can you feel it?'

'I can feel...something,' he replied. There was an imperceptible difference, but he couldn't have said what it was. 'You must be stiff and cramped from lying on this couch. You should drink something.'

She smiled again, a far away look in her eyes and made a snuggling movement against him, which he found oddly touching. 'It is such a luxury to be allowed to *sleep*. And not be wakened by their incessant demands. At times, I have been black and blue from their pinching. Scratched raw by their claws. But no more. Dear God in Heaven, no more.' She sighed, a peaceful, breathy sound. 'I just laid here, for a few moments to enjoy the peace and solitude. But I lost track of time. Well. No matter. What else have I to do now, but rest?'

'You're going to get a terrible crick in your neck if you stay there much longer. Let me help you to your bedroom. You can get washed and changed, while I make tea and sandwiches? I'll bring you a tray.'

'Sweet, kind boy.' She reached up to gently brush his cheek. 'That sounds wonderful. You know, I often think of how lucky I was that it was you, I almost knocked down outside the shop that day.'

'Me, too. Works both ways, you know. I reckon we rescued each other.'

'Rescued? Is that what we did? Yes. I rather think that it was.' She turned her face up towards him. 'I am glad I was able to help you a little, Caleb. I failed so miserably with my own family. I regret that.'

Caleb felt emotion welling in his chest and had to swallow hard. He had never seen her like this; gentle, almost sentimental. 'Come on then, Mrs Stark. Are you ready?' He eased her to the edge of the couch, intending to get her onto her feet. But her legs gave away. She stumbled, clutching at him, so he swept her into his arms.

The feel of her, little more than skin and bones now, reminded him of a blackbird he had rescued from a stray cat in the yard behind the shop. How fragile the bird had felt, its heart ticking rapidly against his cupped palms. In the bedroom, he lowered her onto the bed and made sure she was sipping from a glass of water, before he fetched her walking stick. 'Can you manage? I can help you, if you like?'

He cringed inwardly at the thought of undressing and washing her. He'd never yet had to give her that degree of personal care, even when nursing her through the bout of flu. He really could have done with Jess's help right now.

'No need,' Mrs Stark said, between gulps of water. 'I am

perfectly capable of giving myself a cat lick. But you could sort me out a face flannel, a clean towel and nightdress.'

'No problem.' He smiled at the idea of a cat lick. It was a good name for a quick wash. He went to get the things she wanted, placing them on the bedside cabinet. She had drunk all the water, so he re-filled her glass. 'Sure you can manage? OK then. I'll leave you to it. Back soon.'

'Goodbye, Caleb. My boy,' she said in such a soft voice, that Caleb thought he must have been mistaken.

My boy. She had never called him that before. Trailing a hand behind him in a wave, he headed for the stairs.

CHAPTER 42

IT WAS GETTING dark by the time Jess and Taryn stood amongst the trees at the edge of Windroth estate. Their journey back through Faery had passed in a rapid blur of movement, but she hadn't wanted to linger. The beauty and wonder of their earlier journey had been forever spoiled by all she had witnessed.

From this distance Windroth Hall looked like an impressive dolls house silhouetted against a grey-violet sky in which the first stars glowed. It had been morning when she left and she was surprised to find it was now evening. She had thought the house shabby, bleak and echoing with sad memories, but it felt like a cosy cottage compared to the faery court. Weariness dragged at her. It was more than tiredness. She felt wrung out by all she had seen and wanted nothing more than to climb the staircase, collapse in a spare bedroom and close the door on the world, or rather, on both worlds.

She searched for the right thing to say to Taryn. Something smart and off-hand that would hide how she was really feeling, like; 'I enjoyed the tour, but I didn't think much of your friends.' Or 'Remind me not to sign up for a repeat performance of the mother of all culture shocks.' Nothing seemed adequate. 'OK then. Um…see you sometime,' she settled for, preparing to set off across the open fields.

'Wait!' Taryn was at her side in an instant. 'We must talk before we part company.'

Jess looked at him. 'What's the point? Talking's not going to stop me feeling like I've been chewed up and spat out. I'm going to try *really* hard. And maybe, just maybe, I can make myself forget everything I've seen.'

'I understand that you are distressed. That is to be expected,' he said, his voice softening.

'Distressed? You feel *distressed* when your pet cat goes missing! Try disgusted, horrified, sick to my stomach. Those poor kids. What did they ever do to deserve that? And what about their grieving parents? I bet no one's given them a thought.'

'You are correct in that assumption. The affairs of men are not close to fey hearts. We think of mortals as little more than rats – breeding rapidly and then gone in the blink of an eye. It seems hardly worth wasting breath on them. Even I who have, now and then, lived mortalwise and seen more of humans than many, feel a great void between our races.'

A chill ran down Jess's spine. How could he be so matter-of-fact? His beautiful sharply-angled face had never seemed so alien to her. 'What sort of cold-blooded answer is that? However you dress it up, faeries like *you* torture and murder *children*! And then...then *eat* them, for God's sake. I'm surprised you didn't rush forward to get your share!'

He blanched. 'You judge me harshly. Not all fey are flesh eaters. The practice is repugnant to me. But the courts are bound by the whims of their rulers. Catelysma has developed a taste for bloody entertainment. So her Dark Court reflects that and all it means. It is not only mortals who are endangered there.'

Jess's eyes widened. 'That's supposed to make me feel better? You warned me once about Gentry. Remember? You said they were cruel because they lived a long time and got bored or something. Catelysma makes Hannibal Lecter look like Bambi! I suppose I should pity those faeries, having to do everything she asks, whether they want to or not. Doesn't anyone ever stand up to her?'

'It is impossible for any fey who has sworn allegiance to disobey their Dark Queen. Even the solitary fey must answer her call once an oath is sworn. Only another Gentry is powerful enough to stand against her.'

'So refuse to take the oath! Problem solved!'

Taryn gave her a pitying look. 'If only it were that simple.'

'So basically, Queen Bitch has absolute power?'

'As you so eloquently put it. Catelysma is the planet around which the Dark Court revolves.' His lips twisted in a grimace. 'There are many ways to force the unwilling to swear loyalty. We may struggle on the hook, but we all comply, eventually. Even solitary fey are drawn towards the faery courts to celebrate the seasonal feasts with their own kind. And the Dark Court holds sway in this forest. Only another Gentry would be strong enough to found a Bright Court and challenge Catelysma's rule.'

Alerted to something in his voice, Jess looked at him closely. 'You haven't sworn allegiance to Catelysma, have you?'

'I despise her and her cruelty,' he said, his lips twisting. 'I will *never* serve her. But I walk a knife edge between kindling her desire and her anger. Keeping her hopeful of conquering me, offered some protection to those she would use against me. But with her patience wearing thin, I fear that battle is near lost.'

'So that's what was going on back there. I thought you were just flirting.' Jess was beginning to realise how little she knew about the complicated rituals of a faery court. A horrible thought entered her mind. 'That red faery. You know her, don't you? What's the story with her?'

'Red faery? Ah, I see why you would call her that.' He sighed deeply. 'Her name is...was... Anira. My lady was gentle and sunny of nature. We were lovers, but over time, the fierceness of our passion faded. Anira and I remained close friends. She was as dear to me as a sister. Catelysma knew this. I assume that she decided to punish me for my tardiness in pledging myself to her, so...' he paused and pain passed fleetingly across his face, 'she...she ordered Anira to swallow a draft of sanguine-leaf. Anira had no choice but to obey her queen.'

Jess screwed up her face in sympathy. 'Not good. Right?'

'Sanguine-leaf is a deadly poison. It has the effect of causing blood to slowly ooze from every pore in the body, until death comes as a welcome release. Can you imagine how terrified Anira would have been? How hopeful that I would hear of her suffering and arrive at court in time to petition the queen for an antidote? But a vital quest kept me away. By the time I returned, it was too late. Shocked I saw my sweet lady barely a breath away from death. No antidote in Faery could have helped Anira. It was only that knowledge that stopped me throwing myself at Catelysma's feet and begging her to accept my fealty.'

A vital quest. Jess knew what that quest was. Taryn had been mortalwise, looking out for her, glamoured as Mike and living in the underpass. Unknowingly, she'd had a hand in what happened. Her heart hurt for Taryn who'd been in an impossible situation. The strength of will he'd displayed in masking his anger and grief, while facing down Catelysma, and keeping Jess safe into the bargain, was nothing short of amazing.

'I'm sorry, I'm so sorry,' she said, knowing how inadequate that sounded.

He nodded acknowledgement of her words breathing a sigh that made him shudder. 'By displaying Anira at the apple feast, so all could watch her dying moments, Catelysma sent a powerful message to me and any unsworn fey who dare to oppose her. I cannot stop thinking that Anira died because of my stubbornness. I killed her,' his voice broke.

'No. You're wrong!' Jess burst out, furious on his behalf. 'It wasn't your fault. Catelysma killed Anira. She's vile and twisted and enjoys making people suffer. You have to stop beating yourself up. If you do that, Catelysma wins. Is that what you want? We humans have a saying; Don't get mad. Get even.'

The livid bruise stood out on Taryn's cheek. Tears had tracked through the drying blood on his cheek. 'You speak wisely, Jess,' he said, lips thinning to expose shiny, somewhat pointed teeth. With a look of determination, he ran a hand over his face and then looked briefly at the blood and tears on his hands, before bending swiftly and scooping dew from the grass. By the time he had finished washing, he had composed himself.

'Forgive me for my moment of weakness. I have no wish to burden you with my sorrow. I will endeavour to take comfort in knowing that Anira is beyond harm, dwelling in the Far Summer Lands of our Ancestors.' His starkly beautiful face was expressionless.

'That's the only way,' Jess said, touched that he would even think of apologising to *her*. She wished she could tell him that losing someone stopped hurting after a while. But she would have been lying. She still felt a pang whenever she thought of Lisa. And Lisa was still alive and well, even though her college friend was as good as dead to her. 'Taryn?' she asked thoughtfully, after a pause when neither of them spoke. 'You once told me to avoid the faery courts because they were dangerous. It was obviously a massively big deal for you to show your face at the Dark Court. So, why take me there?'

'I had a good reason, as will become clear. But first I must beg your forgiveness a second time. I had no idea that mortal children had been procured. I deeply regret that your first encounter with your own kind was so trying for you.'

Jess blinked at him, feeling as if a distance of light years stretched between them. 'My own kind? Catelysma? Those murderers.' She shuddered. 'I am *nothing* like them! Any of them. I know some humans can be scumbags, but fey are no better. They might even be worse! No offence, Taryn. But fey-born or not, that's my first and last visit to Faery.'

'You may decide otherwise, when you have heard all I have to say,' he said calmly. 'For you speak truly. You are unlike the Dark Court fey. Or any other fey I know of. You are unique.'

Jess was intrigued despite herself. 'Is this another of your riddles? Tell me then. But keep it simple.'

'I will endeavour to do so. The reason I took you into the Dark Court was to confirm something I suspected. Do you recall when you first shed your glamour and revealed your fey form?'

She nodded. How could she forget the moment when her life changed forever? 'It was in the underpass. After you gave me that dried berry drink. What about it?'

'I noticed something about you immediately. You were fey, but with a difference. Something...other. I had my suspicions then, but they were so unlikely, that I discounted them. Those suspicions remained, however, and would give me no peace. I turned the problem over and over in my mind, trying out different theories and possibilities, but I could not shake my first conviction. Finally, I was forced to accept the evidence of my own eyes. And to accept the impossible.'

'I knew it!' Jess said, exasperated. 'Don't you *ever* give a straight answer?'

He smiled thinly. 'It is not in the nature of the fey. But, for your sake, I am trying. Truly.' He paused. 'Well then – how is this for directness? You have mixed blood, Jess. You are the child of fey *and* mortal parents. I needed to be certain before I told you. Now I am.'

'What? *What?* That's impossible. You just said so yourself.'

'It is so rare as to be *almost* impossible,' he clarified. 'I told you once that the glamour on you was the strongest I had ever seen. That was my first mistake. The original glamour, that keeps the fey-born safe in the world of men, however well-woven, would have weakened long ago from the iron and chemicals in the air eating away at it. *You* rebuilt your glamour, and maintained it, using your own latent power. Your personal glamour, incredibly strong and vibrant as it is, is what I saw. Do you have any idea how rare this is, Jess? You can only have inherited the ability to do this from an unusually powerful, high-born fey parent.

'You were born in Faery, I am certain of it. If only because of the need for the protection of glamour, when you were consigned to live mortalwise. You were exchanged for Alice Morgan's own baby. I am not sure why she was chosen as your foster-mother. But I do know that fey blood breeds true and will always be dominant within you. Jess? Jess, are you listening to me?'

She nodded, automatically ticking off mental bullet points. *I was born in Faery? I am a changeling. Alice's human baby girl - the real Jess - was most likely killed to make room for me. I have one human and one fey parent.*

Was Alice attacked by an elf and made pregnant? Or had she been seduced by a fey lord's beauty? But then another thought. Was it Rob Morgan who'd done the deed with a faery? That would explain his nightmares, his guilt. But not his desertion of Alice, after baby Stella died.

'So, what am I?' she asked. 'Is there even a name for me? Like a mongrel, half-breed or sludge-blood – given what you lot think of humans?'

He spread his hands. 'Ugly, meaningless words. You are Jess Morgan. Although you will have a true name in Faery. One day, you will find out what that is. And then you will come into your true power.'

'Oh, wow! I can't wait!' she drawled, resorting to sarcasm, her default mode whenever she felt out of her depth. It was a bad habit, but she couldn't resist. 'Just call me Ms Rumpel-stiltskin! Will I get a magic wand, too? In the story books faeries and humans have affairs and babies all the time. Maybe my dad was a frog prince? Mum gave him a kiss and – bonus! There he was - sex on legs, with wings!'

He didn't laugh. 'Crude mortal fantasies, born of half-truths and ignorance. This is serious, Jess. You are in great danger. The truth is that highest-born fey only rarely give birth to young. Their wombs seem unable to nurture a babe. Some lower-born fey reproduce readily, but even then many infants are sickly and perish. It is one reason why the practice of stealing mortal babies arose. Grieving fey mothers hoped to adopt and raise them in Faery. But mortals face many dangers at court, not least from jealous Gentry and rarely survive for long, as you have seen.'

Jess winced, not wanting to think of the scene of carnage she had recently witnessed. She was doing her best to forget that, whatever Tayrn said about learning from it.

'As to mortal and fey couplings,' Taryn went on. 'They did take place in ancient times and, *very* occasionally a baby would result and grow to adulthood. Such a creature of two worlds had special qualities. Many solitary fey oppressed by cruel Gentry found themselves drawn to those of mixed-blood, banding together around them to live in wild camps, hailing them as their leaders. Gentry, wary of any challenge to their rule over the traditional courts, looked on these enigmatic leaders and their wild camps with great suspicion. A great war in Faery was sparked by Lord Natus, the last known child of a fey man and a mortal woman. Natus's ambition outgrew the wild camp he founded. He gathered an army, took it upon himself to overthrow a Shadow King, the despotic ruler of a Dark Court. It was his downfall. Even those Gentry who opposed the Shadow King sided with him against Natus and his followers.'

'What happened?' Jess asked.

'The killing was savage. Nothing of its measure was ever seen in the Blessed Land. Death reigned supreme. Bodies of the slain, piled up; a bitter harvest, poisoning rivers and streams. Scrags and redcaps grew bloated on the free bounty. The stench was a pall that shuddered the heart of every creature with breath still in its body. Gentry gave no quarter. They slaughtered entire villages of those who harboured Natus's stricken supporters. Some solitary fey, wounded and in hiding, were driven to eating the blood-stained clay of battlefields, lest they starve. It is said that numbers of these fled to Catelysma and other Gentry, and swore fealty to save their skins. And that is how the taste for blood spread amongst the Dark Courts.' He shrugged. 'But I do not know the truth of this.'

Jess was appalled. So much death. 'But peace was restored?'

Taryn nodded. 'Eventually, the pendulum swung back, as it must. Balance was restored. New laws set in place. No challenge to any fey court, either Night or Bright, will *ever* be countenanced lest it be presented by a solitary Gentry, man or woman, to the High Gentry at the Midsummer revels, when all of Faery royalty gather together.' He gave Jess a wry smile. 'Odd as it may seem to you, Gentry set great store by blood-line, ritual and the rightness of things. For the ruling families, deviation from the accepted rule leads to disaster. Poor Natus was charismatic, undeniably brave - and foolhardy to listen to bad advice. There never *was* a chance of him advancing any higher and being accepted as a nobleman, despite the fey blood running in his veins. You can never rise to become Gentry. You are only ever born to it. Natus's challenge to overthrow a Dark Court ruler was doomed to failure. He perished on the battle field, with hundreds of thousands of his followers. The reverberations of Natus's defeat resounded over a millennium, one result being that mixed couplings amongst all high-born fey and mortals were forbidden. Any transgression is punishable by death.'

Jess had been listening closely, in fascination. Natus. He sounded like the hero of some video game. He had been like her, apparently. Shame that she had been born a thousand years too late to meet him. 'If that's true, about it being forbidden for fey and humans to sleep together, what makes you think that you're right about me?'

'Because, I was able to put my theory to the test,' he replied. 'High-born solitary fey travel from far afield to the apple feast. I thought to find some imprint of you on one of them. But something entirely...unexpected happened. Something I could never have foreseen.'

'What?' Jess asked. 'You spotted my faery mum or dad at

the Dark Court? You did, didn't you? I can see it in your face. Why didn't you tell me when we were there? I could have been introduced!'

'I have already told you of the danger,' he answered obliquely. 'I was afraid of how you would react. To have revealed yourself would have put us both at risk.'

'I'm not some little kid, Taryn!' she blustered, furious that he'd kept such vital information from her. 'I've been looking after myself since I was four years old – a four year old human, anyway! I've a right to know stuff that concerns me.'

Taryn's silver eyes softened. 'You have, indeed. But this is no small thing. You may need time to encompass it.'

She felt like punching him. 'For fu...Would you *just* tell me?'

'Very well. I...I looked on Catelysma and saw what should have been staring me in the face all along, if only I had not been distracted by Anira's plight. Luckily your glamour is so powerful it even shields you from the Dark Lady, or you would not be standing beside me now.'

Jess felt her scalp crawl. 'What are you telling me? Catelysma's not...? You're not telling me that she...she's my... No! You're wrong. You have to be!' She shook her head wildly, her glamoured brown hair whipping against her face.

'It is true, Jess. Catelysma's blood, the rare and ancient blood of Gentry, runs in your veins. The Shadow Queen herself gave birth to you. Of that there is no doubt in my mind. You are more of a threat to the rulers of Faery than ever was Lord Natus. Should your presence become known, the news will spread throughout Faery like wildfire. Exiled fey and those who have resisted the dominance of Gentry, will flock to your side, with more readiness than they ever did to him. The kings and queens of both Dark and Light courts will petition for your death before you grow strong enough to challenge their rule.'

Jess listened in stunned silence. *Queen Bitch is my mother.* This was *so* not what she had expected. Of all mad things she had been forced to accept, this was by far the most insane.

Taryn continued with his reasoning. 'I am astounded that Catelysma's womb quickened and cradled a babe to term.' He shook his head slowly. 'Even more that she was able to keep such a forbidden birth secret. If it became evident that she has a living daughter, born of a liaison with an unknown mortal, her sovereignty, and possibly her life, would be in peril. Even Gentry must abide by some laws. For reasons I cannot yet fathom, she allowed you to live and exchanged you for Alice's human baby Jess. I can only assume that she expected you to perish while living mortal-wise...'

Alice is not my real mum. Catelysma is. Then I had a human father. But who was it? The suspicion she had already felt, about Rob Morgan took deeper root within her. Alice had said he was a beautiful man. She had spoken of Rob's nightmares, his terrible guilt, after Stella died. It would make a skewed kind of sense. But his desertion of his young family remained a mystery. She couldn't go there. Not yet. Not with so much else whirling in her mind. She zoned back in to what Taryn was saying.

'... why then, would she have put such a powerful protective glamour on you? It would have been easier to allow you to gradually weaken and fade.'

'Problem solved, eh?' Jess felt sick. She swallowed hard. 'Catelysma, could pretend it never happened.' *I, never happened.* 'So why didn't she finish the job?'

'I have not all the answers. Neither, I suspect, does the hudskin who asked me to attend to your welfare while you dwelt mortalwise. Although... I begin to wonder,' he said thoughtfully.

'Rewind a minute! Hudskin?' Jess queried. It was the first time Taryn had used that word. In the underpass, after she had saved Lisa and had first learned about glamour and her feyness, Taryn had mentioned that a good friend of his had asked him to watch over her. Sixteen years ago, in mortal time, he'd said, Jess recalled. 'This...hudskin creature. *He* asked you to look after me?'

Taryn nodded. 'But *he* is a *she*. Ninka Minka, the Hudskin, is a solitary fey. A wise and gracious being of the deep forest who appears at court only when her special talents are required. The hudskin tribe was hunted to extinction in these parts by Gentry, consequently Ninka has no love for Catelysma. Ninka is expert in herb craft, hunting, and has arcane powers known only to her lost tribe. She once did me a great service. So I was happy to render to her the favour of watching over you. Her reasons for this, she kept to herself. And I did not ask.'

'Why not?' Jess was mystified by such an obvious omission.

'It was enough that I agreed to her request. She did not owe me an explanation,' Taryn said, rather huffily, Jess thought.

'Well, I'd have asked her! Ninka obviously knows more about me than she's letting on! I need to talk to her!'

'I agree, but that may have to wait. It takes time in Faery to locate a being who does not wish to be found. If Ninka does indeed know more about you than she is willing to impart, you may be assured she will keep that knowledge close to her heart.'

'That's OK then,' Jess said, dryly. 'I'll just take your word for that, shall I?'

'Yes,' Taryn said with perfect seriousness. 'It is well indeed, that we can trust Ninka. For Catelysma must not know that you have survived. Still less, that you have returned to Faery. Until the time is right.'

'Right for what?' Jess asked, suspiciously. 'I'm not the least bit interested in faery politics, if that's what you're getting at! This is not my fight! And don't compare me to Lord Tatus, or whatever his name was. I'm not special or strong enough, to ever be that important. And I sure don't want one single person - or fey - to die because of me!'

'*Natus.*' Taryn corrected, softly. He seemed perfectly calm, his sculpted features immobile. 'You think you are not special? Allow me to persuade you otherwise.' Sinking to his knees, he bowed his head, so that his silver hair swept forward. Placing his folded hands on his breast, he closed his eyes. 'I, Taryn Neath Redfeather, by the power of my true name, do swear sole allegiance to you, the Lady Jess Morgan or whatever true name is yours. My whole life, heart and my sword are yours to command....'

'Oh, God. No, Taryn!' Jess wailed, as she realised what he was doing. She reached out a trembling hand, but stopped just short of touching him. 'Get up. Don't do this...'

'...and I do pledge to protect you, to obey you without question,' he went on unhurriedly. 'And to accept no other Gentry as my Sovereign Lady, save you, as long as I draw breath. I have spoken,' he finished. Raising his head to her, she saw that his eyes were as radiant as stars. 'It is done, my dear lady. Freely and with a light heart.' Reaching out, he lifted the hem of her dull, mud-coloured robe and brought it to his lips. 'Command me as you will.'

'I don't want this! Any of it! I won't have this put on me. OK? Just leave me alone, Taryn. I told you. I'm done with Faery!'

She backed away slowly as Taryn rose to his feet. He inclined his head, his face expressionless. 'Your word is my pleasure. I will be waiting, my Lady.'

Jess made a sound of exasperation. 'Oh, just…do whatever you want!'

She whirled around. Her feet barely brushing the tops of the grass, she sped away from him in a rapid blur of colour and motion. She had no idea where she was going. To her horror a sob lodged in her throat and threatened to burst from her in a low keening wail.

She had never felt so alone.

CHAPTER 43

O N HIS WAY back to Windroth, Caleb called into the library on impulse. To one side of the self-service machines for borrowing books was an area with tables, plastic chairs and a vending machine. He sat at an empty table with his styrofoam cup of coffee. Taking a sip, he grimaced. The only good thing about it was that it was cheap.

'Mind if I sit here?'

Caleb looked up to see a girl with short red-brown hair wearing an animal-print, fake-fur gilet over a black T-shirt with a silver, Celtic knot design. Her black jeans were tucked into buckled black biker boots. She had a round face and friendly blue eyes. There were huge rainbow-coloured plastic hoops in her ears.

'Help yourself,' he said, smiling.

'It's ages since I was in a library,' she said. 'This is more like a supermarket.' She wrinkled her nose, nodding towards the machines, one of which was bleeping as a customer placed books on a square pink pad. 'Robots or what?'

There was something about the girl. Caleb couldn't have said what. He was certain he'd never met her before, he'd have remembered. But there was a glint in her blue eyes that reminded him of someone.

'Can I...erm get you a coffee?' he asked on impulse, surprised at his own nerve.

'Nah. Don't drink the stuff. But I appreciate the offer.'

They were silent for a few moments, while he drank coffee and she sat looking into space as if deep in thought. He wondered what was troubling her. And why he was somehow certain that something was. *Takes one to know one*, he supposed. Perhaps misery was like invisible ink, which became a stain when it met the matching chemical stimulus in another person. There was a stillness to the girl that was unusual. Most people were constantly fiddling with hair, biting nails, waggling a crossed leg.

She turned her head and caught his eye. Caleb felt himself reddening at being caught staring.

'Read any good books lately?' she said with a disarming grin. 'Hey! Someone had to say it,'

'Yeah.' They both laughed. 'Don't have time to read. Too busy doing...other stuff,' Caleb said.

'Yeah? Like what?'

'I'm an artist,' he said. 'It takes up all my time.'

'Cool. I'm a big fan of art. What medium do you work in?'

'Ink, crayon, charcoal. I do detailed drawings, from nature mostly. Black and white, in an illustrative style, a bit like woodcuts. That's why I'm in town. I don't come in that often. I've just shown some of my drawings to a lady in a gallery down the road. I couldn't believe I dared. But she wanted... all of them.'

'Congratulations, Caleb.'

'Thanks.' He frowned, puzzled. 'How do you know my name?'

'We met once. I looked... a bit different then.'

That accounted for the familiarity he felt. When and where had they met, he wondered? He was about to ask, when she spoke again.

'I don't like being in town either. I was wandering around

by myself, trying to decide what to do…' She paused, cast her eyes down. '…trying to make sense of the car crash my life has become. And I saw you come in here. So I followed you. I'm not really sure why…'

He wasn't sure how to respond. Should he feel flattered? She might be a stalker or a psycho. But his instincts told him otherwise. He was intrigued by her and wanted to know more. 'Car crash, eh? Sounds pretty heavy.'

'And then some,' she said, smiling although the corners of her mouth quivered as if she were very close to tears.

'What happened?'

'That's the million dollar question.' She shook her head from side to side. 'I'm not sure you'd believe me. *I* don't even believe me!'

'Try me? What have you got to lose?'

She put her head on one side, her face perfectly serious now. He thought he saw faint lines of strain around her eyes. 'You mean it? You really want to know?'

He nodded, folded his arms on the table top. 'I'm not in a hurry.'

'OK.' She chewed at her bottom lip. 'This might be the worst idea I've ever had.' Glancing around, as if checking that no one was looking their way she reached out and curled her fingers around his bare forearm.

Caleb felt his stomach lurch as if he stood on a cliff edge. A sensation, like a mild electric shock ran up his arm and he only just managed not pull away. Something was happening to the girl's face. Her features blurred as if they had been painted on water. He saw the rounded features sharpen, the blue eyes narrowed and turned greenish-hazel. The short reddish hair spread outwards into a nimbus of tangled dark hair. At the same time he was enfolded by her perfume. He suppressed a gasp as it flooded his senses; warm and spine tingling, spice and moss. Longing kindled in the base of his belly.

He felt his eyes widening in disbelief. 'Jess? *Jess*. It's really you! What the hell?'

'It's called glamour,' she said with a feral grin. 'The ability to change your appearance in any way you want.'

Caleb shook his head in confusion. An inrush of joy constricted his heart and quickened his pulses. *Jess was here. She had sought him out.* Somehow he managed to stay calm and not alter his expression. 'How did you just do that? Make yourself look so different? Did you hypnotise me or something?'

She shook her head. 'It's something I'm able to do now.'

'Like a magician's trick?'

'Not exactly…'

'Because it was pretty good,' he went on, still too rattled to think straight. 'Beyond amazing, in fact! Where did you learn it?'

'It's not a trick,' she said, deadpan.

It had to be. She was having a laugh at his expense. There was no other explanation. He was starting to feel foolish and let down. Was this garbage all she could come up with, after that dramatic statement about her messed-up life? He'd actually felt sorry for her, invited her to confide in him, when all along she'd been playing him. *Just like Sharon.* He'd thought Jess was different.

'So are you going to tell me what happened after you dumped Alice at Windroth?' he said, coldly. 'And why you took off without a word to me…or…or anyone. Did you find some New Age festival that springs up on the common at this time of year? Well I hope you had a good time learning stupid circus tricks with the crusties and sad old hippies you've been hanging out with! Because it was me who had to deal with the mess you left behind!'

Jess glared at him. 'What mess? What are you on about?'

Anger flickered within him. She'd obviously not given a thought to how her absence affected anyone else. 'Just before I left for town, I found Mrs Stark collapsed on the couch in her studio. She'd hardly eaten or drunk anything in days. I'd assumed that Alice was taking care of her. How wrong was I? Your mum's been completely out of her skull. She's probably necked half of Ivy's drinks cabinet. I'm guessing it didn't help that she had no idea, *when* or *if*, you were ever coming back. Enough carnage for you?' He was on the point of getting up and storming out of the library. Jess's expression stopped him.

She looked genuinely shocked. 'Oh, crap. Mum was doing so well. Ivy, is she…'

'She was OK, when I left. No thanks to you.'

'But…but how…I've only been gone a few hours.'

'A few hours? You kidding? Try almost five *days*.'

'Five days? Time must be different there,' she murmured, frowning in puzzlement.

'Where's "there"?' Caleb asked, exasperated. She wasn't making any sense. 'Where *have* you been? What's going on, Jess?'

'It's…complicated. I want to tell you. But I'm scared, Caleb. Scared that once you know, you'll hate me. And…and I don't think I could bear that.'

His anger evaporated in the face of her vulnerability. She looked lost and confused. He had a sudden urge to put his arms around her.

'Jess,' he said seriously. 'Whatever it is, I won't hate you.

I couldn't.' He needed to understand, to prove to himself that his growing attraction to her was not misplaced. 'Imagine that I'm a stranger if it helps,' he suggested.

The ghost of a smile passed over her face. 'It doesn't. Nothing can.' She blew out her breath on a long sigh. 'Look. Can we get out of here?'

'OK.' He stood up. 'I know a place. Near the river. I used to go there sometimes to draw, when I was still working at the shop.'

'Sounds like a plan.'

Outside the library, he unlocked the padlock and lifted his bike free of the rack. 'If you sit on the crossbar, I'll give you a lift.'

Jess wrinkled her nose, eyed the bike with distaste. 'No thanks. I react badly to metal. You ride. I'll jog.'

'Fine.' He shrugged, colouring. She probably thought he was trying for a grope.

As he set off through the side streets, heading towards the new shopping centre, Jess fell into a rhythm beside him. He expected her to drop back after a short while, but she easily kept pace, loping along beside him with long-legged, almost animal grace.

They passed shops and cafes, shaded by trees and then came to a break in the buildings, where a short lane ended at a fence bordering a field. Caleb dismounted to navigate the stile. Jess ran straight past him, and without missing a step, vaulted over the fence. Impressive. She wasn't even breathing hard.

He stowed his bike behind a bush. They made their way down the overgrown track to where brambles and nettles had grown thickly over the summer into an almost impenetrable jungle. 'There's used to be a proper path here. We might not be able to get through to the river.'

'No problem. I'll go first.' Jess plunged ahead, wading through chest-high greenery, reaching out to pick late blackberries and popping them into her mouth. There was a vibrancy about her that had been absent in the library. Was it his imagination or did a channel appear to open up around her?

Caleb stepped into the space she had made. Trailing brambles sprang back to snag at his jeans. Nettle stings pricked him through his clothes, but he emerged relatively unscathed onto the sloping bank. The river's fresh, muddy smell transported him back to the first time he had discovered this place. The bank eventually gave onto a small flat semi-circle of grass, shaded by a twisted willow with its roots in the river. With the shifting screen of tall, reed mace to one side, it was a natural haven of privacy.

Jess sank down onto the grass. Raising her knees, she looped her arms around her bent legs. He could see the stain of blackberry juice on her fingers. Her eyes, slitted against the sunlight, glittered like chips of green glass. She was very still.

Caleb sat cross-legged beside her. Silence stretched between them. He sought for something to say, to lighten the moment. 'Don't you just love it here? It was my sanctuary, before I started going to Windroth.'

She turned to look at him, her face softening as if she were casting off the vestiges of a waking dream. 'What's the story with Windroth? Why are you there?'

He smiled inwardly at her directness. It was refreshing. He told her about his first meeting with Mrs Stark. How they had become unlikely friends and how he used to cycle over to visit on his days off. He told her too about how he hated the shop, the tension between him and his dad. Which only got worse after Mum died. 'Being able to come to Windroth, sit in the grounds drawing, kept me sane. After Dad and I had a massive row, I walked out for good, with just the clothes on my back. It was Mrs Stark's idea for me to stay in the old summer house.'

'I never thought of frosty old great granny as a lifesaver.'

'Can't vouch for what she's like with anyone else. But she's been good to me. I'll always be grateful.' He gave her a sideways glance. 'Do you still think I'm a gold-digger?'

She shrugged. 'I was just spouting off. It's what I do. So that when people let me down, I don't have to feel bad. If I don't get close, they can't hurt me.'

'So cynical and so young,' he said dryly. But he was touched by her admission. Something inside him sympathised with it.

'Yeah, well. If you were me, you'd understand.'

'I'd like to. Understand, I mean. Isn't that why we came here?'

She looked away, stared straight ahead. A breeze blew back her mass of dark hair revealing a profile that seemed carved from white marble. 'This was a mistake. I don't want to drag you into my nightmare. You've got enough going on, without getting involved in my problems.'

'It's a bit late for that, don't you think?' he said, with a wry grin. *I am so involved. And have been since the first moment I set eyes on you in the hospital car park. I'm in deep. Way beyond my better judgement and I don't care that nothing about this makes any kind of sense.*

She searched his face, as if looking for some hidden meaning. Two high spots of colour streaked her prominent cheekbones. 'I'm…I'm not used to anyone caring what I do. Anyone besides Mum, anyway.'

'You'd better get used to it,' he said evenly. 'Because I'm not going anywhere.'

'You mean that?' She gave a tremulous smile.

'I never meant anything more in my life.'

'Oh.' Dappled sunlight coming through the willow softened her expression. She believed him. She looked very young, and very scared. 'Once you've...um seen. There'll be no going back. For either of us.'

She wasn't making much sense, but he didn't care. 'Sometimes you have to take a gamble, right?' Caleb said softly, resisting the urge to reach out and gently run the backs of his fingers down her pale cheek. He'd already said far more than he'd meant to. Probably made a total idiot of himself. But he didn't regret a word.

Jess was silent for a long time. He didn't hurry her. She closed her eyes and sat with her head bowed, resting her chin on her knees. When she sat up and turned to him again, he saw that she had made up her mind.

What she said next was so far from what Caleb had been expecting that he couldn't take it in and just sat there, looking at her blankly.

'So,' she asked on a long exhalation. 'What do you know about faeries?'

CHAPTER 44

Ivy woke abruptly, with a familiar feeling of dread. She struggled against it, trying to escape back into the peace and calm of the past few hours. Then she remembered. *They* had gone. No longer need she lie there, trying to muster the strength to get up and go and start work in her studio. No longer would the clamour of tiny voices accompany every second of her day and intrude upon her sleep. Her tormentors had no power to force her to their will. She did not entirely understand why, but she was free of them, at long last, as she'd told Caleb, though she could see by his face that he had no idea what she was talking about.

She tried to push herself into a sitting position, but her back was stiff from having fallen asleep in an awkward position on top of the bed. She managed, by digging in her heels and taking most of her weight on her palms, to move backwards in a series of small shunts. The satin eiderdown impeded her progress and she had to have two short rests to catch her breath before she began moving again, but eventually she had negotiated the slippery lumps and bumps and was sitting up and resting against the wooden bedhead.

That her world had narrowed to such small triumphs! She would have laughed at the absurdity, but the effort had exhausted her.

There was someone in her room. Someone tall and very thin silhouetted against the window. Ivy couldn't make out any facial details for the light streaming in behind the figure and forming a corona of brilliance around it. But something was wrong with the image. It took Ivy a few seconds to work out what it was. Caleb had closed the curtains before he left. Light was not pouring *into* the room. It was part of the figure's composition.

'Who are you? What do you want?' she asked, startled that her voice was so weak and shaky. She didn't sound like herself at all.

'Did you think I had forgotten our bargain, Ivy Elizabeth Stark?' asked the figure, every detail of his vivid, unearthly face suddenly as clear as if it were lit by a spotlight.

Ivy's terror distilled into something without a name. She had carried the image of him in her mind since that forest meeting, all those years ago, tried to exorcise it, by painting him, again and again. Now, he was here before her, unchanged and fiercely beautiful.

'You,' she whispered.

'Ah, you remember. How gratifying a sop to my vanity.' He smiled unpleasantly. 'I know not how you dismissed the host I sent to attend you. No matter. I have come to collect that which is mine.'

Cold sweat trickled down Ivy's back, beneath the white cotton nightdress, as the figure moved slowly toward her. 'Leave me alone,' she ordered in a stronger voice. 'You can do nothing to me now.'

'You are not my concern, old woman. I have it on good authority that the child of your daughter's daughter, the first child of your blood to be been born on this hallowed soil since we made our compact, has returned.'

'No. You're wrong!' Ivy burst out, as the beautiful, mismatched eyes she still sometimes saw in her nightmares pinned her with a pitiless gaze.

He went on as if she had not spoken. 'Jess Morgan is staying in this house, as is her mother, who lived here and gave her birth. You see then, how accurate is my information? My spies have sharp eyes. You *will* fulfil our compact. Give her to me.'

She had tried to keep them away with her coldness though she had often found it almost impossible to suppress her feelings, particularly after Rob had vanished. And now the two of them had returned; her granddaughter and her great granddaughter.

She lifted her chin in defiance. 'I have not seen Alice or Jess for years.'

'How I do detest the lying tongues of mortals.' His voice was slippery as silk and as cold as the grave. He pointed one long white finger at her throat. 'Favour me with the truth, Ivy Elizabeth Stark. I will have the girl's true name and whereabouts.'

Ivy tried to lie. She felt a movement in her throat, a sharp, prickling sensation as if she had swallowed a fishbone. Sounds clawed upwards, scraping the soft lining of her cheeks and lips. She gasped with pain, could not stop her lips shaping words .

'Jessica Anne Morgan is staying here in my house,' she croaked.

He laughed unpleasantly. 'Continue, if you please.'

Blood filled Ivy's mouth. She coughed, attempted to swallow and felt it bubbling from her mouth, but this time there was no prickling or scraping in her throat as she answered honestly. 'Jess was here. But she has gone. Left us, without a word.'

Jack's eyebrows knitted in a frown. Suddenly he was standing pressed up against the bed, looming over her tall and impossibly thin. He placed a hand either side of her, leaning heavily on the folds of her dressing gown, so that the thick fabric tightened against her and pinned her to the bed. It felt as if a tree had fallen on her.

'What trickery is this?' he demanded. 'Tell me true! Quickly, before I teach you what it means to defy me!'

'Not...lying...,' Ivy uttered through clenched teeth, a low moan escaping her. She could barely breathe for the agony in her body. No one could stand this much pain. It would be over soon, she thought. Her hands bunched into fists, her heels working uselessly as his sharp face hovered above her.

He leaned closer, as if in fascination. 'How dim your light is growing, old woman. Barely a glimmer now in the approaching flatlands of your long dark night. Fragile hot-blood. Merely a breath. And then - gone. Hardly worth the trouble.'

Ivy fought down a sob at his cruel taunting. She could smell his breath, caramel, cinnamon and something dry and ancient, like stone. For a moment, she thought he was going to kiss her cheek and had just enough strength left to cringe away. He laughed, abruptly. In a single, sinuous movement, he reared back and straightened to his full height. As the pressure on her was removed and blood surged once more through her cramped veins, Ivy screamed. For a moment consciousness almost deserted her. Blackness pricked with stars filled her vision, before her sight cleared again.

'Well – I have always enjoyed the hunt. I will find Jess. Be assured that things will not go easy for her when I do!' His voice was fainter now.

Half-conscious, Ivy was aware of a faint breeze from the direction of the window. There was a single flash of light. A fluttering noise. And then, silence.

How easy it would be to drift away, but she resisted that easement with every fibre of her being.

No. Not yet. Jess was in danger. She must warn her. 'Pull yourself together, woman. Do not be so feeble!' she said aloud. Having given voice to her feelings, she became practical and took stock of the situation.

From where she sat in the centre of the huge old bed, even the tiny journey to the edge felt as daunting as if it were ten miles. Well, no sense in putting off the inevitable. Leaning forward slowly at the waist, she braced herself on her knuckled hands. So far, so good.

'Do get on with it, you ninny,' she urged stoutly, blinking away tears as she began shuffling sideways, caterpillar-like.

It was disconcerting, trying to bully into action numb legs that felt as heavy as lumps of wood. The dratted eiderdown kept rucking up beneath her into slippery ridges, hampering her progress, but she kept on, shuffling and wriggling, dragging the stupid feather-filled thing with her. Eventually she was half-sitting, half-lying close to the edge of the bed. The side of the heavily carved, wooden headboard dug painfully into one shoulder blade, but she was too flushed with triumph to notice. The section of eiderdown on which she was still sitting now drooped over onto the rug. If she could only somehow swing her lower half around, until her feet rested on the carpet, she might be able to wriggle her feet and toes and regain some feeling in her legs. And then she would push against the bed with her hands, straighten her elbows, and attempt to stand up.

But she was trembling badly now from her exertions and cold all over, which made no sense at all. Surely she ought to have been sweating like the navvies working on the railways in her youth. 'Damn and blast old age! It is a filthy, dirty trick,' she grumbled.

A wave of weakness swept her. She drew in long deep

breaths until it passed. If she sat here dithering for much longer, she was going to lose her nerve completely. Oh, but she was so tired. What little strength she had mustered was fast fading. Time to admit that there was no possibility of standing up, let alone walking. Very well. Only one thing for it. She grasped handfuls of eiderdown, gathered herself for one final heave and let her body fall sideways, so that she toppled onto the floor with a little grunt of distress.

A figure swam in front of her. As she blinked, it resolved into a tall dapper man, with a yellow waistcoat and striped tie beneath his flannel suit. 'Go on, old girl. You can do it.'

'Ralph?' Ivy's eyes filled with tears. 'It really is you. Oh, my dear. I am so sorry that I could not be the wife you wanted.'

'Never mind that,' he said in his familiar clipped voice. 'I know it was not your fault. Do not be frightened. I am here. Chin up now.'

Biting her lip against her protesting joints, she rolled onto her stomach, levered her weight onto her forearms and began, slowly and painfully, to drag herself towards the bedroom door...

* * * * *

After she had finished her strange and dark tale, Caleb sat silently, words failing him. Jess stood up. And did something. Something she called dropping the glamour.

'Oh, my god! *God.* You're a...You really are!' His jaw sagged as he looked at the shimmering, unearthly creature, which was somehow still Jess, but at the same time *so* not! 'Are those...?'

'Wings. Yeah,' she said, shyly. 'They come with the outfit. So...what d'you think?'

'Um…Not sure,' he said faintly. 'Give me a minute.'

He was having difficulty taking in the marvel of softly glowing skin, so fine that he could almost see the blood vessels and bone structure beneath it; the skinny, elongated limbs and spidery-fingered hands; the tips of long, knife-like ears that showed through her shaggy halo of green and silver hair. And those alien eyes; the entire space between her eyelids flooded with a green so pale it was almost white. How did someone even begin to view the world without pupils?

This was beyond surreal. His hand trembled as he pointed to the skeins of gently moving light framing her head and shoulders; blue, green and violet. Not light, but shimmering membranes that seemed covered with delicate lace and edged with gauzy streamers that seemed to fill the air with warm sweet perfume.

'Do…um those work?'

'Stupid things!' she said, irritably flexing a shoulder. A ripple passed over her wings. They sank down, out of sight. 'Don't know. It's not been high on my list of fey things to find out. I think they might be just decorative. Not all fey have them, mostly only high-born ones, I think. Oh, wait. I did see a whole lot of tiny folk with wings, in Faery…' She stopped and chewed anxiously at her bottom lip. 'How insane this all is. I wish I could wind back the clock. But I…I can't. This is who…what I am, behind my cloak of glamour. You're the only person, I've told. The only… human…who knows the truth.'

Implying that something *inhuman* also knew? Caleb didn't even want to go there. His shock quota for the day was already so far into the red it was nearing overload. He was having enough trouble trying to absorb the sheer enormity of what he was seeing. *She's a faery. They really exist.* His thoughts churned, but he couldn't shape a single coherent sentence.

'I think rabbit caught in the headlights, about covers the look on your face.' Jess smiled tightly, but her lips twisted as if she was painfully aware of how exposed she was. 'At least you haven't taken off, screaming at the top of your voice. That has to be a good sign, right?'

Caleb heard the plea in her voice and struggled to find the right words. Something was required of him, but he didn't know if he was up for this. He felt a mad urge to laugh. The girl he was so drawn to that he could hardly think about her without catching his breath wasn't even human. He couldn't tear his eyes away from the shifting strands of green in her tangled cloud of hair. It was incredibly beautiful, he realised, wondering how it would feel against his skin. Would her pale lips be hot or cold on his? He averted his gaze, suddenly embarrassed by his inappropriate thoughts.

With no change of pace or with anything to mark the fact, Jess's glamour was restored. She looked exactly like the girl he recognised - the solidly human Jess, with her quirky, charity shop dress sense. She was wearing the layered black skirt, rose-printed tights and buckled biker boots she'd been wearing days before in the kitchen at Windroth.

'There. I'm just me again,' she said, planting her hands on her hips in a gesture that was typical of the Jess he knew – or thought he had. She'd taken a massive leap of faith by revealing herself.

'So, what now?' she asked, in a small voice. 'Say something.'

'Phew! I'll try. I'm still stunned, who wouldn't be? But... I feel privileged too, that you allowed me to...see.' He chose his words carefully, knowing that only complete honesty would do. She'd see straight through any attempt to patronise her. 'I'm not saying it's going to be easy for me to accept all this. Far from it, but I'll get there. What I can promise, is this. Your secret's safe with me, Jess. I swear it.'

'It's hard for me to trust anyone. I've been let down by almost everyone in my life, especially guys. You're different, Caleb. Somehow…I do trust you.'

He nodded, touched and gratified that she'd let her guard down, allowed him to penetrate that prickly exterior of hers. He had the feeling it was a first for her.

'Good. Because, I want you to.' And I want to be worthy of that trust, he realised, with surprise. 'What d'you think? Shall we take a massive risk and be totally honest with each, from now on?'

'Sounds like a plan.' She smiled, her narrow willow-green eyes - human eyes - softening. 'You have an advantage. Faeries can't lie. I don't think they can anyway…' her brow furrowed as she appeared to consider this statement. 'Try me. Ask me something. Go on.'

Caleb wished he'd paid more attention to the fairy books in Mrs Stark's bedroom bookcase. But what he'd read had seemed such an improbable mixture of myth, horror and superstition that he wondered how much truth they contained. He thought hard. What did he want to know?

'Did you always know that you were a…a faery?'

She shook her head. 'I thought I was a weird kid with a whole lot of stupid allergies to chemicals and food, but mostly metal. I was always able to *see* lights and colours around things, but I never told anyone. Sometimes I even thought I'd *made* things happen, but it was always muddled and kind-of just out of reach of my understanding. And then everything changed, a few weeks back. A solitary fey, a faery, glamoured as a homeless guy living in the underpass near our flat, helped me.'

'You had a *faery* living near you?'

'On and off, for ages, apparently, but I never knew. I thought he was just a regular guy, down on his luck. A real trip, isn't it? Lots of fey live mortalwise – that's what they call it when they live alongside humans in towns and cities. Mike – that was his name then – saved my life, after Mum's junkie boyfriend, Leon, kidnapped me. Leon locked me in a flat, kept me drugged so I couldn't escape. But that's another story.'

Caleb was taken aback by this bleak glimpse into her life. And he thought he'd had it hard. 'I never thought of faeries living in towns? Are there any around us now?'

'Yes. Everywhere. In the trees, grass and the water. They're a different breed from the fey I've met. More elemental, not like the court fey. Do you want to see them?'

'What do I have to do?' he asked, warily.

'Try touching me.

Caleb reached out his hand, felt Jess's long skinny fingers curl around it, encompassing his entire palm and fingers in a cool, dry clasp. With the image of her unglamoured, other-self still sharp in his mind he almost expected her to feel wispy and insubstantial as smoke. But she felt reassuringly solid. Completely human – he'd have said, if he didn't know better.

And then his eyes widened, and all thoughts fled. The world around him shifted sideways. He gasped taking in the symphony of enhanced colour and movement. Tiny glowing beings, like fireflies with trailing legs, flitted amongst the grass and other plants which, in their turn, shone like stained glass illuminated by sunlight. He saw more of the beings, subtly different in form, clustered thickly in the willow's branches. Beneath the river were pale girls, their long, weedy hair flowing with the movement of the water. One of them appeared above the surface and beckoned him in, fish eyes gleaming coldly and her parrot-like beak snapping. He heard her laughter, chuckling and bubbling on the breeze and then she dived, kicking up pale legs, dotted with scales as big as silver coins, and ending in ragged fins.

'Seen enough?' Jess let go of his hand.

Caleb reeled, almost losing his step as his vision returned to normal. 'That was beyond amazing! I never dreamed... Never imagined...'

'Me neither,' she said, with a narrow grin. 'My education has just been fast-tracked. Not that I'm any kind of expert. I've just had a bit longer than you to get used to all this. Incidentally, the fey I saw at Windroth are different again, from those you just saw in the grass and the river. I don't know why they were attacking Ivy, when Alice and I got there.'

'*Faeries* were attacking Ivy?'

'Yes. They shot darts into you. That's why you collapsed. I had to suck out the fey poison in your blood. I think it made some kind of connection between us.'

'A connection? So that's why I can see faeries when we're touching?'

'Maybe. I don't really know. I'm on a steep learning curve too, remember?'

'You made them leave, didn't you? I was fighting them...' he remembered, 'there was a noise – like a bell ringing...'

'Yes. I ordered them to go and not come back. Never expected it to work. But it did.'

Something was puzzling Caleb. 'Why would faeries want to hurt Mrs Stark?'

'Already said, I don't know that either. She's been painting faeries from life for years, maybe most of her life. I've seen some of her best paintings. They're amazing, full of faery stuff.

Some of it pretty twisted. But something must have gone wrong, recently. Otherwise, why would the fey turn against her? Maybe Ivy did something to offend them. All I'm certain of is that some pretty strange things have been going on at Windroth. And I intend to find out why.' She paused. 'But first things first. I need to get back there. See what's happening with Mum and Ivy. I've been away too long.'

CHAPTER 45

THEY FOUND HER lying on the floor, her head turned to one side, the collar of the dressing gown masking the lower part of her face. Her arms were bent up close, one to either side of her chest. Her thin bare calves, sticking out from beneath the folds of the nightdress she wore beneath the dressing gown, ended in fluffy pink socks. The incocngruous and pathetic sight struck Caleb to the quick. They should have been there.

'Maybe she had a heart attack and fell out of bed. Look. There's a bed cover on the floor.' Jess pointed across the room. 'She must have been trying to get help, but wasn't able to walk.'

'Maybe.' Caleb said, uncertainly. 'I don't know. Something just feels…wrong. I can't explain it.' Jess looked sharply at him and he saw a subtle change in her expression. 'Don't you think?'

'I'm not sure. Maybe.' She said it in a way that made him think there was something she wasn't telling him.

His skin tingled with suspicion. 'I've a right to know if there's something odd going on here! Oh God. Tell me it wasn't one of your lot again.'

'Hey, what's with this "my lot" ? I don't know any more about this than you. You believe me, don't you?'

At the spark of hurt in her eyes, which she quickly suppressed, Caleb felt a start of guilt. 'Yes, of course. I didn't mean that. I'm just in shock. I can't believe she's dead.'

'Caleb.' Jess glanced meaningfully towards the open door,

through which her mum was advancing with measured steps. 'She doesn't know about me,' she whispered. 'And I don't want her to. Not yet.'

He had completely forgotten about Alice Morgan. Had she heard their conversation? Would it make any difference if she had? By the state of her, he didn't think so. He nodded at Jess, to show he understood.

Jess's mum was visibly trembling. 'Ivy... was still alive, when I...I got to her. I was asleep in my bedroom when I heard her calling for help. I came as quickly... as I could. I don't know how long...she'd been lying there...'

Caleb managed to stop himself saying something seriously unhelpful. But he'd known what state Alice was in when he'd left for town. And he'd still gone.

'Go on, Mum.' Jess prompted. 'You heard Ivy calling for help? What happened then?'

Alice looked at her daughter, seemed to dredge up words from thick fog. 'She...she wasn't moving. Tried to turn her over. Too heavy. She was...trying to say something. Had to bend close. Ivy said, something like... "Tell Jess. Watch out for... Jack". Yes, that was it. She made me promise...tell you. You're in danger from a man...called, Jack.'

'Jack? I don't know any guy called that.'

Alice blinked. 'I held...her hand. Told her I was there. Not... worry about anything. She went quiet. And...and then she gave a sort of long sigh. Stopped breathing.' A sob erupted from her. She cupped her hands around her mouth and nose as if she could force the sound back inside. 'Always hated her. But for it to end like this...'

'You were with her. To give her comfort,' Jess said.

Caleb moved closer, patted Alice's shoulder awkwardly. 'I'm sorry, Mrs Morgan.'

As Alice nodded, Jess threw him a grateful look. She slipped an arm around her mum's shoulders and helped her gently out of the room.

On her return she stood for a few moments examining the body carefully.

'I didn't see it before. But from this angle…there's blood on the floor beneath Ivy's chin.' Bending down, she moved the dressing gown collar aside.

'Leave her alone, Jess,' Caleb said, uncomfortably. 'She probably bit her tongue when she fell. What difference does it make now?'

'Exactly. Ivy's not going to mind if I move her, is she? *She* left that warning message for *me*, remember? There could be some clue, something else to find out. Once other people start taking over and removing her body, I'll have lost the chance. You don't have to watch if it'll freak you out.' Even as she was speaking, Jess had slipped her hands beneath the old lady's shoulders and was gently rolling her onto her back. The paper white face, strangely unlined now, the sunken eyes and blood-smeared lips and chin were revealed.

Caleb swallowed hard, having difficulty holding it together. Mrs Stark looked better than he'd expected. Her face was calm and somehow peaceful.

Reaching out, Jess gently laid the back of one hand against Ivy's right cheekbone. Suddenly she retracted her hand as if had been burned. 'Glamour!' she cried. 'It's all over her!'

'What? *What?* Shit. I knew it. Those…those monsters came back and finished the job.' Caleb bunched his hands into fists as impotent rage swept through him. 'Faeries murdered Mrs Stark.'

'It's not that simple,' Jess said. 'Listen to me. Are you listening?'

'What are you *talking* about? How can any of this be simple?' He ran a hand across his face, attempted to calm down. 'OK. I'm listening.'

'Take a close look at her. She doesn't look like someone who suffered an attack, does she? There are no signs of skin darkening from poison dart wounds, at least not that I can see without undressing her.'

'You're not thinking of...!' Caleb cried, horrified.

'No. Of course not. What do you take me for? What I'm saying is, she wasn't killed by the same, fey-swarm we saw in her studio.' She took a breath. 'It was someone else. A high-born faery has been in this room.'

'That's insane! How can you know that? It's pure guess-work.' He was beginning to be exasperated by her amateur sleuthing.

'That blood on her mouth. It reeks of powerful glamour. You want me to prove it to you?'

Caleb didn't, but he found himself moving closer. 'Yeah. Show me.' *This is* such *a bad idea*, he thought, even as he reached out and encircled one of Jess's wrists with one hand.

Immediately, a smell filled his nose and mouth and seemed to pour down his throat. It was like vanilla cheese cake; the spicy smell in Gran Farmer's kitchen when she was making Christmas pudding; the sharp breath of the night air, woven into Sharon's hair on the night of the rave; all this and more, blended with flowery oils into a symphony that would have made a perfumer's fortune. But there was something else, ancient and powerful, beneath those heady scents which he could not identify. Deep inside him, a hunger awoke that spoke to him of possibilities beyond his wildest imaginings. His vision swam and he blinked hard as fear unfolded tendrils deep in his belly.

Glamour. It smelled like, heaven and hell.

'Caleb. You can let go now.'

Jess's voice seemed faint, far away. He ignored it, drew in another deep breath of that amazingly complex smell. Felt his heartbeat drumming in his ears so loudly they hurt. Or was it the base notes of some hypnotic music? Sinking into it, he opened himself up to the silk-lined abyss.

Want more. More. Yes. Let it all come.

'Enough!' Jess's long fingers, strong as corded steel wire prised his hand free.

Caleb clawed desperately at her wrist, trying to catch hold again. Redness hovered at the edge of his vision. She gently nudged him away with her tapered fingertips. But he reeled backwards, panting, as if he'd been slammed into a wall. He was aware of her face gradually swimming back into focus. The hectic pace of his heartbeat slowed. His shoulders sagged from the acres of emptiness cramping his belly.

'God, I'm sorry, Caleb. I didn't know that would happen. You have no defence against raw glamour. Why would you? I should have filtered it. I'm such an idiot!'

Lost. Gone. Need more of it. Is this how it felt to be a faery? To be soaked in glamour, through and through? 'Hey. Forget it,' he grunted, heat rising into his face. His hands were trembling. He felt hollow and sick at heart for something he had glimpsed, but could never have. He felt stupid and ashamed. How weak was he? He forced himself to meet Jess's eyes. 'You made your point. A powerful faery was here, in this room.'

'So, we agree? And whatever it wanted, I think Ivy resisted it.'

'So it what – tortured her?'

'I don't know. Maybe. Ivy could have bitten her tongue when she fell onto the floor. The fey have other ways of making you tell the truth.' She looked thoughtful. 'True names are important to them. Once they have it, it gives them power over you.'

'How do you know that?'

'What? Oh, from something that happened with Taryn. It's not important. But you might want to remember what I told you. *Never* give any faery your full name.'

Caleb was calm now, his thoughts clear. *As long as he didn't think about that incredible scent and the way it made him feel.* He made a metal note to guard his own name. 'So it was this...Taryn – who was in Mrs Stark's bedroom? What did he hope to gain by questioning a helpless old woman?'

Jess shook her head. 'Not Taryn. He's a loyal friend. You remember I told you about Mike, the faery who lived in the underpass? They're one and the same. Taryn's the faery name he goes by. That's not his full name, of course...' She paused, her thoughts appearing to turn inwards again.

A gesture that was not lost on Caleb. Taryn seemed to hold a special place in her affections. He felt a flicker of pain he couldn't identify, certainly didn't want to examine too closely. 'You've no idea who this other faery could have been?'

'No.' Jess reasoned. 'I just don't get it. What could any high-born faery have wanted from a sick old woman?'

Suddenly, the whole thing became clear to him. Caleb wondered that he hadn't made the connection earlier. His grief must have clouded his judgement.

'It wanted to know about *you*. Think about it. Your mum told you that Ivy said you had to watch out for, Jack. She naturally assumed Ivy was talking about a man. But Ivy wasn't. It was a faery!'

'Oh, God. Of course!' Glancing down at the dead woman, Jess's mouth twisted with emotion. 'Jackryn Fleet! Ivy probably only knew him as Jack. She painted him many times...'

How did Jess know the faery's name? He wasn't sure he wanted to know.

'... There has to be a story behind that. Did he have some kind of hold over her? And where do I come in? I don't get it. What can he want with me?' Jess's face crumpled. 'Oh, Ivy. You were so brave to defy him. Why did you do that? You hardly knew me.'

'Maybe she knew more than you thought. Or she assumed that you'd be able to fill in the gaps, given time?' Caleb offered quietly. 'Who knows? But I don't think you're going to find all the answers here.'

Jess stared into space, suddenly silent and still, perhaps reaching out with some faery sense of which he was unaware. She clearly had her own agenda and it didn't include him.

He could feel suppressed grief beginning to weigh on him like sleeplessness. Mrs Stark had gone. There was just that small, empty husk on the carpet from which the spark of life had so obviously departed.

'Are you done?' he asked Jess, tersely. 'Because I don't know about you, but I can't bear to see her lying there like that a moment longer.'

'No. You're right. We need to do right by her.' To his surprise, Jess swooped down and placed a kiss on Ivy's forehead.

Caleb bent and scooped the eiderdown up from the floor. Wordlessly, they each took two corners of the bulky cover and gently laid it over Mrs Stark's body. And then, by unspoken agreement, went out and closed the bedroom door.

CHAPTER 46

NINKA WAS SITTING cross-legged on a straw bale in a shadowy corner of the tack room. She liked the smells in here; polished harnesses smelling of beeswax and honey and damp saddles newly cleaned with herb-scented soapwort. From the open door, she had a good view of the main stable block. It was a good hunting day, cold, crisp and clear, so most of the individual stalls were empty.

She scrubbed at the mud stains on the saddle blanket in her lap with a small hotchi-spine brush. Her sensitive hunter's ears picked up a tiny noise. She looked up frowning. Moments later a tall figure strode in through the main stable door, his footsteps leaving no mark on the beaten earth floor.

Taryn. Fabe had sent word of the faery lord's appearance at the apple feast, but Ninka had not anticipated a visit from him, especially in this place. They had met seldom when he returned to Faery in between living mortalwise, secrecy being paramount.

Laying aside the harness Ninka rose and went to meet him.

'Lord Taryn. Have you a mind to ride today?' she said formally, in case any of the stable fey happened to be in earshot. One never knew who would carry tales. But a quick glance affirmed that they would not be overheard.

'Lady Ninka Minka.' He greeted her with small bow.

She flushed with pleasure at the unaccustomed courtesy. 'It is not advisable to address me so. You could be laughed out of here and I whipped for the arrogance of accepting a title I do not deserve.'

'Although deserve it you do. None more so,' he said, his voice heavy with meaning. 'I must confess my surprise at learning that you are in the service of Jackryn Fleet.'

She shook her head. 'I am not. I choose to stay here to be close to Aerith.'

He nodded. 'The new chief huntress. Is that wise?'

Taryn was one of only three fey, the others being Fabe and Crowle, who knew that the mortal babe given into her care by Catelysma had survived to young adulthood. He also knew that it was only Ninka's arcane skills that masked Aerith's humanity and allowed her to pass in safety through Faery. But no fey, only Ninka herself had any idea that Aerith was anything more than an ordinary forest foundling. The one being who knew of her beloved's true parentage, thought her long-dead. And that was how it must remain.

'Not wise or prudent,' Ninka said, unhappily. 'I worry that Catelysma, or one of her spies, will cross our path. All this time I kept Aerith safe. It is my misfortune that she has come to Jackryn's notice.'

She did not voice her other fears. That Aerith was enjoying the benefits of her position rather too much, along with the flattery of the handsome, high-born lord. A fragment of conversation, from a previous day, rose to her mind. 'Do you know that he almost caught me anointing myself with the masking oil,' Aerith had told her, laughing delightedly. 'I told him it was a special perfume blend.' Ninka was aghast.

All night she had lain sleepless, chafing and worrying, mentally sifting details for any subtle sign of their fortune's souring.

If she detected even a hint of danger she would race

headlong into the forest's depths, taking Aerith with her; even if Ninka had to bind and gag the girl and use her shape shifting skills on them both. She realised that Taryn had asked her a question about their lodgings and was awaiting an answer.

'We have a chamber above the stable,' she told him. 'It is richly appointed. Aerith delights in it.'

Taryn nodded. 'Have you and Aerith ventured into the court?'

Ninka shook her head. 'Fabe keeps me larded with all the news, since I am no longer welcome there.'

'How so?' he asked.

She realised that he might not have heard the story of how Catelysma had banished her from court, assigning her to permanent care of Aerith, after her once pretty plaything's appearance had so revolted her. Ninka told him all about it; how she had disguised the child and pretended she wanted rid of it.

Taryn threw back his head and laughed. Sunlight coming through a narrow, crystal skylight in the wooden roof struck sparks from his loose silver hair. 'What a clever trickster, you are! It is rare for any fey to get the better of the Dark Lady.'

Suddenly Ninka wearied of this talk of trickery and danger. The area between her shoulder blades twitched uncomfortably, as if anticipating the sting of an arrow. She changed the subject. 'It seems that you are also out of favour. On account of your continued refusal to acknowledge Catelysma as your sovereign.'

His lips thinned. 'And did you hear that the queen's wrath had fallen upon the Lady Anira?'

She nodded. 'I was greatly saddened to hear it.'

'By the time I set eyes upon her, my poor lady was near death, displayed beside the thorn throne as a clear warning to all who would choose autonomy over servitude to a heartless monster!' He paused, his white face haggard. 'Anira is gone. But I honour her sacrifice. I will *never* serve Catelysma as my queen.'

Ninka did not offer unwelcome words of comfort. Only time would bring that. Instead, she uttered a gentle word of warning.

'Catelysma is pitiless when angered. You have defied her publicly. I fear she will be ever more devoted to pressing you into her service. Have a care for *all* those you value.'

'You echo my thoughts,' he said bitterly. 'How many solitary fey are in my position, or will be ere long? Those who, by right, should have the freedom of choice to stand alone. Where is the justice?'

'Justice?' Ninka grimaced. 'Not a word Gentry hold in high regard.'

'You speak truly.' His voice was low, intense, sharp-edged as a hudskin-forged blade. 'Catelysma changes our laws to suit her own ends, administering punishments at will for imagined slights. But she, like others of her ilk, is not above *all* laws. The solitary fey, once sworn, have no recourse but to obey their sovereigns. For who is able to remain free, or powerful enough, to act against Gentry? But I tell you this, my hudskin friend. Justice may sleep in Faery. But a time *will* come when revenge awakens and overflows our land like the waters of a breached dam. Then let the high families of Gentry tremble!'

Ninka could not conceal her shock. She cast her eyes around nervously. 'Take care, for you speak of treason.'

Two brawny, hedge puckles appeared from the back of the stable, trundling wooden barrows of soiled straw. The faintly almond scent of faery horse urine hung in the air. A hob with over-large ears like a bat came through a side door, leading a sleek white horse towards a stall. Ninka saw a sly look came over the hob's face as it glanced toward her and Taryn. The puckles, noticing the hob's interest, turned questing snouts in their direction.

After his outburst, Taryn seemed sunk within himself, as if lost in thought. He stared ahead, his eyes unfocused.

'Taryn,' she hissed under her breath. 'We are observed.' She had to get him out of there, before he said something that endangered them both.

He recovered his wits in an instant. 'Accompany me to the fields, hudskin,' he ordered loudly. 'And none of your puny excuses! Your work can wait!'

Ninka pretended to flinch. 'As you will, Lord Taryn.'

As Taryn strode out of a side door, she assumed her habitual crouch, scurrying along as if having difficulty keeping up with his determined, long-legged stride. Behind her the bat-eared hob tittered. The puckles made rude noises, blowing bubbles of snot. Taryn glowered at them over his shoulder until they slunk back to work.

The faery lord's tall, whipcord frame filled Ninka's view as he crossed the stable yard ahead of her. His cloak of velvet-black talpa skin, embroidered with whorls of silver thread, billowed in the cold wind, which contained a hint of snow. The chill in the air, thought Ninka, mirrored Taryn's bleak mood.

In all of their long association, she had never seen him like this. Had the death of Lady Anira cut him so deep that the unhealed wound festered on the heart? It was one thing to refuse allegiance to Catelysma, quite another to talk of challenging Gentry's entire rule.

Lord Taryn had always been the mildest of the faery nobles, using charm and wit to avoid conflict and keep Catelysma at arm's length, although none doubted his steadfastness, intelligence and strength. While Jackryn Fleet and most other lords thought it beneath them to even acknowledge Ninka, Taryn had always been respectful and kind to her. Which was why she had chosen him for an ally, after she had stumbled upon that dangerous secret.

They were headed for the path leading to a clearing enclosed by thick hawthorn. A number of sleek ruby-eyed horses were cropping the short grass. At their approach, the largest of them raised its head, twitching its ears forward. Its silver mane was loose, streaming over one powerful shoulder in shimmering waves. Ninka recognised it as one of Jackryn Fleet's favoured mounts.

Taryn made a soft clicking noise with his tongue.

The powerful horse nickered a response. It cantered towards him on silent, silver-shod hooves that barely brushed the tops of the grass. Taryn held out his cupped hands and the horse snuffled its nose into them, huffing warm breath. 'Blezantine,' he crooned.

Ninka blinked her surprise. 'You know this horse?'

'I bred him myself. We were inseparable until Jackryn won him from me by trickery. I was about to leave Faery for a while, so I left Blezantine here, knowing he would be well taken care of. I will claim him back, when the time is right.' He stroked the horse's elegant nose and then reached up to pat his cheek. 'Well, Blez, my fine lad. What say you? Do you remember your true master?'

The horse's fierce red eyes gentled. Huffing out another snort, he stretched out his long neck and stood quietly with his forehead resting against Taryn's chest.

'You have your answer.' Ninka smiled, holding her ground, trying not to feel intimidated by the enormous animal.

After a few moments, Taryn stepped back and slapped the horse's shoulder. 'Off you go, Blez. Join your companions.' He stood watching as the horse whirled. Kicking up its heels and tossing its silken mane, it streaked back to the small herd.

Ninka stared into the field. 'Fabe mentioned a young fey woman who accompanied you to the apple feast,' she commented. 'It was curious that when I asked, she was not able to describe her.'

Taryn turned to Ninka, his smile fading. She sensed the excitement he was trying to hide. 'My companion passed unnoticed, leaving no imprint of herself upon the court. Even Catelysma paid her no heed.'

Ninka drew in her breath. 'How so? Such a glamour must be powerful indeed.'

He grinned. 'It is. More than even she realises. You have experience of it yourself, for you came upon this same young woman, in the woods bordering fields near Windroth village.'

'I? I met no fey stranger.' Ninka frowned, casting her mind back. There had been that terrifying encounter, with the mortal with true sight. She remembered how shocked she had been at its lack of response to her warding signs. And then, with a blinding flash, she understood. 'It was she! Glamoured to look mortal! I was completely deceived. Are you telling me... it was the changeling?'

He nodded. 'Jess is aged about sixteen in mortal years, a time there when she is considered to be a woman. Which is perhaps why her fey blood has lately awoken within her.'

'Jess.' The mortal name always felt strange on Ninka's tongue. It was wrong, somehow, too short, too sibilant. She felt a thrill of horror at Taryn's recklessness. It was an effort to keep her voice soft and reasonable. 'Why did you say nothing of this to me?'

'I did not keep it from you intentionally. The life Jess led mortalwise has been harsh and joyless. More so, of late. I thought it important to remain there, to guide and instruct her.'

She nodded. 'I can see the sense in that. But why bring her into Faery? I cannot think it wise to introduce such a fledgling to the Dark Court.'

'I had my own reasons for doing so. I wanted to prove something to my own satisfaction.' He sounded defensive, a little pompous.

'Indeed?' So he was not entirely free of the faery lords' natural arrogance. 'And did you?'

'Jess does not frighten easily. And she was glamoured. I knew she would be safe enough, if I kept her close. Ah, the things she can do! So much more than you or I could ever have imagined. She is remarkable.'

He was being evasive. Did he know more than he was prepared to say? Taryn's eyes shone with pride and affection. He was bound to feel a special bond with Jess; he had been her friend and confidant for much of her growing time away from Faery.

Anticipation tempered with fear stirred within her. She must assert herself, before he ran away with the idea that Jess was his sole responsibility. 'Where is she now?' she asked curtly. 'I must see her. You have her, somewhere safe?'

The edges of Taryn's sharp cheekbones flushed red. 'She has fled again mortalwise. Professing to want nothing of Faery. Or...of me. To my chagrin. I underestimated the effect of the court on *her*,' he said abashed. 'I am sure this is merely a temporary set back.'

'The poor girl is probably still riding the nightmare in her sleep. You made a serious error of judgement. Have you any idea of what you have set in motion?' Ninka's belly twisted with anger.

Taryn said nothing. At least he had the grace to look shamefaced. 'I acted in haste. I was wrong. I see that now.'

Ninka could only imagine how Jess had felt. Any creature born in Faery, would be indelibly imprinted by its struggle to survive in the mortal world where iron sickness and tainted air ate away at fey glamour. No doubt Jess was as strong and remarkable, as Taryn said. She had to be, to have survived. But the transition to her new life, and position, in Faery would be difficult in the extreme. It ought to have been slow and measured, tempered by good counsel. Ninka's counsel. The dangers Jess had faced mortalwise, were nothing to what awaited in Faery.

Yet Taryn had imprudently cast her directly into the vicious theatre that was the Dark Court, where entertainments were as bloody as they were twisted.

Words of condemnation rose to her lips, but she did not voice them. Instead, she said reasonably, 'In the circumstances, I think it best for Jess to have returned mortalwise. And to stay there. Faery is not kind to the unwary and innocent.'

Taryn gave her a sharp look. 'No. Jess must return. And soon. She has to!'

'Must?' Another small warning bell sounded in Ninka's mind. Earlier he had spoken of treason. 'Why must she return? What is going on, Taryn?'

He lowered his gaze, appeared to consider. 'I beg your indulgence a while longer, my friend. On my honour. I will tell you all. But, first, I must know why *this particular* changeling is so important that you asked me to protect and watch over it? I have never asked you this, trusting that it was none of my concern. But now, Lady Ninka, I do ask, most humbly. Will you tell me?'

As she glanced up at him, her anger and disappointment faded. Misguided, impatient, Taryn might be, but he was honourable and steadfast. It could not have been easy for him to spend so long mortalwise in service to Jess. She would need his loyalty and his strong arm in times to come. And so would Jess.

'Give me a moment, to consider,' she said.

Her head was spinning with the pace of it all. She had known this moment would arrive, but events had overtaken her. With Taryn beside her, Jess had already travelled through the Blessed Lands on her way to the Dark Court. By the blood of Gentry, the enormity of that fact again struck fear into Ninka's soul. The ancient fey rituals of acceptance and protection had yet to be performed. Was it possible that Jess could have passed unnoticed, leaving no footfall, no scent trail of her passing on the very fabric of Faery?

No. Ninka did not think so, for one second.

But then, Jess was unique. Her glamour *was* astonishing. Who knew what her capabilities might be? She needed time to speak to Jess. To tell her all she knew. To enable her to hear the words that would bring her into her full power.

But first, there was Taryn.

'Very well. Lord Taryn. What is done, is done. For your loyalty and the service you have given, you are owed the truth. Shall we walk? This may take a while.'

Taryn seemed about to speak, but then thought better of it. 'Very well.'

As they moved off, Taryn shortening his stride to match hers, Ninka began to cast her mind back. 'It began almost sixteen spans ago in human time,' she told him. 'When I was roaming the forest...'

Running. Leaping. Grass beneath her paws, sounds of growing things in her long ears. Ninka relished the sense of freedom as she flashed across a clearing and down into a moss-lined hollow. Further down, down. Into a wide cutting, formed when, long ago, winter storms caused ancient trees to uproot. Ferns grew on the steep slopes, along with plants bearing purple-veined, pitchers, filled with enticing liquid in which unwary insects drowned. Along the grassy base of the cutting she loped, over fallen trees, lichen-covered, hollowed into caves and half fallen to dust and then, up an incline, to navigate thick, twisted tree roots that bullied the hillside out of shape. In and out of them, ducking into damp hollows, blackening her skidding paws on leaf mould. And then running again, heart beating beneath her ribs, muscles flexing beneath her slender, brown fur flanks. Deeper, ever deeper, into the tangled green heart of the wildwood where even the fey hunt could not easily penetrate.

This was Ninka's domain. This place nurtured her, cradled her being, as it had always done for those of her kind. Here was freedom and ancient knowledge. She was entirely at ease, powerful in her own right and far from the cursed court and all the perversities of Gentry rulers.

The canopy of overhead branches was thick here, a living lacework, that made an enemy of light. What light did manage to penetrate filtered in pale strands that were absorbed by bleached, attenuated plants dotting the forest floor. Ninka paused to nibble a crescent from a blue-flushed toadstool.

And that was when she heard it.

The noise was contained, deadened by the thickness of trees. Sounds did not penetrate far, this deep into the wildwood. Yet it was unmistakable. A woman's cries; thin and hollow. Ninka froze, nose twitching, long sensitive ears swivelling. Rarely did she come upon other fey, apart from the occasional wood brownie, or one of the little grey men who toiled underground and whose shadows were occasionally to be glimpsed at the stony entrance to one of their burrows.

Hesitantly, Ninka edged forward. She could hear panting, followed by a deep groan. She trembled. Whoever this woman was, she was in great pain, perhaps badly injured. Had she been borne here by abductors, attacked and left for dead? Ninka's first instinct was to break cover, assume her hudskin form and offer her services.

But something felt wrong about this. Badly wrong. She hesitated. Still glamoured as a hare, she crept under thick ferns on silent paws. Edged closer.

The slender, fey woman was squatting against a tree. Even though she was clothed in a rough brown robe, it was clear she was finely made with long, pale limbs that gleamed softly like a pearl. Her arms were spread. She gripped the thick twisted roots on either side of her with clawed fingers. Her mass of sweat-darkened hair had fallen forward to screen her face. As a convulsion shook her, she loosed a deep groan that ended on a scream.

Ninka had attended many forest births and on one rare occasion the lying in of one of the court faeries. There was only one reason why a high-born faery gave birth in secret. The babe could only be the issue of a forbidden union with a mortal. Such matings were rare indeed. Few fey were reckless enough to flout the law, which might demand the death of the parents as well as the destruction of the half-blood child. This woman must have been seduced by the brief, hot-blood flare of a mortal's beauty. Ninka wondered who he might have been. And what qualities the mortal possessed to so ensnare this faery woman.

And then the woman threw back her head and let out another shriek. As her face was revealed, a piece of wood clamped between her bared teeth, Ninka's blood ran cold.

Catelysma! By the ancient, unsullied blood of Gentry!

The Dark Queen bore down, groaning. Her white face shone with exertion, agony stealing her matchless beauty. She gave a final screech as something pale and wet slid to the forest floor in a rush of blood and fluids. Collapsing sideways, she sagged against the tree trunk and lay there gasping.

Hidden beneath the ferns, Ninka trembled. If news of this birth ever came to light, it would be the ruin of the Dark Queen, for even Gentry were not above the cardinal law against mixing fey and human blood. Best to creep away now, while she still had the chance. Should Catelysma discover herself observed, Ninka's life would be forfeit.

Ninka was about to melt into the undergrowth, when a movement caught her attention. On the leaf litter, the pale thing that had issued from the queen's body, was twitching. It was curled, chrysalis like, within an envelope of thin pearly skin, through which limbs and the ridges of a backbone were faintly visible. Ninka could not help staring at the mixed-blood *thing* in fascination. She saw a tiny hand press against the glimmering membrane and then a finger appeared through a rent, which gradually widened.

As the creature within struggled free, Ninka was put in mind of a tiny serpent she had once watched emerge from its leathery egg. With a final thrust the babe was flushed out of the collapsed membrane onto the leaf litter. It lay on its side, wet and pale of limb, with spidery hands and feet. Its face wizened as a dried apple, mouth and eyes mere slits. Strands of dark hair clung to its skull and there was a silky fuzz of the same hair across its narrow shoulders and down its backbone. From its lipless mouth there arose a thin cry.

At the sound, Catelysma's head jerked towards her babe. She shuddered, her face bound by repulsion and horror. Perhaps she had not expected it to live. Thrusting back her tumbled hair, she rose shakily to her feet, took a few paces towards the hollow bole of an oak, wherein was trapped a small pool of rainwater.

Ninka had hesitated too long. The moment to escape was lost. She could only watch, hardly daring to draw breath.

Catelysma stripped off her plain brown robe. Scooping up handfuls of water, she splashed her face and body, before washing the birth fluids from her thighs and nethers. Once dressed again, she began moving around, collecting twigs from the forest floor. When she had collected a bundle, she secured it with strands of ivy. Ninka watched in puzzlement as glamour flowed over the twig bundle. Catelysma now held *another* babe, human-looking this time, with fair hair and rosy limbs.

A stock-changeling? Ninka blinked, even more confused. What was the queen about?

Catelysma then went over to her own new-born. She looked down at it, her face twisting with emotion. Bending down, she scooped up the faery babe with her free hand, encircling its waist in her long tapered fingers. Its head flopped back on its thin neck and it let out a wail, arms and legs working. Two shining tears rolled down the queen's pale cheeks and dripped onto the babe. Glamour flowed over it, so that the skinny, wrinkled fey thing filled out, became more human-looking, with a head of glossy dark hair.

Now it appeared that the queen held two healthy *mortal* babes.

Ninka's curiosity was beginning to mitigate her fear. She had expected Catelysma to smother the life from her babe and bury its body, if not banish it to nothingness with incendiary glamour. She could not imagine what the queen was about. She dared to move, ever so slightly, to see clearly through the fronds.

The queen was tearing broad strips of fabric from the hem of her robe. She packed moss around each of the babes, before tightly swaddling them. Cradling them, one dark and one fair, in the crook of one arm, she set off without a backward glance, through the wildwood.

On impulse, and much against her better judgement, Ninka followed at a distance…

'*Two* babes?' Taryn said, when Ninka had finished speaking. He looked astounded. 'One fey-born and the other a *stock* changeling? I do not understand.'

'I did not either, not at first. After I followed Catelysma and saw what she did with the babes, the pieces of this puzzle came together.'

'You saw what Catelysma did with the babes?' Taryn fell silent, waiting for her to enlarge on this shocking statement.

'That is as much as you need to know for the present.' Ninka gave him a level look. 'You already suspected that Catelysma was Jess's mother, did you not? That is why you took her to the Dark Court.'

Taryn lowered his gaze, chastened. The fact that she was keeping vital information from him must have stung his pride.

'I had my suspicions. I guessed that Jess was the child of

mixed fey and mortal blood,' he told her. 'There was something *other* about her form when she first shed her glamour before me. She was a true-changeling who had been foisted upon an unknowing Alice Morgan. But it was not until I saw Catelysma and Jess side-by-side that all became clear to me.'

'I see. And does Jess know of this?'

He looked uncomfortable.

'You told her that Catelysma gave birth to her,' Ninka said wearily. 'Could you not restrain yourself from flaunting your knowledge?'

He raised his chin, looked down his narrow-boned nose at her. His eyes were chips of flint. 'She had a right to know!'

'Argh! A murrain on your meddling!' Ninka raged. 'Jess is not ready to be cloaked in her true power. There is work to be done, before she ever set foot in Faery! But we are too late. In your cursed arrogance, you have put lives at risk. Jess's life and the lives of others.'

His mouth gaped in devastation. 'By all the stars. What have I done? I regret not seeking your counsel sooner. On my oath, it will not happen again.' He stood with bowed head, dejection in every line of his tall, thin form. 'I do most humbly beg forgiveness. Shall I kneel, the better to plead my case?'

Ninka's fingers itched to slap his handsome face, but there was no doubting his genuine dismay. She clicked her tongue in impatience. 'Enough of this courtly posturing! You faery nobles!' she grumbled. 'Let us be done with useless humility. It avails us nought. There is much work to do, if we are to salvage anything from this morass of your making.'

He nodded, squared his shoulders, his composure regained. 'I am your devoted servant. And, despite what you may think, Jess's safety and well-being are paramount to me.'

'On that, at least, we agree.' Ninka took a breath, clearing her thoughts.

'What must I... we do?' he asked.

'You will return mortalwise. Seek out Jess. Use whatever methods you must to persuade her, but bring her to my forest dwelling.'

'Consider it done.' Taryn turned, about to do as she instructed. He hesitated, his face clouding. 'You said I have put "other lives are at risk"? Gentry forgive me for that, for I cannot forgive myself.' He closed his eyes briefly and then looked at her. 'May I know, which lives?'

'You may not,' Ninka said, in clipped tones. 'I have the matter in hand. I suggest you devote yourself to the task before you.'

A spasm ticked in his taut pale cheek. 'Lady Ninka Minka.' He whirled and left, without another word.

* * * *

As Ninka made her way back towards the stables her mind was full of all she must do. There were preparations to make to ensure that Jess had all the protection and sovereign power due to her. She hoped there would be time, before the inevitable visitation.

She must venture deep into the forest, gather things she needed. If Aerith would come with her, so be it, but she did not feel confident of her power to separate the girl from the uncertain patronage of Jackryn Fleet. Ninka would have to trust in fate, and her belief in Aerith's own good sense, that her beloved would be safe enough without her protection, until she returned.

But her heart quaked within her. The time when long-buried secrets surfaced approached with the inevitability of the moon's rising and setting. And then, her beloved Aerith could be as imperilled in Faery, as if she stood naked and exposed before the thorn throne in the Dark Court.

Ninka resolved to do all she could to keep Aerith's true mortal origins secret, even if her own life were to depend upon it.

CHAPTER 47

IT WAS CALEB she wanted to spend time with Jess realised. They were growing closer. It was what she wanted, more than anything. He was clean, open, unsullied. In stark contrast to some aspects of her recent experiences in Faery. She needed someone like him in her life.

What she had seen at the Dark Court still preyed on her mind. Bloody, troubling images she was desperate to forget, clouded her thoughts. Despite what Taryn had told her, she refused to accept that Catelysma, the Bitch Queen from Hell, was her mother. It was insane. Stuff like that only happened in movies. But Taryn was so convinced it was true, he'd sworn undying allegiance to her. And told her his true name into the bargain. Which, after he'd resisted the pressure Catelysma had put on him, and paid so dearly for it with the loss of Anira, was a truly big deal

The way he'd fallen to his knees and spoken to her like some kind of goddess, still made Jess cringe. She suspected that he had some agenda of his own. Perhaps he saw her as an avenging angel - a pawn in the politics of Faery? Or did he plan to expose her as the forbidden child of Gentry and mortal blood? And so bring down the harsh judgement of Catelysma's peers upon her? It would be an effective and devastating act of revenge. In a way, she wouldn't blame him.

Taryn had been the one constant in her life. And now that relationship had been transformed forever. Jess wasn't sure what she thought of him any more. Taryn was a faery lord, like Jackryn Fleet, and in her limited experience of the lords, they were self-serving, arrogant and pitiless. After all, most of them took their lead from their Dark Queen.

Jackryn must be involved in whatever had happened at Windroth. He'd been so eager to find out more about her that he'd tormented a dying woman. She burned with fury at the faery lord's cruelty. How dare he set foot inside Windroth Hall! One day he would pay for what he'd done. She owed it to Ivy, her mum too, to lay the past to rest.

But she couldn't face what carnage she might uncover. Not yet. A part of her felt guilty for leaving so much of importance unresolved. But a larger part of her was simply scared by a burden that felt too heavy for one person.

It was still a shock to get her head around who – *what* – she had become. Barely a heartbeat ago she'd been an ordinary girl, without any great prospects, living on the Limefields Estate, where girls of a similar age led mundane lives. Their main aim to get out of their skulls every weekend, maintain their false nails or save up for breast enlargements, so they could chase a few moments of fame on Reality TV; just like thousands of similar girls up and down the country. Jess sighed, thinking that she'd settle for an uncomplicated life like that, in a heartbeat.

She screwed up her nose. Well, maybe not the plastic surgery.

She came to a decision. For the time being, until she felt ready to address the issues surrounding Windroth, she would bury all knowledge of fey beings, and Faery, deep inside her, lacquering it with layer upon layer of glamour. She envisioned it sleeping there in the darkness, gleaming like a dragon's egg. Who knew? Maybe if she never spoke of that stuff again, it would all go away. Her pulses quickened as she thought of Caleb. At least with him, she still *felt* human. It might be only a pretence, but she felt desperate to cling to it for as long as possible. And to refuse, absolutely, to dwell on the fact that the poisonous blood of a pitiless tyrant was coursing through her veins.

Grabbing a bag of fruit and nuts and a banana, she clumped downstairs, calling out, 'Just coming!'

The hail had turned to heavy rain by the time she and Caleb left the kitchen. She matched Caleb's pace as they jogged past the old orchard on their right, through the gate in the wall and navigated the neglected kitchen garden. Lifting her face, she opened her mouth to catch the rain, enjoying the sensation of the coldness on her tongue and skin.

She glanced at the glasshouse, Caleb pointed out as they passed it, making a mental note to explore it some time. And then she was ducking through the archway in the wall, entering his small private world.

Rain was kicking up tiny spouts from the pond, drumming on flat lily pads that almost covered the water's surface, slicking the weathered stone of the old fountain. Overlooking the far end of the pond, the summer house stood like a miniature Gothic gatehouse, the scale of it far more to Jess's taste than rambling Windroth Hall. This whole enclosed garden, with its formal structure softened, but not overcome by the same air of decay that marked the rest of the grounds.

'Wow! Look at this place!' She was in love, totally charmed. Her bleak mood had dissipated entirely as if this unexpected gift of a garden had worked some alchemy on her. She felt carefree and mischievous, something she rarely experienced. Looking sideways at Caleb, she noticed how serious he looked. She wanted to see him smile. Maybe playing a trick on him would make him laugh in that silly, creaky way of his that made her heart turn over. The impulse to…tease him. It was new to her.

'Last one inside the summer house is a scabby monkey!' she cried, speeding past him.

'A scabby what?' he spluttered.

She chuckled. It had worked. The look on his face was priceless.

'Hey! Wait!' He yelled, running after her.

She reached the summer house before him, took the steps to the veranda in one leap. But as she fumbled to open the door, the latch stuck and she lost precious seconds.

The scuffing of Caleb's trainers sounded softly behind her. 'Loser!' he cried, triumphantly, gently shouldering her aside.

She didn't resist, though she could have overpowered him with the tip of one pinkie. This was *so* what she needed. Silly, aimless…wonderful. Just a boy and a girl messing around. She had never done this. Never wanted to, until Caleb. Something that had been crushed down tight inside her began to unfurl. She concentrated her senses, tested it, found to her surprise and delight that there was *nothing* fey, about *that* particular blossoming.

Caleb grasped the door handle. She took advantage of his concentration to edge close again, so he was pressed against the side of her body. The side of his hip nudging hers on a level, legs matching hers in length. He was longer at the waist, which gave him the extra height. They were a good fit, she realised, with a jolt of heat to her belly.

He flashed her a sideways grin, gave the door latch an expert twist. 'There's a knack to it. You have to twist and push at the same time. There!'

'Is that right?'

She couldn't resist jostling him, so they were wedged together in the doorway and neither could enter. For a moment they fought for supremacy, neither willing to give way. 'Who's the loser now?' she cried, triumphantly, gaining ground, easily holding Caleb back, until he surprised her by grabbing the waistband of her cargos and hauling her backwards.

'Ow! Not fair. Wedgies are cheating!' she giggled, easing the taut fabric from between her bum cheeks.

'Yeah? What do you call, using turbo-speed to get a head start on me?'

'A girl's prerogative!'

He gave a shout of laughter. 'Yeah, right! I'm never going to win, against you, am I?'

'You might. Actually, no! Why don't you just give up!' Jess was choking with laughter. She had both arms braced against the door frame now, was jiggling her body from side to side attempting to prevent Caleb from ducking past.

'You want to play dirty? Huh? Do you?' He tickled her armpit. As she collapsed against him snorking and gulping, he encircled her slender hips with one arm dragging her through the door.

Jess screeched, unable to stop herself falling as they tumbled together into a heap on the floor. At the last moment, Caleb twisted so that Jess landed on top him, cushioning her fall. They lay there, chests pressed together, breathing hard, trying to catch their breath. Rain from her tangled wet hair dripped onto his face, but he didn't wipe it away.

Seconds ticked by. Jess could smell Caleb's skin, feel the heat of his body, every contour of it suddenly more precious to her than she could ever have imagined. Looking into his eyes, she saw the darker brown flecks around the edges of the caramel coloured irises. Beautiful, like inclusions in amber. This had stopped being funny. She should move, break this spell. But she didn't.

Caleb's eyes became intense, his expression questioning and unsure. 'Jess?'

It was that hesitancy, more than if he'd been confident and taken the lead that decided it. Before Jess knew what was happening, she was leaning forward, cupping the sides of his head with her long-fingered hands and pressing her mouth to his.

His mouth was firm and warm, opening readily beneath hers. She tasted him tentatively at first, liking the unique sensation of slick warmth, and the way, when they moved apart for a second his breath hitched. Then they were kissing again and he began exploring her mouth in turn. The tips of their tongues met, shied away. The kiss went on, becoming deeper, more insistent. Caleb lifted his hands, caressed her back and then moved up to her shoulder blades.

Touched her tightly furled wings. Jess tensed, her senses swimming at the building of sensation. Deep down in her belly, the heat multiplied, matching the pressure in her wing membranes. They were swelling now, becoming engorged, pulsing. She gasped against Caleb's mouth, drowning, as the cresting of pleasure threatened to overwhelm her.

This was wrong in so many ways. It was time to stop. Now.

'Wait!' She drew back, pushing against his chest. She rolled off him, sat on the floor with her back to him, let out her breath in a dizzy rush. 'Sorry. I…I didn't mean to jump you like that.'

'I'm not complaining. I've been dying to kiss you for ages. But I didn't dare make the first move.' Caleb rose slowly to his feet, reached down to take her hand.

Jess didn't need help getting up, but she took his hand anyway. The old-fashioned gesture was sweet and appealing. The sort of thing, pretty blonde 'girlie' types expected from their boyfriends. She had once seen a girl from college pointedly sitting in a parked car, until her boyfriend came around and opened her door for her. She remembered feeling disgust as the obviousness of the girl's gesture, while also thinking that no boy was ever likely to treat her that way. But she had been wrong about that, as with so many other things.

She and Caleb stood hand in hand, facing each other, but with space between their bodies. She looked down at her feet, unable to meet his gaze. 'Was it...um. You know, OK?' she asked, shyly, her usual bravado deserting her. What a stupid question. He must think she was a total moron.

He smiled. 'Oh, yeah. Much more than, just OK? How was it for you?' he joked.

She found herself grinning, grateful that he had turned this around with humour, eased the awkward moment. 'It was...unique,' she said honestly, her chin still tucked into her chest, and then added before she thought better of it, 'Not that I've anything to measure it against. Boys haven't exactly been queuing up to ask me out...or anything else. '

'Really? They must be mad.'

She could have kissed him again, for that remark alone. Closing her eyes, she let herself sag forward and lean against him. His lips brushed her hair, a tiny caress but she felt echoes of it all the way down to her toes. Longing twisted in her with a terrible giddy anticipation she couldn't seem to quash.

She was aware of the ridges and hollows of his collar bones, the hard muscles of his chest. And was again gratified by the way his breath grew swift and shallow at her closeness. She could hear his heartbeat speeding up; sense the rush of blood through his veins that gave a flush to his skin. Despite his strength and vigour, he seemed so fragile. So human.

Gone so soon. Hardly worth the breath. Fragile hot-blood. The dismissive faery terms jumped into her head.

They had never seemed more appropriate. Grief for his brief mortality rioted through her. And grief for herself; the monster who still thought she could hide behind her human self. How much of that original hot blood, which she'd once had in common with Caleb and the rest of the human race, remained in vessels circulating with alien fluid? She found herself re-evaluating everything she thought she knew and everything she wanted out of life.

All because of him.

This wasn't flirting any more, she thought incredulously. It was beyond serious. She was scared, completely out of her depth.

'Wait? What you just said. Are you telling me….That was your first kiss?' Caleb seemed to have only just absorbed what she'd told him.

Jess gave a shaky grin, attempted to harness her scattered thoughts. 'Yeah. How lame is that?' she burbled. 'Last girl in the school to get a bra too.' *God, what was she saying?*

'This is so cool!' he said delightedly. 'I love it. Sweet seventeen and never been kissed.'

'What did you just say?' She pulled back, jerking free, as a memory surfaced with painful intensity.

He frowned, let his hands drop to his sides. 'Jess? What's wrong?'

'Nothing. Only…I've just realised. Today is my birthday. I'd completely forgotten about it. What with Ivy dying and…and all the stuff that's been happening to me. Mum hasn't even remembered. I thought *she* might have. It's her job, isn't it?' She wrung her hands, started pacing the room. 'I'm *eighteen*, Caleb. That's a landmark in any girl's life, right? According to all the songs and poems written about it being a special age. Like, magical and "now you're a woman or an adult anyway". Whatever else, I have a right to feel special, in a kind of normal human way, don't you think?' To her horror, she burst into tears.

'Sorry. I don't know what came over me.' Jess said when she could speak again. She wiped her eyes with the white, monogrammed cotton handkerchief Caleb handed her. *Who even used those things any more?* Gulping, she finished mopping up and went to sit on the edge of his bed, twisting the damp cotton square between her hands. 'I'll wash this. Let you have it back,' she murmured, distractedly.

'Keep it. It's one of Ralph's. I've got dozens. Feeling any better, Birthday Girl?'

She nodded, wrinkling her nose. 'A bit. Shit, how pathetic, am I? I can't remember the last time I cried about anything.'

'Well, maybe it was time you did. From what I've seen you take everything on your shoulders, like you're the only person around who can fix things. You don't have to do that any more. I'm here now. I can help. I want to.'

She gave him a watery smile. 'You've already done loads. Ivy's funeral. Been patient with Alice You have to be the kindest, most practical guy in the world.'

'Cheers. Sounds really boring...'

'It's a compliment. I've been taking care of me and Mum since I was a little kid. I *so* wished that someone would make all the bad stuff go away. Just for once.'

He came closer. The bed dipped as he sat beside her. He

draped one arm around her shoulders, waved the fingers of his free hand in the air, in a mock magician's gesture. 'Shazam! There you go. All the bad stuff's history.'

'Shazam?' Was he for real? It was crazy and silly, such a very *human* word for magic, but so poignant that she something long-standing inside her thawed. She sighed and rested her head on his shoulder.

'Happy Birthday, Jess,' he said softly. 'I'm sorry you don't feel special, because you are. I don't mean just in a, Wow! You're-a-faery, kind of way. I mean, plain special. No, not plain anything. You couldn't be plain, if you tried. You're stunning, actually. And you don't even realise it. Ballsy too, in a way I happen to think is really amazing. You must know I can't stop looking at you. I thought I was being so obvious about it. I love how you look. The way you dress to please yourself. And the way you don't take any shit from anyone. I've been bottling all this up and I'm probably going to regret spilling it all out later. But hey, in for a penny, right?' He paused, let out a shaky breath. 'I think I should stop now, before I dig myself an even deeper hole.'

'Yeah. I'd quit while you're ahead, if I were you!' She laughed, more touched by his outburst than she cared to admit. 'Bottom line? I like you too, Caleb. More than is probably good for either of us. And I can't think of anyone, I'd rather spend my birthday with. Or anywhere, come to that.' She chewed at her bottom lip. 'I'd *never* do anything to harm you. You'll always be safe with me, Caleb. Cross my heart. Faeries can't lie, you know,' she said, suddenly serious as she realised that she meant every word. For no reason she could fathom, it was important to her that he know that.

'Erm...got that. Loud and clear.' Caleb nodded, looking a

bit puzzled. 'Have to say. It wasn't exactly the reaction I was looking for after my oh-so-eloquent declaration.'

'Sorry. Best I can do for now.' She leaped to her feet and then bent and quickly kissed his cheek to soften her words.

He looked surprised and pleased. 'Fair enough. So, what do you want to do now? Your choice. Sit on the rug in front of the stove? Eat? Just hang out here for a while. Or you could allow me to draw you?'

His eagerness for the latter was palpable. Jess hadn't the heart to tease him by pretending reluctance. 'Since you've been so patient, up to now, how can I refuse?'

'You mean it? Aw, brilliant!' Caleb's smile illuminated his whole face.

He moved towards a rickety table that stood to one side of the wood-burning stove. There was a drawing pinned to the wall above it.

'Looks like you've been practicing,' she nodded towards the drawing.

Caleb went to the cupboard in the corner, gathered a heap of drawings and dumped them on the table. Jess began leafing through them. Every single one of them was of her. Some were head and shoulder studies, others were full-length sketches. She couldn't help feeling flattered, even though she didn't entirely recognise herself in the elegant lines and stylised poses.

Caleb watched as she examined them, a tide of red climbing up his neck. 'I started drawing you after I saw you in the hospital car park. It was only a glimpse, but I couldn't stop thinking about you. Usually I'm brilliant at remembering details of faces. It's a special skill – a brain thing. But I couldn't seem to capture your expression from memory. As you can see, I got a bit obsessed with trying.'

'Maybe you'll do better, from life. How do you want me?'
Jumping to her feet, she stuck out one hip and put her head
on one side. Positioning a finger at the corner of her mouth,
she pursed her lips in an exaggerated pout. 'Like this?'

'That is truly awful!' he said, spluttering. 'Something more
natural, if you can manage it. It's not that easy to hold a pose.
You should probably sit or lie down. Make yourself comfortable.'

'Fine. I can do that.'

While Caleb gathered materials, she kicked off her boots and
wadded cushions against the metal headboard. The smell of
wood and clean linen was mixed with the iron-reek of the
metallic stove and bedstead. But glamour muted her usual
reaction to it. Relaxing against the cushions, she stretched out
her legs. There was a hole in one of her black and white striped
socks. One long tapering toe poked through it. She tucked the
offending foot self-consciously beneath the other one.

'That's good.' Caleb nodded his approval at her pose. 'Do
you want anything before I start? A drink? You might be
sitting in that position for a while.'

She shook her head. 'I'm fine. You go ahead.

'OK. I probably won't talk much. I'll be too busy concentrating.' His voice was already slightly distant as he settled
himself in one of the kitchen chairs and pinned a sheet of
paper to a wooden drawing board. He held a pencil at arm's
length, squinting, taking measurements, adjusting proportions, and then applied himself to making marks on the page.

Silence fell.

Jess eased the tension from her muscles and tried to relax.
She loved this quaint one-roomed place which was also his
studio. Everything seemed arranged to please the eye, the
mis-matched old furniture somehow working in harmony.

The contrast between Caleb's workspace and Ivy's chaotic studio couldn't have been more marked. He worked on, every now and then pausing to blend something on the page with a finger or select a different pencil. When he looked over to study her, his expression was at once vague and intense, as if he was not only seeing her as a subject to draw, but attempting to capture something of her true essence. It was disconcerting at first, to be the object of such sustained attention, but after a while, Jess got used to it and enjoyed the companionable silence.

Eventually time began to drag. Being told to stay completely still, fostered a perverse desire to wiggle her hands and feet and pull silly faces. She controlled herself with difficulty. If Elizabeth Siddal could bear to lie in a bath of water for months while Millais painted his *Ophelia*, surely she could do this. Completely unaware of his subject's struggle, Caleb seemed to have retreated into a world of his own. After what felt like another hour had passed, Jess could contain herself no longer. Despite her glamour, the faint heat of iron-burn was beginning to penetrate through the barrage of cushions.

'OK. You can look now.' He turned the chair slowly towards her.

Jess launched herself off the bed, boredom forgotten. The drawing was a full-length study. She looked relaxed, long-limbed, her hair a wild tangled nimbus that framed her narrow, sharp face. The light from the window fell all down one side of her face and body, leaving the other half in shadow. It was a shock to see herself reflected through Caleb's eyes. Was she really that arresting? The planes and hollows of her face were delineated, with a sure touch. He had made her look exotic, mysterious, with her high-cheekbones and narrow, upward slanting eyes.

She could see that the drawing was very good indeed. It was as if she were laid bare to the observing eye, but there was something about the tilt of her chin that threw out a challenge, too.

'What do you think?' he asked tentatively, moving to stand beside her.

'Honestly? I'm kind of uncomfortable about the way you've made me look. It's like me, but *more* than me, somehow.'

His face fell. 'So you hate it?'

'Did I say that?' She rounded on him. 'I love it. I absolutely freakin' do! It's totally amazing, Caleb.'

A slow smile spread over his face. 'Good, because I think it's the best drawing I've ever done. It's yours, if you want it. A birthday present.'

'No! You're serious? I can keep it? Oh, wow! I am *so* going to treasure it.' She held out her arms. 'Come here, you talented person, you.'

He was grinning, his brown eyes shining with pride, as he moved into her arms. 'I do hope you're going to take advantage of me, again.'

'You wish! My boyfriend the artist,' she breathed softly. She kissed him, a gentle, grateful brushing of his lips, with only a hint of their earlier passion.

'Is that what I am? Your boy friend?'

'Do you want to be?' she asked.

Instead of answering, he slid his arms around her waist, held her tight and kissed her deeply. His hands moved upwards and her wings again quivered with anticipation, flexing and swelling. The exquisite sensation brought Jess up short. *High-born, fey and mortal. Forbidden to mate.* However you dressed it up, they were the facts. Look what happened when the rules were broken. *She* happened. A creature with a foot in two worlds and who belonged to neither. She was something, Other. Even more so, than poor doomed, Lord Natus had been; the half-blood who's ambition had prompted a terrible war in Faery. And look what had happened to him.

But did that mean she must deny herself any happiness? Could fate be that cruel? Jess knew this was madness, but she was weary of trying to be sensible, of reasoning things out. She had been starved of affection, of the loving touch of someone who cared for her, who actually found her oddness beautiful. And Caleb did. He accepted her, as she was, even having seen her unglamoured. She had been waiting for someone like him.

'Wait.' she pushed him away, gently disentangling herself from his embrace. He gave a murmur of complaint and would have reached for her again, but she neatly sidestepped to avoid him. 'Listen to me, please, Caleb. I don't even know if this can work. You and me. I'm scared of what I am. I have no idea what I might be capable of. There's danger…more than you know. This could be the biggest mistake of my entire life. Of yours, too.'

'I'm willing to take that risk,' he said, softly. 'I think it's worth it. Don't you?'

The tiniest hesitation. 'Yes. Yes, I do. Caleb I…'

'Come here.' He leaned forward to draw her into his arms.

At that moment, there was a faint sound. Jess whipped around, looked towards the door. Through the glass, she saw the outline of a tall thin figure. Gripping Caleb's arm she thrust him behind her to shield him from the faery lord who stood outside on the veranda.

CHAPTER 48

BRIEFLY HE CAUGHT a glimpse of something that seemed formed of light and movement, like a figure in armour caught between the pulsing beats of a strobe light. Strands of silver, blue and pearl-white streamed upwards from the region of its shoulders. Silver eyes without pupils blazed from a narrow white face. His stomach twisted with alarm. The creature was entirely alien.

Jess let go of his arm. Caleb saw the creature with human vision.

Instantly, the figure resolved into a tall young man with tousled fair hair, wearing jeans and a printed, red T-shirt.

'What the...Who the hell is that? Jess! No don't...' Caleb reached for her, but his hand closed on thin air, as she flashed past him in a blur.

'It's OK, Caleb. I know him,' she called, over her shoulder.

He watched in astonishment as she wrenched open the door and addressed the glamoured faery in familiar tones, with a trace of irritation.

'Taryn? What are you doing here? I thought I told you I was finished with Faery and everyone in it.'

'My Lady.' The fair-haired guy gave a shallow bow. 'If I am not mistaken, your final words to me were, "Just do whatever you want." Hence, I am here.'

'I'd forgotten you were so literal. 'So - what? You decided to come mortalwise for a jolly?' Jess said, sarcastically. 'Or are you checking up on me?'

'A "jolly? Your parlance continues to confound me.' Taryn shook his head slowly. 'Your welfare is indeed my prime concern, but there is another purpose for my visit. You may wish to take your ease while we talk of this. If you would invite me into your dwelling?'

'It's not my place. It's Caleb's. You'll have to ask him. But I'm forgetting my manners.' Jess stood in the doorway, with one foot inside the summer house and the other on the veranda. 'Caleb, meet Taryn. Taryn this is Caleb.'

'Hi,' Caleb raised a hand. 'Good to meet you, Taryn.' How did you greet a faery lord? Should he bow? Offer to shake hands? Neither felt right, so he did nothing.

So this was the faery that had lived beneath an underpass, disguised as a human called Mike. He had watched over Jess, helping, advising and protecting her while she was growing up and still believed herself to be human. One of the good guys, apparently, if there was such a thing. From his limited knowledge of faery dealings with humans he was finding it difficult to connect the words 'good' and 'fey'. Taryn had a weird way of speaking. To Caleb's ear it was oddly mannered, like a bad actor reading from Dickens.

'Charmed to meet you, also,' Taryn said. The light-grey eyes assessed him coldly. The faintly amused expression made it clear that he was only being polite for Jess's sake.

Caleb looked away first. It was disconcerting to have the faery lord's full attention fixed on his face. Even glamoured as human, Taryn had an unsettling other-worldly beauty. He felt an unwanted stab of jealousy. It was impossible not to be drawn towards Taryn's startling good looks. Surely Jess was not immune.

'Go on. Ask him then,' Jess prompted, as Taryn stood with his arms by his sides. 'Caleb won't bite.'

'As my Lady wishes. Caleb, I request that you favour me with an invitation to enter your dwelling,' he said, through gritted teeth.

Caleb's mouth twitched. It appeared that the faery was unable to enter the summer house without his permission. If he made it welcome, one time, did that mean it was free to enter at will whenever it wanted, like when he was sleeping or washing himself? Maybe even walk in on him and Jess? The thought of it gave Caleb the creeps.

'No, I don't want him in my place,' he decided, looking at Jess. 'He can stay out here.'

'Fine. It's up to you,' Jess said, grinning.

Caleb stuck his hands in his pockets, regarding the faery lord levelly. It felt good to assert himself. It seemed to him that faeries had had a lot of their own way around here. Maybe he could redress the balance in some small way. But his brief flare of triumph was extinguished by the twist of anger on the faery's fine-boned face, which he quickly masked as he turned to Jess. Caleb felt a stir of consternation as he realised he'd just made an enemy.

'Very well. It is of no matter,' Taryn said stiffly. 'May we walk? What I have to say is for your ears only.'

'You can tell me in front of Caleb,' Jess said. When Caleb did a double-take and would have objected, she held up one hand. 'No, Caleb. Whatever it is, it concerns you, too. You already know almost as much about me as Taryn. I don't want us to have any secrets.'

Taryn did not attempt to hide his consternation. 'I cannot think that wise.'

Jess shrugged. 'I trust him. Caleb's OK. He's my friend. I want you to treat him as such. See that no harm comes to him from any fey. Understand?'

'As you wish.' Taryn darted a glance of pure malice at Caleb. His expression made it clear that he thought Jess was insane. As he glanced through the open door of the summer house, he spotted the drawing board still propped on its chair. His eyes widened in shock. 'This mortal has stolen your image! I must advise you, most strongly, to destroy it forthwith.'

'It's just a drawing! A birthday present,' Jess said. 'What's the big deal?'

'In Faery, images of the fey are not made permanent. Some imprint of the subject's glamour will have been trapped within any work during the making. I fear that it is dangerous, particularly for one such as you,' he paused meaningfully, 'to keep this...scribbled object. Should it fall into an enemy's hands it could be used to cause mischief. And much worse.'

'Lighten up, Taryn! It's an amazing drawing. I love it and I am *not* destroying it,' Jess said stubbornly. 'I'll hide it somewhere safe. Locked in an iron box or something. I'd like to see any faery risk getting its fingers burned to stumps to get at it.'

Taryn didn't look happy, but he inclined his head. 'Dramatic perhaps, but efficacious. Well then, shall we?' He gestured to the wicker chair, that Caleb often sat in to watch the sun setting over the forest in the distance.

Caleb studied Taryn with interest. He noticed that the glamoured faery lord's hands were relatively large, his pale fingers elongated, tapered, like Jess's. They weren't deformed to the extent that they'd be easily noticed. His eyes, too, were slightly elongated and uptilted. Caleb thought it interesting that some, subtle tell-tale marks of fey, remained imprinted on Taryn's human disguise. Those who knew what to look for might recognise the signs of a glamoured faery. He stored the information away for a later time when it might be useful.

Jess sat in the chair. Taryn moved with fluid grace to sit cross-legged on the deck of the veranda. Caleb sank down opposite him, taking care to keep his distance.

'Well?' Jess prompted. 'What *did* you come here for?'

Taryn paused, took a breath, looking sideways at Caleb before he spoke. 'The Lady Ninka sent me to seek you out. She requests that you come with me to her forest dwelling.'

'The hudskin who originally asked you to watch over me? Why does she want to see me?'

Taryn looked embarrassed. 'It appears that I acted rashly in taking you into Faery. You were not fully prepared. There are things that must be done. Things of which I had no knowledge.'

'But Ninka does?'

He nodded. 'I assume that you are not averse to meeting with her? As I recall, you expressed a wish to speak with her.'

Jess nodded. She gave Taryn a shrewd look. 'Ninka *sent* you here to bring me back? Like in, *ordering* you? Sounds like she was pretty hacked-off with you.'

'She was furious. With good reason. It pains me to say this, but I may have endangered you, unknowingly. I acted in haste, which I do most earnestly regret. On my oath, it will not happen again.' He paused, his face sorrowful. 'If you will come with me to see Ninka, many things will be made clear to you. And, I am certain, reparation made for my errors.'

Caleb had been listening in appalled silence. Now he looked directly at Taryn. 'You messed-up and put Jess in danger? Why should she trust you now? Or this Ninka, person?'

Taryn turned to him, his eyes the colour of lead. 'I respect my lady's wishes to protect you from all harm. But that does not give you governance over me. I am not required to answer you.'

Caleb leaped to his feet, fists bunched. He was sorely

tempted to punch the faery's smugly beautiful face. But there'd be little satisfaction in hitting someone who was sworn not to hit him back.

'Leave it, Caleb. I need to go back into Faery with him. Now.'

'Then I'm coming, too!'

'Impossible!' Taryn rapped. He laughed harshly. 'Have you seen what is left after a lamb is thrown to wolves?'

'He's right,' Jess said. 'It wouldn't be safe for you in Faery.'

'And it is, for you?' he countered.

'I'm not completely unprepared, remember? And I have Taryn.'

'Him?' Caleb scoffed. 'He doesn't seem to know what he's doing!'

Taryn rose fluidly and stood facing Caleb. 'I would gladly die before I let any harm come to her! Can you say the same?'

'All right, you two. That's enough peeing up trees,' Jess said.

Catching Caleb's glance, she rolled her eyes in Taryn's direction, but he couldn't make himself see the joke. The faery lord wouldn't harm him because Jess had asked him not to, but he obviously despised him and thought him weak and useless. *Well ditto.* Would it have made any difference if he'd allowed Taryn admittance to the summer house? Probably not.

Jess leaned forward in her chair speaking softly. 'Caleb. I have to find out who I really am and what that means to me. I can't do that if I'm worrying about you. Besides, I need you to be here for Mum. She's no good on her own. You've seen that. Tell her I had to go away for a while. Make something up. She knows I like you, so she'll trust you. Keep an eye on her for me, yeah?'

Caleb wanted to argue, but he knew she was right. She stood up and moved closer. Reaching out, she stroked his cheek.

He turned into her hand, kissed her palm and heard the slight, inward hiss of the faery lord's disapproving breath. As Jess stepped away, a rush of protectiveness, like he'd never experienced, hit him. Caleb looked at Taryn. 'Take care of her, right? Or you'll have me to deal with.'

The faery looked back at him, his mouth set and his expression cold and remote. If he'd been human, he'd had said something like, 'big deal.' Caleb had never felt more ineffectual.

'We should be going now,' Jess said. 'Will you do something else for me?'

'Name it,' Caleb said.

'See whether Mrs Stark has a metal chest or a safe where you can put my drawing. Lock it away, just in case. I'll look forward to seeing it again when I get back.'

He nodded. 'Sure. No problem. Be careful, Jess. Don't take any silly risks.'

'Do not presume to order her, mortal,' Taryn said, coldly.

Jess ignored the faery lord's comment. 'Me, take risks? No way. I'll be back as soon as I can. Cross my heart.'

He could only watch, feeling helpless as Taryn stood back and allowed Jess to precede him down the veranda steps.

They walked side by side towards the far end of the garden. Two tall, slender beings. The colours of the sky and grass shifted over them, so that they appeared part of the landscape. The way they moved had nothing of humanity about it. For a moment, Caleb thought that he saw tiny white flowers springing up behind Jess in the wake of her footprints, but he couldn't be certain.

She turned and waved. Even as Caleb lifted his hand in return there was a displacement of the air around her and Taryn. They faded, became as insubstantial as mist. And then were gone.

He stood there for a while longer, taking deep breaths, willing himself to be calm. To have found Jess and then, possibly, to have lost her, in such a short time. It was almost too much to bear.

Stop it, he told himself. *She's coming back. She promised. Faeries can't lie, remember?*

It didn't help much. But it was all he had. Turning, he went into the summer house and unpinned the drawing from the board. Taryn had said it could be used against Jess. Was it only this one, drawn directly from life that counted? Just to be certain he gathered up all the other less successful drawings he'd made from memory, and rolled them up together.

Closing the door firmly behind him, he headed towards the main house. Alice Morgan would be back soon, she might even be back already, and he still had to think up a feasible excuse for Jess's absence.

CHAPTER 49

NINKA WAS ON her knees, thrusting her digging stick deep into the rich loam. After extracting a fleshy tuber she plucked pinkish nodules from the root hairs, before reburying the main root structure. The nodules went into the pouch at her belt, with all the other seeds, stems and leaves she had collected.

She had been at this task since before moonrise the previous evening. Many of the plants she needed were most potent with sap at the time of high tides in Faery. It was now a little after sunrise, and Ninka finished gathering the last of the leaves and stems, which needed the dew upon them. She had eaten nothing and not slept for almost two days. Though her eyes were gritty and she was dizzy from hunger, she welcomed the fact that this work was demanding of her attention. It distracted her from thinking about Aerith, what she and Jackryn Fleet might be doing in the chamber over the stables.

So much was at stake that she must set aside worries about her beloved. If Taryn was not able to persuade Jess to come to her, Ninka would have to travel mortalwise. She crossed that great divide only infrequently, while foraging, having no love of that iron-blasted land. But she must do whatever was necessary to bring to completion that which had begun in the forest more than sixteen human years since.

Having almost collected most of what she needed, Ninka breathed a sigh of relief. Her sorex-fur lined boots crunched over frost-rimed twigs and grass, as she filled a small leather bottle from a stream. Many of the trees had lost their leaves, bare branches pricking a sullen sky, the colour of bleached bone. She drew in a breath of air and tasted the approach of winter on her sensitive tongue. Soon every twig in the forest would be glazed with ice, underground dwellers slumbering safely beneath a blanket of snow.

In the cold season, the tree dryads, mountain Divas and river girls grew sluggish, as did much of life in the landscape of Faery. Ninka felt the grip of fear. Time to complete the necessary ritual grew short. If she did not soon take Jess before the sentinel oak, the investiture must wait until leaf-spring-out. And by then, it could be too late.

If Catelysma was not already alerted to the fact that a new dawning was imminent in Faery, she soon would be.

Ninka shivered as she turned homewards, the icy wind seeking out the smallest gaps in her clothing. Her wrists, hands and bare legs above her boots were chilled to the bone. Fool not to have brought her fur-lined cloak.

Head down, she bustled onwards, accompanied only by the rustling of the fern leaves overhead. She was eager now to be about her business inside her dwelling. By the time she reached the fallen tree, the sun was visible as a vague, grey-yellow disc through threads of gathering cloud.

Once inside the wickerwork hut, she went directly through the leather curtain and into the cave. She had earlier laid a fire in the central pit. Before long a blaze was sending shadows leaping up the stone walls. Ninka heated pebbles to use as pot-boilers in the flames, while collecting vessels from a shelf.

She laid out the materials on a flat stone. Some she had gathered, others stored in jars and boxes. Seeds, powdered barks and oils. All must be done in the rigid order laid down by whist-women of her lost hudskin tribe. Knowledge not used in centuries, and not needed, until now. When the pebbles were hot enough. Ninka carefully dropped them into a vessel of stream water. When the surface began bubbling and steaming, she added ingredients, until a thin film of oil rose to the surface. Skimming it off with a flat stick, she transferred it to a shallow stone bowl. The process was repeated over and over, until she had a small pool of colourless oil in the bowl. She added a pinch of this, a sprinkling of that, all the time softly murmuring; now and then, drawing arcane finger-shapes in the air.

It was when engaged in such work that she felt her loneliness most keenly. By rights, there ought to have been three ages of hudskin whist-women at work; an aged wise-woman, one of child-bearing age, and a virgin apprentice. But Ninka was all there was in these parts, perhaps all there ever would be anywhere. She must do the best she could to honour those who had gone before her, and pray it would be enough.

Soon, the cave filled with a pungent smell. In the centre of the shallow bowl there began a glow, which grew brighter until the oil gleamed with the purity of gold. Ninka set the oil aside. It needed to cool. While it did, she could finally eat.

Loading a large fresh leaf with strips of cured cervid, she added a sprinkling of dried berries and a pinch of powdered fungi, before folding it and hunkering down next to the fire to eat. Much restored by the food, she rose and went to fetch a small leather bottle from a basket in her wicker hut. She chose one with an oak stopper, carved into the shape of an acorn. She decanted the golden, lukewarm oil into the bottle, stoppering it firmly, before slipping it into her tunic pocket.

Soon after, she set about clearing up; carefully returning

pots, jars, boxes to their places on wooden shelves. She yawned. It was warm in the cave and Ninka's eyelids drooped. She had decided to curl up next to the fire pit, when she heard a faint sound.

Instantly, she was alert, her knife-shaped ears swivelling towards the source of the sounds. She moved soundlessly through the cave and into the hut. Two figures were just emerging from the trees at the far side of the clearing. Ninka's pulses quickened as she recognised Taryn. The young woman with him, so straight and tall and with a look of determination on her narrow, pale face, was the same one she had mistaken for a mortal with true sight.

Interesting that the girl had chosen to enter Faery still clothed in her human form, when Taryn must have warned her of the danger if any curious fey had happened to see her. Was this a display of rebellion or stubbornness? If Ninka had not known better, she would indeed think Jess entirely human. Her glamour was powerful, beyond imagining.

Jess Morgan. No longer a changeling struggling to survive in a hostile environment, but one of Faery's own, returned to Her hallowed earth.

Now that the moment of their long-awaited meeting was almost upon her, Ninka felt a rush of uncertainty. That which must be accomplished might be beyond her. It was so very long since she had been required to do such deep work. Her feet began edging backwards of their own accord. There was a secret exit, at the rear of the cave. How easy it would be to slip away, take no part in what was to happen.

No! This burden could not be lifted from her. There was no one else who could do this.

Ninka stopped dead, fighting for calm. She seemed to hear the thin cry that echoed through the trees that day in the forest. Imprinted on her eyelids, was a brief remembered vision of the scrawny, spider-limbed babe clawing its way out of the pearly membrane while its exhausted mother turned her face away. Jess had been an innocent, born into turmoil. She had not asked for any of this. She deserved the truth. And Ninka must ensure that she had it – most of it, at least. But first, there was the ritual of naming, when the true, fey-born changeling, returned to her homeland, would finally come into her power. After that, well – the work really began. This child of two worlds' life would be set on a course beyond her own control.

Ninka's part in securing Jess's birth right, would be over. She could, once again, melt into obscurity. Except for the one thing that troubled her deeply. How to ensure that Aerith was kept out of all this? It was bad enough that Jackryn Fleet was enamoured of his new huntress, something Ninka had hoped would be short-lived. But with Jess entering Faery, Aerith would be doubly-imperilled. The two young women, unknowingly linked as they were by shared, part-parentage, must never meet. For who knew what memories might surface? Ninka's dearest wish was that she and her beloved could disappear back into the deep forest. Live there, far away from the courts, the cruel machinations of capricious Gentry and the lingering trail of a Dark Queen's secrets, betrayal and murder.

Taryn and Jess were closer now. Ninka patted her scalp lock; the few coarse hairs were still neatly plaited, secured with binder twine sewn with red beetle wings. Glancing down, she saw that her tunic was creased and had a grease stain near the hem. There was no time to change into finer garments. She set her cloak around her shoulders. And then, gathering her wits, drew herself to her full height and went forth to greet the young woman who might be the Hope of all Faery, or Her Nemesis.

Jess checked her stride. One moment she was looking at the fallen tree, which almost filled the clearing below a steep bank covered in an impenetrable screen of brambles and ivy, and the next a small figure morphed directly out of the branches and began walking towards her and Taryn.

The creature was wearing a cloak, secured across its chest by a broad, leather strap. Large pointed ears stuck up through coarse brown hair that was scraped to one side of the broad little skull and gathered into a plait beside one ear. As Jess took in the details of keen black eyes, rounded features and reddish-brown skin, her jaw dropped.

'The shape-shifter in the woods! But...we've already met,' she exclaimed.

Ninka smiled, revealing a double row of sharp little teeth. 'Indeed. It was my misfortune that I did not realise who stood before me.'

Jess smiled in return. She caught the hudskin's scent and remembered that pleasant mixture of earth, wet leaves and sweet animal muskiness. This time Ninka's expression was friendly and watchful, not bound by terror as at their earlier encounter.

Should she apologise for her insensitivity? Better not. Reminding everyone of her earlier idiocy wasn't a good start.

'Lady Ninka. I'm very pleased to meet you,' she said, warmly, hoping it was the right thing to say.

'And I you, Jess Morgan. I must confess, that I wondered if this day would ever come. To see you here before me, returned to the land of your birth. And so strong and vital, gladdens my heart.' Ninka's voice was light and faintly accented.

'My life hasn't exactly been a picnic, up to now,' Jess said wryly. 'But from what I've seen of Faery, I don't expect it to suddenly become a piece of cake.'

Ninka frowned. She threw a confused look at Taryn.

'My Lady anticipates problems of adjustment,' he translated.

Ninka's face cleared. She nodded, smiling at Jess. 'I hope to be able to allay any fears in that direction.'

Jess felt herself warming to this small creature. She hoped Ninka might be able to answer the questions that had been tormenting her for so long. 'Taryn says you know a lot of stuff about me. You asked him to watch over me, when I was growing up.'

Ninka nodded. 'That is so. We have much to discuss. But first, will you take some refreshment?'

'I'll pass if it's OK. I'd rather get straight down to business.'

'Your pardon. I am not sure...' Ninka flicked another confused glance at Taryn.

'My Lady is charmed by your offer of hospitality,' he supplied. 'However she is eager to know what information you have in your possession. And how it may be of interest to her.'

'Ah, indeed.' Ninka's face cleared. She turned back to Jess. 'I will be glad to furnish you with everything I know. May I suggest we first complete the ritual, which will bring you into your true power? For every moment spent in Faery without being clad in your true, bright raiment imperils you.'

'Ritual?' Jess said, nervously, remembering what she had seen at the Dark Court. If this had anything to do with sacrificing human children or spilling fey blood for the pleasure of it, she'd be out of here before anyone could stop her.

Taryn seemed to know what she was thinking. 'Do not be alarmed. Ninka's methods are not those of the Dark Courts.'

'Indeed they are not!' Ninka said, emphatically. 'I have no love of she who sits upon the thorn throne. You need only to stand before the sentinel oak and drink an herbal infusion I have prepared. What then transpires will be between you and the Oak Dryad.'

'Dryad?'

'The elemental being, which inhabits the oak.'

'That's it? All I have to do?' Jess said, relieved that it sounded fairly simple. She wasn't sure about meeting an elemental, whatever that was, but Taryn would be close by if she needed help.

Ninka's sharp black eyes twinkled. 'Deep magic need not be complex.'

'OK then. Let's do it,' Jess decided. 'And then will you tell me everything you know?'

'As much as I can. On my honour,' Ninka promised. 'Come then. All is prepared.'

Jess hesitated, still uncertain. She liked Ninka, but could she trust her? She recalled again that when it came to the fey, nothing was as it seemed. She glanced sideways at Taryn. Catching her eye, he nodded reassuringly.

They dipped down into a valley, where a river bubbled over large stones and then climbed a steep hill beside a waterfall that foamed into a deep pool. Descending down a series of flat rocks, with the water thundering down beside them, they eventually reached a broad, pebbled bank and found the going easier for a while.

Jess spotted a grove of trees with bluish, leathery leaves that grew in clumps, like wide spreading hands. Taryn saw her looking. 'Sanguine trees,' he told her, his expression bleak. *Sanguine-leaf, which Catelysma had forced Lady Anira to eat.* Jess shuddered. She had been curious about the trees and would have liked to examine them more closely, but now their beauty was forever spoiled for her. Ninka pressed onwards and she did not slacken her pace.

After what seemed like a very long time, Ninka stopped in front of two ordinary looking birch trees. 'Through there is a portal,' she announced. 'Portals are hidden in plain sight all over the Blessed Land. By using this one, we will shorten our journey. If you will permit me.' Ninka linked hands with Jess. 'We must hold tight, if we are not to become separated and emerge at different places in Faery.'

Her small hand felt warm and slightly rough, like the scuffed pads of a dog's paw. Taryn gripped Jess's other hand. Although she looked closely, she could see nothing to distinguish the birches from thousands of other similar trees.

As they stepped between two birches, dead silence fell. Grey mist swirled around Jess, so that she could hardly see Taryn and Ninka. The mist was cold and thick, pressing against her mouth and nose. She gasped, finding it hard to breathe for the oppressive weight on her chest. Strands of mist seemed to penetrate her nose and flow into her lungs. She started to choke. In her panic, she tried to pull her hands free, but her companions held on tight. Just when Jess's vision had darkened and she began seeing stars, they burst forward into bright greenish light.

As soon as Ninka and Taryn dropped her hands, Jess fell gasping and coughing to her knees. She clawed at her face, tearing away sticky spider-web strands of mist that had formed a thick layer over her mouth and nose.

'My lady!' Taryn was at her side, helping to pull shreds of the stuff from deep inside her throat as she retched and choked.

The sticky strands on their fingers crumbled to dust and trickled away. Jess dragged long shuddering breaths of clean air into her lungs, the pressure gradually easing from her chest. Still speechless, she smiled her thanks.

Taryn rounded on Ninka, his face implacable. 'If you ever endanger my lady again, your life is forfeit. I vow it. Dear friend to me or no!'

'Taryn! Don't!' Jess reached up and gripped his arm. 'I'm fine.'

Ninka gave Taryn a searching look, but made no comment. She stood by calmly, unmoved by his threats. 'The discomfort will soon pass,' she assured Jess. 'Forgive me. I underestimated the effect of the fey mist on you. Soon, nothing in the land of Faery will harm you. Come. We are close to our destination.'

Still tight-lipped, Taryn extended a hand, helped Jess to her feet. She had a flashback to earlier at the summer house, when Caleb had made a similar gesture. At the thought of him, she felt a pang, followed by a rush of emotion. *My boyfriend? Could it be true? Impossible thought.*

She wondered what Caleb had told her mum, about where she had gone and why. How much time had passed, since she entered Faery this time? Two hours, twenty-four, two days? Ivy's funeral was soon. She wanted to be there.

Ninka was moving again, but more slowly now. Taryn walked at Jess's side. After the experience of going through the portal, he seemed especially watchful. The trees here seemed familiar. More light penetrated to the forest floor, so that a variety of plants competed with the usual brambles and nettles. Here and there a sapling straggled upwards. Ahead of her, Jess could see the gigantic oak, which dominated the small clearing. She had stood here, just a few days ago, before

Taryn led her into Faery. A short walk from the oak, was the forest's edge which bordered the fields at the limit of Ivy's estate. She realised that they had just travelled in an enormous circle

Windroth Hall was almost in sight, albeit in the otherworld. Between those weather-worn, red brick walls were the two people she valued most in all the world. The knowledge both cheered her and gave her pause. She stood at a crossroads. Even now she could turn her back on Faery. What if she was to leave? Leave all the secrets intact, flee mortalwise and bury herself there forever? She could glamour herself human, build a new life for herself. And Caleb.

'Come, Jess Morgan. Your destiny is at hand,' Ninka called from the fractured light beneath the spreading canopy of the oak.

After a moment, Jess nodded. Useless to deny the truth any longer. She had to do this. It was her destiny. She would finally be certain of her place in both worlds. Only then, would she feel in charge of her own life and able to make considered choices.

Taryn smiled his approval. He had shed his human glamour as he entered Faery, unlike her. His feyness shivered around him like mist around a waterfall, softening and blurring the outline of his true form. He looked like an angel in a Burne Jones painting. Too perfect to be real. His silver hair, blown tight to his head by the cold wind, resembled a shining helmet.

'All will be well,' he whispered. 'Do not be afraid.'

'I'm not afraid,' she replied. 'I'm freakin' terrified.'

Jess took her place beside Ninka. The hudskin handed her a small, dark-brown bottle, which felt warm from having been pressed against her small body.

'You know what to do?' she asked Jess.

Jess nodded. 'How hard can it be?' *Stand beneath this oak and drink whatever herbal potion was in the bottle.*

'Very well. When Taryn and I have stepped away out of sight, withdraw the stopper,' Ninka instructed. 'Drink all that is within, Jess Morgan.'

'Wait! You're leaving me here, by myself? What if I do something wrong? I might end up getting turned into a grasshopper or...or a mouse turd!'

Taryn gave a snort of laughter, quickly controlled.

Jess glared at him. 'It's all right for you. I'm taking a huge leap of faith here!'

He was immediately serious. 'Your pardon I beg. If you wish it, I will remain here.'

'What transpires is for Jess alone,' Ninka said, firmly, turning to Jess. 'Have courage, Jess Morgan. All is as it should be. Drink the potion. Every drop. You need do nothing more, but wait. Is that clear?'

'Crystal,' Jess murmured grumpily. 'You go, Taryn. I'll be OK.'

Why did Ninka keep calling her by her first name and surname? It didn't feel as if it was accidental. She had no more time to wonder why that might be. Ninka and Taryn were already moving away in different directions.

There was still time to call Taryn back. He would have to return, if she asked him to. Hadn't he sworn to obey her every command, without question? An interesting thought occurred to her. Why not make *him* drink that stuff on her behalf? But she knew she wouldn't do that. This was her journey to take. She watched in silence, until he and Ninka were swallowed up by the trees.

Alone now, beneath the towering bulk of the ancient tree, the only sounds the soughing of the wind through its topmost branches and the accompanying creaks and groans of the living wood. Time to drink whatever was in the bottle. Jess took a deep breath. For all she knew, it could be poison. What was even in the stuff? *Eye of bat, snot of toad, pee of hedgehog.* Oh, God this wasn't helping. She eased the acorn stopper from the small leather bottle, brought it to her nose and sniffed tentatively.

It smelled pleasantly of herbs, vaguely sweet like honey. Perfectly innocuous.

'Right. Here goes nothing.'

Tipping up the bottle, Jess swallowed, once, twice, three times. The liquid slid down her throat like warm syrup. Remembering Ninka's instruction to drink it all, she shook out the last couple of drops onto her tongue.

And then, she waited for something to happen. Nothing did.

Except that silence fell. A deep silence, which was more than a general absence of sound. Not a single leaf, no blade of grass moved. There was no birdsong and not the faintest breath of wind. Total sensory shutdown.

A sense of anti-climax crept over Jess. Was that it? How ridiculous to have made such a fuss. She was about to call to Ninka and Taryn to return.

When everything changed.

A silent pulse rippled all the way through the oak's massive branches. It was as if the entire tree had just given itself a shake. A loud creaking filled the clearing, as bulges jutted from areas high up on the bark. An arm appeared from one bulge and then a shoulder; on the opposite side, another arm and a second shoulder. Gradually, the elemental's upper body slid free from the tree and appeared to hang there, still half-clothed in robes formed by the living wood. Around its head root-like excrescences moved gently. Pushing down with the heels of its hands, it slowly heaved one massive gnarled leg free and then the other, until finally, it stepped onto the grass.

Jess looked up at the towering figure whose vastness, soared above the trees and almost filled the forest clearing. Its face and body were deeply scored and covered with many knots and whorls. Here and there were patches of lichen, greeny-grey and mustard yellow. Beetles crawled in and out of crevices in the bark skin and small white moths, circled around the neck.

The figure shuddered and appeared to be falling forward. Startled, Jess leaped sideways, ready to run, but before she could take another step, there was a silent collapsing motion, a telescoping downwards. She caught a strong smell of green wood and sap. A tall, slender woman stood before her, her skin entirely formed of tiny overlapping leaves, like the scales on a snake. Root-like hair and robes of grass and moss swirled around her in a wild nimbus. The leafy features constantly melted and then reformed, alternating between youth and extreme old age.

'Jess Morgan.' The voice was hollow and thready, as if the words had been conjured from a great distance. The dryad extended a pale arm and opened twiggy fingers to expose a gnarled and deeply rutted palm in the centre of which grew a single pale flower.

Jess felt enveloped by an energy in which there was depthless wisdom and kindness, tinged with compassion. She gulped, completely overwhelmed.

'Yes, I'm Jess,' she faltered. 'And...and you are?'

'Arboria Petra,' the dryad intoned.

'Arboria Petra.' Jess inclined her head. 'I am honoured to meet you.'

The scaly features moved, overlapping into a smile. 'You are known to me, Child of Faery. You stood before me a short span since. I have something for you. Come close. Accept what is yours.'

Jess took a hesitant step forward. The dryad nodded encouragingly as Jess plucked the flower from the centre of her palm.

Instantly that deep, unearthly silence blanketed her. A warm sensation flowed down Jess's arms, travelled downwards through her lower body and flowed out through the soles of her feet. She had a sense of it continuing on down, penetrating deeply into the sacred earth beneath her and connecting to the very pulsing heart of the land. She felt her head tipped backwards. From a gap in the clouds, a column of light streamed down and pierced Jess's forehead. Light burst from her eyes, ears and nose. Just when she thought she would scream with the intensity of the pressure in her head, the light blinked out.

She didn't realise that she was weeping. After a few moments, she wiped her eyes. The dryad was watching her, her face still, serene. Opening her arms wide, she gestured for Jess to step into her embrace. Jess did so. The smell of wood and sap was overpowering.

Reaching out one twiggy finger, the dryad placed it on the centre of Jess's forehead. When she spoke, her voice was softer than a summer breeze, yet Jess heard every word with perfect clarity.

'Welcome. Damiana Seelie Firethorn, sovereign being of Faery, for now and always.'

Damiana. My true name. 'Now I belong…here,' Jess murmured.

The dryad's hands lit gently on her shoulders, before it took a step backwards. 'Almost,' she whispered, her face compassionate.

As another blast of power swept through Jess, she cried out and sank to her knees. This new force worked within her, as if soldering every vein, sinew and bone. She felt it fortifying and strengthening her body from head to toe. And somehow, she knew that she was becoming wholly fey, while the last fragments of her humanity were being ripped apart.

No. She would not give up that which was so much a part of her. Without the traces of mortality in her blood, she might become as cold and pitiless as her bitch queen of a mother. That was never going to happen. Gathering the shreds of her glamour, Jess wrapped it shield-like around a tiny part of herself. The secret humanity within her shrank to the size of a pearl. She placed it safely, deep inside her heart. She felt the powerful force tempering her, as if she stood inside some alembic vessel. It washed around the secret pearl, but left it intact. Seconds later, she felt the last filaments of that internal heat cooling, withdrawing. Finally it faded.

Jess slowly rose to her feet. She was tingling from head to foot.

At that moment, the deep silence that had accompanied the ritual, shattered. A cacophony of voices filled the air, all harmonising into one long triumphant note of unbearable sweetness. Beneath her feet, Jess felt a vibration like a slow, deep heart beat. Clouds roiled overhead, a charcoal tempest slashed by silver. Jagged lightning flashes, fragmented the sky. Day slid into night. Star trails streaked the darkness and the moon rode in a continuous arc, as if the world spun on its axis. The sun rose and it was day again.

Birdsong filled the air. Somewhere in the depths of the forest a stag barked a challenge.

'There,' the dryad said, on a long outward breath. 'Faery

embraces her newest Bright Daughter.' She opened her arms wide. 'Behold.'

Jess stood in silence, as with a rustling like the sound of a mighty river in spate, every tree in her line of sight bowed towards her. She would have raised a hand in acknowledgement, but she felt unable to move a muscle.

Points of light began swirling around the dryad. She spread her grassy skirts in a deep curtsy and bowed her head so low that her crown of twigs brushed the ground. As she straightened, the overlapping particles of her face arranged themselves into a smile.

'Should you ever require my counsel, Lady Damiana, call upon my name.' It was a whisper on the breeze.

'I will remember that, Arboria Petra,' Jess replied.

The dryad's form began to dissolve into clouds of whirling leaves. There was an uprush of movement as the being swelled into her former vastness. Jess had a glimpse of massive limbs, pocked with lichen, looming cathedral-like above the clearing. And then the elemental melted into the oak and was gone.

Jess did not know how long she stood there alone. It could have been moments or hours. Some time later, she became aware of movement. From out of the trees, Ninka and Taryn walked slowly towards her.

Ninka was sobbing openly and Taryn's eyes were wet, his face white as milk.

Jess smiled, held out her hands to them, and took a single step. She saw Taryn's expression slide into concern as he sped towards her in a blur of movement.

And then. Damiana Seelie Firethorn, who had lately been plain Jess Morgan, crumpled to the ground in a dead faint.

CHAPTER 50

JESS OPENED HER eyes to find Ninka and Taryn looking worriedly down at her. She was lying on something soft. A quick investigation showed it to be Taryn's cloak, spread on top of some piled bracken that rustled as she moved.

Neither the massive sentinel oak nor the clearing was anywhere in sight. Thick brambles and vines surrounded them on all sides, while closely grouped trees soared high overhead. She had a vague recollection of being scooped up in Taryn's arms and then a sensation of being borne away at preternatural speed.

Jess pushed herself up onto one elbow and looked around. 'What happened?'

'Your senses were temporarily overcome,' he explained. 'And who could blame you.'

'That's not what I meant,' Jess said, sitting up. As usual Taryn had taken her literally. 'I mean, I get that I'm officially part of Faery now. That's a good thing, right? So how come you two look as if someone just died?'

'If I may be permitted to answer?' Ninka said solemnly. 'We, your loyal friends and subjects, rejoice that your majesty's illustrious presence in Faery has been formally announced to all. But that very fact must be a matter for immediate concern.'

Your majesty? Illustrious presence? Jess's stomach lurched with foreboding. She was fully aware that something momentous had just happened. After all, you didn't have a cosy chat with an elemental every day of the week. She thought she had a grasp of what was at the heart of Ninka and Taryn's concern, but her brain seemed to need a kick start.

'So one new faery entered Faery?' she said stalling for time. 'Big deal. It can't be that rare, can it? Why would anyone be that bothered about me?'

Taryn looked sideways at Ninka, his face incredulous. 'Is it possible that she truly does not know?'

'Know what?' Jess said. Her head was starting to pound. She turned to Ninka. 'Would you just tell me straight? What am I missing?'

'Very well. You now stand among the Gentry. Like calls to like, in Faery. Which means that *every* ruler of *every* court, Bright and Night, is now aware of your presence. There will be widespread shock and anger. The naming and investiture of Gentry has always been accompanied by great ceremony, after the most auspicious time is decided and after due announcement. But you have burst upon Faery, like...like a comet in the firmament, seemingly from out of nowhere. The eyes and ears of royalty, and those who serve them, will be following your every move. Until you prove otherwise, you are assumed to pose a threat. From now on you can trust no one.'

Gentry. She was *Gentry.* Everything narrowed to that moment, that word.

'Well that's just great isn't it? One minute I'm something special. And the next its open season and I'm the bait! I'm not even full Gentry. I'm a half-blood. Tell her, Taryn. You worked it out!'

'It is as my Lady says,' Taryn answered obediently, looking uncomfortable.

Ninka nodded. 'Catelysma is your mother. I know this.'

Jess rounded on Taryn. 'You *told* her? What the hell for?'

'He does not deserve your anger,' Ninka spoke up in the faery lord's defence. 'I discovered the facts about your birth for myself, long ago. Taryn came much later to the knowledge.'

Jess folded her arms and set her jaw. 'Yeah? Well it still feels like I'm the only one around here who's got no idea what's been going on!'

'I have vowed to tell you everything, I am able to, about your origins,' Ninka reminded her. 'Do you desire that I do so?'

'Oh, I *so* do!' Jess said struggling for calm. She thought of all the years, painful years, when she'd beaten herself up for being different. She thought she had heard everything. But it seemed there were still more shocks to come. 'Just don't give me any freakin' fey riddles. OK?'

Ninka glanced at Taryn, who stood by impassively. She turned back to Jess. 'You wish me to speak freely?'

Jess deliberated about whether to ask the faery lord to gather wood for a fire or find something for them to eat, anything that would take him out of earshot. But he'd sworn the oath of service by the power of his true name. She recalled how he had even warned Ninka against harming her, when they navigated that portal earlier. His loyalty seemed absolute. She needed to believe that. It was time she placed her trust in him.

'Stay, Taryn.' She gestured for him to sit. 'You've been keeper of my secrets for so long. A few more aren't going to make much difference.'

He nodded and sank down to sit cross-legged on the forest floor.

'Well then. Where to begin,' Ninka said as if to herself.

'There is no doubt that Catelysma is your mother. With my own eyes, I saw her give birth to you…'

Jess listened in silence as Ninka began to tell her what she had seen in the forest when glamoured as a hare. She felt the hudskin's terror and fascination as she realised what she had stumbled upon. She heard how, after the birth, the Dark Queen had fashioned a stock changeling out of sticks so that it looked human. And then had glamoured her own new-born to also resemble a human babe.

'*Two* of us? One a live baby and the other, made of sticks? Both made to look human. But why? I don't understand.'

'Neither did I. At first. Catelysma swaddled the babes and set off with them through the forest.' Ninka's voice deepened and grew soft, as she finally divulged the dangerous secret she had kept within her for so long. 'So I decided to follow her. And I saw where she went…'

Deep in the forest, Catelysma moved more rapidly than an arrow from a bow. Ninka needed to use all her hare's senses to keep track of the Dark Queen, despite Catelysma having so recently given birth.

It was already getting dark. By the time the queen approached the forest's edge, a gibbous moon had risen to cast its silver light over the fields of crops and pasture that stretched into the distance beyond the trees. Catelysma stopped and turned around, her eyes raking the undergrowth.

Ninka huddled in a shallow depression, pulse racing. Had she betrayed herself with the slightest sound? Flattening her long ears along her narrow back, she closed her eyes, lest moonlight should glint on them and betray her hiding place. Moments later, she heard the soft rustle of the queen's robe as she continued.

Opening her eyes, Ninka saw her already at the far side of a field of crops. She followed, keeping low to the ground. After some time, she saw Catelysma approaching a stretch of grassland, planted with ornamental trees, which led on to gardens with clipped hedges, gravel paths and flowerbeds.

Ninka's terror of being discovered was now subsumed beneath her curiosity. The queen's destination was the big house, visible at the top of an incline as a black shape against the moonlit sky. There were lights in some of the windows. Windroth Hall. The place was known to Ninka.

Why was the house of interest to the Dark Queen? Surely it was beneath the notice of Catelysma, who did not concern herself with the bland doings of mortals.

Ninka had visited the outskirts of Windroth's grounds on occasion as they were rich in forage and rare roots. She had glimpsed the mortals who dwelt there, seemingly few indeed, for so large a dwelling. A small woman, with grey hair and a deeply-lined face who exuded a feverish, hectic energy; a muscular dark-haired man – unusually fair of face for a mortal, who cut lawns and did work around the place; and, having arrived only lately, a sweet-faced young woman, barely more than a girl, over whom hung an aura of great sadness.

She had discovered a secret too. The man and young woman were lovers. Ninka had watched them lying naked in the long grass, engaged in love-play. Usually her interest in mortals quickly gave way to boredom, but she had found herself charmed by the intensity of their affection.

Now she watched from the shelter of a crumbling stone urn, as the queen approached the imposing front porch of the house. Without breaking her stride, Catelysma passed immediately *through* the front door as if it were made of mist.

Ninka was deeply shocked. How could this be? No fey

could enter a mortal dwelling lest invited. Even Gentry were subject to that law. There was some mystery about Windroth, but she had no time to wonder at it. If the Dark Queen had been granted ingress why not other fey? Ninka loped forward, bunched her muscles and jumped at the door. She melted through the solid wood, emerged into an open space with a high ceiling. The floor, patterned with many coloured squares, was hard and cold under paw.

There was a steep staircase of dark wood. Glimpsing the faint, flickering afterglow at the head of the stairs, Ninka scampered after Catelysma. She kept to the deep shadows, her paws making no sound on the wooden treads. There was a flat area and a corridor, with a confusing number of closed doors. She was just in time to see the queen glide silently through the facing door at the far end. Ninka paused, before following Catelysma.

She knew at once that the darkened bedroom was occupied. Could hear regular breathing, coming from the sleeping figure in the large wooden bed. A chorus of lighter, more rapid breathing rose from two infants occupying cots with barred sides, placed nearby a source of warmth. The bitter reek of hot iron from the device giving out heat was mixed with human smells; sleepy skin, soap and clean linen.

Taking cover beneath the bed, Ninka watched the queen reach into the first cot and pick up a rather long, thin baby with black hair. She then placed her fingers over the mortal infant's nose and mouth. Ninka sensed the speeding up of the tiny mortal heart and the internal struggle for life, before the infant stopped breathing. It had died without a murmur. Catelysma threw the small body to the floor, where it lay in a cold shaft of moonlight, its features still flushed and the dark hair sleep-damp. A moment later, the tiny corpse crumbled to dust and blew away.

The queen lifted a fold of her robe to reveal her own glamoured newborn. Ninka saw that it looked *exactly* like the babe she had just killed. Catelysma placed the fey-born counterfeit in the cot. It fitted exactly into the tiny warm depression so recently vacated.

And so the forbidden royal child was foisted cuckoo-like upon the young mother who lay asleep, all unknowing that her own babe had been murdered.

Ninka was still puzzled by Catelysma's actions, but not overly dismayed. Exchanging stock changelings, and sometimes sickly fey young, for healthy mortal babes had a long tradition in Faery, albeit it was rare in recent times. The exchange had been made. That ought to have been an end of things. But the queen's next action caused her to frown in confusion.

Catelysma bent over the second cot, scooped up the human infant and placed it securely in the crook of her arm. This babe was rosy-cheeked with blonde hair that looked pale in the moonlight. Ninka could see the pink bodysuit it wore, decorated with a design of some kind of dancing animals. It cooed softly as the queen enfolded it in her robe, before placing the newly-made, stock changeling in its place. This second changeling, formed of sticks and leaves, now took on the resemblance of the chubby, fair-haired human babe.

Both of the young mother's twins had been replaced by imposters; one true, fey-born, the other a bunch of glamoured sticks, although she would never know it. Her cuckoo-children were both clothed in identical copies of the little pink suits.

Ninka expected the queen to throw the tiny blonde mortal to the floor, where it would crumple to dust in the moonlight as its dark-haired twin had done. But she did not. Cradling the mortal babe, Catelysma stole across the room to the window.

Why would the queen kill one mortal babe and allow the other to live? Ninka could make no sense of it.

Catelysma's back was turned to the bed. Ninka saw an opportunity to leave. She was about to edge out from under the bed, plunge through the house and flee across the fields before Catelysma emerged. But at a sigh from the sleeping mother, the queen whirled around, her eyes flooding black and a snarl marring her perfect face.

A shriek of terror lodged in Ninka's throat. Too late to escape unseen. Panicked, she leaped sideways, to where a bedside chair stood in deep shadow and squeezed behind the cushion. From the faint traces of warm milk, perfumed powder and sweet infant breath, she knew this was where the mortal sat to nurse her young.

Her heart stirred with pity. What terrible thing could the young mother have done to have brought such punishment upon her?

The queen's robes rustled. She moved to stand close to the bed. Although almost faint with terror, Ninka risked peering around the cushion. The faint pearly glow outlining the queen, illuminated the sleeping woman's face. The soft bloom of motherhood on her was as sweet as a briar rose. Where was the dark-haired man? Ninka wondered. He who this girl-woman had lain with in the long grass? Ought he not to have been sleeping beside her?

And then all thought fled as she caught sight of Catelysma's face. The queen's expression of fury was terrible. She reached out a hand, her elongated, tapered fingers hovering just above the sleeping woman's face. Ninka fully expected her to strike the mortal, or pinch the breath from her and leave her lifeless, as she had done with the first of the woman's babes. The queen appeared to fight for control. She slowly withdrew her hand.

'No. Better you should live. Your punishment is for you to raise *my* child,' she hissed. 'The forbidden child *he* unknowingly seeded in my eternal womb. Which glory and wonder was cheapened and sullied by his seeding two mewling brats in you! Cursed, base born hot-blood, too fair of face for his own good! Much woe may it bring you, mortal woman, to watch *both* of your assumed off-spring wither before your eyes! And may your treacherous, errant husband live in continued fear of my anger. I have spoken.'

Ninka was deeply shaken. The words of binding! Nothing could now be undone.

The queen gave a bitter laugh, but to Ninka's surprise, her face crumpled and she loosed a deep groan of misery that held such pain and disappointment that Ninka trembled to hear it. Dashing away tears, Catelysma tossed her streaming hair over her shoulder. Her robes billowed around her, like sails buffeted by an icy wind. The child in her arms stirred, its small blonde head moving as it began to stir. The queen's head dipped towards it, her beautiful face bleak as midwinter. Ninka saw one pearly teardrop fall unnoticed onto the tiny upturned face. Ignoring the infant's cries, Catelysma streaked forward comet-like, plunged through the closed door and bore the baby away.

The queen's impassioned words rang in Ninka's head. She would need time to weigh and absorb them. But one thing she did know. By the queen's own admittance, this mortal girl was being punished unfairly. Why should she suffer because of the actions of others? She could not know that her lover, the dark-haired mortal, had lain with Catelysma. To lose both of her babes. It was too cruel. Ninka knew that there was no hope for the 'stock' changeling. Having no essential substance, these always faded quickly.

But the other, being true-fey – even if of mixed-blood - had a chance of life, even though Catelysma clearly meant for it, too, to perish in infancy.

Ninka leaped to the floor, scampered over to the cot on silent paws, to where the queen's glamoured new-born lay, snug beneath the covers, sleeping peacefully. Poor innocent. It had not chosen such a sorry destiny.

Reaching for her glamour, she drew her hudskin form around her. She then reached her hand through the bars of the nearest cot. The babe turned its face towards her and opened willow-green eyes that glowed against the pale-pink sleep-suit. The glamour Catelysma had set upon it was strong; maybe strong enough for it to survive a few mortal spans, but glamour alone would not grant enough protection for this unique infant to endure an entire life-span spent mortalwise. Without stopping to think of the wisdom of her actions, Ninka raised her hand. Forming arcane shapes on the air, she murmured words of power. Tiny points of light materialised in the air around the babe. They shimmered with swirling moving colours, as of soap bubbles in the sun. Each of the lights sank down to settle gently upon her, like raindrops captured on fur, and slowly dissipated. A nimbus of bright gold light flared briefly around the infant's head and then was gone.

She had done all she could. At least one of the mortal mother's babes was safeguarded. Ninka found herself wondering what would happen to it. Would it live or perish after all? Its life in this sere, barren world that reeked of iron and stone would be hard and joyless. Poor little, cursed half-blood. Neither one thing nor the other.

Backing away from the cot, she conjured her glamour, shifting shape into a hare. In a trice she was stretching sinewy brown limbs, leaping back through the bedroom door. All was quiet inside the house, but for the sound of a ticking timepiece. She lost her way and had to wind through endless dark rooms, before she emerged onto the moon-washed gravel path. Catelysma was nowhere in sight. Trembling with relief, Ninka headed deep into the forest and her dwelling, where she could ponder on all that had happened. She only hoped that the queen would not demand her presence at court, to take advantage of Ninka's seamstress skills. She would need time before she could face Catelysma's piercing, all-knowing gaze without faltering.

On impulse, she took a detour. She was still mindful of that half-blood babe and what might become of it as it grew to adulthood amongst mortals. Her thoughts worried at her like the throbbing of a torn finger nail. With a flick of her tail, she plunged into the thick undergrowth and went in search of Taryn, her long-term friend, and the only faery lord she knew she could trust.

Jess let out the breath she felt she had been holding inside for the longest time. It was an effort to speak.

'Oh, my God...' She paused, trying to get her thoughts in some kind of order. 'So, it was all her, Catelysma? *She* killed the real baby Jess, so that I could take her place?'

Ninka nodded. 'She did. I was witness to it.'

'She murdered an innocent baby out of spite, because she wanted to punish my mu...' She faltered, wasn't sure what to call Alice any more. 'Catelysma didn't intend me to live, either?'

'That is true,' Ninka agreed. 'Even though, I think she felt pride that she could give birth to a living baby. She said that her mortal lover had "seeded it in her womb, unknowingly".'

Jess blinked. 'Unknowingly? So she hadn't told him? He didn't know Catelysma was pregnant with...' She couldn't bring herself to say, *with me*. She settled for, '...with his child.'

Ninka nodded again. 'I think no one knew the truth, until I overheard her in that bedroom. Three of us, besides the queen, share her dangerous secret. You, Taryn and I. Catelysma knew her position would be imperilled if anyone discovered she, Sovereign Gentry born, had brought forth a child of mixed-blood. You were the living evidence of her crime. She could not keep you.'

'Why didn't she just kill me? It's not like she'd think twice about it,' Jess said, bitterly. She felt a twist of revulsion, recalling the queen's avid face as she watched the human children being tormented and killed at the apple feast; Catelysma's triumph at publicly displaying the dying agonies of Lady Anira.

'I too wondered that she allowed you to live,' Ninka confessed. 'But then Catelysma's own words explained everything. Her jealousy was stronger than her fear or her fury. She could not bear that her mortal lover, the father of her child, who she would have assumed worshiped and venerated her, had fathered *twin* girls on his young mortal wife. The blow to her pride would have been devastating.'

'But - how could she know that Alice was pregnant with twins?' Jess asked.

Ninka's eyes were soft, her expression pitying. 'Because *he* told her. Your father. The queen's lover. You already know his name.'

'Rob Morgan.' Jess's thoughts rioted as she confirmed what she had already suspected. Rob. The man Alice had adored. The only man she had ever truly loved.

'Yes. I returned to Windroth briefly, after that night. I saw your mortal foster-mother, Alice, walking in the garden. The dark-haired man was with her that time. I heard them call each other by name. Alice was frantic because one of the twins was very sick. She was sobbing as if her heart would break. I was puzzled because the man did not comfort her. I sensed that he wanted to, but could not for some reason. His face seemed frozen. More with horror than distress, I recall.'

As if Rob guessed that Catelysma was responsible? Jess swallowed hard. 'When that twig-thing in my half-sister Stella's cot shrivelled or whatever it did, it would have seemed to Alice like a cot death.'

'I know nothing of this...cot death,' Ninka said frowning. 'But otherwise, yes. It is as you say.'

'Poor Alice.' Jess shook her head slowly, imagining Alice's devastation as she discovered the assumed Stella's pale lifeless body. 'But you said Catelysma took the *real* baby Stella with her? Maybe Stella's still alive in Faery? Did you try to find out? Did you ever see her there?'

Ninka paused, took a breath and briefly closed her eye. Jess sensed her inner struggle. She seemed to be searching for the right words. It was not surprising. What she had witnessed so many human years ago had affected the hudskin deeply.

'Ninka?' she queried softly. 'What happened to Stella? What did Catelysma do with her?'

Ninka passed a hand over her mouth. She did not meet Jess's gaze. 'Her fate...is uncertain,' she said, at length. 'It is generally assumed that she is dead. Such playthings brought into Faery do not fare well. You have seen a little of what happens to mortals at the Dark Court?'

A look passed between Ninka and Taryn; of joint concern, Jess assumed. Taryn seemed about to speak, but at a gesture from Ninka, thought better of it.

Jess suppressed a shudder. 'I wish I could forget. But I still hoped Stella was alive. You know? For mum... Alice's sake. She never got over losing one of her daughters. Rob left us soon after that. Alice thought he couldn't live with the grief and what it had done to the two of them. He seemed to blame himself for it all.'

'A tragedy indeed.' Ninka nodded gravely.

'Why couldn't Rob have been stronger?' Jess burst out. 'When he met Alice she was already fragile. Thousands of miles from where she'd been born, still struggling to get over losing her parents in a car crash. And Ivy Stark, her grandmother, was cold and remote. Alice said Rob brought her back to life. She really loved him. Adored him. And she thought he loved her back. But he betrayed her in the worst way. Just because he couldn't keep his bloody jeans zipped!'

Ninka said nothing.

It was Taryn who spoke up. 'I hesitate to defend him. But Catelysma is hard to resist. As many a discarded faery lord could tell you. When she became desirous of your mortal father, she would have gained power over him. Probably after tricking him into giving her his true name. He may not have had a choice but to comply with her wishes.'

'And Catelysma put a binding curse on Rob Morgan, so he would live in continued fear of her anger. That would be enough to steal any mortal's wits,' Ninka reminded her.

Jess suspected she was right, but she wasn't ready to let Rob off that easily. 'He deserved it, for what he'd done to Alice! So what, if he had an affair with Catelysma? It was over, wasn't it? He could have come clean. Alice would have forgiven him. I know she would. They could have worked it out, somehow. He was the love of her life. No one forced him to run out on her, when she'd just lost a baby. That was really harsh. I can't forgive him for that.'

'Is it possible that your mortal father was afraid for Alice and their remaining daughter? He may have feared that Catelysma would do them harm,' Taryn suggested.

Ninka nodded. 'Taryn could be right. Rob was unaware that the original twins were already gone. Both replaced by changelings. He believed that Stella, his human daughter, had died naturally, although he possibly suspected that the queen had a hand in that. He thought that you, Jess, were his human child. And by leaving, he was protecting his wife and remaining daughter from Catelysma's jealous wrath. He may even have tried to draw her anger onto him alone.'

Jess was forced to admit that possibility. If it were true, it meant that Rob wasn't heartless and weak, as she'd always thought. What he did, may have been the ultimate sacrifice. She shook her head slowly. 'I'll never understand fully why my father did what he did. I wish I could speak to him. But that's never going to happen.'

Ninka shook her head sadly. 'I know nothing more about Rob Morgan. Or where he went.'

Jess fell silent, weary of trying to make sense of it all. She knew she'd probably be dreaming about all this for weeks, but for now she wanted to mentally file it away, until she spoke to Alice; because she, most of all, deserved the truth.

'It is a sad story indeed,' Taryn commented, with another sharp look at Ninka. 'I knew only part of it, until now. Would that I could ease the burden of it for you, my lady.'

There was something unspoken between the two of them, but Jess had had enough shocks for the present. Besides, they'd known each other a long time. They were allowed their personal secrets.

She threw him a grateful look. 'But you already have. You and Ninka. Between you, you protected and watched over me my entire life. I owe you both more than you'll ever know.' She looked at the hudskin. 'You risked your own life and Catelysma's anger to help me. My faery bitch-mother wanted me to shrivel from iron-burn and choke on the poisoned air, when I was living…mortalwise. But, you, Ninka, made me strong enough to survive. You saved my life. I'll never forget what you did for me. And for Alice.'

She got up and went over to Ninka. Gathering the hudskin in her arms, she lifted her to her feet. And then gave her an enormous hug, while kissing the top of her head. 'This is from both of us. Me *and* Alice –' Ninka stood there stiffly, her hands by her sides, until Jess let her go. She cast her eyes down, her broad cheeks flushed deep-red and a shy smile lifting the corners of her mouth.

Jess smiled at the little creature who was so brave, wise and possessed of such grace. And then there was Taryn steadfast, a bit arrogant and over-protective but loyal to a fault. She realised how very dear these two were becoming to her. Catelysma might have destroyed one family, but she was fast gathering a new one around her. With Caleb and Alice, that made four people she valued.

Well, two mortals and two fey, she thought, with an ironic twist of her lips.

'Queen Bitch's going to get one big shock when I turn up at court and out her in front of everyone,' she said through gritted teeth.

At the look of frozen horror on both Ninka's and Taryn's faces, Jess gave a shout of laughter. 'Got you there! Don't worry. I'm not about to go stomping straight into hell-under-the-hill. I've more important things to do first.' She was only sounding off anyway, giving voice to something that might never happen. She hadn't decided yet whether to stay in Faery. At the moment that was not at the top of her agenda.

Ninka grinned, nervously. 'I am much relieved to hear that. A question, I beg?'

'Ask me anything,' Jess said. 'I'll answer if I can.'

'Your true name? Assuming the oak dryad told you it, how do you wish to be addressed?'

That was actually two questions, Jess thought, if she was being picky. But she was glad to change the subject. 'Yes, she gave me my true name. Obviously I'll never tell it to anyone.'

'No, indeed,' Ninka agreed. 'One's true name is the greatest jewel. The power of it will depart from Faery, only when the final breath leaves your body. So, Jess Morgan. How do you wish to be known henceforth?'

Jess paused, worried that the moment she spoke the new name aloud, she would be giving up her humanity. She remembered how she had safeguarded those precious shreds of mortality, during the ritual, and knew they would anchor her mortalwise, whatever happened. She made a promise to herself that she would *never* be ashamed of her mixed identity.

She took a deep breath. 'Damiana. Call me…Damiana. I'll probably keep plain, Jess, for when I'm with Alice and Caleb.'

She noticed Taryn's brief expression of disapproval at the mention of Caleb. There would never be much love lost between the two of them. But the faery lord said nothing. Leaping to his feet, he bowed low. When he straightened his sharp-boned face was aglow.

'My Lady, Damiana. Bright Queen. Truly named! And wedded to this Blessed Land. Let none say otherwise. Oh, what turmoil there must be in all the Courts of Faery!' He sounded delighted by the notion.

Ninka too, smiled, but her sharp eyes seemed wary. And there was a look of discomfort about the way she held herself. Something still troubled the little hudskin.

Jess thought she knew how Ninka felt. She'd put on a good show, but she wasn't at all sure about her new status. *Gentry. Faery Royalty.* It was totally insane. But what was the use of having power and status if she couldn't use it to ensure her personal happiness and the happiness of those she cared most about?

She stood up. 'I have to go home. I mean go... mortalwise.'

Taryn moved to her side, instantly alert.

Jess shook her head. 'No, I mean alone.'

'Is that wise?' Ninka asked. 'If I may suggest, in the circumstances it would be prudent to take Taryn with you.'

Jess shrugged. She turned to the faery lord. 'OK. You can come, but only if you stay out of the way. I have a funeral to go to.'

'As you command.'

Ninka bowed from the waist, one small hand placed on her heart. 'Until we meet again. Fare you well, Lady Damiana. Taryn.'

CHAPTER 51

CALEB STOOD IN front of the dressing room mirror putting on a black tie. Alice had insisted he come into the house and make use of Ralph's en suite. 'You can't keep using that old wash-house next to the kitchen,' she'd said. 'It makes sense to use Ralph's bathroom. Jess told me Ivy gave you all Ralph's clothes. I'm fine with that. In fact, why don't you move into his rooms? That summer house will be freezing, come the really bad weather.' Caleb had only used the wash-house because Mrs Stark hadn't wanted him hanging around the house, which he now knew was because of the danger to him from the fey host that plagued her. Now they were gone, the danger was no more. But he was reluctant to leave the sanctuary of his own private living space and studio.

'Thanks. But I prefer to live in the summer house,' he replied. 'It's warm enough with the stove. And I like being by myself to work.' But he had allowed himself to be persuaded to use Ralph's bathroom. It had been a luxury to have a bath, wash his hair and shave in comfort.

He thought now of Jess, remembering how it felt to hold her, kiss her. The faintly grassy scent of her pale skin and the intoxicating spice and moss perfume of her hair. How unreal it was to see the human glamour melt away as they touched. To drown in jade eyes with no pupils, to feel her long, long fingers cupping his face as she pressed her spoon-cold lips to his. He shivered with longing.

Looking in the mirror he was dismayed at the tangled mess he'd made of the tie. 'Oh, crap,' he muttered, ripping out the knot. He prepared to start again, forcing himself to concentrate this time.

Caleb caught a swift movement in the mirror, barely a flicker from the corner of his eye. Even as he half-turned, Jess spun up behind him and slid her arms around his waist. Her hair was twisted into messy bunches, bushy as fox tails. She wore a purple, fake-fur jacket over a long-sleeved top and black leggings.

'Wow! Smart outfit!' she said, approvingly. 'Except for the tie. It looks like a dog's chewed it.'

She came back. To me. My God. She really did. He felt her small hard breasts searing him through the thin cotton of his shirt. Her thin arms encircled him like a vice, clinging just a little too long for a casual embrace. In them he read her relief to be back and her need of him. *Me too*, he answered silently. The unspoken language of their bodies more potent than words.

'I know. I'm rubbish with ties. Never wear 'em. I don't see the point.' He knew he was grinning like an idiot at this inconsequential exchange when he wanted to say something deep and meaningful, but he didn't care. She was here, looking like a normal girl - until they touched. Teasing him in that silly kid way he found totally charming.

She nuzzled the back of his neck. 'Mmm. You smell nice. Did you think I wasn't coming back?'

Yeah! ''course not,' he said.

'Liar.' She gave him a playful dig in the ribs. 'I meant it when I said you can trust me. Remember that.'

'I'll try to.' He met her eyes in the mirror and made a silent vow to have more faith in her. In them. 'It's hard though, when I don't know where you are. How long you'll be gone. Or what you're doing,' he said honestly.

'Oh, I had some formal faery…stuff to do. I couldn't get out if it, or I'd have come back sooner,' she said in a way that made him think she was seriously downplaying whatever it was that had happened. 'You remember Taryn mentioning Ninka, the hudskin, who sent him to fetch me? Turns out I'd already met her once, in the woods near the village, when I was glamoured as human. Totally freaked her out! She thought I was a human with true sight.'

'Is there such a thing?'

'Apparently. But it's beyond rare. Maybe for some unusual people, it's like… when we're touching and you're able to see what I see? But I don't really know. Or care that much, right now.'

She tossed her head, releasing another waft of perfume that made his senses swim. 'So this, Ninka. What's she like? Can you trust her?'

'She's great. I totally love her. She told me everything. Who I really am and what happened here, at Windroth, around the time me and my twin sister were born. She was actually there when my faery mother made the switches.'

'Switches? Like – in the plural?'

Jess nodded. 'I wasn't the only faery changeling. But I survived. The one that took the place of Stella didn't. For some reason my faery mother took the human baby Stella into Faery. Ninka thinks that she…died there.' He saw her shudder. 'I don't even want to think about how it happened. So my foster-mum, Alice, actually lost *both* of her real daughters, well before the presumed cot death.'

'That's tragic.' He shook his head slowly.

'Yeah, it was,' Jess agreed, bleakly. 'I don't know how to begin to tell Alice. And then there's me - her only living daughter. Who is actually nothing at all to do with her. Not even human.'

'But she has a right to know the truth, doesn't she?' Caleb asked. 'Everyone does.'

'Despite the damage it might do? What if it destroys her completely?' Jess blew out her breath, rested her chin on his shoulder, so that one of her bunches was crushed against his cheek. She pulled a face in the mirror. 'It's been difficult enough for me to adjust to all this. Heck – I'm still reeling from the insane shock of it all! Think what it might do to Alice, to find out that everything she believed is a lie. Actually. Can we leave it there? I can't talk about this any more, right now. Sensory overload.'

'Yeah, 'course. Whatever you want. I'm...I'm just glad to have you back safely.'

He caught her glance in the mirror, feeling a jolt as their eyes connected. He couldn't help wondering what splendours those eyes had looked upon in the world of Faery. How could he compare? Plain Caleb Farmer, aspiring artist who lived at Windroth on sufferance. And didn't even own the clothes on his back.

'Caleb. What is it?' Jess asked, frowning.

'Nothing.' He attempted to shake off his stupid insecurity. She was here with him, because she chose to be, wasn't she? 'Just that. I want you to know. You don't have to tell me anything if you don't want to. I've never gone along with that we-don't-have-any-secrets-from-each-other garbage. Personal space is important, especially head-space, right? People are allowed their secrets. I totally respect that.'

She grinned. 'Couldn't agree more. But that's why I *will* tell you stuff. I feel like I could tell you anything and you wouldn't judge me.' She paused, a look of uncertainty crossing her face. 'You do believe in *us*, don't you?'

He was caught between renewed delight at having her

pressed up against him and guilt for the nagging doubts that plagued him. He thrust the latter aside. Turning into the circle of her arms, he slipped his hands inside her fur jacket and drew her close. The feel of her narrow torso and slender waist sent a pang of mixed tenderness and desire through him. She seemed too fragile for the weight destiny had placed upon her.

'It's a stretch, but I'm trying. We're the odd couple, remember?' he said.

'I know. Pretty cool, isn't it?'

Caleb bent to brush his lips against hers. Her lips parted easily beneath his. The kiss was nothing like casual, containing within it a depth that re-assured him of the intimacy between them in the summer house. He would have been happy to keep on kissing her, but after a moment, she pulled back from him gently.

'So, I assume the funeral's today?' Jess nodded toward the suit jacket on its hanger, looped over the wardrobe door. 'What's the plan?'

'There's a car coming to collect us in...' Caleb checked the small carriage clock on the mantelpiece opposite '...about an hour. The service is at St Giles church in the village and then on to the cemetery. It's about five minute's drive. Alice found instructions in a folder Ivy left. Ivy's to be buried with Ralph. They have a joint plot. Oh, and she found some letters, too. She said she was going to show you them, when you got back.'

Jess nodded. 'Yeah? Wonder what's in them. It's good that Ivy's going to be with Ralph. She'll finally be at peace.' She was quiet for a moment, fleeting sadness pulling at the corners of her mouth. She brightened with an effort. 'So, we haven't much time before we give great grandma a proper send-off. You'd better let me at that tie!'

Caleb lifted his chin as Jess flipped the ends, folding them into a neat knot, which she then slid it up into place.

'There.' She gave the tie a small tweak. 'Much better.'

He turned to check it in the mirror. 'Perfect. I knew you'd know how to do it.'

'I'm a girl of many talents.' She paused. 'I should go and find Alice. Tell her I'm back, before I get ready. See you downstairs?'

He turned to watch her walk across the room. In the bedroom doorway, she looked over her shoulder and smiled. A second later she popped her head back in. 'By the way. What did you tell Alice about where I went?'

Caleb gave her a sheepish grin. 'I said you'd met up with some guy you knew from college. He'd got one spare ticket to a music festival. It was yours. But you had to leave right away.'

'At this time of year? And she believed you?'

He shrugged. 'Seemed to. Anyway, she doesn't seem to have been worried about you. Not like last time. And she hasn't been drinking as much, as far as I can judge. Alice's been going through Ivy's papers. Getting organised. Making lists of stuff.'

'That's enough to keep a whole team of people occupied,' Jess said with a wry grin. 'I'm hoping she's turned a corner after that relapse. She'll do it, in the end. I know she will.' She smiled suddenly. 'OK then. I've been to Frostbite Download? I'll try and remember that!'

Jess found Alice in the sitting room. To her relief, her mum's face was smooth and firm, the puffiness around her jaw and neck much reduced. Her eyes were no longer bloodshot and the yellow tint was fading from the whites. She wore discreet make-up and her dark hair was twisted into a loose bun at the nape of her neck. A cameo brooch was pinned to the lapel of a smart navy-blue dress Jess had never seen before.

'I feel good,' Alice told her. 'The best I have for a long, long time. I've been trying hard. Doing things—keeping busy is the secret.' She smiled, looking a bit awkward. 'I know it's early days, but something feels different this time. Coming back here was hard but it's helped.'

Jess didn't reply.

'There's a cottage hospital, just outside the village,' Alice went on. 'I saw it from the taxi when I went into town. It has a psychiatric wing. I've made some enquires. They offer treatment for addictions. It made me think. After the funeral and when things settle down a bit. Well...it's an option.' Their eyes met in silence.

'I want to make you proud of me.'

'I'm already proud of you.' Jess swallowed hard.

'Caleb and I didn't get off to a very good start. I fell off the wagon almost as soon as I arrived here. I'm not proud of that. But these past few days, we've talked for hours. He's kind, a good listener. No wonder Ivy was fond of him. Here. This is something you must see.'

Alice extracted two sheets of thick cream paper from a large envelope. She handed them to Jess. 'This concerns you.'

Jess began to read. The letter was hand-written in sepia-coloured ink and dated a few months back. As she read on a dawning haze of disbelief made the words swim before her eyes.

'Is this for real? Ivy's left Windroth Hall, to *you and me*?' Jess sank into a nearby chair..

Alice moved to stand beside her. She put a hand on Jess's shoulder. 'I couldn't believe it, either. When I think of the

514

squalid flats we lived in. All those times we did a runner when we couldn't pay the rent. The times we hid from bailiffs. And you, having to scrabble about in bins behind supermarkets for ready meals and sandwiches. I could cry when I remember how bad things got. How bad I'd made them. And now this.'

They were rich. A new start. Freedom in the world of mortals. Ivy had even taken care of Caleb. He had been left a sum of money, the summer house and five acres of land.

Jess leaped to her feet and grabbed Alice. Her mum clung to her. They jumped up and down like lunatics, squealing delightedly. After a few minutes Alice subsided, gasping for breath and staggered laughing to collapse on the sofa. Jess joined her and put her arm round her.

'I hope I haven't been too bad a mum. I didn't always…'

'Don't. OK?' Jess held her tight.

Alice got up. She picked up two sealed envelopes from the writing desk, each addressed in Ivy's neat hand in the same sepia-coloured ink. 'One's for you, the other's for Caleb. Ivy left me a similar letter. It had more or less the same stuff in the letter you just read, but it was personalised. I expect yours and Caleb's are similar.'

Jess stuck the letters in the pocket of her purple fake-fur jacket as she headed for the door.

Alice called after her. 'I almost forgot. How was the music festival?'

The abrupt change of subject, took Jess by surprise. 'Oh…erm. The usual. Cool bands. Too many people. Toilets a total gross-out. Good thing I had tons of wet wipes,' she improvised madly. 'I'm dying for a hot shower. Laters!' she called, escaping swiftly.

Did lying by omission count when applied to faeries? She

hoped not. Because she wasn't going to tell Alice any of the stuff Ninka had experienced first hand. Not now. Maybe, not ever.

How would it help Alice to know that her beloved first-born, baby girl had died a lonely, possibly terrible death, in Faery, instead of being a victim of cot death? Or that Rob Morgan, who she'd loved with all her bruised young heart, had not only deserted her, but had betrayed her and fathered a child on a powerful, vengeful woman; who wasn't even human? It was the kind of thing that could destroy even the most level-headed person. Alice, still in the earliest stage of recovery, couldn't cope with any more emotional baggage.

Neither would Jess reveal details of her true parentage. She wasn't comfortable with having Catelysma's blood – the ancient, pure-blood of Gentry - running through her veins. There would be serious repercussions from the Dark Queen's union with Rob Morgan, should it ever come to light. The thought of what she might have to deal with, who she might have to confront, chilled her to the bone. But that was for the future. And she would not be fighting any battles, alone. Not any more.

One thing she was certain of. She would always think of Alice Morgan as her mother – not just, her foster-mother. OK, Alice hadn't always been able to protect her from danger or provide them with a safe home. But she had cuddled Jess when she woke from nightmares, never judged her or tried to mould her in any way. She had put up with Jess's moods and stroppiness and allowed her to be herself. Alice hadn't got everything right, by any means, but she'd done perhaps the best she could.

By contrast, Catelysma had given up all claims to Jess, when she'd foisted her, helpless and new-born, on the rival for her mortal lover's affections in the hope and belief that Jess would perish mortalwise, taking the evidence of the Dark Queen's transgression with her. Only Ninka's intervention had prevented that.

For Jess was certain of one thing - her existence mortalwise, and that awaiting her in Faery - must be kept separate. She made a silent promise to use everything in her power to protect the humans she loved.

She had to get herself ready for the funeral, and quickly. She had a shower and let glamour flow down over her damp bare limbs, clothing her in autumn-toned ruched silk and tightly-fitting velvet. On impulse she added antique jet jewellery – it seemed fitting. By the time she was descending the stairs, her feet were no longer bare. The spiked heels of pointed-toed ankle boots beat a timpani note on the hall tiles.

Squaring her shoulders, she flexed her folded and flattened wings so that they nestled comfortably beneath her jacket. She was ready to see Ivy off in style.

CHAPTER 52

THE CAR HOLDING Caleb, Jess and Alice drew up in front of St Giles church; a squat, oblong building of honey-coloured stone, with a square bell tower. Stone benches lined two sides of a front porch with an impressive studded-oak door.

Caleb got out of the car and held the door open for Jess and Alice. It was bitterly cold. He was glad of the overcoat he wore, rather self-consciously, over the suit and the two pairs of thick socks which stopped Ralph's shiny black shoes slipping about. As they walked together towards the church, he glanced across at Jess, pulling a wry face and fingering his lapels. She smiled encouragingly as if to say, 'You look fine.'

She looked fantastic and, unlike him, completely at ease in one of Ralph's tail coats, over a calf-length skirt of ruffled material that gleamed amber and brick-red and a tightly-fitting, golden-brown velvet jacket. A choker of some shiny-black material accentuated the long, pale oval of her face. On her feet were green ankle boots and she'd done something clever with her hair, which made her look older and effortlessly stylish.

Moving closer to Jess, he whispered, 'Is it safe for you to enter a church?'

'What? Because I'm supposed to be unholy or something?' she said, frowning. 'Do you believe that?'

'No. Maybe. I don't know - or care, actually. I hate labels. It's not that. There's an awful lot of stuff about dealing with faeries. How to banish or…or harm them. It got me thinking how much of it's true. I need to know this stuff. To… keep you safe,' he admitted.

'Oh I get it. You've been reading more of Mrs Stark's books.'

'Yeah,' he admitted, defensively. 'I wanted to understand. To know whether you can creep up on a faery if you…'

'Turn your coat inside out, so they won't be able to see you?' she finished for him, green eyes dancing at him. 'I remember that from a book I read as a kid.'

'Isn't it true?'

She suppressed a snort of laughter. 'I have no idea. We could try it sometime, if you like. Might be fun! Look. It's sweet of you to worry about me. I love that you care. You know that, right?' She squeezed his arm briefly. 'But you don't have to try to protect me. I'm definitely *not* a story book fairy. Anything but.' Her lips curved in an enigmatic smile that seemed to contain just a shadow of something dark and powerful.

'My mistake!' Caleb joked, grinning to hide his discomfiture at that brief glimpse of levels within her, of which he knew nothing.

He felt way out of his depth; *again.* Would that ever change, he wondered. He had a sudden acute sense of how bizarre his life had become. Had he really just had a serious conversation about the safety of faeries going into church? He wondered whether it was possible to do a crash-course in faeryality.

Jess had quickened her steps and linked arms with Alice. They walked ahead of him into the stone porch. Caleb joined them. Just inside the church door, the three of them paused, so that the vicar could exchange a few words of welcome, before they walked down the nave and took their seats in the front pews.

Jess slanted a smile at him. 'It's OK, all mourners, human and fey, are welcome,' she whispered. 'I can sense that the ground here has been sacred for thousands of years – well before this church. The fey walked this land once. It recognises me.'

Caleb gave her a bemused look. *The land recognised her?* Why not? It was no more difficult to believe than the fact that she had wings hidden beneath her glamour. Glorious wings that were the softest, silkiest things he had ever touched. That fanned a faint scent of flowers towards him. That grew warm and throbbing beneath his fingers.

He swallowed hard, harnessing his thoughts, began flipping through the leaflet he'd picked up from his chair before sitting down. On the front was a scanned image of a youthful Mrs Stark, wearing a light summer dress and hardly recognisable with dark hair and softly rounded features. Alice was reading her order of service leaflet, too. She looked sideways at him and smiled. He smiled back.

In the shadow cast by her formal navy-blue hat, Jess's mother looked a little strained, but there was an underlying sense of calm self-possession about her too. He had a glimpse of how she'd be without alcohol in her life. Over the past few days, while Jess was away, he'd found himself warming to Alice.

The vicar's voice, asking them to stand, interrupted Caleb's thoughts. He rose to his feet, along with Jess and Alice as the coffin was carried in. How small and narrow it seemed, hardly big enough to contain the body within.

Mum's funeral service had been in the small chapel of the 'crem.' Soft-hearted, emotional she'd been, lacking a practical head on her shoulders, the Farmers used to say. They couldn't push her around any more. *Love, you, always will.*

Caleb swallowed. He ran a finger around the inside of the old-fashioned collar of Ralph's dress-shirt which was rubbing uncomfortably at his neck.

He'd had a rather rushed conversation with Jess, on their way outside to meet the funeral cars. She had told him about Mrs Stark's bequest. When he'd expressed shocked disbelief, she'd given him the personal letter the old lady left for him. He'd read it in the car on the way here. The tone of the letter so warm, her wishes for his future as an accomplished artist so fond. Bless Mrs Stark.

It was frigid in the small nave. Candles glowing from sconces on the stone walls providing small pools of light, but no heat. He rubbed his hands together to try and warm them. The cold of the stone floor seemed to penetrate the bones of his feet even through his layers of socks. Incense smoke swirled, in the air above the coffin on the trestles. The pungent resinous smell made him feel queasy. He remembered that he'd skipped breakfast. Shivering, Caleb forced himself to concentrate as the service progressed through prayers and readings. He mouthed replies in the right places, joined Alice and Jess in the hymns, which echoed hollowly in the small church. The service was mercifully short. They were soon emerging, stamping their feet into the dim greyness of the bitter cold afternoon.

St Giles cemetery was some miles out of the village. Their car followed the hearse carrying Ivy's coffin. Caleb was glad of their car's heated interior. The short church service had cast them all into sombre mood and none of the three spoke as the car turned in through the ornate cemetery gates. Once again, they battled the icy wind, as they picked their way across gravestone-studded grass to the recently dug oblong, draped on all four sides with sheets of astro-turf.

Caleb paused for a moment next to Ralph's weathered headstone, the words on it blurred and indistinct. The huge mound of excavated earth from the new grave was piled beside it. It exuded a flat smell of damp loam. He gave a brief nod of respect, silently hoping that Ralph approved of Caleb's use of his extensive wardrobe.

He moved to stand beside Jess and Alice as the vicar arrived. Soon the prayers were completed and to the familiar words of 'Ashes to ashes, dust to dust...' The coffin holding Ivy Stark's mortal remains was lowered carefully into place.

'Goodbye, Mrs Stark. Sleep well,' Caleb murmured, as he sprinkled a handful of dried rose petals onto the coffin. With the old lady's passing, an episode of pivotal importance in his life had come to a close. But there was a sense of rightness about it. He preferred not to think of her lying on the bedroom floor, but to remember the last conversation he'd had with her. Mrs Stark had seemed peaceful and free of care, softer and almost affectionate, able to relax after so many years of torment.

Caleb went and stood to one side, giving Jess and Alice some privacy as they said their final farewells and sprinkled more rose petals. Alice was crying quietly into a bunched tissue. Jess stood with her, as they spoke a few last words of thanks to the Vicar.

The wind blew through Caleb's hair, whipping it into his eyes, nipping at his ears like sharp knives. He cupped his hands and warmed them with his breath, wishing he'd thought to wear gloves. As he turned up the collar of his overcoat, he caught sight of a tall young man in dark clothes, his messy fair hair tumbling about his face, standing leaning against a tree. Even from this distance the man's sharp-featured good looks were striking.

Taryn. Caleb felt a stir of irritation. Had the faery lord been in church? He hadn't noticed, but Taryn could well have been lurking at the back in the shadow of the carved wooden screen around the stone font. Why hadn't Jess mentioned that she'd brought her tame wolf back with her? Or perhaps Taryn had insisted on coming, so he could keep watch over her. The hint of ownership in that concept, made him burn with anger. *She might be your concern when she's in Faery, but when she's mortalwise, she's mine.* Caleb looked steadfastly at the figure beside the tree. He knew that Taryn was aware that he was being watched, though he gave no indication of it. That sharp, pale face remained devoid of expression as his gaze skimmed across Jess and moved on to rove through the rows of headstones and memorial statues before raking the trees that ringed the cemetery's perimeter.

Caleb got the unspoken message. He seemed to hear the faery lord speaking in that oddly formal way of his. 'You are of no concern to me, mortal. It is she, who matters. Only she. My lady, whose service is my life.'

A fragment of something Alice was saying to Jess, caught Caleb's attention and he looked away from the figure beside the tree.

'…something I have to do before I leave.'

Caleb saw that Jess was following her mum. He glanced back at the figure beside the tree, but Taryn had gone. Good. Caleb gave a mental shrug and with a stir of curiosity went after Alice and Jess.

Jess's mother wove between headstones, looking left and right, until she gave a small sound of distress and dropped to her knees. Scrabbling at the long grass and ivy, she tore it away to reveal a mud-streaked, white marble headstone in the shape of a teddy bear. The carved letters still retained traces of their original gilding.

Caleb read the inscription; *Stella Isabel Morgan. Beloved daughter of Alice and Robin. An angel. So cruelly taken from us.*

From the tiny amount of time between the birth and death dates, it was obvious the child had died as a baby.

The grave of Alice's dead daughter. Stella. Jess's twin sister, who'd been stolen away into Faery and a changeling left in her place.

Alice took a spray of pink fabric rosebuds from her handbag. She leaned forward to lay the small posy on the grave. Jess, her face pale, stood by, her eyes resting anywhere but on that sad little grave. As Alice turned and walked away, she looked more at peace, as if the gesture had offered her some relief.

A shiver of disgust snaked down Caleb's spine at the realisation that the grave held not the bones of a beloved child, but a rotted bundle of some foul faery material, the glamour that had tricked a young grieving mother, long since shrivelled to dust. Apparently the real Stella had died in Faery, probably un-mourned, perhaps unburied. No one seemed to be sure about the details.

As if alerted by some thread of his thoughts, Jess looked sharply at him.

His revulsion was so great that, for a moment, he couldn't meet her eye. This was what faeries did. They might trick you into believing they were beautiful, but they were ugly inside. Ruining lives on a whim, tormenting humans for the fun of it, plunging young mothers into the most desperate grief without a thought. Cold, capricious beings, with no care for humanity, they were vile. Hateful. *Hateful*. The word thrummed through Caleb.

He curled his hands into fists, his nails grazing his chilled palms, alarmed by the strength of his emotions. If he felt this way, where did that leave Jess?

None of what had happened to Alice was Jess's fault, he

reasoned, trying for calm. Jess was as much a victim of circumstance as was Stella. But while Stella had perished, Jess had survived with the help of another faery. *A faery* had helped Jess. So then, maybe they weren't all evil? But, like humans, were good, bad, indifferent - all shades of grey, in fact?

Composing himself, he raised his head and was brought up short by the perception sharpening Jess's face. He could tell that she knew *exactly* what he'd been thinking about Stella. She understood, but there was no hint of blame in the line of her mouth. Just acceptance. If he'd have spun round and stalked out of the cemetery and never come back, she'd have made no move to stop him.

But he hadn't gone and left her. And he wasn't going to. Ever.

'I'm fine with this. All of it,' he said in a low voice, smiling, as he gave her to understand that his momentary anger and confusion had passed.

Then something caught his eye over Jess's shoulder. A motionless figure stood next to a metal water trough, fretted by the spidery shadows of blowing trees.

'What?' Jess asked, spinning round. 'It's only Taryn. I told him to keep out of the way.'

'I suppose he thinks he is doing that,' Caleb said dryly. 'I saw him earlier. Why's he here?'

'Good question.' Jess rolled her eyes. 'I didn't think he needed to come, but Ninka insisted I bring a guard. While I was in Faery, things...changed for me.'

'Changed? How?' he asked.

'It's...complicated. But the short version is that I'm...erm sort of important there now. The Gentry, who rule the faery courts, know about me. Or they soon will.'

'And they're not pleased?' he guessed. 'So what? You're in danger from angry faeries now? Like Mrs Stark was?'

'Not *exactly* like that. But yeah. According to Ninka, I could be very attractive to any casually passing bounty hunter. Except that I'm not helpless against them, like Ivy was. Look. I know it's a pain having Taryn hanging around. But I'm kind of stuck with him, for now at least, until I get my head around how all the stuff in Faery works and just how I fit in there. *If I fit in.* I haven't decided what I'm going to be doing in the future. Taryn needn't bother us, though. We can go to the summer house. He can't come inside. Anyway, I'll send him away, so we can be alone. Like, Sha-zam! Your word. Remember?' she waved her hand, grinning to lighten her words. 'Promise. OK?'

Caleb could see that she was expecting him to laugh and agree. But he couldn't seem to let it go. 'And he'll do whatever you say?'

'Yeah, 'course.' Jess nodded. 'He has to.'

He could see by her face that she wished he'd change the subject. He set his jaw stubbornly. 'And why exactly is that?' he asked, giving her a mutinous look.

'Because… Taryn's sworn an oath of allegiance to me. I didn't ask him to. It was… pretty embarrassing, to tell the truth. But it's what faery lords do to those who have the right to rule over them.' She met his eyes, plainly ill at ease. 'OK. That's about half an answer. I know. But please, don't ask me anything else, Caleb. Because I'll have to tell you the truth. And you might not like what you hear. You trust me, right? You said you were happy that I was back here? Me too, times about ten million. With you, I can be plain Jess Morgan and not… someone else. Some*thing* else entirely. I want to keep that feeling for as long as I can. You and me against the world, two worlds even! Tomorrow everything could change. And I don't mean just in Faery. We've only just buried Ivy. Today is *her* day. Can we concentrate on that?'

Caleb was appalled at himself. Hadn't he told her, barely a couple of hours ago, that she didn't owe him any explanations? He'd babbled on about personal space being important. Pompous arse. And now here he was asking questions, demanding answers he had no right to.

'Yeah. 'Course. I...I don't know what I was thinking.' He lifted a hand to lightly brush her cheek. 'What do you see in me, eh? I'm a class A dickhead.'

'Hey! No you're not. Well... maybe just that much,' she teased, holding up a finger and thumb, spaced apart to indicate a tiny amount.

'OK. I deserve that.' Caleb grinned in response.

Alice had paused a short way from Stella's grave. She was dabbing at her eyes with a damp tissue. 'Are you two ready?' she asked, with a watery smile. 'I could murder a cup of tea and a sandwich in front of a roaring fire. The car will take us back.'

Jess nodded. 'We'll come with you.'

The three of them fell into step, heading for the car park. One of the funeral attendants was standing next to the hearse. He came over to speak to Alice.

Caleb and Jess left them talking and carried on more slowly. He glanced towards the water tank, where Taryn had been standing, but he'd gone. He scanned the cemetery for any sign of the faery lord. But couldn't see him.

He was turning back to Jess, a question on his lips, when without warning a tall figure materialised from nowhere. It advanced rapidly towards them through a nearby avenue of gravestones. At first, Caleb thought it was Taryn. He frowned, aware of a kind of buzzing, an alarm, an awareness he couldn't yet understand.

And then, it hit him. The air of menace that preceded the

figure like a faint smell one noticed before it bloomed into a full-blown stench. The man was moving in a staccato unearthly way, the distance being eaten up as if between the beats of his long-legged steps as well as with the normal motion of walking. Caleb had seen both Taryn and Jess move like that. The stranger wore a long flowing coat, unbuttoned and blowing open to reveal a black shirt and jeans. His maroon hair and pale skin showed vivid against his dark clothes. Caleb just had time to register that there was something oddly unbalanced about the up-tilted eyes, before the man placed himself squarely in front of Jess.

Caleb didn't think twice. 'Hey!' he shouted, leaping forward, ready to protect her.

Moving faster than seemed possible, the faery lord casually flicked one arm backwards, catching Caleb across the chest. Caleb gasped, winded. It felt as if he'd run headlong into a tree trunk. Arms flailing, he was flung sideways as if he weighed no more than a small child. And then everything shifted into slow motion. His shoulder connected with the back of a wooden bench. He tumbled over it, bounced off the slatted seat and crumpled to the damp grass. Dimly, through a haze of pain he heard Jess scream.

'Caleb!'

And then in a voice that seemed to echo like cracking ice, his assailant said,

'Jessica Anne Morgan. You will come with me.'

CHAPTER 53

JESS WAS SLOW to react. Concern for Caleb uppermost in her mind.

She made to move toward him, but there was something wrong. The sound of the wind was silenced. Trees bent sideways had become static, scribbled charcoal drawings against a backdrop of cloud printed sky. Alice and the funeral attendant were motionless beside the hearse, like a freeze-frame in a movie.

A long white hand gripped Jess's upper arm, digging in painfully as she was jerked backwards. She whipped around, found herself pulled up close to a muscled body as hard as wood. The human glamour he wore softened his sharp features, but Jess knew she was looking into the enigmatic face from her favourite Krast painting. The face she had glimpsed in the crowd at the Dark Court. His mismatched eyes, one emerald and the other gold, blazed with triumph.

Jackryn Fleet. Ivy's tormentor. Architect of the chaos that had rained down upon her and laid Windroth under a curse.

Jess's lip curled with contempt. She glared defiance at the faery lord as she placed her palms on his chest and pushed hard. Jackryn Fleet staggered backwards, only just managing to keep hold of her arm. She saw his lips tighten in surprise.

'You will obey me, child of the daughter of Ivy Stark's daughter!' he ordered. 'For I have the calling of you.'

'Like hell, you do! Get the fuck off me!' Jess spat, even as she was aware of a blur of light and movement beside her.

Taryn was there, holding a gleaming bronze blade to the faery lord's throat. 'Stand down, if you would live to draw another breath,' he said, dangerously quiet.

As Jess wrenched her arm free, she had the satisfaction of seeing Jackryn Fleet's face go blank with shock.

'You defy me? I do not understand…'

'I bet you don't!' Jess crowed. 'You thought it would be easy to bully me, the way you did Ivy Stark, didn't you?'

'Why so concerned, mewling slut?' Jackryn sneered. 'The mortal woman gained much from our compact. Riches, fame, the things you hot-bloods value above all else. She ought to have been well content.'

Taryn drew back his arm and punched Jackryn in the mouth. 'Do not dare to insult my lady! Your life already hangs in the balance!'

The faery lord rocked back on his heels. Blood from his split lip ran down his chin. He spat a froth of redness onto the ground. Backhanding his mouth, he glared hatred at Taryn. 'When did *you* become enamoured of mortal girls? I thought you more discerning. Have you forgotten Lady Anira so soon?'

Taryn's pale skin flushed as he leaned in towards Jackryn. Lodging the tip of the bronze blade more tightly beneath the sharp jawbone, he exerted pressure. A trickle of blood ran down the white neck and pooled at the coat collar.

'Say the word, my lady,' he hissed at Jess through gritted teeth.

'Wait. Don't kill him. Yet.' Jess moved closer to Jackryn. Of course, he thought she was human. He could not see through her glamour. She decided not to disabuse him of that notion, but to turn it to her advantage. 'And you. What did you gain from this…compact, with my great grandmother?'

Jackryn ignored her. 'You allow your tame mortal to question me?' he said to Taryn. 'She must be skilled indeed in bed-sports. How base have you become that you sully yourself with her?'

Taryn's lips thinned, but he did not rise to the other lord's taunting. 'You will answer her. Or die. Your choice.'

Jackryn smiled disarmingly, despite the knife point buried in his skin. 'Very well.' He looked at Jess, not bothering to hide his disgust. 'I simply wished to safeguard a mortal dwelling which stands close to a portal to Faery.'

Jess frowned. 'Windroth Hall's been here for hundreds of years. It must always have been close to Faery. Why the sudden urgency to change things?'

Jackryn looked surprised, perhaps by the level of her knowledge. She saw him slide hostile eyes towards Taryn, who he obviously held responsible for telling her too much. Masking his expression, he grinned wolfishly, displaying teeth filed to sharp points. 'Mortals,' he said lightly. 'Always thinking to find reasons for everything. Need there be one?'

'Maybe not. But if that's all there was to it, why is it so important for me to come with you?'

'Because you are mine…' Jackryn winced as Taryn's knife bit deeper. 'I speak only the truth.'

'Go on,' Jess urged. 'Why do you think you have power over me?'

'As part of our agreement, Ivy Stark pledged to give me the first of her bloodline to be born on Windroth soil. That is you, Jessica Anne Morgan. You are tied to Windroth. With you in my possession, I will have enduring blood rights over the house and lands. No matter which mortal hands Windroth might pass into, or even be it razed to the ground, as long as I have you, the path opened to Faery, remains ever so.'

Jess deliberated. Not quite accurate. *Stella had been born a few minutes before her twin-sister,* she remembered Alice telling her. *So Jackryn's claim to Windroth, would have been through her. But since the real Stella was long-dead, assumed to have perished in Faery, according to Ninka – and Catelysma had murdered the real baby Jess in front of her – any bargain Jackryn had made with Ivy was null and void.* But she wasn't about to tell the faery lord that, until she had found out everything he had to tell her.

She had worked some of it out for herself.

Because of the curse on Ivy, Windroth became a direct portal into Faery. The traffic must have been two-way, allowing faeries to enter the house without express invitation. Which was how the host of tiny fey was able to crowd into Ivy's studio; and how Catelysma had been able to enter the house via the front door, and Ninka too, that time she had followed her. Jess remembered how puzzled the hudskin had been about that. (It was also possible, of course, that Catelysma had forced Rob Morgan to allow her access to Windroth, which seemed very likely, given how terrified Jess's human father had seemed that the queen would harm Alice and his remaining daughter.) Jess understood why it would be important to ensure that Windroth remained a portal between two worlds, but was that the whole story? Jackryn was clever and slippery. She sensed there was an unwritten sub-text to all this.

'I think you planned to build on what you'd already set in place. With me, you could take over Windroth. Maybe turn it into an enclave of Faery here in the mortal world.' Jess mused aloud. She saw by the alarm the faery lord was trying so hard to hide, that she was on the right track. 'But why would you do that? Did you want to found a court outside Faery? *You* haven't the power to do that alone. Maybe you wanted to impress someone...who has.' And, out of nowhere, she understood. 'That's the answer, isn't it? Who was it? Tell me,' she asked sweetly, already knowing the answer but wanting to hear Jackryn say it.

Jackryn's face worked as he attempted, and failed, to evade the direct question. His eyes blazed as his lips shaped the words. 'She whom I serve. Night Queen of the Dark Court.'

'Catelysma!' Taryn said. 'All begins to make sense. He is an ex-lover of hers. No doubt he hoped to rise again in her favour by gifting Windroth to her. Perhaps sit beside her in the nightmare court they would found together mortalwise. What a triumph that would be.'

Jackryn let out a howl of anger. 'You tarnish my lady's name before this mortal who knows far too much about the fey! How dare you speak of hallowed things to her? Traitor! You are a disgrace to Faery. How the Blessed Land must weep with fury! You had best kill me now. Or when we next meet, I will carve the living flesh from your bones. Feed your liver and eyeballs to the scrags, while you - '

'Oh, shut up a minute. I'm thinking,' Jess ordered, extending a tiny thread of glamour.

The effect on Jackryn was instant. A dark flush stained the fierce faery lord's cheeks. A tendon twitched in his neck as he tried to speak and found he could not. His look of helpless outrage was almost comical. Jess saw Taryn's lips twitch. She signed to him to do nothing as she turned her attention inwards, began slotting together the final pieces of the long-standing puzzle.

It appeared then, that Jackryn Fleet had acted alone in

making his compact with Ivy, gambling that Catelysma's delight at the novelty of his gift would outweigh any censure against his meddling. And it might have worked, had not the queen, herself, unknowingly set in motion the events that ruined her scheming courtier's plans.

Jackryn Fleet could not have known about Catelysma's secret affair with Rob Morgan or that it resulted in a forbidden child. It was Catelysma who had ensured that both human babies born at Windroth were dead, both replaced by change-lings. Jess could only imagine Jackryn's dismay when Alice suddenly quit Windroth, disappearing with her remaining baby girl. For reasons unknown, he had not pursued them. But had instead played a waiting game. And his patience had been rewarded – so he thought. How he must have exulted when he learned that Alice and Jess had returned to Windroth, giving him a second chance to secure Windroth as a gift to Catelysma.

At the irony of it, Jess began to laugh softly at first and then more loudly, until her mocking laughter rang out across the cemetery. 'All your plotting. It's come to... nothing,' she gulped, wiping at her eyes with the satin cuffs of Ralph's tail coat.

She flicked away the glamour from Jackryn, wanting to hear his reaction when he realised he had lost.

Anger mottled the faery lord's cheeks. 'What is this?' he spluttered. 'Stop. I command you!'

'She is not for you to command!' Taryn adjusted his grip on the knife.

Jess finally managed to catch her breath. 'You'll never have Windroth.'

Jackryn Fleet's stained-glass coloured eyes narrowed. 'By the sun and stars, mortal filth! You dare to laugh at my expense?' His voice cracked on a note of fury.

A muscle ticked in Taryn's cheek as he prepared to thrust the blade upwards. 'I warned you.'

'No!' Jess ordered. 'I don't want his blood on my hands. Enough of it's been spilt mortalwise and in Faery. Let him go.'

Emotion, twisted Taryn's face, but he nodded shortly and lowered the knife.

Quicker than blinking, Jackryn drove his shoulder into Taryn, throwing the faery lord off balance. His dark coat fell away, into a pool of oil at his feet. A sword appeared in his hand, the finely-worked length of it flashing like crystal.

In the instant it took Taryn to recover, Jackryn had turned to face Jess. Loosing a cry from between clenched bloodied teeth, he sprang at her, sword raised.

Jess saw her death written on that implacable white face. But the power of her glamour had already ignited, thrumming through blood vessels, sinews and skin to her fingertips. With a tiny internal gesture, the effort of it less than if she were brushing away a cobweb, Jess launched a burst of magic at Jackryn.

There was a sound like thunder. Jackryn's sword burst into flames, became an explosion of ash which stranded in the air like wood smoke. The faery lord cried out in agony, looking in horror at his blackened sword hand. Blanching he staggered, sank slowly to his knees beneath the weight of the enchantment she had placed on him.

'It's over.' Jess looked down at him. 'Crawl back to your nightmare queen. Knowing that you have failed, is punishment enough. Stay away from me and mine from now on. That's an order.'

Jackryn trembled all over as his face worked with pain and confusion. He cradled his shrivelled, still-smoking claw in the crook of his other arm as he scrabbled backwards. Impotent fury had ripped away at the shreds of his glamour, revealing all his stark feyness. The plains of his face had sharpened and his high-bridged nose looked beak-like against bone white skin. Tips of pointed ears stuck up through the purple-red hair that lay against his hollow cheeks and blade-like jaw like skeins of silk.

He lifted a haunted face to Jess, his expression turning into incredulity as realisation dawned on him. 'You are fey. High-born and solitary! How is it that I could not perceive this?'

Jess held his gaze. 'You might try looking out of the corner of your eye,' she suggested. 'Sometimes that works with seeing through glamour. Can't promise, though. Yours is a total mess, by the way. I'd fix it, if I were you. Before things here go back to normal. We're in a cemetery, remember? And you look like an extra in a low-budget zombie movie!'

Taryn had recovered. He stood close by, sword drawn and watchful. He would not make the mistake of underestimating Jackryn Fleet again.

'I do not understand. Who are you, if not Jess Morgan, child of Ivy Stark's blood-line? Favour me with an explanation, I beg,' Jackryn panted, his voice emerging with an effort from between dry lips.

'Since you ask, so nicely. I am, Other,' Jess said. Which was no lie, although only part of the truth. Let him try and figure it out. Faeries loved their riddles, didn't they? 'Go now. It's over. The portal to Faery remains in the forest, as it always has, but entrance to Windroth Hall is by invitation only from now on.'

'I advise you to heed my lady's words,' Taryn said coldly. 'Leave. Before she thinks better of the mercy she cedes you. Were it left to me, your carcass would already be food for corvids.'

Jackryn shot the other faery lord a look of pure venom. With an effort he rose unsteadily to his feet, voided a shuddering breath. His sword hand was destroyed. As Jess watched, glamour covered it in a finely worked gauntlet of chased silver, set with moonstones. Turning to Jess, Jackryn placed the metal hand flat against his breast and bowed stiffly, eyes flat as coloured pebbles.

'We shall meet again. I look forward to your appearance in Faery,' he said with stiff formality. 'Perhaps at the midwinter feast, my lady...?'

'You may call me, Damiana,' Jess supplied. Her lips twisted with pure devilment. She couldn't resist saying, 'See you in court! By the way, give my regards to my...to Catelysma.'

If Jackryn noticed her hesitation, he gave no sign of it. 'I shall convey your compliments. The Dark Lady takes a keen interest in any unsworn, high-born fey who chance to enter her domain. Especially one with such glamour as yours.' He gave a curt bow. 'Lady Damiana.' Turning on his heel, he strode past the patch of dark oil on the ground, which swirled into the air in a flurry of crow's feathers, before resolving into a long dark coat that settled around the faery lord's shoulders.

Jess and Taryn stood watching as the tall figure entered the nearby avenue of gravestones, his unearthly, uber-fast movements painting smudges on the air so that he had faded from sight, long before he reached the screen of trees at the cemetery's border.

'I'd love to be there when Catelysma discovers what Jackryn's been up to. From what I've seen she's a total control freak. I reckon she'll take a dim view of anyone laying enchantments on people without her knowledge.' Jess grinned. 'Perhaps someone ought to tell her?'

Taryn nodded agreement, but he looked dismayed.

Sensing a long involved conversation about how he had failed to protect her, Jess forestalled him. 'Look. I don't want you to beat yourself up about what just happened, OK? Nobody's perfect. End of.'

'Your forbearance is more than I deserve. I will never fail you again,' Taryn said seriously. 'I swear it.'

'Good enough,' Jess said in a tone of finality. She felt light-headed with victory. She had told Caleb that she wasn't helpless in Faery and now she had proof. Since her acceptance into that other world her glamour seemed to have magnified in strength. Coiled within her, the slumbering presence of her enhanced being was now as much a part of her as her bones and organs. The summoning of her power had been effortless. She'd hardly used a fraction of it, but the disabling effect on Jackryn had been instant. Of what else might she be capable?

'Jackryn Fleet will cosset his anger. I fear that you have made a dangerous enemy,' Taryn warned.

'Yeah? Well he's made one too,' Jess said, tossing her head. 'Admit it, I was impressive.'

Taryn raised his eyebrows. 'There is no doubt of your considerable talents. You are clever. A commodity more useful than power alone, for one who has the right to rule in Faery. And you have a sharp mind. Perhaps, though, one might beware of cutting one's self?'

'Taryn? Surely that's not a criticism?' Jess asked, mouth quirking.

'Perish the thought.' The faery lord bowed low, extending one hand in a flourish. 'Merely an observation, Bright Lady.'

'Don't call me that in front of Caleb, OK? When I'm mortalwise, I'm just plain Jess. He knows that things changed for me, when I was in Faery. I've mentioned that I'm…kind of special there. And he knows that you're sworn to protect me. But I don't want him to know that I'm Gentry and what

538

that actually means. Not yet. Heck, I don't even know what it means!'

'As you wish.' Taryn's face was impassive.

A breath of wind stirred a strand of loose hair against Jess's cheek. The sound of traffic outside the cemetery resumed. Nearby, branches of trees rustled. Overhead clouds scudded across the gun-metal sky.

At the sound of a muffled curse, Jess turned to see Caleb rising to his feet just beyond a wooden bench. She hurried towards him, without a second thought and didn't see the look of disdain that tightened Taryn's face, before the colours of the trees and grass flowed over him, lending him instant invisibility.

'Caleb! Are you hurt?'

He grimaced, rubbing his shoulder. 'Just my pride, I think.' He whipped around, eyes scanning the cemetery. 'That bruiser in the long coat! He was fey, wasn't he? What happened to him?'

'It was Jackryn Fleet. Don't worry. He's gone now.'

'What? *What?*' Caleb said horrified.

There was a long mud stain on Caleb's overcoat. Jess reached out to brush at it with her long fingers. 'Sorry. I'm just making it worse. It'll brush off when it dries...'

Caleb looked baffled. 'What are you doing? Leave that,' he said, impatiently, batting her hand away. 'Jackryn Fleet? My God! Isn't that the faery Mrs Stark warned you about? The one who was in her bedroom just before she died? Why was he here? What did he want?'

'Me, as it happens,' Jess told him, sheepishly. 'Turns out he'd made a sort of pact with Ivy. In return for fame and fortune, Ivy agreed to give Jackryn a child of her bloodline who was born at Windroth. He thought it would give him the right to lord it over her house and land. All the faery problems at Windroth stemmed from that pact. It became like a curse to Ivy, destroying her family, her health and leaving her with only the obsession to paint. But it's all over now. We dealt with Jackryn Fleet, me and Taryn. Taught him a lesson he won't forget it in a hurry.' She couldn't help the note of pride that crept into her voice. 'You don't have to worry about JF. He won't be back.'

Jess smiled, mimed dusting off her hands, taking Caleb's silence for acceptance. She didn't notice the set of his jaw, her quicksilver thoughts already running on ahead of her.

All she wanted was to get back to Windroth, where she and Caleb could relax together in the summer house. They'd had no time, before the funeral, for a proper discussion about Ivy's generosity and what it would mean for their future and for them, as a couple. There was no reason for her to go back to Faery. She was looking forward to spending time with Caleb, to both of them getting to know each other. Doing ordinary things, like watching a movie, cuddling up together in front of the stove in the summer house; taking long walks over the hills and stopping at the café in the village. And to other things....discoveries which, just the mere thought of, made her shiver with longing.

Over Caleb's shoulder, Jess could see that Alice had just finished speaking to the funeral attendant. Her mum began walking towards them as the driver got into the empty hearse and drove slowly towards the cemetery gates. She gestured to her mum, signifying for her to get into their car and giving her to understand that she and Caleb would follow shortly.

Alice waved, nodding and opened the car door.

'Ready? Let's go,' Jess said, attempted to link arms with Caleb.

He shook her off. 'Do you think I'm a complete idiot?' he said with an intensity that brought her up short. 'Let me get this right. Some murderous faery turns up here in broad daylight. Knocks me down and tries to drag you off. I *conveniently* get amnesia. And so does Alice, by the look of it. And you're trying to tell me that *nothing much* happened?'

'Not exactly...nothing, if I'm honest,' Jess chewed at her lip. 'It could have been tricky. But it wasn't. It's done with. Finito. What's the point of worrying you with all the gories?'

'Great. So what am I, invisible? Is this how it's going to be, from now on? You keeping things from me? Shielding me from danger, as if I'm a helpless child?'

'No. Maybe. I...I don't know,' Jess replied, confused. 'Look. There's no rule book. I'm making this up as I go along. I'm not always going to get it right. I'm doing the best I can. I'm sorry if you feel left out. OK? Can we go now? Alice's waiting.'

'*Left out*? Like I haven't been invited to the picnic, eh? How pathetic do you think I am?' Caleb closed his eyes, drew a deep breath. 'I just feel so freaking useless. It's hard...you know? Knowing that I can't protect you.'

'You don't need to. I've got Taryn for that,' she said, before she thought better of it.

'Exactly,' he said bleakly. 'All your needs are met. So where *exactly* does that leave me?'

She sighed, exasperated and just managed to stop saying something seriously unhelpful, about injured male pride. Instead, she grabbed his hand, slipped it inside the breast of Ralph's old tail coat and placed it on her velvet jacket, directly above her heart.

'Right here.'

Caleb's face changed, softening but somehow becoming more intense, as he felt her heart beating against his palm. As Jess let go of his hand, it dropped to his side.

Stepping close, she reached up and looped her arms

around his neck. Tipping up her face, she brought her mouth close to his, but stopped just short of touching him. When he would have kissed her, she held him back.

'Wait. I want you to feel something.'

She breathed in Caleb's breath, tasting the warm humanity of him and extending a miniscule shred of glamour, so that their mixed return breath was cool, green and pungent as menthol. It was a joining both simple and complex; a link at some level beyond blood and bone to where there is nothing but space. A reaching out into an expression beyond words, beyond understanding. They stood enveloped in their own singular world, which had no name, but was more than the sum of their two parts.

'Taste that? That's us. Me and you. Mortal and fey mixed. We've made something new...something, other. Can you tell where I stop and you begin?'

'No. I...I can't.' He drew back to look at her. 'I'm a jealous idiot, but I'll try harder to believe in us. Can you do that...that...breath thing again?'

'What this? Oh, yeah.' She grinned, this time adding a touch more glamour and a hint of roses and musk.

Caleb's closed eyelids fluttered as he breathed deeply. She felt him tremble against her as the glamour penetrated deeply into his core. 'Oh, Jess,' he shaped her name on a small groan of wanting.

But she still held herself back from him. 'It's you I want. No one else. Whatever happens. Is that clear enough for you?'

'Crystal,' he sighed, happily.

And Damiana Seelie Firethorn, new Bright Queen of Faery, leaned forward and granted him sole access to her lips.

Fey and mortal conjoined, forbidden, dangerous but not impossible. No. Never impossible.

Afterword

SNOW HAD BEEN falling for hours. The cleared paths and newly cut lawns of Windroth iced by a fluffy white frosting which was ten centimetres thick, and counting. Structures of trees, hedges, fences were indistinct in a monochrome world where familiar contours were softened and blurred.

Inside the summer house it was dark, but for the roseate glow leaching from the gap around the stove's door. Jess padded silently across the wooden floorboards, glamour flowing downwards to transform her white cotton Victorian nightdress into jeans, warm sweater, antique flying-jacket and boots. At the door she glanced over her shoulder at the sight of Caleb sleeping peacefully, one arm flung across the pillow, his hair a black ink stain against the linen.

Jess slipped outside, closing the door behind her. Caleb ought to be safe while she was gone, but just to make certain she extended her fingers and cast an invisible net of enchantment to cover the summer house. Her order forbidding any fey to enter Windroth's buildings without permission still held, but that didn't mean they couldn't come knocking.

She set off through the silent white garden, the froth of dark hair spilling over the shoulders of her coat, gathering a lace of snowflakes. Moving swiftly, she went through the archway into the old kitchen garden, passing the shrouded glasshouse and raised beds before going through the wooden gate in the ivy-covered wall. Emerging into the old orchard, she paused and looked down the length of lawn.

Windroth Hall, the whole gorgeous, ugly Gothic splendour of it filled her vision. Falling snow and the greyish light conspired to paint the house ghostly – like a tintype photograph, all silver and haze. There were no lights at any of the windows. Alice would be in bed long since. The freezing air was seasoned by the acrid tang of iron from the scaffolding caging one wing of the house, the metal ringing with a sullen note and adding to the many impressions flooding her senses. Sleeping trees, their branches brittle with withdrawn sap; animals and insects locked deep inside hard earth; in the forest itself, the ancient oak dryad, Arboria Petra, a drowsy presence.

Jess loved the feeling of the world shutting down, becoming dormant. The feeling that she and Caleb were cocooned within their own private enclave. They were still getting to know each other, still by turns awkward and shy. These past few months since the funeral, time had seemed held in suspension. Which suited her perfectly. She had begun to believe that things could always stay this way. The human glamour she wore all the time now felt weightless, a comfortable body suit which she might never again remove. She was completely happy, she realised with a shock of surprise. Once she would never have believed that her restive teen spirit could settle like this. Windroth, and all it offered, was the only reality she wanted or needed. She had ordered Taryn back to Faery where he was staying with Ninka in her forest dwelling. She had only to call on him and he would be there instantly. As the weeks passed, the world of Faery began to feel more and more like a bad dream.

Until tonight. When something had woken her abruptly.

She'd jerked upright, muzzy-headed with sleep, heart

thudding. The sense of impending danger making her palms wet. The *something* was approaching. She could sense it, prowling like a hunting beast. Impossible to lie there huddled beneath the duvet and blankets, waiting while Caleb slept. Whatever *it* was it was powerful, posing a danger to everyone she cared about. She had to go and meet it.

So now Jess moved onwards, silver-shaded Windroth Hall and its grounds at her back. Every sense alert, she plunged towards the quilted white patchwork of fields, stitched across by interlocking tracks of birds and animal. Beyond the fields, the forest. Dense, ancient and snow-bound.

And the source of what had come stalking.

Suddenly, as Jess approached the first trees, a wall of snow exploded outwards, forming into a giant white hand which reached for her. Quicker than thought, she extended an arm, with her palm held upwards and the snow-hand fractured into a million tiny particles that powdered the ground. A shrill scream of rage splintered the air. Jess stood her ground, fear and adrenaline pumping through her.

Seconds passed.

Out of nowhere, a blizzard came raging, tearing at her hair, half-blinding her before whipping the tresses into a wild tangle above her head. Jess held herself in readiness, knowing instinctively that there was more to come. She was right. Racing towards her out of the maelstrom, came razor-sharp spikes of ice, long as spear heads. She threw a net of glamour around her, a silver cage of closely woven links. The ice spears crashed into it, exploding into glass-like fragments and falling away harmlessly.

Silence fell abruptly. Jess dissolved the silver cage, flexed her shoulders, tossed her halo of hair back and stood ready, a smile of growing confidence on her face. Two nil, so far. Bring it on.

At first nothing happened. And then, a few metres away, a column rose from the snow. It began spinning, ice crystals swirling as if trapped inside a child's snow dome. Light flashed, streaming outwards. Within the light, a tall slender shape formed. A faery woman stepped forward and advanced towards her.

She was more splendid than Jess remembered from their one brief meeting. A symphony in shades of white. Who knew there were so many? Milk-coloured hair, pearly skin, high-collared fur cloak - the colour of bleached-bone and velvet robes in shades of ivory. All was punctuated by a single lock of black hair, among the white that flowed onto the snow behind her. This lock was plaited, woven with diamonds and clasped with silver.

Winter colours, like an ermine, Jess thought, moved by the power of the faery's incredible beauty, despite the dread that curdled her stomach.

Why had the queen come here, alone, when she had countless faery lords to obey her every wish? Jess's insides might be numb with terror, but her fingertips were warm, still vibrating with glamour as if alerting her to the fact that her power was on-alert, undimmed.

What now? Was it to be a stand-off?

Catelysma spoke first. 'I had word of your glamour. You do not disappoint, Lady Damiana…?' she said, silkily.

'Glad you approve,' Jess said. 'I assume Jackryn has been telling tales at court.'

'It is customary to exchange greetings with full titles, when high-born fey first meet their sovereign,' the queen admonished, her mouth briefly thinning with displeasure.

Jess ignored the invitation to give up her name. What did

Catelysma take her for? 'Yeah? Is that before or after you try to kill me?'

'Kill you? Merely games, my dear. You are equal to them, so where is the harm?' The queen smiled again, charmingly, loosing a small bell-like note of laughter. 'But you are correct. Lord Jackryn Fleet did, indeed, give me word of a young solitary fey woman who has lately entered my domain.'

'Thought he would. Couldn't help himself, could he? Although it didn't need *him* to tell you about me, did it? You already knew I'd been into Faery. Jackryn doesn't know the whole story. Is that why you've come here, all alone? To find out exactly who I am? Well – aren't I the lucky one?'

Catelysma frowned, but chose not to comment. She said instead, 'You are young and brash. A mere breath away from insulting. But I forgive you – this once. Come now. Announce yourself fully. Swear into my service. Become my loyal subject. And I will allow you to live, despite the…interesting damage you did to my Lord Jackryn.'

'That's big of you!' Jess felt her lip curl with derision. 'I've seen what you do to those who serve you at your Dark Court. I'll pass on your offer. I think I'd rather take my chances.'

The queen's perfect face twisted with fury. Blackness flooded the space between her eyelids. 'You dare to refuse me? Who are you that sets foot upon the Blessed Land and leaves an imprint such as has not been felt in an age?'

'Don't you know me?' Jess asked. 'Well – I guess it's been a while since you dumped me mortalwise. I was different then. Small, helpless, unwanted. Forbidden.'

Slowly, an expression of horror replaced the fury on Catelysma's face. Shock robbed her of her natural grace. She staggered backwards, her feet catching in the long fur cloak, so that she almost toppled sideways. The white strands of her hair whipped upwards, dissolved into clouds that boiled around her in a tempest in which icicles chimed in jarring, discordant notes.

'No! *No!*' she cried, white to the lips. Her eyes dark wounds in the almond-sliver face. 'By all the eternal stars...It cannot be...You are dead, long since!'

'You wish,' Jess said. There was a bitter taste in her mouth. 'Hello... mother, dear.'